喚醒你的英文語感！

Get a Feel for English !

喚醒你的英文語感！

Get a Feel for English !

New TOEIC 新制多益

奇蹟筆記書

全真練題本

　　隨著多益測驗題型更迭，筆者與時俱進大量研究各題型翻新要點，緊扣最新考情趨勢，全新編訂本著作。本書包含兩回完整模擬測驗及詳盡解析，題型、長度、頻出考點、陷阱題設計方式等皆致力於維持最高擬真度；聽力測驗的錄音檔亦比照實測包括美、加、英、澳四國口音，協助應試者熟悉各國音調，跨越常見的聽力題瓶頸。除此之外，特邀「理解式文法」大師王復國親筆操刀之精闢易懂的逐題解析更是本書的重大養分。

　　投報率最高！愈沒時間愈要擠出時間完成本書所收錄的 400 道試題，你一定做得到！建議讀者在考前二十天集中使用本書，儘量在比照實測的時間限制下作答，並務必詳讀解析，一一檢視自己對於平易題是否已完全掌握？針對困難題是否已知破解？若是猜對或感覺模稜兩可、不太確定的題目，請再確認一遍以加深印象；即便答錯也不要慌張，仔細地做記號提醒自己在所剩無幾的考前日子裡再多看幾次，至少能揪出自己較不擅長的題型，進而在實際應試時妥善分配解題時間。利用本書的嚴選試題反覆自我測驗，有助於強化臨場反應，進一步盡最大可能完全發揮透過研習本書所積攢的實力，讓挑燈夜戰的分分秒秒不白費。祝福各位讀者應試順利，一次就考出目標分數！

本書使用方式

答題用紙置於卷末，請自行撕下使用。

各代表錄音內容採美國、加拿大、英國、澳洲口音

01-01 數字代表音軌編號

聽力測驗 MP3 音檔請刮開書內刮刮卡，上網啟用序號後即可下載聆聽。網址：https://bit.ly/3d3P7te，或掃描 QR code

貝塔會員網

CONTENTS 目錄

前言 Preface ·················· 2

關於多益 About the TOEIC L&R Test ······ 4

全真測驗

第一回
LISTENING TEST ·············· 6

READING TEST ················ 18

第二回
LISTENING TEST ·············· 48

READING TEST ················ 60

完整解析

第一回
解答總覽 ····················· 89

LISTENING TEST

    PART 1 ·················· 90

    PART 2 ·················· 92

    PART 3 ·················· 97

    PART 4 ·················· 110

READING TEST

    PART 5 ·················· 120

    PART 6 ·················· 126

    PART 7 ·················· 131

第二回
解答總覽 ····················· 163

LISTENING TEST

    PART 1 ·················· 164

    PART 2 ·················· 166

    PART 3 ·················· 171

    PART 4 ·················· 184

READING TEST

    PART 5 ·················· 194

    PART 6 ·················· 200

    PART 7 ·················· 205

聽力測驗 MP3 曲目對照表 ·············· 239

※ 2022 年 01 月資料

「多益 TOEIC」是美國教育測驗服務社 ETS 針對非英文母語人士所研發的英語能力測驗，每年全世界有數以百萬計的人報考。多益測驗成績具國際公信力，足以體現應試者在實際溝通情境中的英語能力，也是許多企業、教育單位及政府機構招聘新進員工、遴選內部晉升或海外派任職員時所採用的鑑別門檻。

☆ 多益題型架構

多益分為下列七大題型，共有 200 題，考試時間共兩小時。

	聽力測驗 LISTENING TEST 45 分鐘 / 100 題				閱讀測驗 READING TEST 75 分鐘 / 100 題		
	Part 1	Part 2	Part 3	Part 4	Part 5	Part 6	Part 7
題型	照片題	應答題	簡短對話題	簡短獨白題	單句填空題	短文填空題	文章理解題
題目數	6	25	39	30	30	16	54

部分考題與商業有關，但不需要專業知識亦可作答。

☆ 評量分數

應試者使用鉛筆在答案卡上作答，答錯不倒扣，總分範圍在 10 到 990 分之間。多益測驗沒有分級，因此也沒有所謂的通不通過或合不合格。

☆ 報名方式與費用

一般考生採網路或 APP 報名，報名費為 1600 元（追加報名費為 1900 元）。低收入戶家庭人士或其子女免報名費，測驗日時年滿 65 歲以上者僅需 800 元。

☆ 測驗日期與考區

在台灣，原則上每個月會舉辦一次 TOEIC 考試。不過各地舉辦時程不同，詳情請至官網確認。

▲ 本頁資訊以官網最新發布訊息為主，請參閱 / 洽詢：

〔官方網站〕http://www.toeic.com.tw

〔客服信箱〕service@examservice.com.tw

ACTUAL TEST

1

全真測驗

第一回

01-01 ▶ 01-58 **LISTENING TEST** 006

READING TEST 018

※ 答案卡置於本書末，請自行撕下使用。

LISTENING TEST

The Listening test allows you to demonstrate your ability to understand spoken English. The Listening test has four parts, and you will hear directions for each of them. The entire Listening test is approximately forty-five minutes long. Write only on your answer sheet, not the test book.

PART 1

 01-01 ▶ 01-07

Directions: For each question in PART 1, you will hear four statements about a picture. Choose the statement that best describes what you see in the picture and mark your answer on the answer sheet. The statements will be spoken only once, and do not appear in the test book.

Example

Sample Answer

Statement (C), "They are sitting around the table," is the best description of the photograph, so you should mark (C) on your answer sheet.

1.

2.

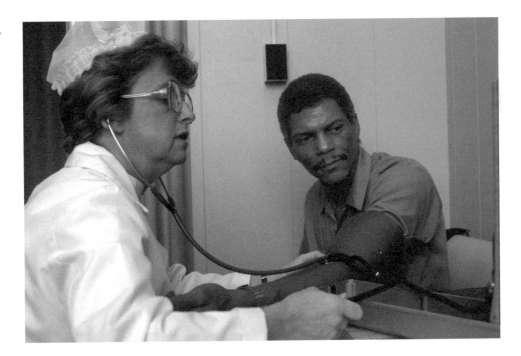

GO ON TO THE NEXT PAGE ➤

3.

4.

5.

6.

GO ON TO THE NEXT PAGE

## PART 2

01-08 ▶ 01-33

Directions: In PART 2, you will hear either a statement or a question and three responses. They will be spoken only once, and do not appear in your test book. Choose the best response to the question or statement and mark the corresponding letter (A), (B), or (C) on your answer sheet.

7. Mark your answer on your answer sheet.

8. Mark your answer on your answer sheet.

9. Mark your answer on your answer sheet.

10. Mark your answer on your answer sheet.

11. Mark your answer on your answer sheet.

12. Mark your answer on your answer sheet.

13. Mark your answer on your answer sheet.

14. Mark your answer on your answer sheet.

15. Mark your answer on your answer sheet.

16. Mark your answer on your answer sheet.

17. Mark your answer on your answer sheet.

18. Mark your answer on your answer sheet.

19. Mark your answer on your answer sheet.

20. Mark your answer on your answer sheet.

21. Mark your answer on your answer sheet.

22. Mark your answer on your answer sheet.

23. Mark your answer on your answer sheet.

24. Mark your answer on your answer sheet.

25. Mark your answer on your answer sheet.

26. Mark your answer on your answer sheet.

27. Mark your answer on your answer sheet.

28. Mark your answer on your answer sheet.

29. Mark your answer on your answer sheet.

30. Mark your answer on your answer sheet.

31. Mark your answer on your answer sheet.

01-34 ▶ 01-38

Directions: In PART 3, you will hear several short conversations between two or more people. After each conversation, you will be asked to answer three questions about what you heard. Choose the best response to each question, and mark the corresponding letter (A), (B), (C), or (D) on your answer sheet. The conversations do not appear in the test book, and they will be spoken only one time.

32. Where most likely does the woman work?

(A) At an airport
(B) At a golf course
(C) At a shuttle service
(D) At a train station

33. Why is the man calling?

(A) To book a flight
(B) To inquire about a room
(C) To arrange transportation
(D) To schedule a delivery

34. What does the woman say will cost extra?

(A) Changing the pick-up time
(B) Traveling on a weekday
(C) Using a credit card
(D) Transporting oversized luggage

35. Where most likely is this conversation taking place?

(A) In a bicycle shop
(B) In a hotel lobby
(C) In a bus station
(D) In a luggage store

36. What is the problem?

(A) An order is late.
(B) An item is damaged.
(C) The customer cannot wait.
(D) The merchandise is the wrong size.

37. What does the man offer to do?

(A) Lower a price
(B) Offer a refund
(C) Replace a part
(D) Order a replacement

38. What does the man want to do?

(A) Sign up to use the gym
(B) Renew his membership
(C) Get a new card
(D) Use the swimming pool

39. Where most likely is the conversation taking place?

(A) At a sports center
(B) At a school
(C) At a computer store
(D) At a car rental company

40. What does the woman give the man?

(A) An access code
(B) A student ID card
(C) An application form
(D) A temporary pass

41. What does the woman say about the Newvis Clearset?

(A) It is very popular.
(B) It is somewhat outdated.
(C) It is difficult to use.
(D) It is no longer for sale.

42. What does the man request?

(A) A registration card
(B) An updated manual
(C) A new warranty
(D) A full refund

43. What does the woman suggest the man do?

(A) Call a customer service number
(B) Email a company
(C) Visit a Website
(D) Purchase a television

GO ON TO THE NEXT PAGE ➡

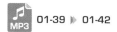

44. Why does the woman talk to the man?

    (A) To ask him to attend a conference
    (B) To persuade him to give a presentation
    (C) To discuss his plans for the weekend
    (D) To invite him to an event

45. What does the woman say is important?

    (A) Visiting an art museum
    (B) Booking a hotel room
    (C) Making a quick decision
    (D) Arranging transportation

46. What does the man agree to do?

    (A) Join a group of coworkers
    (B) Help the woman get tickets
    (C) Reserve seats for the conference
    (D) Consider the woman's suggestion

47. What are the speakers discussing?

    (A) A department meeting
    (B) A new schedule
    (C) A budget proposal
    (D) A computer purchase

48. What does the woman say about the software?

    (A) It is expensive.
    (B) It is outdated.
    (C) It is too slow.
    (D) It is overpriced.

49. What does the man decide to do?

    (A) Research a product
    (B) Support a proposal
    (C) Make a recommendation
    (D) Explain a policy

50. Why did the man call the woman?

    (A) To look for work
    (B) To ask about an experiment
    (C) To arrange a tour
    (D) To introduce a professor

51. What does the woman mean when she says, "we are a little understaffed at the moment"?

    (A) The lab doesn't currently have any workers.
    (B) She may have a position for the man.
    (C) The staff require additional training.
    (D) She doesn't have time to talk with the man.

52. What will the woman do next?

    (A) Schedule an interview
    (B) Write a recommendation
    (C) Call a colleague
    (D) Email a resume

53. What type of service does the woman's company provide?

    (A) Interior design
    (B) Accounting services
    (C) Legal advice
    (D) Office management

54. What does the man say he wants to do?

    (A) Open a new accounting practice
    (B) Consult with a financial advisor
    (C) Hire a moving company
    (D) Meet with a designer

55. When will the man sign the lease?

    (A) Later that day
    (B) The next week
    (C) The next month
    (D) Whenever it is convenient

56. Where do the speakers most likely work?

    (A) At a shipping company
    (B) At a factory
    (C) At a store
    (D) At a warehouse

57. What does the man mean when he says, "we're looking at next week"?

    (A) It will take several days to make the packaging.
    (B) The order can't be shipped this week.
    (C) He will arrange a meeting in the near future.
    (D) They will start manufacturing the order next week.

58. What will the woman include in her email?

    (A) A design idea for the new packaging
    (B) A document with the latest specifications
    (C) A revised manufacturing schedule
    (D) An explanation for the delay in shipping

59. What are the speakers mainly discussing?

    (A) Places to take visitors to their city
    (B) Ways to get from the airport to the hotel
    (C) Possible locations for a welcome luncheon
    (D) Plans for an upcoming sales conference

60. What problem do the speakers have?

    (A) They are unable to confirm some hotel reservations.
    (B) They haven't found a location for an important event.
    (C) They can't find a large enough space for a conference.
    (D) They don't have time to arrange airport transportation.

61. What does the woman suggest they do?

    (A) Book a restaurant for a farewell dinner
    (B) Get in touch with a hotel
    (C) Use a catering company
    (D) Reschedule a social event

West Wing		East Wing
Conference Room	4th FL.	Management Offices
Accounting	3rd FL.	Sales / Marketing / IT
Cafeteria / Break Room	2nd FL.	Kitchen
Reception	1st FL.	Meeting Rooms

62. Who most likely are the speakers?

    (A) Office movers
    (B) Truck drivers
    (C) Computer installers
    (D) Cafeteria workers

63. Look at the graphic. Where is the man currently working?

    (A) On the first floor.
    (B) On the second floor.
    (C) On the third floor.
    (D) On the fourth floor.

64. What are the speakers probably going to do next?

    (A) Load up a truck
    (B) Meet in the sales office
    (C) Install some equipment
    (D) Move a refrigerator

GO ON TO THE NEXT PAGE →

Jeb's Sporting Goods
1121 Kingstone Pl., Newcastle

Exchange Receipt
February 12 16:28 pm

RETURNED
25L Highlander Backpack, Purple $20.00
Tax $ 2.00
* * * * *   * * * * *
Total $22.00
* * * * *   * * * * *

EXCHANGED
25L Highlander Backpack, Orange $20.00
Tax $ 2.00
* * * * *   * * * * *
Total $22.00
* * * * *   * * * * *

Restocking Fee $ 5.00
* * * * *   * * * * *
Total $ 5.00
* * * * *   * * * * *

Thank you for shopping with us.
No refunds or exchanges without a receipt.

Category	Issue	Number of Complaints
1	Registration	66
2	Passwords	132
3	Navigation	23
4	Purchasing	71

68. Where do the speakers most likely work?

(A) At a credit card company
(B) At an architecture firm
(C) At an online store
(D) At a data management company

69. Look at the graphic. What category of complaint are the speakers discussing?

(A) Category 1
(B) Category 2
(C) Category 3
(D) Category 4

70. What will the speakers do next?

(A) Contact affected users
(B) Start collecting data
(C) Simplify the registration process
(D) Review customer complaints

65. What problem does the woman mention?

(A) She purchased the wrong color item.
(B) The product is defective.
(C) She already used the product.
(D) The store doesn't offer exchanges.

66. What does the woman say recently happened?

(A) She started a new job.
(B) She exchanged some currency.
(C) She purchased a bicycle.
(D) She changed her method of commuting.

67. Look at the graphic. How much additional money will the woman be asked to pay?

(A) $2
(B) $5
(C) $20
(D) $22

PART 4

 01-48 ▶ 01-52

Directions: In PART 4, you will hear several short talks. After each talk, you will be asked to answer three questions about what you heard. Choose the best response to each question, and mark the corresponding letter (A), (B), (C), or (D) on your answer sheet. The questions and responses are printed in the test book. The talks do not appear in the test book, and they will be spoken only one time.

71. What type of service does the speaker provide?

(A) Vehicle storage
(B) Car rental
(C) Order processing
(D) Automobile repair

72. What does the woman mean when she says, "You won't find them for less than that"?

(A) She is offering the lowest price.
(B) She is trying to find a smaller size.
(C) She is willing to help him look.
(D) She is expecting the man to call.

73. If the listener wants the service, when should he return the call?

(A) Within the hour
(B) By five o'clock
(C) Before closing time
(D) Any time this week

74. Why is the listener going to travel?

(A) To meet some clients
(B) To go sightseeing
(C) To attend a trade show
(D) To visit a branch office

75. What does the speaker plan to do first?

(A) Apply for a visa
(B) Book airline tickets
(C) Reserve a hotel room
(D) Arrange a tour

76. What does the speaker have to confirm?

(A) Travel dates
(B) Hotel requirements
(C) A passport number
(D) Frequent flyer miles

77. What is the purpose of this event?

(A) To promote a new restaurant
(B) To showcase student achievements
(C) To celebrate a talented chef
(D) To thank local food producers

78. According to the speaker, what can be found in the program?

(A) Names of the instructors
(B) A description of the institute
(C) Profiles of the chefs
(D) Information about the ingredients

79. What will happen at the end of the event?

(A) Instructors will hold a cooking demonstration.
(B) Farmers will talk about locally grown food.
(C) Guests will attend a dessert reception in the kitchen.
(D) Students will answer guests' questions.

80. What is the purpose of the announcement?

(A) To explain an upcoming merger
(B) To introduce a new manager
(C) To discuss a recent acquisition
(D) To report on a business competitor

81. What does the man mean when he says, "Don't say we're not ambitious"?

(A) He wants listeners to wait until he has finished.
(B) He feels his company has an aggressive strategy.
(C) He takes a conservative approach to business.
(D) He hopes employees will support the decision.

82. What does the man ask listeners to do?

(A) Print out a marketing report
(B) Attend a training session
(C) Review an online document
(D) Take advantage of Mr. Chang's visit

GO ON TO THE NEXT PAGE ➡

83. What does the Sebastiani School specialize in?

    (A) Music education
    (B) Online marketing
    (C) Computer programming
    (D) Library science

84. According to the advertisement, what do students like most about the Sebastiani School?

    (A) Flexible schedules
    (B) Low prices
    (C) Excellent instruction
    (D) Online resources

85. What is scheduled to happen on July 1?

    (A) Alumni will perform for the students.
    (B) A graduation ceremony will be held.
    (C) Faculty and students will be available to talk.
    (D) Registration for the next term will begin.

_____

86. Why is the woman calling?

    (A) To ask for a favor
    (B) To announce some good news
    (C) To express her gratitude
    (D) To change her appointment

87. What does the woman imply when she says, "Perfect timing, I know"?

    (A) She thinks the party was scheduled at the right time.
    (B) She believes all the guests will arrive on time.
    (C) She feels the appointment is inconveniently scheduled.
    (D) She doesn't want to change the time of the game.

88. Why is the woman looking forward to next week?

    (A) Her ankle will be healed by then.
    (B) An important game will be played.
    (C) It is her turn to organize the party.
    (D) She plans to give Beth a gift.

89. According to the speaker, what is happening today?

    (A) A new bridge is being opened.
    (B) A lightning strike is being reported.
    (C) A storm is passing through the area.
    (D) A river is flooding its banks.

90. What does the speaker mean when she says, "It's really something else"?

    (A) The storm is quite extraordinary.
    (B) The wind is more dangerous than the rain.
    (C) The forecast was for sunny skies.
    (D) The situation is being closely monitored.

91. What are listeners advised to do at 9:30?

    (A) Evacuate their homes
    (B) Avoid unnecessary journeys
    (C) Contact local authorities
    (D) Listen to a broadcast

_____

92. What does the speaker want to focus on this year?

    (A) Lowering operating expenses
    (B) Writing accurate reports
    (C) Increasing sales revenue
    (D) Cutting capital-intensive investments

93. What does the speaker request help with?

    (A) Opening offices
    (B) Collecting data
    (C) Emailing information
    (D) Operating equipment

94. What will the listeners receive by email?

    (A) A blank template
    (B) A detailed spreadsheet
    (C) A formatted budget
    (D) A completed report

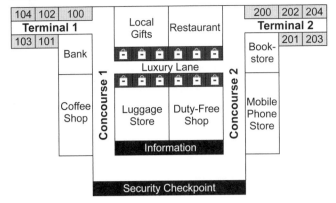

IT Equipment Request -- New Employee					
Name	Department	Start Day	Desktop	Laptop	Mobile Phone
Jordan Yee	Sales	June 4		✓	✓
Dex Findler	IT	June 4			
Ben Kim	Marketing	June 4		✓	✓
Pam Bundy	Design		✓*		✓
* Notes:					
			Authorization: Kayla Sayers		

95. Who most likely are the listeners?

(A) Tour group members
(B) Construction crew workers
(C) Airport employees
(D) Flight attendants

96. Look at the graphic. Where will the listeners be unable to go?

(A) Terminal 1
(B) The coffee shop
(C) The bookstore
(D) The duty free shop

97. What does the woman advise the listeners to do?

(A) Walk up Terminal 2
(B) Go immediately to the gate
(C) Relax at the restaurant
(D) Browse the gift store

98. Look at the graphic. Which employee does the speaker need more information about?

(A) Jason Yee
(B) Dex Findler
(C) Ben Kim
(D) Pam Bundy

99. What does the speaker assume will happen?

(A) The listener will revise the document.
(B) The designer will require special software.
(C) Dex Findler will request a mobile phone.
(D) Kayla Sayers will return his call.

100. What is the listener asked to do if there is a problem?

(A) Install some software
(B) Submit a form
(C) Contact a manager
(D) Send a text message

This is the end of the Listening test. Turn to PART 5 in your test book.

GO ON TO THE NEXT PAGE

READING TEST

In the Reading part of the test, you will read several different types of texts and answer a variety of questions. The Reading test has three parts, and directions are provided for each of them. You will have seventy-five minutes to complete the entire Reading test. Answer as many questions as you can within the time allotted. Write only on your answer sheet, not the test book.

PART 5

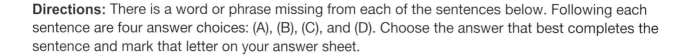

Directions: There is a word or phrase missing from each of the sentences below. Following each sentence are four answer choices: (A), (B), (C), and (D). Choose the answer that best completes the sentence and mark that letter on your answer sheet.

101. Grassley Audio is excited to ------- the release of the DJ500 line of headphones.

(A) announcing
(B) announce
(C) announced
(D) announces

102. The lecture will be followed ------- a question and answer session.

(A) after
(B) then
(C) as
(D) by

103. The IT department will require employees to ------- change their password.

(A) formerly
(B) regularly
(C) previously
(D) recently

104. All employees who sign up for the training session will receive an email confirming their ------- for the event.

(A) register
(B) registers
(C) registered
(D) registration

105. Snyder Inc.'s annual 5K Fun Run is this Saturday, and all employees and their families are welcome to -------.

(A) challenge
(B) accompany
(C) participate
(D) adjoin

106. To schedule an appointment with Ms. Jackson, either call her assistant ------- fill out the online form on her website.

(A) and
(B) if
(C) or
(D) but

107. Please transfer all calls to Ms. Ginsberg, who can assist Mr. Chen's clients while ------- is unavailable.

(A) his
(B) himself
(C) him
(D) he

108. The ------- policy is just one part of the sales agreement.

(A) return
(B) returnable
(C) returned
(D) returning

109. Guests of the CEO will be seated ------- the long table near the window.

(A) among
(B) in
(C) at
(D) on

110. The restaurant they took us to had some of the most ------- dishes I've ever had.

(A) memorial
(B) memorable
(C) memorizing
(D) memorized

111. All musical instruments must be promptly returned to the band manager ------- the scheduled practice has been completed.

(A) once
(B) soon
(C) immediately
(D) often

112. To avoid damaging the equipment, it is important to follow the instructions ------- when cleaning the device.

(A) care
(B) careful
(C) carefully
(D) caring

113. Mr. Burroughs was hired to ------- the writers and artists who design our greeting cards.

(A) explain
(B) supervise
(C) order
(D) create

114. Gooseberry Inc. will open an office in Paris in preparation for an ------- into the European market.

(A) expanding
(B) expanse
(C) expansion
(D) expand

115. The Instagoo mobile device is ------- quick in opening most apps.

(A) remarkable
(B) remarkably
(C) remarked
(D) remarks

116. Mr. Baxter is proposing a ------- strategy for increasing our market share among teenagers.

(A) different
(B) various
(C) furious
(D) insistent

117. Enter your email address below if you would like to receive regular updates ------- our products and services.

(A) regard
(B) regards
(C) regarded
(D) regarding

118. ------- the sales team and the technical staff are available to reply to customer inquiries.

(A) Because
(B) While
(C) Either
(D) Both

GO ON TO THE NEXT PAGE

119. During the remodeling, the copy machine will be ------- located in the hallway near the meeting rooms.

(A) partially
(B) temporarily
(C) normally
(D) permanently

120. We were not immediately able to offer a complete ------- of what went wrong.

(A) explain
(B) explainable
(C) explanation
(D) explained

121. The location of Ms. Chee's retirement party ------- to the Balboa Grill.

(A) has been moved
(B) to be moving
(C) being moved
(D) has been moving

122. Only managers are required to attend the sales workshop, but ------- in the customer service seminar is mandatory for all employees.

(A) consistency
(B) arrival
(C) improvement
(D) participation

123. The redesign of the website ------- to increase user interaction, but actually it had no measurable effect.

(A) intend
(B) intended
(C) intending
(D) was intended

124. Over half of all new hires this year were made _____ referrals from current employees.

(A) because
(B) through
(C) since
(D) though

125. Free product training, follow-up calls, and similar ------- ensure better customer retention.

(A) practices
(B) practiced
(C) practical
(D) practically

126. Shipping costs are ------- calculated based on the weight of the order and the desired speed of delivery.

(A) competitively
(B) automatically
(C) similarly
(D) significantly

127. The purpose of the meeting is to decide ------- the department can reduce costs in the coming year.

(A) only
(B) how
(C) even
(D) so that

128. When opening a new retail outlet, location is always the most important -------.

(A) consequence
(B) movement
(C) reduction
(D) consideration

129. Rather than purchasing new computer equipment, the consulting company recommended upgrading our software -------.

(A) enough
(B) instead
(C) otherwise
(D) either

130. Several restaurants near the office offer a discount to those with a ------- employee ID card.

(A) mutual
(B) accountable
(C) valid
(D) prudent

PART 6

Directions: There is a word, phrase, or sentence is missing from parts of each of the following texts. Below each text, there are four answer choices for each question: (A), (B), (C), and (D). Choose the answer that best completes the text and mark the corresponding letter on your answer sheet.

Questions 131-134 refer to the following email.

From: Joe Shlabotnik, Director of Water Safety, Green Valley Lake

To: All Lifeguards and Junior Lifeguards

Subject: Water Safety Training

Date: Thursday, April 22

The bathing beach at Green Valley Lake will open for the summer ------- on June 1. To prepare
131.
for the season, weekly training sessions will be offered at the Boathouse each Saturday afternoon

in May. Junior lifeguards ------- to attend all four sessions. -------, we also encourage senior
132.   **133.**
lifeguards to come by to refresh their skills and share their knowledge with less experienced staff.

At Green Valley Lake, we believe that learning together leads to better working relationships, and

those relationships help create a safer environment for our community. -------.
134.

Best regards,

Joe Shlabotnik

---

131. (A) this month
(B) as usual
(C) recently
(D) at first

132. (A) expects
(B) expected
(C) expecting
(D) are expected

133. (A) At once
(B) Therefore
(C) Of course
(D) Especially

134. (A) We hope all Green Valley lifeguards take advantage of this
opportunity.
(B) Thank you all for organizing such a memorable event.
(C) We look forward to having another successful school year.
(D) The next training session will be emailed to you on Saturday.

GO ON TO THE NEXT PAGE

Questions 135-138 refer to the following notice.

Zeblen Consulting regularly surveys our clients to research how we can improve the ------- we offer them. To make working at Zeblen as fulfilling as possible, we're now asking our own employees those questions. The responses you provide will help us improve ------- company **136.** culture and work environment. -------. **137.**

The survey was designed by Mittleman Research, and it is available at mittlemanresearch.com/ zeblen. Please visit that ------- and complete the survey by Friday. You will not be asked for any **138.** personally identifying information and all responses will be completely anonymous.

135. (A) serve
(B) services
(C) serving
(D) servicing

136. (A) its
(B) their
(C) our
(D) that

137. (A) To give just one example, we could provide more trees and plants in the office.
(B) We hope that all employees will find time to attend the workshop.
(C) Clients will be asked how Zeblen can better meet their professional needs.
(D) Topics include advancement opportunities, compensation, and workplace support.

138. (A) company
(B) site
(C) evaluation
(D) report

Questions 139-142 refer to the following notice.

-------. The north elevator will be closed during the month of October and the south elevator will
139.
be closed all of November. These closures are annoying, but necessary to ensure the safety of
everyone in the building.

Let's work together to minimize the disruption. First, try to avoid using the working elevator in
the morning and evening when it is most in demand. Large items, ------- bicycles, should only be
140.
transported when there is no one else waiting. If you live on one of the lower floors, take the stairs
whenever possible. Most importantly, please be ------- of others. Lines will be long, and we should
141.
be especially mindful of the needs of older residents and those with young children.

Thank you for your -------. If you have any questions or concerns, please contact the property
142.
manager.

139. (A) All tenants are kindly asked to take the stairs until further
    notice.
(B) Be advised that bicycles are not allowed to be transported
    in the elevators.
(C) Please note that elevator maintenance this fall will cause
    some inconvenience.
(D) Building management would like to remind everyone to
    remain calm.

140. (A) example of
(B) include
(C) unlike
(D) such us

141. (A) considerate
(B) prominent
(C) familiar
(D) magnificent

142. (A) proposal
(B) cooperation
(C) advice
(D) suggestion

GO ON TO THE NEXT PAGE

Dr. Sembla Nyad
Templeton University
872 Skylab Rd.
Austin, Texas

Dear Professor Nyad,

It is my distinct pleasure to invite you to be a featured speaker at the Sunnyvale Technology Summit this year. Your research on the history of social media is essential to the discussion of this year's theme, which is "The future of online communities." If you are -------, perhaps we could **143.** discuss topics for a possible talk over the phone.

Speakers are not directly compensated, but we will gladly ------- travel and hotel expenses. More **144.** importantly, the summit is a place to meet people. Our ------- is to bring together leaders from the **145.** academy, business, and government for far-reaching discussions on the interplay of technology and society.

-------. Details about the summit are available at our website: sunnyvaletech.com. Please feel free **146.** to call me anytime if you have any questions.

Sincerely,

Timothy Jessup
Director, Sunnyvale Technology Summit
t.jessup@sunnyvaletech.com
(512) 555-3667

143. (A) interest
(B) interested
(C) interesting
(D) interestingly

144. (A) receive
(B) require
(C) restrict
(D) reimburse

145. (A) mission
(B) sponsor
(C) experiment
(D) dilemma

146. (A) I have included a check to cover your expenses.
(B) I am sure you will enjoy working at Sunnyvale.
(C) I do hope that you are able to join us this year.
(D) I encourage you to decide on the theme as soon as possible.

Directions: PART 7 consists of a number of texts such as emails, advertisements, and instant messages. After each text or set of texts there are several questions. Choose the best answer to each question and mark the corresponding letter (A), (B), (C), or (D) on your answer sheet.

Questions 147-148 refer to the following job announcement.

~~ IT Analyst Wanted ~~

Tenz Personal Help Desk is seeking a motivated IT professional with excellent interpersonal skills for a full-time off-site position. Tenz delivers personalized on-demand IT support via online chat and video conferencing to residential customers and small businesses. In addition to having comprehensive, up-to-date technical knowledge of the hardware and software our customers use, the successful candidate must be able to communicate patiently and effectively with customers who may not have technical knowledge. To be considered, you must have a computer with a video camera and a reliable Internet connection. Tenz analysts work from home, but this is not a flexible or freelance position. Working hours are 8 AM to 5 PM Interested applicants should complete the online form at tenzpersonalhd.com/careers by May 15.

---

147. What is stated as a requirement for the job?

(A) Visiting customer homes and small businesses
(B) Ownership of the proper equipment
(C) The ability to repair computer hardware
(D) Experience working as an off-site employee

148. What does the announcement indicate about Tenz?

(A) It is a successful and growing business.
(B) It mainly employs freelance workers.
(C) It will make a hiring decision by mid-May.
(D) It expects employees to be sociable.

GO ON TO THE NEXT PAGE

Questions 149-150 refer to the following text message chain.

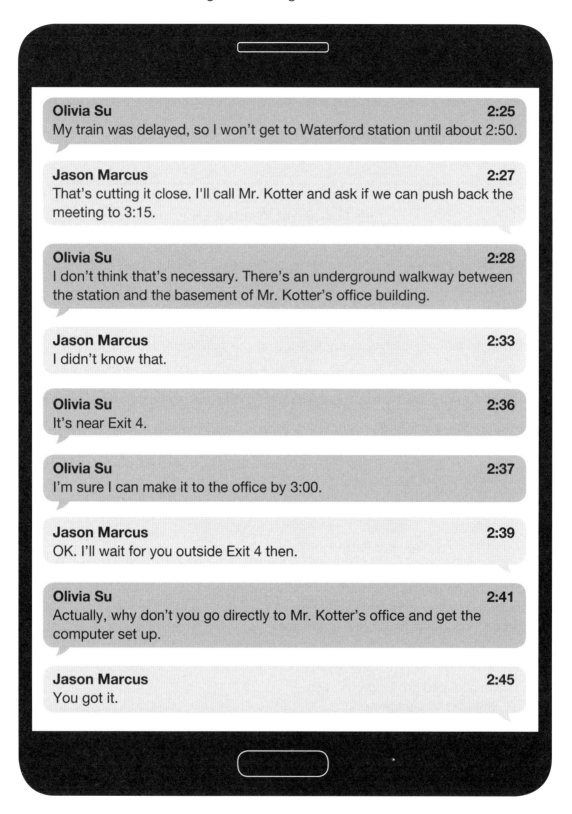

Olivia Su   2:25
My train was delayed, so I won't get to Waterford station until about 2:50.

Jason Marcus   2:27
That's cutting it close. I'll call Mr. Kotter and ask if we can push back the meeting to 3:15.

Olivia Su   2:28
I don't think that's necessary. There's an underground walkway between the station and the basement of Mr. Kotter's office building.

Jason Marcus   2:33
I didn't know that.

Olivia Su   2:36
It's near Exit 4.

Olivia Su   2:37
I'm sure I can make it to the office by 3:00.

Jason Marcus   2:39
OK. I'll wait for you outside Exit 4 then.

Olivia Su   2:41
Actually, why don't you go directly to Mr. Kotter's office and get the computer set up.

Jason Marcus   2:45
You got it.

149. What is suggested about Ms. Su?

(A) She is familiar with Waterford Station.
(B) She works for Mr. Kotter.
(C) She wants to postpone the meeting.
(D) She prefers to meet with Mr. Kotter alone.

150. At 2:45, what does Mr. Marcus mean when he writes, "You got it"?

(A) He believes Ms. Su will arrive on time.
(B) He knows Ms. Su will bring her computer.
(C) He will follow Ms. Su's suggestion.
(D) He thinks Ms. Su should contact Mr. Kotter.

Tip-Top Millinery

Hats Fun & Formal

Returns and Exchanges

Item: *Velbo Sun Hat, Red*   **Customer Name:** *Mary Popper*
Customer Code*: *2*

Reason for return:
☐ Wrong Size   ☐ Change of mind   ☐ Damaged
☑ Other: *Purchased as gift for friend who had the same hat*

Action Taken: *Returned in good condition for full cash refund*

Sales Associate: *Patt Morrison* **Authorization:** *Jo Clancey*

For exchanges, this from must be signed by the sales associate. For cash refunds, this form must be signed by the sales associate and the owner.

* ❶ new   ❷ returning   ❸ member   ❹ VIP

151. Who most likely is Jo Clancey?

(A) Ms. Morrison's friend
(B) A salesperson at the store
(C) The owner of Tip-Top Millinery
(D) The designer of the Velbo Sun Hat

152. What does the document indicate about the customer?

(A) She will purchase a different hat.
(B) She often returns items to the store.
(C) She exchanged the hat for one of equal value.
(D) She has been to the store before.

GO ON TO THE NEXT PAGE

From:	Charles Nelson
To:	Kumiko Eden
Subject:	New Employee Sales Performance

Dear Ms. Eden,

I did a quick evaluation of the monthly sales revenue generated by new hires, which you can see below. The data seems to support your speculation that the training program is not functioning effectively. After six months, new staff are still far from reaching the company average of €5,625. Equally concerning is the flat sales performance during their first three months of employment.

There are some limitations to the data. I haven't accounted for seasonal sales fluctuations or employees who left the company during their first six months. Nevertheless, it does suggest that management may want to make some changes. It would be premature to recommend a particular course of action, such as outsourcing the training program or replacing it with a mentoring system.

We might even consider eliminating it, but those decisions will require further research. Let me know how I can help.

Best regards,
Charlie

New Employee Average Monthly Sales Volume							
Sales Revenue (Euros)	5,001-6,000						
	4,001-5,000						
	3,001-4,000						
	2,001-3,000						
	1,001-2,000						
	501-1,000						
	0-500						
		Month 1	Month 2	Month 3	Month 4	Month 5	Month 6

153. Why is Mr. Nelson writing the email?

(A) To brainstorm new marketing strategies
(B) To gather data about sales performance
(C) To report a preliminary analysis
(D) To recommend a solution to a problem

154. What is indicated about the training program?

(A) It is not meeting management's expectations.
(B) It will be replaced with a mentoring system.
(C) It should be outsourced to a consulting company.
(D) It will be eliminated if performance does not improve.

Questions 155-157 refer to the following article.

All the Buzz about the New Hornet
By Mika Sanchez

SAN JOSE, CA (July 26) – After months of rumors, eBe Mobile Solutions announced this morning that its flagship smartphone, the Hornet 1, is now available for purchase. The Hornet represents a major gamble for the company—not only did eBe completely redesign the phone, they reimagined the purchasing process as well. — [1] —.

The phone's six-inch screen covers the entire front side, except for a small speaker and camera at the top. It is a stunning technical achievement, but perhaps even more innovative is what lies—or doesn't lie—beneath the screen. When ordering their Hornet 1, users can save money by removing features that they don't need, for example the fingerprint scanner or the headphone jack. At the same time, they can pay to upgrade their phone with components they want, such as a better camera, a larger battery, or more memory. — [2] —.

Once a global leader in smartphone sales, eBe has been struggling to maintain market share in recent years. Some analysts have expressed concern about whether eBe can deliver its customized phones in a timely manner. They warn that eBe may have rushed the Hornet 1 to market in order to beat competitors, who generally release new models in August and September. — [3] —.

Jenny Yu, spokesperson for eBe, said, "We believe the Hornet 1 is an unprecedented achievement not just for eBe, but for the entire mobile communications industry." — [4] —.

155. What is indicated about the Hornet 1?

(A) Its components have all been upgraded.
(B) Its screen covers the entire front side.
(C) Some of its features are optional.
(D) Most of its users will save money.

156. What is reported about eBe Mobile Solutions?

(A) It has chosen a risky strategy.
(B) It can deliver its phones quickly.
(C) It is a global leader in smartphone sales.
(D) It will release its flagship product soon.

157. In which of the positions marked [1], [2], [3], and [4] does the following sentence best belong?

"All told, the Hornet 1 comes in more than one hundred configurations."

(A) [1]
(B) [2]
(C) [3]
(D) [4]

GO ON TO THE NEXT PAGE

Questions 158-160 refer to the following memo.

Memo

DATE: February 2

We are excited to announce the hiring of Janice Kropotkin, who will serve as our new director of communications. Ms. Kropotkin comes to us with twenty years of experience in public relations, most recently a five-year appointment as press secretary for Mayor Quinn. Before her public service, Ms. Kropotkin worked for a decade as a spokesperson for Charmine Industries, and before that as an ombudswoman for the Daily Pilot newspaper.

Ms. Kropotkin will give a short talk on Friday afternoon at 4:30 in the employee cafeteria. She plans to discuss her experiences as well as outline her plans for the future. If you have questions about the direction of the department, she would be happy to address them. Ms. Kropotkin also plans to use the meeting as an opportunity to solicit feedback on the company website, a redesign of which will be her first major project. Members of the marketing and sales departments are strongly urged to attend.

---

158. In what field does Ms. Kropotkin specialize?

    (A) Online communication
    (B) Public relations
    (C) Industrial planning
    (D) News reporting

159. For how many years did Ms. Kropotkin work for Charmine Industries?

    (A) 5
    (B) 10
    (C) 15
    (D) 20

160. What is NOT scheduled to happen at the gathering?

    (A) Food and drinks will be served.
    (B) Opinions will be collected.
    (C) A brief presentation will be made.
    (D) A question and answer session will be held.

Questions 161-164 refer to the following online chat discussion.

Vacarro, Kristen [2:02 PM]
So, it's already Wednesday. We need to figure out if we can get the prototype quadcopter up and running before Stan and I leave for the toy show on Friday.

Vacarro, Kristen [2:03 PM]
I promised Toy Star I'd show them something special. They have over 200 stores now—I'd hate to disappoint them.

Henderson, Stan [2:05 PM]
The hardware is ready. I modified the body of the drone to accept the new camera. It's not perfect, but it should be good enough for a few demonstrations.

Jin, Alpha [2:18 PM]
The software is a work in progress. The camera has a lot of new functionality that I'm trying to make accessible with our current hand controller.

Vacarro, Kristen [2:20 PM]
Our flight departs at noon. Is that going to be enough time?

Jin, Alpha [2:22 PM]
I'll have the coding done by Thursday night, but I'll need at least one day for testing. A failed demonstration is worse than no demonstration.

Vacarro, Kristen [2:24 PM]
OK, it looks like we're going to have a non-functional prototype. We'll just have to make do.

Henderson, Stan [2:29 PM]
Hang on. We're meeting with Toy Star Saturday afternoon, right? What if I postpone my flight by a day?

Vacarro, Kristen [2:31 PM]
You'd have to make it to the conference center before 4:30.

Henderson, Stan [2:31 PM]
It's worth a shot. If Alpha is in, I'll get my flight changed.

Jin, Alpha [2:32 PM]
Let's do it.

---

161. What kind of business do the chat participants likely work for?

(A) A camera maker
(B) A toy manufacturer
(C) A software firm
(D) A toy store

162. When will Stan Henderson travel to the show?
(A) Wednesday
(B) Thursday
(C) Friday
(D) Saturday

163. What will Ms. Jin most likely do next?

(A) Change her flight time
(B) Repair a camera
(C) Work on some software
(D) Perform some tests

164. At 2:24 PM, what does Kristen Vacarro mean when she writes, "We'll just have to make do"?

(A) They are determined to finish the project on time.
(B) They must immediately make another prototype.
(C) They have just enough work for each of them to do.
(D) They will manage despite imperfect circumstances.

GO ON TO THE NEXT PAGE

The South Coast Gardening Cooperative
Give Your New Lemon Tree a Healthy Start!

Congratulations! With proper care, the lemon tree you have just purchased will bring you joy for decades to come. Take a moment to familiarize yourself with this amazing plant.

Overview
◆ This three-to-four-year-old tree is ready to be removed from its container and planted in the ground.
◆ Select a sunny spot at least two meters away from buildings, fences, or other trees.
◆ Make sure the place you choose has good drainage—wet soil can damage the roots.
◆ Analyze the soil. Lemons are acidic, but the trees grow best in neutral soil.
◆ After you have found the perfect location, dig a wide, shallow hole. Carefully remove the tree from its container and plant it together with the potting soil.

Care
◆ For the first several weeks, water thoroughly every other day. After the adjustment period, water weekly: more in summer, less in winter.
◆ If the tree does not bear fruit or otherwise appears unhealthy, call us. Our experts can suggest a suitable fertilizer as a first step.
◆ If problems persist, we can arrange to visit your tree to observe the soil conditions, root system, and other factors, such as pests and diseases, that may be affecting its health. Current fees for these and other services are available at southcoastgardeningcoop.org/services.

165. What is described in the Overview section?

(A) How to choose a suitable plant for the soil
(B) How to care for the tree in its container
(C) How to select and prepare an area for planting
(D) How to provide the optimal amount of watering

166. According to the instructions, what should people do before beginning to work?

(A) Drain the area
(B) Test the soil
(C) Dig a hole
(D) Remove the container

167. Why are people advised to visit the cooperative's website?

(A) To receive a fertilizer recommendation
(B) To view the prices for inspections
(C) To schedule a visit to the cooperative
(D) To request an expert phone consultation

Questions 168-171 refer to the following email.

From:	afithian@ppleup.com
To:	<All Employees>
Subject:	Plans for February
Date:	January 14

Everyone at headquarters is looking forward to welcoming the 64 colleagues from across town who will be working here in February while the midtown office is being renovated. It'll be a tight squeeze, but we've found space for everyone.

The Market Research and Communications teams will appropriate all five meeting rooms on the second floor. Everyone will have to be creative about finding meeting space—or finding reasons not to have meetings.

Customer Service and Technical Support team members will be using spare desks downstairs in the IT, Operations, and Purchasing departments.

Because members of the Sales and Business Development teams are issued laptops, we're asking you to work remotely. If you're in the area, we've reserved the meeting room at Phil's Coffee all month. Phil's is in the Packer Building across the street from HQ. The meeting room is in the basement and it seats 12.

As a reminder, the company is still offering two additional days off for every three days of vacation taken in February. It's a great time for a holiday!

Finally, no additional parking can be made available. Paid parking in the area is not cheap, so please consider bicycling to work, using public transportation, or carpooling. If you need a ride or can offer a ride, click here to be taken to the company's ride-sharing board. Help out if you can.

There will undoubtedly be some inconveniences, but this will also be a wonderful opportunity to get to know our colleagues better. Let's make the most of it.

Sincerely,
Alissa Fithian

168. What is the purpose of this email?

(A) To welcome a group of new workers
(B) To announce the opening of a new office
(C) To assign work spaces to employees
(D) To explain a remodeling project

169. The word "appropriate" in paragraph 2, line 1, is closest in meaning to

(A) correct
(B) take control of
(C) look out for
(D) allocate

170. Where is the Operations Department located?

(A) On the third floor
(B) On the second floor
(C) On the first floor
(D) In the basement

171. According to the email, what are employees discouraged from doing?

(A) Using a laptop
(B) Meeting in a coffee shop
(C) Taking a vacation
(D) Paying for parking

GO ON TO THE NEXT PAGE

Burnett Investment Research

476 5th Avenue
New York, NY 10018
burnettresearch.com

November 18
Mr. Tajima Hideki
Health Insights International
5-7-13 Minami-Azabu
Minato-ku, Tokyo 106-8575

Dear Mr. Tajima:

We were very pleased to learn that you have agreed to transfer your referral agreement from TPR to Burnett Investment Research. When Burnett acquired TPR, we made a commitment to honor all existing contracts and agreements, but of course agents such as yourself maintained the option of upgrading. We think you made the right choice. — [1] —.

Please review the Burnett referral agreement, which I have signed and enclosed. The commission rate and payment schedule we offer are identical to those in the TPR agreement. Also unchanged are the global pharmaceutical industry reports, which will continue to be produced by TPR and marketed under the name "Burnett-TPR." — [2] —. The new agreement makes available to you Burnett's extensive list of research reports. Our focus on medical services and equipment has in recent years been expanded to include consumer-facing companies, especially those specializing in fitness-tracking, digital records management, and nutritional supplements. We believe these additional resources will be of interest to your existing clients, and will allow you to expand your current client base. — [3] —.

As for the TPR agreement, I have signed two copies of a Mutual Termination letter. Please sign one and return it to us together with a signed copy of the Burnett agreement. Both documents should reach us before December 31. I am looking forward to working with you as we embark on this promising new endeavor. If you have any questions or concerns, please do not hesitate to contact me. — [4] —.

Sincerely,

John Most

John Most
Business Development Manager, Burnett Investment Research

Enclosures

172. Why did Mr. Most send this letter to Mr. Tajima?

    (A) To announce an acquisition
    (B) To suggest an investment strategy
    (C) To describe the terms of an agreement
    (D) To inquire about a contract

173. What did Mr. Most send with the letter?

    (A) A research report
    (B) An investment guide
    (C) A referral agreement
    (D) A client list

174. The phrase "embark on" in paragraph 3, line 3, is closest in meaning to

    (A) commence
    (B) agree with
    (C) invest in
    (D) cooperate

175. In which of the positions marked [1], [2], [3], and [4] does the following sentence best belong?

"Fund managers and financial advisers will benefit from research conducted by our global network of investment strategists."

    (A) [1]
    (B) [2]
    (C) [3]
    (D) [4]

GO ON TO THE NEXT PAGE

⊠

From:	June Wai
To:	stanley.roper@rivercityrentals.com
Subject:	Four apartments in June
Date:	April 17

Dear Mr. Roper:

I spoke with you earlier on the phone about possibly renting apartments for the four researchers who will be visiting Renjex's River City laboratory this June. As requested, I've noted the names and requirements of each of our visiting colleagues.

- Janet Wood: requires access to public transportation and nearby amenities
- Cindy Snow: prefers a simple, inexpensive option
- Jack Tripper: will be living with his wife
- Lana Shields: would like a quiet neighborhood

Our campus is located in the Arts District, so apartments in that area would be ideal, but Forrest Hills, where I reside, is a lovely, peaceful area. And I suppose Ms. Wood would prefer something more centrally located.

We'll need the apartments from June 1 to June 30. Ms. Snow will be staying until July 5, but can stay in a hotel for the final few days, unless special accommodations can be made. I'm eager to have this taken care of, so I'd appreciate it if you could let me know what you have available by April 20. I look forward to hearing from you soon.

Best regards,
June Wai
Administration Supervisor, Renjex Labs

 River City Short-Term Apartment Rentals

List of Apartments

Location ▼	Apartment ▼	Type* ▼	Rent ▼	June ▼
Forrest Hills	Shadow Point Apartments #111	Studio	$590	Available
Arts District	Topanga Suites #206	Studio	$680	Available
Town Center	City Garden #912	Studio	$975	Unavailable
Waterfront	Vista Tangento #306	1 Bedroom	$825	Unavailable
Town Center	City Garden #1401	1 Bedroom	$1,115	Available

* Studio apartments are single-occupancy only. One-bedroom apartments may have up to two residents, but in that case a monthly $50 service fee is added to the rent to cover the increase in utilities.

176. Why did Ms. Wai send the email?

(A) To request materials for a laboratory
(B) To promote her company in the city
(C) To inquire about available apartments
(D) To get information about visiting researchers

177. What is suggested about Janet Wood?

(A) She intends to get a driver's license
(B) She has recently moved to River City
(C) She currently commutes by subway or bus
(D) She will not have access to a car in June

178. What area of the city would Lana Shields likely prefer?

(A) Forrest Hills
(B) Arts District
(C) Town Center
(D) Waterfront

179. When is Mr. Tripper expected to move out?

(A) April 20
(B) June 1
(C) June 30
(D) July 5

180. What is indicated about one-bedroom apartments?

(A) They are more expensive than studios.
(B) The cost of utilities is not included in the rent.
(C) They are more expensive if there are two residents.
(D) They are more likely to be available than studio apartments.

GO ON TO THE NEXT PAGE

Questions 181-185 refer to the following webpage and email.

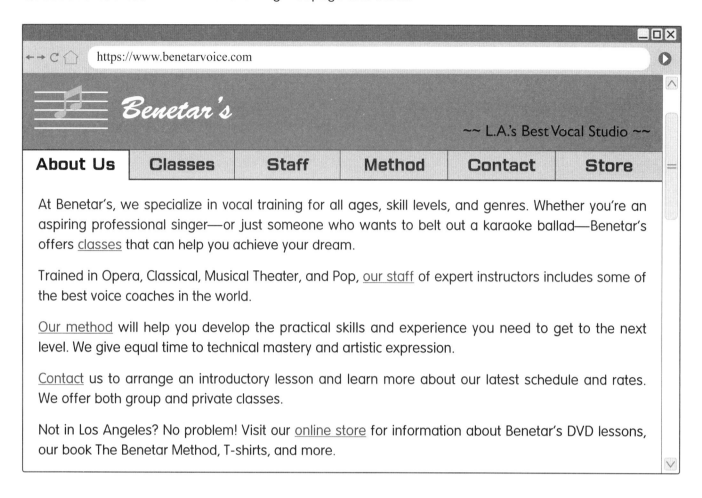

At Benetar's, we specialize in vocal training for all ages, skill levels, and genres. Whether you're an aspiring professional singer—or just someone who wants to belt out a karaoke ballad—Benetar's offers classes that can help you achieve your dream.

Trained in Opera, Classical, Musical Theater, and Pop, our staff of expert instructors includes some of the best voice coaches in the world.

Our method will help you develop the practical skills and experience you need to get to the next level. We give equal time to technical mastery and artistic expression.

Contact us to arrange an introductory lesson and learn more about our latest schedule and rates. We offer both group and private classes.

Not in Los Angeles? No problem! Visit our online store for information about Benetar's DVD lessons, our book The Benetar Method, T-shirts, and more.

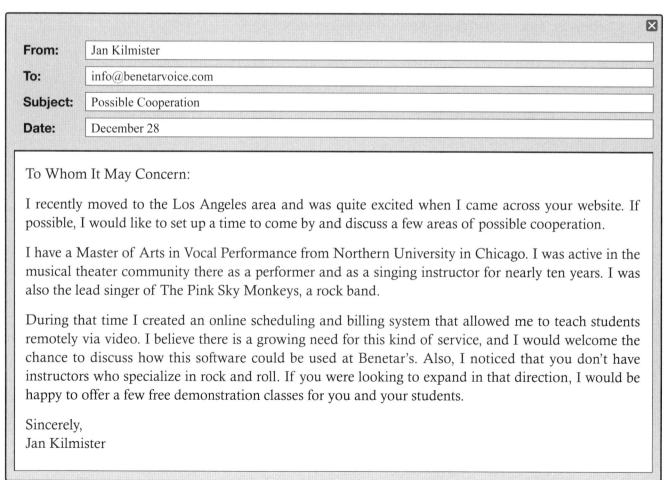

From: Jan Kilmister

To: info@benetarvoice.com

Subject: Possible Cooperation

Date: December 28

To Whom It May Concern:

I recently moved to the Los Angeles area and was quite excited when I came across your website. If possible, I would like to set up a time to come by and discuss a few areas of possible cooperation.

I have a Master of Arts in Vocal Performance from Northern University in Chicago. I was active in the musical theater community there as a performer and as a singing instructor for nearly ten years. I was also the lead singer of The Pink Sky Monkeys, a rock band.

During that time I created an online scheduling and billing system that allowed me to teach students remotely via video. I believe there is a growing need for this kind of service, and I would welcome the chance to discuss how this software could be used at Benetar's. Also, I noticed that you don't have instructors who specialize in rock and roll. If you were looking to expand in that direction, I would be happy to offer a few free demonstration classes for you and your students.

Sincerely,
Jan Kilmister

181. What is NOT suggested about Benetar's?

    (A) It has teachers from all over the world.
    (B) It trains singers in several styles of music.
    (C) It focuses on technical mastery.
    (D) It offers singing classes for children.

182. What is indicated about Benetar's?

    (A) It has recently relocated from Chicago.
    (B) It offers private classes on the Internet.
    (C) It sells merchandise on its website.
    (D) It posts its most recent schedule online.

183. What style of singing offered by Benetar's is Ms. Kilmister most qualified to teach?

    (A) Classical
    (B) Pop
    (C) Musical Theater
    (D) Rock

184. What is suggested about Ms. Kilmister?

    (A) She has a degree in software development.
    (B) She prefers to teach group classes.
    (C) She plays guitar in a music group.
    (D) She would like to work at Benetar's.

185. What does Ms. Kilmister ask about?

    (A) The procedure for registering for classes
    (B) The rates for online instruction
    (C) The software used by Benetar's
    (D) The future plans of the studio

GO ON TO THE NEXT PAGE

Keynote Speaker Profile

Penny Rosemont has been involved in the creation of over a dozen video games in her long and storied career. Below are a few highlights.

Vegetable Mayhem
As lead game designer, Ms. Rosemont was responsible for creating the unique social aspects of this communal farming game, which are generally credited with sparking its world-wide success.

Diamond Moonshot
The game pairs two players from different countries who must work together to build a spaceship and fly it to a diamond-shaped moon. It was Ms. Rosemont's first time serving in the role of creative director.

Birdie Derby
To develop this racing game, Ms. Rosemont started her own company—Massive Penny Gaming. The new CEO scored a huge global hit with this game that pits large "flocks" (actually teams of up to 1,000 players) against each other in massive round-the-world races.

Rainbow Dream
More a critical success than a commercial one, this educational game teaches players the skills they need to make their own video game. To progress to the highest levels, advanced players need to show beginners how to accomplish various technical tasks.

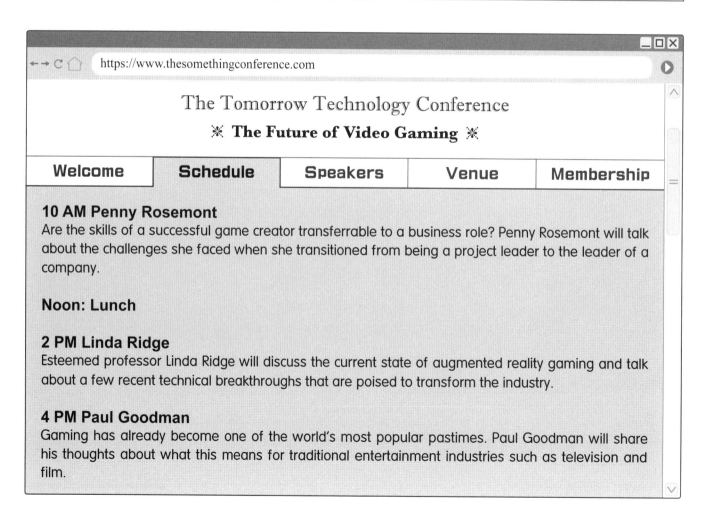

https://www.thesomethingconference.com

The Tomorrow Technology Conference
※ The Future of Video Gaming ※

| Welcome | Schedule | Speakers | Venue | Membership |

10 AM Penny Rosemont
Are the skills of a successful game creator transferrable to a business role? Penny Rosemont will talk about the challenges she faced when she transitioned from being a project leader to the leader of a company.

Noon: Lunch

2 PM Linda Ridge
Esteemed professor Linda Ridge will discuss the current state of augmented reality gaming and talk about a few recent technical breakthroughs that are poised to transform the industry.

4 PM Paul Goodman
Gaming has already become one of the world's most popular pastimes. Paul Goodman will share his thoughts about what this means for traditional entertainment industries such as television and film.

From: rgruder@tttc.com

To: penny.rosemont@mail.mpg.com

Subject: Many thanks!

Date: October 1

Dear Ms. Rosemont,

I would like to thank you for your compelling presentation. Everyone at the Tomorrow Technology Foundation was impressed by your ability to weave your personal story into a larger discussion of the evolution of the business side of gaming. It was truly inspirational.

And thank you also for your patience as we dealt with the microphone issue. I'm not sure I would have been so gracious had it been me up there on the stage. If we are fortunate enough to have you back to speak next year, rest assured that we'll change the batteries before your talk, not during it!

Thank you again, and please do keep in touch.

Roberta Gruder

---

186. What is one common feature in all of Ms. Rosemont's games?

(A) They connect players from different countries.
(B) They focus on teaching technical skills.
(C) They have generated significant revenue.
(D) They require players to work together.

187. Which game did Ms. Rosemont discuss at the conference?

(A) Vegetable Mayhem
(B) Diamond Moonshot
(C) Birdie Derby
(D) Rainbow Dream

188. What is indicated about the keynote speech?

(A) It was interrupted by a technical problem.
(B) It was scheduled for the end of the day.
(C) It was recently added to the schedule.
(D) It was delivered by a respected professor.

189. In the email, the word "compelling" in paragraph 1, line 1, is closes in meaning to

(A) required
(B) forceful
(C) reasonable
(D) practical

190. What is probably true about Ms. Gruder?

(A) She is employed by a video game company.
(B) She will give a presentation the following year.
(C) She is the organizer of the conference.
(D) She had a problem with the microphone.

GO ON TO THE NEXT PAGE

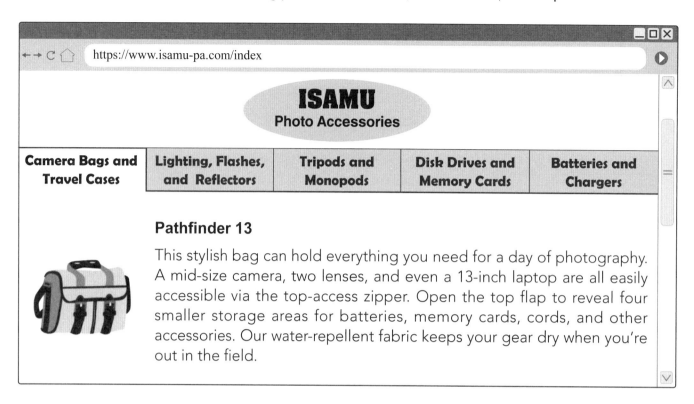

ISAMU
Photo Accessories

Camera Bags and Travel Cases	Lighting, Flashes, and Reflectors	Tripods and Monopods	Disk Drives and Memory Cards	Batteries and Chargers

Pathfinder 13

This stylish bag can hold everything you need for a day of photography. A mid-size camera, two lenses, and even a 13-inch laptop are all easily accessible via the top-access zipper. Open the top flap to reveal four smaller storage areas for batteries, memory cards, cords, and other accessories. Our water-repellent fabric keeps your gear dry when you're out in the field.

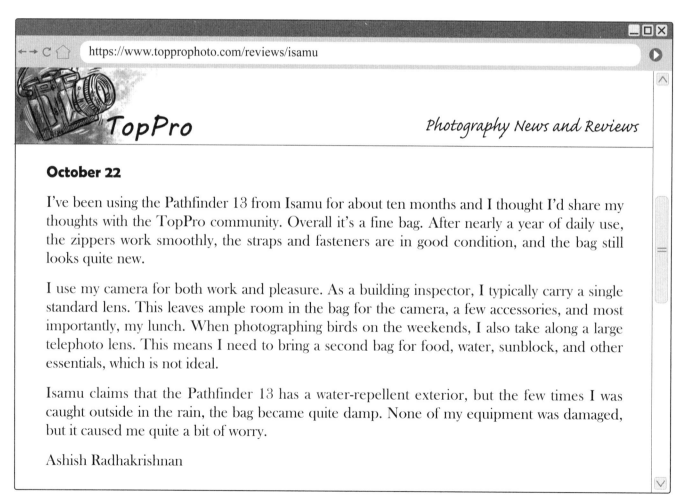

TopPro   *Photography News and Reviews*

October 22

I've been using the Pathfinder 13 from Isamu for about ten months and I thought I'd share my thoughts with the TopPro community. Overall it's a fine bag. After nearly a year of daily use, the zippers work smoothly, the straps and fasteners are in good condition, and the bag still looks quite new.

I use my camera for both work and pleasure. As a building inspector, I typically carry a single standard lens. This leaves ample room in the bag for the camera, a few accessories, and most importantly, my lunch. When photographing birds on the weekends, I also take along a large telephoto lens. This means I need to bring a second bag for food, water, sunblock, and other essentials, which is not ideal.

Isamu claims that the Pathfinder 13 has a water-repellent exterior, but the few times I was caught outside in the rain, the bag became quite damp. None of my equipment was damaged, but it caused me quite a bit of worry.

Ashish Radhakrishnan

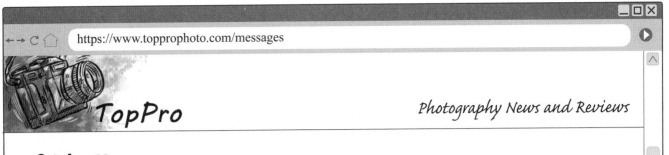

https://www.topprophoto.com/messages

TopPro

Photography News and Reviews

October 23

Dear Mr. Radhakrishnan,

Thank you for your review of the Pathfinder 13. The team here at Isamu welcomes feedback—both positive and negative. I'm sorry that you were worried about the safety of your equipment. We're proud of the Pathfinder's water-repelling properties, and unless your bag was submerged, your camera was likely quite safe. You noticed water on the exterior of the bag because we placed the weather coating on the inner-most layer. This is something we will clarify in our upcoming catalog and online marketing materials. Also, please note that we do offer inexpensive rain covers on our website.

As for the size, we've decided to expand the Pathfinder line. In January, we will introduce the Pathfinder 15. More spacious than your model, it should have room for all of your weekend gear. If you agree to review the Pathfinder 15 for the TopPro website by the end of this year, we would be happy to send you one to keep. Either way, please do get in touch with me and thank you again for your review.

Martha Larsen, Isamu Customer Service Supervisor
m.larsen@mail.isamu.com

191. What does Mr. Radhakrishnan write about his Pathfinder 13?

(A) It is large enough to use for work.
(B) It was purchased recently.
(C) It caused his camera to get wet.
(D) It is stylish and spacious.

192. In the review, the word "claims" in paragraph 3, line 1, is closest in meaning to

(A) asserts
(B) admits
(C) demands
(D) realizes

193. What does Ms. Larsen offer to Mr. Radhakrishnan?

(A) An inexpensive rain cover
(B) A free catalog
(C) A new camera
(D) A larger bag

194. What must Mr. Radhakrishnan do in order to receive a gift from Ms. Larsen?

(A) Visit a website
(B) Write a review
(C) Call customer service
(D) Return a product

195. What does Ms. Larsen indicate about the water-repellent coating?

(A) It is quite safe for customers to use.
(B) It allows a camera to be safely submerged.
(C) It is located on the inside of the bag.
(D) It will be introduced in the coming year.

GO ON TO THE NEXT PAGE

Attention All Orchestra Members

I'm thrilled to announce that Fontella Fox will be joining us on stage for our concert on Saturday! The current plan is for Ms. Fox to close the concert with two songs—her recent hit "Look Out" and another song to be announced. I'll work out the song arrangements with Ms. Fox's music director before our rehearsal on Friday. We'll only have that one chance to practice, so be prepared to stay as long as it takes.

This is a wonderful opportunity for us to perform with a talented and versatile pop singer. Let's make the most out of it. In the meantime, please listen to "Look Out" and be ready for anything!

From:	Gozen Steimer <g.steimer@ffenterprises.com>
To:	Sally Tase <sallytase@greensboroughorch.org>
Subject:	Saturday concert
Date:	Thursday, July 2

Dear Ms. Tase,

It was great talking with you. I just wanted to confirm what we discussed on the phone. Ms. Fox will take the stage after the "William Tell Overture" and immediately perform "Look Out." After the song, you will introduce her, she will greet the audience, and then the show will end with Ms. Fox's performance of "My Oh My."

I've attached sheet music for both songs. You'll probably have to make some adjustments, but I'm sure we can work out any issues when we meet on Friday. Ms. Fox is really looking forward to this event! If you have any questions, please give me a call.

Gozen Steimer
FF Enterprises, Music Director

Surprise Guest at the Bijou

The Greensborough Orchestra ended its season on a high note at the Bijou Concert Hall last night. After a lively two-hour program of French and Italian opera favorites, pop star Fontella Fox took the stage and charmed the audience with a couple of songs from her latest album, *Too Few*. Backed by lush layers of strings, Ms. Fox's voice took on a warmth that is sometimes missing from her studio productions.

The enthusiastic crowd demanded an encore, and Fox returned to the stage with conductor Sally Tase. After a few words with the musicians, Fox and the orchestra launched into "Habanera," the famous aria from Bizet's opera *Carmen*. The crowd responded to Ms. Fox's operatic debut with a standing ovation.

Ms. Tase later confirmed that Saturday was the first time the orchestra played "Habanera" with Ms. Fox. "I knew that Fontella had some classical training, but until that moment on stage, I had no idea she sang opera!" Tase said. "I think the concertgoers really appreciated the spontaneity and sense of adventure she brought to the evening."

— By Marcel Dubois, Music Criti

196. Who most likely posted the notice?

(A) Fontella Fox
(B) Sally Tase
(C) Gozen Steimer
(D) Marcel Dubois

197. What are orchestra members instructed to do on Friday?

(A) Attend a rehearsal
(B) Announce a new song
(C) Meet with a music critic
(D) Arrive earlier than usual

198. What is indicated about the orchestra members?

(A) They are accomplished singers.
(B) They performed an unrehearsed song.
(C) They are fans of Fontella Fox.
(D) They publicized the concert.

199. What is true about Fontella Fox?

(A) She is a professional opera singer.
(B) She teaches the audience to sing in a variety of styles.
(C) She sang three songs at the concert.
(D) She asked the audience to sing with her.

200. What does Mr. Dubois indicate about the concert?

(A) The orchestra mostly played unfamiliar songs.
(B) It was the conductor's debut performance.
(C) The audience joined in singing the final song.
(D) It was the first time Fontella Fox sang opera publicly.

Stop! This is the end of the test. If you finish before time is called, you may go back to Parts 5, 6, and 7 and check your work.

ACTUAL TEST

2

全真測驗

第二回

02-01 ▶ 02-58 **LISTENING TEST** 048

READING TEST 060

＊ 答案卡置於本書末，請自行撕下使用。

LISTENING TEST

The Listening test allows you to demonstrate your ability to understand spoken English. The Listening test has four parts, and you will hear directions for each of them. The entire Listening test is approximately forty-five minutes long. Write only on your answer sheet, not the test book.

PART 1

 02-01 ▶ 02-07

Directions: For each question in PART 1, you will hear four statements about a picture. Choose the statement that best describes what you see in the picture and mark your answer on the answer sheet. The statements will be spoken only once, and do not appear in the test book.

Example

Sample Answer

Statement (C), "They are sitting around the table," is the best description of the photograph, so you should mark (C) on your answer sheet.

1.

2.

GO ON TO THE NEXT PAGE

3.

4.

5.

6.

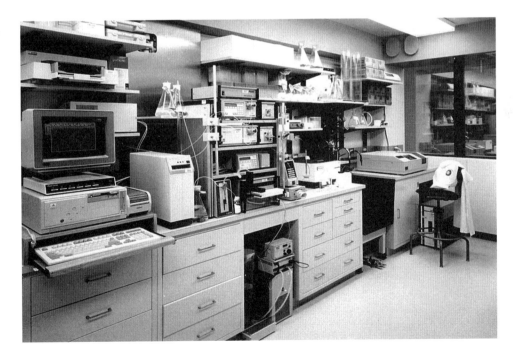

GO ON TO THE NEXT PAGE ➤

02-08 ▶ 02-33

Directions: In PART 2, you will hear either a statement or a question and three responses. They will be spoken only once, and do not appear in your test book. Choose the best response to the question or statement and mark the corresponding letter (A), (B), or (C) on your answer sheet.

7. Mark your answer on your answer sheet.

8. Mark your answer on your answer sheet.

9. Mark your answer on your answer sheet.

10. Mark your answer on your answer sheet.

11. Mark your answer on your answer sheet.

12. Mark your answer on your answer sheet.

13. Mark your answer on your answer sheet.

14. Mark your answer on your answer sheet.

15. Mark your answer on your answer sheet.

16. Mark your answer on your answer sheet.

17. Mark your answer on your answer sheet.

18. Mark your answer on your answer sheet.

19. Mark your answer on your answer sheet.

20. Mark your answer on your answer sheet.

21. Mark your answer on your answer sheet.

22. Mark your answer on your answer sheet.

23. Mark your answer on your answer sheet.

24. Mark your answer on your answer sheet.

25. Mark your answer on your answer sheet.

26. Mark your answer on your answer sheet.

27. Mark your answer on your answer sheet.

28. Mark your answer on your answer sheet.

29. Mark your answer on your answer sheet.

30. Mark your answer on your answer sheet.

31. Mark your answer on your answer sheet.

## PART 3

02-34 ▶ 02-38

Directions: In PART 3, you will hear several short conversations between two or more people. After each conversation, you will be asked to answer three questions about what you heard. Choose the best response to each question, and mark the corresponding letter (A), (B), (C), or (D) on your answer sheet. The conversations do not appear in the test book, and they will be spoken only one time.

32. Where do the speakers most likely work?

(A) A taxi service
(B) An airport
(C) A hotel
(D) A train station

33. What change does the woman mention?

(A) Employees will start work earlier next month.
(B) Visitors will be met when their flight arrives.
(C) Staff can be picked up at the train station.
(D) The city bus will run more frequently.

34. What must the man provide?

(A) A flight schedule
(B) A bus pass
(C) A taxi voucher
(D) A shuttle reservation

35. What does the woman ask the man to do?

(A) Make a call
(B) Send an email
(C) Give a presentation
(D) Join a video conference

36. Why is the woman unable to complete the task?

(A) She has to call a colleague.
(B) She has to attend a meeting.
(C) She has a computer problem.
(D) She has to travel for business.

37. What will happen on Monday afternoon?

(A) Some software will be installed.
(B) Some awards will be given out.
(C) A video conference will take place.
(D) A meeting will be scheduled.

38. What is the man's problem?

(A) He cannot find a place to charge his laptop.
(B) His device suffered some water damage.
(C) He was overcharged for a product.
(D) His computer is not functioning properly.

39. What does the woman ask the man about?

(A) When the computer was purchased
(B) Who most recently used the device
(C) Whether the computer had been damaged
(D) What steps he took to solve the problem

40. What does the woman offer to do?

(A) Refund the purchase
(B) Repair the power cord
(C) Replace a component
(D) Return the device

41. Where does the woman most likely work?

(A) At a hotel chain
(B) At a credit card company
(C) At a restaurant
(D) At a travel agency

42. Why is the man calling?

(A) To complain about an employee
(B) To dispute a charge
(C) To request an upgrade
(D) To cancel a reservation

43. What does the woman say she will do next?

(A) Repair some fixtures
(B) Update a policy
(C) Provide a full refund
(D) Contact the manager

GO ON TO THE NEXT PAGE ➤

Actual Test 2 | PART 2/3

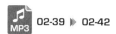

44. What is the company planning to do next month?

(A) Create a mobile-friendly website
(B) Participate in a product expo
(C) Outsource a design project
(D) Upgrade the company database

45. What problem does the man mention?

(A) He doesn't have time for long-term projects.
(B) Database queries do not work on mobile devices.
(C) Webpages are not displaying correctly.
(D) There is no time to build a mobile-only website.

46. What does the woman suggest?

(A) Using a professional designer
(B) Making a mobile-only website
(C) Contracting out website maintenance
(D) Hiring a project manager

47. What does the woman say about the stadium seats?

(A) There is a waiting list for people wanting to purchase them.
(B) Prices for them are listed in the newspaper.
(C) There are a large number of them available.
(D) They are given away during regular business hours.

48. What does the woman tell the man to do?

(A) Visit the stadium
(B) Purchase a ticket
(C) Suggest a price
(D) Rent a truck

49. What does the woman imply when she says, "take it or leave it"?

(A) The stadium closes at the end of the day.
(B) The man needs to arrange delivery.
(C) The price is not negotiable.
(D) The seats can be picked up later.

50. What are the speakers discussing?

(A) Recruiting a new employee
(B) Managing an international project
(C) Preparing for a worldwide expansion
(D) Attracting a global clientele

51. What does the man say staff should be able to do?

(A) Speak a foreign language
(B) Work remotely
(C) Handle evening shifts
(D) Travel frequently

52. What does the man suggest?

(A) Hiring Harry Dent
(B) Working on weekends
(C) Consulting a colleague
(D) Traveling to Asia

53. What kind of tour was just completed?

(A) A food tour
(B) An architectural tour
(C) A historical tour
(D) A boat tour

54. What does the man inquire about?

(A) The types of outings offered
(B) The cost of a private tour
(C) The preferences of a friend
(D) The availability of an activity

55. What will the woman most likely do on Saturday?

(A) Lead a historical tour
(B) Canoe through the harbor
(C) Learn a new tour route
(D) Travel out of town

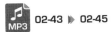
56. What has the woman recently accomplished?

(A) She was promoted to manager.
(B) She secured a large contract.
(C) She designed a new logo.
(D) She launched a new company.

57. What does the man mean when he says, "I really appreciate that"?

(A) He is glad that Fargo Outfitters likes his design.
(B) He is grateful for the woman's acknowledgement.
(C) He is thankful for the team's hard work.
(D) He enjoys the process of creating logos.

58. What does the woman ask the man to do?

(A) Make a reservation
(B) Host a ceremony
(C) Schedule some overtime
(D) Contact some colleagues

---

59. What are the speakers mainly discussing?

(A) A sales seminar
(B) A department merger
(C) A company event
(D) A meeting schedule

60. Who most likely is Ms. Tenner?

(A) The head of sales
(B) The speakers' supervisor
(C) An event organizer
(D) A corporate caterer

61. What do the speakers need to do by Friday?

(A) Organize a meeting
(B) Submit a report
(C) Prepare a picnic
(D) Suggest some ideas

Coleta Fan Co.
Working with us is a breeze!

**Visit us in May and receive
a free handheld fan with any purchase**

1435 Ridge Rd., Mountain Gap, CO   (970) 555-6893

62. Look at the graphic. According to the woman, which information is incorrect?

(A) The name of the company
(B) The advertising slogan
(C) The terms of the offer
(D) The location of the business

63. What does the woman say she is concerned about?

(A) Misleading manufacturers
(B) Bothering the designer
(C) Confusing customers
(D) Misinforming retailers

64. What does the man ask the woman to do?

(A) Visit a website
(B) Contact a manufacturer
(C) Return a call
(D) Email a list

GO ON TO THE NEXT PAGE ➡

FOURTH FLOOR MEETING ROOMS

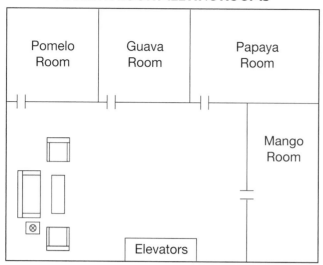

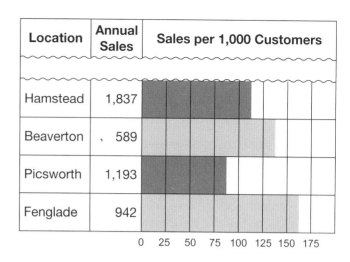

Location	Annual Sales	Sales per 1,000 Customers						
Hamstead	1,837							
Beaverton	589							
Picsworth	1,193							
Fenglade	942							

0 25 50 75 100 125 150 175

65. Where most likely are the speakers?

(A) At a job fair
(B) At a technology conference
(C) At a sales seminar
(D) At a coffee shop

66. How did the woman learn about the position?

(A) From a recruiter
(B) From a newspaper ad
(C) From a candidate
(D) From a website

67. Look at the graphic. Which room will the woman go to next?

(A) The Pomelo Room
(B) The Guava Room
(C) The Papaya Room
(D) The Mango Room

68. Why is the woman speaking with the man?

(A) To report some figures
(B) To receive a bonus
(C) To offer some advice
(D) To recruit a salesperson

69. What happened recently at Kate Stern's location?

(A) A sales conference was held.
(B) A commission was formed.
(C) Some salespeople were promoted.
(D) Some procedures were improved.

70. Look at the graphic. Which location does Kate Stern most likely work at?

(A) Hamstead
(B) Beaverton
(C) Picsworth
(D) Fenglade

PART 4

 02-48 ▶ 02-52

Directions: In PART 4, you will hear several short talks. After each talk, you will be asked to answer three questions about what you heard. Choose the best response to each question, and mark the corresponding letter (A), (B), (C), or (D) on your answer sheet. The questions and responses are printed in the test book. The talks do not appear in the test book, and they will be spoken only one time.

71. Where is the speaker reporting from?

(A) A radio station
(B) A wind farm
(C) A government office
(D) A local residence

72. What does the speaker imply when she says, "city officials required builders to keep turbines at least 2,000 feet from homes, schools, and businesses"?

(A) A requirement was rescinded.
(B) A concern was addressed.
(C) A project was proposed.
(D) A request was rejected.

73. What can listeners do on a website?

(A) Purchase renewable energy
(B) Read a news report
(C) Review a proposal
(D) Sign up for a plan

74. Who most likely are the listeners?

(A) Training professionals
(B) Website developers
(C) Computer security specialists
(D) Publishing company representatives

75. What does the speaker imply when he says, "I brought a few copies with me today"?

(A) He prepared copies of his presentation.
(B) A book is available for purchase.
(C) Participants will have to share the materials.
(D) His lecture notes are incomplete.

76. What does the speaker remind listeners about?

(A) A book on mobile devices
(B) An implementation strategy
(C) A course on network security
(D) An upcoming seminar

77. What does the speaker imply when he says, "That would be a really large group"?

(A) The company cannot accommodate so many people.
(B) The number of guests provided may be incorrect.
(C) The person booking should choose a different activity.
(D) The tour may have to be cancelled or postponed.

78. What does the speaker say he has changed?

(A) The date and time of the tour
(B) The location of departure
(C) The type of museum to be visited
(D) The place where the guests will dine

79. What did the speaker send to the listener?

(A) A museum catalog
(B) A preliminary contract
(C) A restaurant reservation
(D) An alternate itinerary

80. What part of the company does the speaker most likely work in?

(A) User experience
(B) Technical communication
(C) Customer support
(D) Software engineering

81. What are the customers' mostly complaining about?

(A) The interface is confusing.
(B) The manual is out of date.
(C) The new version is overpriced.
(D) The app is difficult to delete.

82. What task does the speaker assign to the listeners?

(A) Conducting customer research
(B) Writing new product documentation
(C) Developing an interactive tutorial
(D) Adding new features to the app

GO ON TO THE NEXT PAGE ➡

83. Why is the speaker calling?

(A) To inquire about an advertisement
(B) To suggest a cheaper shipping method
(C) To negotiate a lower price
(D) To find out the listener's location

84. What does the speaker say she is concerned about?

(A) The selling price
(B) The specifications
(C) The age of the item
(D) The time of delivery

85. What does the speaker offer to do?

(A) Pay for delivery
(B) Contact the seller
(C) Pick up an item
(D) Take an exam

86. What is the purpose of the announcement?

(A) To introduce a colleague
(B) To discuss a job opening
(C) To acknowledge a coworker
(D) To plan for a retirement

87. What was Bob Fletcher hired to do?

(A) Engineer a product
(B) Lead a team
(C) Manage a department
(D) Recruit a staff member

88. What does the speaker encourage the listeners to do?

(A) Suggest a replacement
(B) Organize a party
(C) Prepare some snacks
(D) Attend a gathering

89. According to the speaker, what is a special feature of the radio station?

(A) It is commercial free
(B) It plays many kinds of music
(C) It is owned by the listeners
(D) It only plays requests

90. What does the speaker tell the listeners they can do?

(A) Call the station
(B) Visit a website
(C) Ask a question
(D) Request an interview

91. What will Walter Mac be discussing?

(A) The history of hip-hop
(B) An upcoming concert
(C) His song writing process
(D) The inspiration for a new song

92. What is the announcement mainly about?

(A) Updating security procedures
(B) Launching a cloud-based email system
(C) Using new software tools
(D) Improving coworker collaboration

93. According to the speaker, how can employees get assistance?

(A) By upgrading their system
(B) By searching online
(C) By contacting IT staff
(D) By reading the manual

94. What is an advantage of the new system?

(A) Some employees may work from home.
(B) Instant messaging is built in.
(C) It is easier for the IT staff to maintain.
(D) It takes little time to get used to.

Room	Task
Main Office	- Empty trash cans - Vacuum
Meeting Room	- Wipe the table - Water the plants
Copy Room	- Empty the recycling bin - Fill the copier
Kitchen	- Wash the coffee maker - Clean the sink

Joe's Surf City Ice Cream

10% Off All

| Ice Cream Cones | Frozen Yogurts |
| Ice Cream Sundaes | Iced Coffees |

810 Olive Street   Valid 8/24–8/31

---

95. Why is the speaker traveling to Atlanta?

(A) To join a training session
(B) To assist a manager
(C) To organize a seminar
(D) To attend a career fair

96. What did the speaker leave on the listener's desk?

(A) The key to the office
(B) A sealed envelope
(C) Cleaning instructions
(D) A list of tasks

97. Look at the graphic. Which room will take the most time?

(A) Main office
(B) Meeting room
(C) Copy room
(D) Employee lounge

98. What does the speaker ask the listeners to do?

(A) Participate in a contest
(B) Work extra shifts
(C) Help direct traffic
(D) Hand out coupons

99. Look at the graphic. Which items does the speaker want to sell more of?

(A) Ice cream cones
(B) Ice cream sundaes
(C) Frozen yogurts
(D) Iced coffees

100. According to the speaker, what will happen in September?

(A) The last big event of the summer will take place.
(B) The store will have fewer customers.
(C) The employees will go back to school.
(D) The listeners will have new opportunities.

Actual Test 2

PART 4

This is the end of the Listening test. Turn to PART 5 in your test book.

GO ON TO THE NEXT PAGE ➤

In the Reading part of the test, you will read several different types of texts and answer a variety of questions. The Reading test has three parts, and directions are provided for each of them. You will have seventy-five minutes to complete the entire Reading test. Answer as many questions as you can within the time allotted. Write only on your answer sheet, not the test book.

PART 5

Directions: There is a word or phrase missing from each of the sentences below. Following each sentence are four answer choices: (A), (B), (C), and (D). Choose the answer that best completes the sentence and mark that letter on your answer sheet.

101. The warranty is valid for a ------- of two years from the date of purchase.

(A) time
(B) period
(C) guarantee
(D) certificate

102. ------- her flight arrives on time, we'll have an hour for lunch before the meeting.

(A) Regardless of
(B) No matter
(C) Most likely
(D) Assuming that

103. Our unusual recruiting system was the ------- of our first HR manager.

(A) create
(B) creation
(C) creative
(D) creatively

104. Books purchased ------- Earword Publishing come with a code that allows readers to download an audio version of the text.

(A) with
(B) from
(C) by
(D) for

105. To activate the software, ------- your purchase by completing the form on our website.

(A) apply
(B) sign
(C) produce
(D) register

106. Mr. Tajima's request is not being considered ------- he submitted it after the deadline.

(A) because
(B) reason
(C) due to
(D) caused by

107. Rent near the subway line is more than ------- budget allows for.

(A) we
(B) us
(C) our
(D) ours

108. The entrance is ------- the top of the escalator.

(A) at
(B) up
(C) along
(D) under

109. A human resources consultant helped us refine our recruiting strategy and hiring -------.

(A) positions
(B) managers
(C) accomplishments
(D) procedures

110. With registered mail, the ------- of the letter has to sign a receipt upon delivery.

(A) reception
(B) receiving
(C) receiver
(D) receptionist

111. ------- a rather slow start, we've ramped up production and are now on schedule.

(A) Because
(B) However
(C) Despite
(D) Although

112. The underlying issue must ------- before the contract is signed.

(A) address
(B) be addressed
(C) addressing
(D) to address

113. ------- costs were far lower for the pervious copier.

(A) Maintain
(B) Maintained
(C) Maintaining
(D) Maintenance

114. All of the technology departments ------- R&D are expected to submit a quarterly budget.

(A) except for
(B) as for
(C) in addition
(D) as well

115. ------- we know, the shipment is still in transit.

(A) In regard to
(B) On account of
(C) As far as
(D) In accordance with

116. Mr. Kuzma redesigned the logo to more ------- reflect the organization's mission.

(A) accurately
(B) curiously
(C) temporarily
(D) ordinarily

117. Refunds must be requested ------- thirty days of purchase.

(A) before
(B) within
(C) during
(D) while

118. The source of any data used to ------- your proposal must be clearly cited.

(A) deliver
(B) advise
(C) mention
(D) support

GO ON TO THE NEXT PAGE

119. In ------- the total cost, don't forget to include the cost of the packaging.

(A) calculate
(B) calculating
(C) calculation
(D) calculator

120. Ms. Gutiérrez has ------- flat sales growth in the coming year.

(A) protested
(B) projected
(C) processed
(D) provided

121. Hotel staff are trained to decline some guest requests while also ------- an acceptable alternative.

(A) offering
(B) to offer
(C) has offered
(D) offer

122. This ------- event space can host anything from a business conference to a wedding banquet.

(A) influential
(B) articulate
(C) adaptable
(D) thoughtful

123. Ms. Lee ------- to replace the floor in the break room before the new refrigerator is delivered.

(A) intends
(B) extends
(C) contends
(D) pretends

124. Our study shows that it's ------- common for young professionals to own more than one phone.

(A) increase
(B) increased
(C) increasing
(D) increasingly

125. The sales figures just came in and we can congratulate ------- on another excellent quarter.

(A) itself
(B) yourselves
(C) oneself
(D) ourselves

126. Employees must submit vacation requests three weeks ------- to ensure that all shifts can be covered.

(A) sooner
(B) in advance
(C) up front
(D) ago

127. Customers are given immediate access to the database ------- receipt of payment.

(A) upon
(B) for
(C) until
(D) from

128. The app works quite ------- for a beta version.

(A) hardly
(B) primarily
(C) closely
(D) smoothly

129. Demkay Software sponsors an annual coding contest ------- help recruit potential employees.

(A) to
(B) that
(C) so
(D) can

130. I wrote a formal proposal, which helped me ------- my ideas.

(A) clarifying
(B) clarified
(C) clarify
(D) clarity

Directions: There is a word, phrase, or sentence is missing from parts of each of the following texts. Below each text, there are four answer choices for each question: (A), (B), (C), and (D). Choose the answer that best completes the text and mark the corresponding letter on your answer sheet.

Questions 131-134 refer to the following advertisement.

Try the new Ball Awareness System today!

Sports coaches are always looking for ways to help their teams perform better. That's -------
131.
we've created the Ball Awareness System (BAS). From basketball to volleyball, the Ball Awareness System works with any team sport that takes place within a defined playing area. Players wear special electronic wristbands that provide location data to sensors ------- around the playing field
132.
or court. Coaches can follow the movements of each player in real time via a mobile device app.

-------.
133.

As an added benefit, the BAS wristband also ------- as a fitness tracker. Players can monitor
134.
metrics such as heart rate, calories burned, and distance traveled during the game. To learn about all the ways BAS can help you help your team, visit www.ballawarenesssystem.com today!

---

131. (A) when
(B) how
(C) why
(D) what

132. (A) place
(B) placed
(C) placing
(D) to place

133. (A) Location data is uploaded as soon as the game has ended.
(B) The BAS app uses GPS to track the location of players.
(C) Fans can stay home and watch the game on television.
(D) After the game, players can access the same information.

134. (A) functions
(B) wears
(C) suggests
(D) uses

GO ON TO THE NEXT PAGE ▶

Questions 135-138 refer to the following press release.

Replanter, the office plant provider of choice for businesses throughout the northeast, today announced the Tropicalia package, a collection of attractive tropical plants that will bring life and color to even the drabbest office. These plants were chosen for their beauty, their low-maintenance -------, as well as their ability to grow well in low-light environments. The ------- of the package can
135.   136.
be adjusted to meet the needs of the smallest office suite or the largest corporate headquarters.

The Tropicalia package ------- six months of weekly maintenance visits by our specialists. -------.
137.   138.
After six months, you can choose to have our specialists train you in the care of the plants, or pay a low monthly fee to maintain our professional servicing.

135. (A) requires
(B) required
(C) requiring
(D) requirements

136. (A) size
(B) name
(C) location
(D) performance

137. (A) packs up
(B) looks into
(C) comes with
(D) consists of

138. (A) During this period, you can bring your own plants to the office for display.
(B) They will water and prune your plants, and replace any that are not thriving.
(C) This is the time to consider the benefits of a plant-filled work environment.
(D) A specialist can suggest a package of plants that is just right for your office.

Questions 139-142 refer to the following email.

From: Jetsuna Sakya <j.sakya@springfieldtimes.com>
To: Ruth Horowitz <ruthphorowitz@musicmail.com>
Subject: Your recent letter to the Springfield Times
Date: November 22

Dear Ms. Horowitz,

Thank you very much for your recent letter to the Times ------- to our November 18 article about
                                                        139.
the city's plan to renovate the Springfield Art Museum. You ------- several interesting and I
                                                           140.
think completely original points in the letter, and I was wondering if you would be interested in

expanding your thoughts on the subject into a longer article for the newspaper. -------.
                                                                              141.

If you are interested in writing such a piece, please call me as soon as possible. We would need

to ------- it from you by 4 PM on November 24 so that it could be on our website that evening and
   142.
in the paper on November 25, the day of the next city council meeting.

I look forward to working with you.

Sincerely,
Jetsuna Sakya, Managing Editor
Springfield Times
(541) 565-3227

139. (A) responds
(B) to respond
(C) responded
(D) responding

140. (A) put
(B) did
(C) made
(D) told

141. (A) Your letter will be published with a minor correction.
(B) I could arrange a discount on a two-year subscription.
(C) Our readers are quite interested in the fashion industry.
(D) The ideal length would be about 750 to 1,000 words.

142. (A) receive
(B) borrow
(C) prevent
(D) distinguish

GO ON TO THE NEXT PAGE

Questions 143-146 refer to the following article.

(May 23) — In a bid to revitalize business in Alpine City, the heart of downtown will be turned into a pedestrian-only shopping district. ------- on June 15, Market Street between Lake Blvd. and
143.
Third Street will be completely closed to cars, bicycles, and other personal vehicles. -------.
144.

"This is going to make downtown a more attractive place to visit," says Jamie Ashby, mayor of Alpine. "It will be a safer environment for families, and will cut down on pollution." Some business owners are worried the change will hurt business. Stan Willis, owner of Alpine Hardware, noticed a twenty percent drop in ------- when the street was closed for repaving last year. "If people can't
145.
park near my store, they're less likely to purchase large or heavy items," he said. "I do hope this brings more people downtown. If it doesn't, I'll ------- my business elsewhere."
146.

143. (A) From
(B) Begin
(C) First
(D) Starting

144. (A) Commercial vehicles will be allowed on Market between 10 PM and 6 AM.
(B) Anyone driving on Lake Blvd. after June 15 will be issued a traffic ticket.
(C) Cyclists will be allowed to use Market Street during non-business hours.
(D) Drivers can take an alternate route from Lake to Third via Market Street.

145. (A) customer
(B) damage
(C) revenue
(D) production

146. (A) going to move
(B) have to move
(C) must move
(D) be moved

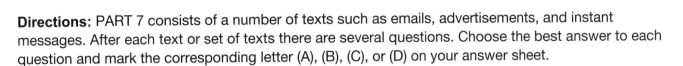
Directions: PART 7 consists of a number of texts such as emails, advertisements, and instant messages. After each text or set of texts there are several questions. Choose the best answer to each question and mark the corresponding letter (A), (B), (C), or (D) on your answer sheet.

Questions 147-148 refer to the following notice.

Savoy Coding Academy Talent Base

Savoy Coding Academy provides comprehensive training in today's most in-demand digital technologies. Companies from startups to established technology firms are finding the skilled programmers they need on the <u>Savoy Coding Academy Talent Base</u>. Every Savoy graduate in our database is certified by Savoy to be proficient in the technical fields identified in their profile. Each member profile also includes a portfolio of completed projects and code samples. Access to the job board website is free of charge and open to all potential employers. Feel free to contact our <u>Career Services</u> department for more information.

---

147. What is the purpose of this notice?

(A) To describe a curriculum
(B) To promote a resource
(C) To initiate a service
(D) To recruit programmers

148. What can visitors do on the Talent Base website?

(A) Submit a job application
(B) Request access to a database
(C) Review current job openings
(D) View a potential applicant's work

Questions 149-150 refer to the following text message chain.

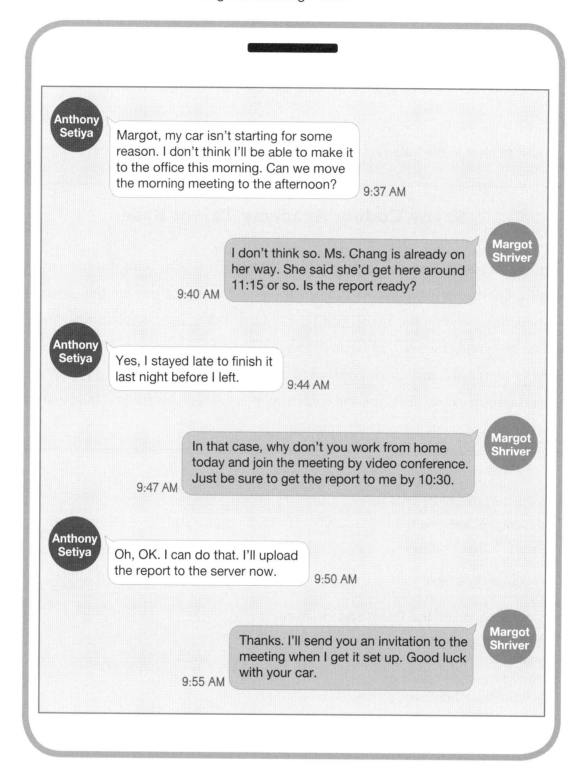

Anthony Setiya — Margot, my car isn't starting for some reason. I don't think I'll be able to make it to the office this morning. Can we move the morning meeting to the afternoon? 9:37 AM

Margot Shriver — I don't think so. Ms. Chang is already on her way. She said she'd get here around 11:15 or so. Is the report ready? 9:40 AM

Anthony Setiya — Yes, I stayed late to finish it last night before I left. 9:44 AM

Margot Shriver — In that case, why don't you work from home today and join the meeting by video conference. Just be sure to get the report to me by 10:30. 9:47 AM

Anthony Setiya — Oh, OK. I can do that. I'll upload the report to the server now. 9:50 AM

Margot Shriver — Thanks. I'll send you an invitation to the meeting when I get it set up. Good luck with your car. 9:55 AM

149. What is suggested about Anthony Setiya?

(A) He sometimes works overtime.
(B) He usually works from home.
(C) He prefers online meetings.
(D) He works for an auto company.

150. What does Margot Shriver ask Mr. Setiya to do?

(A) Postpone a meeting
(B) Complete a report
(C) Schedule a video conference
(D) Send a document

Memo

To: All Emerson Employees

From: George Benson

Subject: Policy Changes

Because of the current influenza outbreak, we are implementing several new policies to protect the health and well-being of our staff, customers, and partners. Please be advised of the following changes:

- All visits to the office by non-employees must be pre-approved by a manger. Whenever possible, communicate with vendors and other partners online rather than face-to-face.
- In-person meetings of more than two people are not allowed for any reason. Please coordinate with colleagues by text or phone.
- If you eat lunch at the office, please do so at your desk, not the break room.
- Employees are required to monitor themselves for flu symptoms, including fever, cough, and sore throat. If you feel unwell or exhibit any symptoms, please do not come to work. Supervisors have been asked to grant all reasonable requests for leave and to facilitate work-from-home when appropriate.

These policies will remain in effect until the end of the month, at which point they will be reevaluated and adjusted. I appreciate your cooperation during these difficult times.

Thank you,
G.B.

151. What is the purpose of this memo?

(A) To ask for donations
(B) To announce new policies
(C) To warn the employees of a disease
(D) To remind all supervisors of a meeting

152. What must a vendor do if he/she wants to visit the company?

(A) Pay an entrance fee
(B) Make an appointment beforehand
(C) Call a supervisor first
(D) Get approval from a manager

GO ON TO THE NEXT PAGE

WHEN

March 5 10:00 AM – 5:00 PM *
March 6 10:00 AM – 1:00 PM

WHERE

Central Library Balboa Room
(**Across from the Circulation Desk**)

Every year, patrons donate thousands of used books to be sold at the Central Library book sale. Revenue from the sale is used to support the library's general fund.

This event is organized by the Friends of Central Library (FOCL), an independent volunteer group. Join FOCL and your $10 membership fee will entitle you to numerous benefits such as a 10% discount at the library gift shop and reduced-price tickets for the library lecture series. Free bookmarks and snacks will be provided by the head librarian throughout the sale.

* **FOCL members are invited to attend the Preview Night on March 4 to get first pick of the books offered during the sale.**

153. What is suggested about the sale?

(A) It will benefit a volunteer group.
(B) The books come from the library.
(C) It is run by the head librarian.
(D) The proceeds will go to the library.

154. What is NOT suggested as a reason to join the Friends of Central Library?

(A) Reduced gift shop prices
(B) Discounted lecture tickets
(C) Free gifts and snacks
(D) Early entry to the sale

START YOUR OWN ONLINE BUSINESS
A SEMINAR FOR NEW ENTREPRENEURS
Saturday, December 4, 10AM–5PM • Fairchild Hotel Grand Ballroom

ONLINE MARKETING	**DISTRIBUTED TEAM MANAGEMENT**	**INTERNATIONAL PAYMENTS**	**CUSTOMER RETENTION**

The Irwin School of Business and Vestco Consulting present this exciting and informative seminar on the factors that determine the success of any new online business venture.

SPEAKERS
- A.J. Freely, Professor of Accounting at the Irwin School of Business
- Denise Chu, Chief Customer Officer at Vestco Consulting
- Francis Tanaka, Author of *Supervising Remote Workers in the Digital Age*
- Wanda Dempsey, Host of the Promotion and Publicity Podcast (via video conference)

Learn the skills you need to launch a successful Internet business. At the same time, learn more about the many exciting benefits of enrolling at the Irwin School of Business.

SEMINAR $75   *Includes lunch*
VIP PASS $120

In addition to the seminar and lunch, VIP Passholders are invited to an exclusive dinner with the speakers and members of the business community. Guests will have the chance to informally present their ideas to business leaders and potential investors.

REGISTER ONLINE at IRWINBSCHOOL.EDU/SEMINAR

155. What is suggested about the seminar?

(A) It is for prospective business owners.
(B) It will primarily be conducted online.
(C) Course credit is available to participants.
(D) Hotel accommodation is included in the fee.

156. Which speaker would most likely discuss distributed team management?

(A) A.J. Freely
(B) Denise Chu
(C) Francis Tanaka
(D) Wanda Dempsey

157. What is mentioned as a reason for purchasing a VIP ticket?

(A) Networking opportunities
(B) A complimentary dinner
(C) Preferential seating
(D) An investment seminar

GO ON TO THE NEXT PAGE ➤

Twin Lakes City Swimming Pool

The Twin Lakes City Parks and Recreation Department has established these rules for the safety and enjoyment of everyone using the pool. Our aim is to create a wholesome and welcoming environment for all our guests.

Overview

Pool hours are 7 AM to 10 PM Lifeguard hours are 2 PM to 8 PM on weekdays and 9 AM to 9 PM on weekends.

Admission fee: $2 for adults. $1 for children 12 and under.

Exercise lanes may be reserved in 30-minute blocks. No more than two consecutive blocks may be registered. Notify a lifeguard or administrator if a lane you reserved is occupied.

Rules

- No running, diving, or horseplay in or around the pool.
- The following items are not allowed in the pool or on the pool deck: glass containers of any kind, pool toys or flotation devices, food and drinks (except water).
- Children under 12 are not allowed in the pool or on the deck when a lifeguard is not on duty.
- Proper swimming attire is required. Shorts and T-shirts are not permitted in the water. Suitable swimwear items are available for sale at the Twin Lakes Mall across the street from the pool. Towels may be purchased at the pool office.
- Do not use the pool if you feel unwell, exhibit cold or flu symptoms, or have a cut or wound.
- Please use the showers provided before and after entering the pool.
- No more than 25 people may use the pool simultaneously. Exit the pool immediately upon lifeguard request.

158. According to the notice, what should guests do after swimming?

(A) Register for an exercise lane
(B) Notify the lifeguard
(C) Use the shower facilities
(D) Return towels to the office

159. What can be done at the City Swimming Pool?

(A) Using pool toys or inflatable devices
(B) Swimming with no lifeguard on duty
(C) Purchasing the required swimwear
(D) Reserving a swimming lane for 90 minutes

160. What information is NOT provided?

(A) The reason the rules were created
(B) The pool's opening and closing times
(C) Recommended reservation times
(D) Details about the necessary attire

Stardust Regency Hotel

Service Assignment

Assignment No.	JGB8675309
Assigned By	Julia Valenzuela
Assigned To	Ty Fenton
Department	☐ Housekeeping ☐ Groundskeeping ☐ Parking and Transportation ☐ Food & Beverage ☑ Facilities ☐ Other (specify) _____
Location	Room 415
Time	March 2, 11:15 AM
Description	A guest reported a malfunctioning air conditioner at 11 AM. She is currently attending a function and will return to the room after 6 PM. Please report back on progress before 5 PM so I can arrange for an upgraded room for Ms. Nakayama if necessary.

Report

I replaced a faulty wall switch. The air conditioner is in good working order now. While inspecting the main unit I noticed the filter was clogged, though this was unrelated to the switch. I washed and returned the filter. I'm not sure who's responsibility it is to monitor and maintain the AC equipment. I think it would be a good idea to schedule a regular—perhaps monthly—visual inspection as part of normal housekeeping duties. If necessary, I can show everyone how to remove and clean the filters.

T. Fenton
March 2, 4:40 PM

---

161. Who most likely is Mr. Fenton?

(A) A guest of the hotel
(B) A housekeeper
(C) A hotel supervisor
(D) A maintenance worker

162. What does the document indicate about Ms. Nakayama?

(A) She requested an upgraded room.
(B) She will attend a function when she returns.
(C) She will stay in Room 415 that evening.
(D) She is expecting a report by 5 PM.

163. What does Mr. Fenton offer to do?

(A) Replace a broken part
(B) Provide supplemental training
(C) Make a maintenance schedule
(D) Perform a monthly inspection

GO ON TO THE NEXT PAGE

Alice Chen	4:42 PM	OK, we're launching six websites in four weeks, so it's going to be a busy month. Let's start with the Mexican restaurant. Any updates?
Ben Wright	4:44 PM	I finally got the images from the photographer and finished the design on Monday. I'm just waiting for the text now.
Alice Chen	4:45 PM	I thought the website copy had already been edited and approved.
Yusef Khan	4:49 PM	That's true for the English text. The translation company's deadline for the Spanish text is Wednesday.
Alice Chen	5:53 PM	OK. Please follow up on that Yusef. And please ask Ms. Lopez if she wants to check the translation. That's the client's responsibility. Anything else?
Daniela Goldblatt	5:56 PM	Well, Ms. Lopez asked me to use a different online reservation system. I spent the morning working on that.
Alice Chen	6:01 PM	Hmm. You know that things like that can significantly affect the cost of the project. In the future, please discuss major changes with the team before starting work on them.
Daniela Goldblatt	6:05 PM	Fair enough, but it was easy to install, and it has some great features. For example, you can also use it to order to-go meals for pickup.
Alice Chen	6:09 PM	I'll take a look at it. I hope we can use this project as an example for other potential clients. New restaurants are always opening up, so they're a great source of new business for us.

164. What kind of business do the chat discussion participants most likely work for?

(A) A web design firm
(B) A Mexican restaurant
(C) A photography studio
(D) A translation company

165. What will Yusef Khan likely do next?

(A) Edit a document
(B) Check a translation
(C) Contact a customer
(D) Set up a system

166. What did the client request?

(A) An online meeting
(B) A phone call
(C) A revised deadline
(D) A new system

167. At 6:05 PM, what does Daniela Goldblatt mean when she writes, "Fair enough"?

(A) She thinks that Ms. Chen is being impartial.
(B) She is pleased the quality of the work is adequate.
(C) She believes that Ms. Chen made a good point.
(D) She is sure the cost of the change is reasonable.

Questions 168-171 refer to the following email.

From: Emilio Negroni

To: Janice Hamidou

Subject: Volunteer Orientation

Date: June 4

Dear Ms. Hamidou,

I am pleased to offer you a volunteer position at the Yonkers Art Museum. Every year, the Museum is fortunate to welcome an exceptional cohort of forty student volunteers from art history departments at universities in the Hudson Valley and beyond. I myself am a graduate of the YAM internship program and hope that you benefit from it as much as I have.

All new volunteers are required to attend a Volunteer Orientation on June 16. Please see the schedule below for details. And please stop by the museum's information desk any time before the orientation to pick up your official volunteer badge. It allows you free access to the museum and will give you the chance to meet other volunteers and become more familiar with the collection.

Please notify us of your participation by registering at the YAM Volunteer website before June 8. If you are unable to serve as a volunteer or if you cannot attend the orientation, please contact me as soon as possible.

Best regards,
Emilio Negroni
Volunteer Supervisor, Yonkers Art Museum

June 16	VOLUNTEER	ORIENTATION
9:00–10:00	Hudson Auditorium	Overview of the Volunteer Handbook
10:00–12:00	Hudson Auditorium	Introduction to the Collection
12:00–2:00	Atrium Café	Lunch
2:00–4:00	Empire Room	Education Training: School Visits and Guided Tours
4:00–6:00	Nordine Hall	Skills Training: Office Support and Patron Outreach

168. What is the purpose of this email?

(A) To announce a program
(B) To offer a position
(C) To welcome a visitor
(D) To delegate a responsibility

169. The word "cohort" in paragraph 1, line 2, is closes in meaning to

(A) apprentice
(B) companion
(C) group
(D) category

170. Where can Ms. Hamidou get her volunteer badge?

(A) The Hudson Auditorium
(B) The Empire Room
(C) Nordine Hall
(D) The Information Desk

171. According to the email, what must all volunteers do before June 8?

(A) Graduating from an art history department
(B) Organizing an orientation session
(C) Confirming their attendance
(D) Contacting the volunteer supervisor

GO ON TO THE NEXT PAGE

New Confuso Device to Launch?

By Martha Wells

TOKYO (July 21) — Analysts predict popular handheld gaming device manufacturer Confuso Industries is preparing to launch a new device sometime this fall. Analyst Dinesh Crampton has been tracking the sales and inventory of Confuso's latest device across several distribution networks and has identified diminishing supplies of the EBOT 5 in North America, Africa, and Europe. — [1] —. It appears that the company is intentionally reducing its stock.

In a research note published by Drummond Securities, Mr. Crampton argues that that the forthcoming device is likely not the EBOT 6 but rather an entirely new device. — [2] —. Another analyst, Maria Puente of Anticip Research, agrees. "Confuso received several large shipments of Isottech's TR50 microchips," Puente said in an interview. "The use of such powerful chips is a clear indication that Confuso is making a significant change."

Crampton believes existing games will function on the new device, but that developers will undoubtedly want to design games that take advantage of the speed and efficiency improvements offered by the new chips. In fact, the recent lack of new EBOT games may be a sign that developers are already working on games for the new device. — [3] —.

Confuso regularly subsidizes the development of new games to coincide with product launches to ensure consumers have ample reason to upgrade. Confuso, which develops games under its Whadabot subsidiary, has not released a new product in over eight months. Ms. Puente cited this to support her forecast, though she notes that Whatabot is not expected to be a major profit center for the company. — [4] —.

172. What is indicated about Confuso Industries?

(A) They are running out of essential components.
(B) They are launching a device in a new market.
(C) They are manufacturing a new computer chip.
(D) They are encouraging developers to create new products.

173. What is NOT given as evidence that Confuso will launch a new device?

(A) Falling stock prices
(B) Diminishing supplies
(C) Upgraded microchips
(D) The lack of new products

174. What is reported about Whadabot?

(A) It often publishes market forecasts.
(B) It is going out of business.
(C) It is owned by Confuso.
(D) It is a major source of revenue.

175. In which of the positions marked [1], [2], [3], and [4] does the following sentence best belong?

"MiG Gaming Studio, which has created dozens of games for Confuso devices, declined to comment for this article but has recently hired over twenty game developers to work on 'an exciting new project.'"

(A) [1]
(B) [2]
(C) [3]
(D) [4]

| About | Furniture | Appliances | Appraisal | Contact Us |

Family owned and operated for nearly fifty years, Floyd's Home Furnishings is your one-stop shop for all your furniture needs. We carry fine contemporary furniture, but also buy and sell high-quality used items. So, whether you need to furnish an entire home or just want to get rid of that old chest of drawers in the basement, Floyd's can help.

And that's not all. We also buy and sell superior quality rugs, light fixtures, and appliances like refrigerators, ovens, and washing machines. Thanks to our exquisite taste and massive selection, there's a great chance we stock exactly what you're looking for—and in exactly the style you like. From heirlooms to air conditioners, from cozy and comfortable to classy and contemporary, we have it all.

Our customers love our <u>Free Appraisal Service</u>. It's simple. You upload a photograph of the item you want to sell, and we'll offer you a price for it the very next day.

Floyd's reasonable delivery service is also popular. Our friendly delivery drivers can bring your purchases right into your home, and for an additional small fee they can help assemble or install every item we sell. Items that we purchase from you will be picked up at your convenience anywhere in the greater Ann Arbor area. We guarantee it!

• Please note that we never buy or sell used mattresses. Also, due to oversupply, we are not currently accepting bed frames.

343 South 5th Ave., Ann Arbor, MI 48104

(734) 327-4200   service@floydsfurnishings.com

GO ON TO THE NEXT PAGE

Contact Us

Name *   Ted Rexroth

Email *   t.rex@ohnochicxulub.com

Phone   (734) 794-6320

Subject   In-Person Appraisal?

Message *

I'm planning to move overseas for work in the near future and need to sell all of my furniture as soon as possible. I live in a small two-bedroom home, but over the years I've amassed quite a large collection.

I noticed on your website that you offer free digital appraisals, but I wonder if the process would be less cumbersome if someone from your store visited my home in person. My place is on the Old West Side, within walking distance of your location downtown. I have some antiques from my grandmother that would be best appreciated in person. There are also some pieces in the attic, which has poor lighting for photography.

Also, I noticed that you said you don't take beds at the moment, but it would be a great help if you could remove the one from my apartment. My landlord insists that the place be completely empty when I leave. I understand that you would be unable to compensate me for it, and I would even gladly provide a reasonable removal fee.

SEND MESSAGE   * **Required**

---

176. What is NOT suggested about Floyd's?

(A) It stocks a diverse range of merchandise.
(B) It purchases stuff from the public.
(C) It is currently selling bed frames.
(D) It guarantees low prices on used items.

177 What is indicated about Floyd's?

(A) It offers a free delivery service.
(B) It specializes in heirlooms and antiques.
(C) It recently opened a new location.
(D) It sells household electric appliances.

178. Why does Ted Rexroth request an in-person meeting?

(A) He believes it would be more convenient.
(B) He intends to purchase a large collection.
(C) His landlord insists that he do so.
(D) His grandmother prefers to stay home.

179. What is suggested about Ted Rexroth?

(A) His family owns a business.
(B) He frequently travels abroad.
(C) He lives close to Floyd's.
(D) He owns his own home.

180. What does Ted Rexroth offer to do?

(A) Photograph some antiques
(B) Pay for a service
(C) Walk to the store
(D) Purchase a bed

From:	Justine Kemp <cto@megaopticaldevices.com>
To:	<All Employees>
Subject:	Professional Development
Date:	December 17

Dear All,

As most of you know, senior management meets annually to identify the key skills Mega team members need to strengthen to increase our competitiveness in the coming year. This system has worked well enough, but it has also led to some inefficiencies. Not all employees needed the training that was provided to them; other employees didn't receive the training they required to thrive in their positions.

To address this issue, we have partnered with Chase/Bender Analytics, a consulting company that specializes in understanding and improving corporate training processes. We want to hear about your experiences, expectations, and suggestions about professional development at Mega Optical. All employees will soon receive another email with a link to an online survey at the Chase/Bender website. Please complete it before the end of the day tomorrow. We won't be making any immediate decisions, but we would like to have some preliminary data this week to help us determine the professional development budget for next year.

Mega Optical values the contributions of all of our team members. I firmly believe that your support of this endeavor will make our professional development program even stronger.

Justine Kemp,
Chief Talent Officer, Mega Optical Devices

Actual Test 2

PART 7

GO ON TO THE NEXT PAGE

Chase/Bender
──── ANALYTICS ────

Mega Optical Devices Professional Development Survey
Preliminary Report ◀ ▶ December 20

DISCLAIMER: Chase/Bender Analytics is still evaluating the survey data and still receiving new data (the response rate as of December 20 stands at 87%). Significant decisions should not be made until the full report with formal recommendations is submitted on January 12.

The conclusions drawn here are tentative, but there are enough signals in the data to allow us to observe a few trends. Two areas in particular stood out as relevant: desired training content and the preferred frequency and duration of instruction.

Content

Frequency/Duration

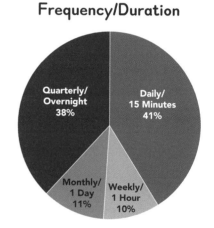

CONTENT: Previous professional development efforts focused on technical skills, but current interest in such training is minimal. A slight majority of employees expressed an interest in foreign languages, though there is no agreement about which languages should be taught. In situations where employees have diverse needs, companies often encourage employees to seek out their own classes and then offer them either full or partial tuition reimbursement.

FREQUENCY/DURATION: Employees overwhelmingly prefer either short daily classes or a quarterly overnight retreat. The frequency and duration of training has a bearing on how the instruction is provided. Short daily lessons are most efficiently delivered as part of an automated learning system. Conversely, an overnight retreat is as much an occasion for socializing and team building as it is for professional development. Moreover, some types of content (like language learning) are best acquired in short daily lessons, while others (such as a leadership workshop) are more suited to an all-day seminar.

181. What is the purpose of the email?

    (A) To explain an assignment
    (B) To request some professional training
    (C) To introduce a company
    (D) To announce a budget

182. In the email, the word "endeavor" in paragraph 3, line 2, is closest in meaning to

    (A) progress
    (B) effort
    (C) strategy
    (D) attempt

183. What is NOT mentioned about the survey?

    (A) It was conducted online.
    (B) It was required of all employees.
    (C) It was administered by an outside company.
    (D) It was written by Justine Kemp.

184. What is suggested in the preliminary report about Mega Optical Devices?

    (A) It should focus on employees' technical skills.
    (B) Not all of its employees completed the survey.
    (C) It offers tuition reimbursement to its staff.
    (D) Employees are expected to know more than one language.

185. According to the report, what type of training is best provided by computer?

    (A) Technical training
    (B) Daily classes
    (C) Leadership workshops
    (D) All-day seminars

GO ON TO THE NEXT PAGE

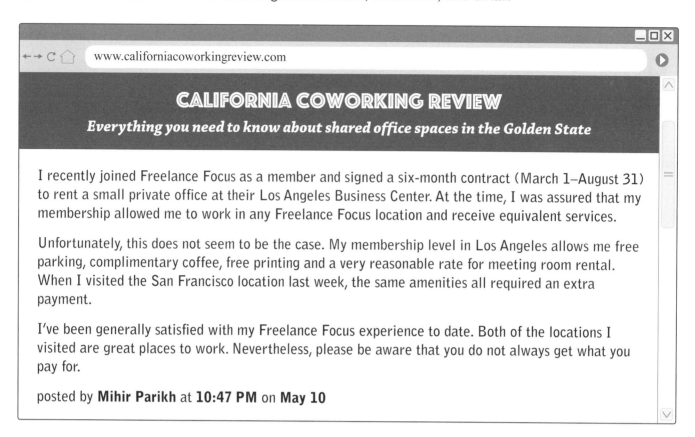

www.californiacoworkingreview.com

CALIFORNIA COWORKING REVIEW
Everything you need to know about shared office spaces in the Golden State

I recently joined Freelance Focus as a member and signed a six-month contract (March 1–August 31) to rent a small private office at their Los Angeles Business Center. At the time, I was assured that my membership allowed me to work in any Freelance Focus location and receive equivalent services.

Unfortunately, this does not seem to be the case. My membership level in Los Angeles allows me free parking, complimentary coffee, free printing and a very reasonable rate for meeting room rental. When I visited the San Francisco location last week, the same amenities all required an extra payment.

I've been generally satisfied with my Freelance Focus experience to date. Both of the locations I visited are great places to work. Nevertheless, please be aware that you do not always get what you pay for.

posted by **Mihir Parikh** at **10:47 PM** on **May 10**

Freelance Focus Workspaces
Rates and Services effective Jan. 1

Type	Schedule	Locations (California)
☐ Desk Rental	☐ Daily	☑ San Francisco
☑ Small Office	☐ Weekly	☑ Los Angeles
☐ Large Office	☑ Monthly	☐ San Diego

San Francisco

Status	Rate	Parking	Drinks	Meeting Room	Printing
Visitor	$710	$12/Day	$1	$45/hour	$0.20
Temporary	$790	$65/Month	$1	$40/hour	$0.10
Associate	$840	$55/Month	$1	$35/hour	$0.05
Collaborator	$950	$45/Month	No charge	$20/hour	No charge

Los Angeles

Status	Rate	Parking	Drinks	Meeting Room	Printing
Visitor	$600	$6/Day	$1	$30/hour	$0.10
Temporary	$710	$2/Day	$1	$30/hour	$0.05
Associate	$790	No charge	No charge	$20/hour	No charge
Collaborator	$840	No charge	No charge	No charge	No charge

From:	customerexperience@freelancefocusworkspaces.com
To:	Mihir Parikh <mp@MHPinfomatics.com>
Subject:	Small Office Rates and Services
Date:	May 11

Dear Mr. Parikh,

I read the comments you posted yesterday about Freelance Focus on the California Coworking Review website. I'd like to apologize for the incorrect information you received when signing up and explain the steps we're taking to resolve the issue you raised.

The company sets minimum standards for each membership level but recognizes that local conditions can vary considerably. This is why we allow each location to set its own rates. I've made our human resources department aware of your concerns and they have committed to ensuring that staff nationwide communicate clearly about this issue with current and prospective members.

At no additional charge to you, I have upgraded your membership to Collaborator level for the duration of your current contract. This ensures that your experiences at the Los Angeles and San Francisco locations will be more uniform.

Please contact me directly if you have any additional questions or concerns.

Duncan Jones,
Director of Customer Experience

---

186. Why did Mr. Parikh write this review?

(A) To request an upgrade
(B) To warn of a problem
(C) To schedule a meeting
(D) To change a policy

187. What is suggested about Mr. Parikh?

(A) He works in more than one location.
(B) He wants to rent a larger office.
(C) He currently lives in San Francisco.
(D) He has recently changed jobs.

188. How much is Mr. Parikh's rent each month?

(A) $710
(B) $790
(C) $840
(D) $950

189. What is true about the two locations?

(A) All members have to pay for printing in San Francisco.
(B) Los Angeles members enjoy a greater range of services.
(C) San Francisco charges less for some services.
(D) Some members pay for parking in Los Angeles.

190. What is provided by the company as a response to the review?

(A) A change in pricing policy
(B) A new training initiative
(C) A membership fee discount
(D) A statewide uniform standard

GO ON TO THE NEXT PAGE

Questions 191-195 refer to the following schedule, text message chain, and email.

GYM NIGHTS

**Tristero Pharmaceuticals &
The San Narciso Scorpions**

Join us for "Gym Nights," when Tristero employees get together after work at the San Narciso High School Gymnasium for a little exercise and a lot of fun. Now in its fifth year, Gym Nights is the centerpiece of our Employee Wellness program. With four different activities featured each week, you're sure to find something to get your body moving. All employees are welcome and there's no need to sign up in advance. All activities are 7–9 PM.

Monday Nights	**Line Dancing** *with* Damian Jones	Whether you're a beginner or an experienced pro, professional dancer Damian "DJ" Jones will get you up and moving around the dance floor. Please wear soft-soled shoes.
Tuesday Nights	**Basketball** *with* Jeff Rambis	Lace up your sneakers and take your game to the next level as the coach of the San Narciso Scorpions leads you through intense drills and fun scrimmages.
Wednesday Nights	No activities scheduled	The San Narciso Scorpions welcome Tristero employees to root for the county's most exciting high school basketball players. The boys' and girls' teams use the gym on alternate Wednesdays.
Thursday Nights	**Yoga** *with* Radha Patel	Practice a pose or simply do some breathing exercises with the owner of the San Narciso Yoga Studio. Please bring a mat.
Friday Nights	**Badminton** *with* Leslie Firth	No racket, no problem! San Narciso Scorpions Athletic Director has everything you need for a friendly game of badminton.

Leslie Firth [9:05 AM]
Hi, Ed. I'm afraid we have to make a few changes to the Gym Nights schedule next week.

Edward van Exel [9:16 AM]
Oh, OK. What's going on?

Leslie Firth [9:18 AM]
A couple things. Jeff is taking next week off to attend a wedding.
Could you get someone to fill in? Or maybe you just want to cancel?

Edward van Exel [9:26 AM]
It's kind of short notice, but I may be able to find someone. What's the other thing?

Leslie Firth [9:31 AM]
The school is going to need the gym on Friday night for an academic awards ceremony.
I should have put it on the schedule at the beginning of the year, but I forgot. That's on me.

Edward van Exel [9:33 AM]
Don't worry about it Leslie. Though I have to say I was looking forward to a rematch. We came so close last week!

Leslie Firth [9:35 AM]
Ha! Maybe next time. At least I'll finally be able to have a Friday night off.
I've already made plans to go out to dinner.

Edward van Exel [9:39 AM]
Enjoy it. I'll let everyone know what's going on and see what I can do about Tuesday.

From:	Edward van Exel <EvE@ tristeropharmaceuticals.com>
To:	<allemployees@tristeropharecuticals.com>
Subject:	Gym Nights
Date:	May 16

Dear All,

I just want to let everyone know about a few changes to the Gym Nights schedule next week.

Due to a previously scheduled event at San Narciso High, there will be no badminton practice on Friday, May 27. Also, because Coach Rambis will be out of town on personal business next week, our very own Stacey Fox from IT will be leading basketball activities on Tuesday. For those who don't know, Stacey is a former Scorpions player who later led the South State Sparks to a collegiate championship. Come prepared! It should be fun.

Other activities will not be affected, and everything should be back to normal for the week starting May 30.

Best,
Edward van Exel
Health and Wellness Program Supervisor
Human Resources Division, Tristero Pharmaceuticals

191. According to the information given on the schedule, what activity provides all the necessary equipment?

(A) Line dancing
(B) Basketball
(C) Yoga
(D) Badminton

192. What is true about San Narciso High School?

(A) It has two basketball teams.
(B) It sponsors "Gym Nights."
(C) It closes its gym every Wednesday night.
(D) It provides free transportation for Tristero employees.

193. Why did Leslie Firth start the text message chain?

(A) To remedy a problem
(B) To respond to an email
(C) To request a day off
(D) To recommend a replacement

194. In the text message chain, at 9:31 AM, what does Leslie Firth mean when she writes, "That's on me"?

(A) She intends to pay for the meal.
(B) She takes responsibility for the mistake.
(C) She is required to attend the ceremony.
(D) She will buy a gift for Jeff Rambis.

195. Who is going to substitute for Coach Rambis?

(A) Damian Jones
(B) Radha Patel
(C) Stacey Fox
(D) Edward van Exel

GO ON TO THE NEXT PAGE

http://www.newflaneurtours.co.uk

New Flaneur
WALKINGTOURS

Beautiful Brompstead at a Leisurely Pace

| Food | Architecture | History | Nature |

Brompstead Architecture Tour

This is an easy 1.5-kilometer stroll through the picturesque town of Brompstead. It begins on the steps of Town Hall and departs at 1:30 every Friday afternoon. Allow two hours. The walk is wheelchair accessible and suitable for all ages. A suggested donation of £5 per person is appreciated, but not required. Highlights include:

Town Hall
This lovely example of Queen Anne style was completed in 1887 and served as the seat of local government for nearly a century. Currently, it is home of the Brompstead Heritage Centre, a gift shop, and a bookstore.

The Provincial Building
An ornate four-storey office building that housed a bank, professional offices, and a private club for Brompstead's business elite. Built in the early 20th century, the Provincial Building is still an entrepreneurial hub, with offices, a start-up incubator, and a coffee shop.

Bronson House
Recently celebrating the 175th anniversary, the home of Brompstead's most famous poet is an exemplar of Early Victorian residential architecture. The upper floors are preserved exactly as Julius Bronson left them. The ground floor features a small theatre where a local actor will recite a few of Mr. Bronson's poems during our visit.

The Spenderton Modern
What do you get when you take a textile mill from the 1800s, convert it into an agricultural machinery factory in the 1900s, and then transform it into a museum of contemporary art in the 2000s? Nothing short of a three-dimensional history of Brompstead built from glass and red sandstone.

The tour ends in the museum's sculpture garden. After the tour, many people choose to visit the museum (tickets £12) or have tea at the nearby Rosemont Hotel.

A New Business for Historical Brompstead

By Alex Cruz

April 22 (Bristol)—I met Abigail Gleason whilst queuing for coffee on the ground floor of the building where I work. Five minutes later, I had a broad understanding of the past century of local history and learned that my office had once been occupied by Chester T. Dunford, a barrister who served as Mayor of Brompstead in the late 1920s.

This was no accident. Ms. Gleason is an historian of some renown. Her company, New Flaneur Walking Tours, is less than a year old, but Ms. Gleason has long been fascinated with historical Brompstead. "I've been collecting stories about this place ever since I can remember," she says. "I'm so pleased to be able to share them."

Ms. Gleason personally leads the History (Thursday) and Architecture (Friday) tours, but she has help on the weekends. Restauranteur Stephanie Liu leads the popular Food Tour on Saturdays and Shannon Quayle, a member of the Brompstead Land Trust, leads a four-hour Nature Walk through Mystic Woods.

A graduate of the University of Bristol History Department, Ms. Gleason was a long-time employee of the Brompstead Heritage Centre. She loves writing but wanted a more personal way to share her knowledge. "I've written countless pamphlets, blog posts, and even a short biography of Julius Bronson, but nothing beats spending time with people," she told me. "I was made for walking and talking, and that's why I started giving tours."

Dear Brompstead Editor,

I was delighted by your story about Abigail Gleason and her company. At my advanced age, I get around by wheelchair, not on foot, but it seems I can still join one of Ms. Gleason's walking tours. It may interest your readers to know that Chester T. Dunford was my grandfather, and that in addition to his government service he was also instrumental in founding the Brompstead Land Trust. He worked tirelessly for the conservation of the Mystic Woods, which is why we can all enjoy that enchanting place today.

If Ms. Gleason has any plans to write another biography, I can think of nobody more worthy than Grandad Dunford!

Sincerely,
Oliver Dunford

GO ON TO THE NEXT PAGE

196. What is one common feature of all the buildings on the tour?

(A) They were initially built for commercial purposes.
(B) They have been adapted for contemporary use.
(C) They were constructed in the 1800s.
(D) They are not generally open to the public.

197. Where does Alex Cruz most likely work?

(A) Town Hall
(B) The Provincial Building
(C) Bronson House
(D) The Spenderton Modern

198. What is indicated in the news article about Ms. Gleason?

(A) She was a restaurant owner.
(B) She teaches History and Architecture at a university.
(C) She used to work in the Town Hall building.
(D) She is a native of Bristol.

199. In the letter, the word "founding" in paragraph 1, line 4, is closest in meaning to

(A) fabricating
(B) preserving
(C) discovering
(D) establishing

200. What is probably true about Oliver Dunford?

(A) He has visited the New Flaneur website.
(B) He was once elected to public office.
(C) He wants to write a book about a family member.
(D) He will apply to become a tour guide.

Stop! This is the end of the test. If you finish before time is called, you may go back to Parts 5, 6, and 7 and check your work.

第一回 全真測驗完整解析

解答總覽

題號	正解	題號	正解	題號	正解	題號	正解	題號	正解
1	D	41	A	81	B	121	A	161	B
2	B	42	B	82	C	122	D	162	D
3	B	43	C	83	A	123	D	163	C
4	D	44	D	84	D	124	B	164	D
5	C	45	C	85	C	125	A	165	C
6	B	46	A	86	A	126	B	166	B
7	A	47	C	87	C	127	B	167	B
8	B	48	A	88	B	128	D	168	C
9	B	49	C	89	C	129	B	169	B
10	A	50	A	90	A	130	C	170	C
11	B	51	B	91	D	131	B	171	D
12	C	52	C	92	A	132	D	172	C
13	B	53	A	93	B	133	C	173	C
14	A	54	D	94	D	134	A	174	A
15	B	55	A	95	A	135	B	175	C
16	A	56	B	96	B	136	C	176	C
17	B	57	B	97	D	137	D	177	D
18	B	58	D	98	D	138	B	178	A
19	A	59	D	99	B	139	C	179	C
20	B	60	B	100	D	140	D	180	C
21	B	61	C	101	B	141	A	181	A
22	C	62	A	102	D	142	B	182	C
23	C	63	C	103	B	143	B	183	C
24	A	64	D	104	D	144	D	184	D
25	C	65	A	105	C	145	A	185	D
26	A	66	D	106	C	146	C	186	D
27	C	67	B	107	D	147	B	187	C
28	C	68	C	108	A	148	D	188	A
29	A	69	D	109	C	149	A	189	B
30	C	70	D	110	B	150	C	190	C
31	C	71	D	111	A	151	C	191	A
32	C	72	A	112	C	152	D	192	A
33	C	73	B	113	B	153	C	193	D
34	D	74	C	114	C	154	A	194	B
35	D	75	A	115	B	155	C	195	C
36	B	76	A	116	A	156	A	196	B
37	C	77	B	117	D	157	B	197	A
38	D	78	D	118	D	158	B	198	B
39	A	79	D	119	B	159	B	199	C
40	D	80	C	120	C	160	A	200	D

1 正解 D

(A) They are boarding a ship.
(B) The boat is tied to the dock.
(C) They are sitting on the shore.
(D) The boat is floating on the river.

(A) 他們正在登船。
(B) 船拴在碼頭上。
(C) 他們坐在岸上。
(D) 船浮在河上。

解析

照片顯示有兩個人坐在一艘漂浮在河上的小船上，因此 (A)「他們正在登船」、(B)「船拴在碼頭上」和 (C)「他們坐在岸上」皆為誤。正確答案是 (D)。

Vocabulary
☐ **board** 上（車、船、飛機等）　☐ **float**（使）漂浮

2 正解 B

(A) The man is checking her blood pressure.
(B) The woman is examining the man.
(C) The man is looking at the woman.
(D) The woman is shaking his hand.

(A) 男子在幫她量血壓。
(B) 女子在為男子做檢查。
(C) 男子正看著女子。
(D) 女子正握著他的手。

解析

照片顯示一名女子正在替一名男子量血壓，選項 (A)「男子在幫他量血壓」明顯主客錯置、選項 (D)「女子正握著他的手」亦與照片不符。另，由於照片中的兩人皆往一旁看，因此 (C)「男子正看著女子」同樣為錯誤。正解為 (B)。

Vocabulary
☐ **examine** 檢查；診察

3 正解 B

(A) They are pointing at the screen.
(B) The men are looking at some data.
(C) They are seated in front of the computer.
(D) The men are touching the monitors.

(A) 他們正指著畫面。
(B) 兩名男子正在看某些資料。
(C) 他們坐在電腦前。
(D) 兩名男子正在觸碰螢幕。

解析

照片中兩位男士正在看電腦螢幕上的資料，其中一人站著，而坐著的那位正用手指著螢幕畫面。選項 (A)、(C) 與 (D) 都犯了「數量」上的錯誤，只有 (B)「兩名男子正在看某些資料」為正確描述。

Vocabulary
☐ **screen** 螢幕　☐ **monitor** 顯示器

MP3 **01-05** ▶ **01-07**

4 正解 D

(A) They are facing each other.
(B) The man is sitting near a copier.
(C) The machines are out of order.
(D) The woman is pushing a button.

(A) 他們彼此面對著面。
(B) 男子坐在影印機附近。
(C) 機器都壞了。
(D) 女子正在按按鍵。

解析　照片中可見一男一女背對背站著，女子正在按影印機的按鍵。(A)「他們彼此面對著面」與 (B)「男子坐在影印機附近」明顯為誤，而因女子正在「使用」影印機，故選項 (C)「機器都壞了」亦不正確。正解為 (D)。

Vocabulary
☐ **face** 面向；正對　　☐ **out of order** 故障

5 正解 C

(A) The pedestrians are wearing hats.
(B) The cyclists are pedaling away from the water.
(C) The path runs alongside the shore.
(D) The bicycles are leaning against some plants.

(A) 行人戴著帽子。
(B) 自行車騎士正駛離水域。
(C) 此路徑沿著水岸邊。
(D) 自行車靠在一些植物上。

解析　照片顯示有幾個人正沿著湖邊騎著自行車，其中有幾位戴著帽子。由於照片中並沒有 "pedestrians"，因此 (A) 為誤，而因自行車騎士是沿湖邊前進，所以 (B) 亦不正確。另，照片中看不到有任何自行車靠在植物上，故 (D) 亦為誤。唯有選項 (C) 的描述與照片相符。

Vocabulary
☐ **pedestrian** 行人　☐ **pedal** 踩踏板；騎自行車

6 正解 B

(A) The exhibition hall is not open.
(B) Several chairs have been provided.
(C) The display is being set up.
(D) Some visitors are standing in line.

(A) 展覽廳沒有開。
(B) 提供了數張座椅。
(C) 展覽正在擺設中。
(D) 有些訪客在排隊。

解析　此照片的場景為某個展覽會場，有些來賓站著，有些則坐在椅子上。(A)「展覽廳沒有開」與 (C)「展覽正在擺設中」明顯為誤。而因照片中並沒有人在排隊，所以 (D) 亦不正確。正確答案是 (B)「提供了數張座椅」。

Vocabulary
☐ **exhibition** 展覽

第 1 回完全解析　PART 1

91

7 正解 **A**

Is the restaurant still open?
(A) It should be.
(B) It opened at 11:30.
(C) No, thanks. I'm full.

餐館還在營業嗎？
(A) 應該是。
(B) 它 11:30 開始營業。
(C) 不用，謝謝。我吃飽了。

解析	本題為 "Yes-No" 問句，說話者詢問餐館是否還在營業，選項 (A)「應該是」為合理的回應，故為正解。選項 (B) 答的是該餐館的「開門」時間，選項 (C) 雖然以 "No" 起頭，但其後的內容與原問題無關，因此二者皆不可選。注意，問句中的 "open" 為「形容詞」，選項 (B) 的 "opened" 為「動詞」，不可混淆。

8 正解 **B**

Do you think she will finish the report before the meeting starts?
(A) I think it's about the new marketing plan.
(B) Not if she doesn't hurry up.
(C) The report starts on page 4.

你認為她會在會議開始前把報告完成嗎？
(A) 我想要談的是新的行銷計畫。
(B) 她要是不趕快就沒辦法完成。
(C) 報告從第四頁開始。

解析	本題亦為 "Yes-No" 題型，詢問對方認不認為「她」會在開會之前完成報告，選項 (A) 答的是會議的內容，選項 (C) 答的是報告的內容，皆答非所問。正確答案是 (B)。注意，不可因聽到 "report" 與 "starts" 就誤選 (C)。

9 正解 **B**

Hasn't Lisa already notified the client of our decision?
(A) I'll be ready in just a minute.
(B) No, she said she'll tell them tomorrow.
(C) Well, she decided to cancel the project.

麗莎還沒把我們的決定通知客戶嗎？
(A) 我只要一下子就會準備好。
(B) 對，她說明天再告訴他們。
(C) 嗯，她決定把案子取消掉。

解析	本句為否定的 "Yes-No" 問句，詢問對方麗莎是不是還沒有把他們的決定告知客戶，選項 (A) 答的是自己的狀況，選項 (C) 則說她（麗莎）決定把案子取消掉，二者皆答非所問。正解為 (B)。注意，由於本句為「否定」問句，因此雖然麗莎「是」還沒有通知客戶，但英文須以 "No" 而非 "Yes" 起頭作答。另，雖然 "decision" 為 "decide" 的「名詞」，但不可誤選 (C)。

10 正解 **A**

Have you received a draft of the proposal yet?
(A) Not that I know of.
(B) I did that last time.
(C) Sure, when is it due?

妳收到提案的草稿了沒？
(A) 如果有的話，我並不知道。
(B) 我上次做過了。
(C) 當然，什麼時候截止？

解析	本題仍為 "Yes-No" 題型，詢問對方是否已收到提案的草稿，選項 (A) 即為正解。注意，"Not that I know of." 表達的是，說話者認為應該沒有，但是並不打包票，因為比方說還沒有查看 email 信箱。選項 (B) 提到的「上次」與 (C) 提到的「截止」皆與原問句無關。

11 正解 **B**

Who's going to take over while Janice is away?
(A) She said she'll be back on the fifteenth.
(B) I think we'll just be on our own next week.
(C) Janice will give us a report when she returns.

珍妮絲不在的時候，會由誰來接手？
(A) 她說會在 15 號回來。
(B) 我想我們下星期得自立自強了。
(C) 珍妮絲回來的時候就會跟我們做一個報告。

解析	本句為 "Wh-" 問句，以疑問詞 "Who" 起頭，問話者想知道珍妮絲不在的期間會由誰接手。選項 (A) 提及珍妮絲回來的時間，選項 (C) 則說她回來的時候會做一個報告，二者內容皆與原問句不相干。正確選項 (B) 雖然沒有直接針對 "Who" 作回應，但是卻間接地表示並不會有人來接手。

12 正解 C

When did Sam leave the office last night?
(A) I think he got a better offer from another company.
(B) He wants to schedule a meeting for 7:30 tonight.
(C) I don't know. He was still working when I left yesterday.

山姆昨晚是什麼時候離開辦公室的？
(A) 我想有別家公司對他開出了更好的條件。
(B) 他想把會議排定在今天晚上 7:30。
(C) 我不曉得。我昨天離開的時候，他還在忙。

> 解析 本題亦為 "Wh-" 問句題，以疑問詞 "When" 起頭，問話者想知道的是山姆昨天晚上什麼時候離開辦公室。選項 (A) 提及某家公司開出了更好的條件，與選項 (B) 提及山姆想把會議排定在七點半，皆與原問句無關。本題應選 (C)，回話者表示由於昨日自己離開時山姆還在忙，因此他並不知道山姆是何時走的。

13 正解 B

How much do they charge for that service?
(A) They'll pay half now and half upon delivery.
(B) It's a small percentage of the total amount.
(C) The payment goes directly into our bank account.

他們的那項服務要收多少錢？
(A) 他們會現在付一半，另一半在交件時付。
(B) 收總金額的些微百分比。
(C) 付款直接進到我們的銀行戶頭。

> 解析 本句仍屬 "Wh-" 問句，以疑問詞 "How" 加形容詞 "much" 起頭，問話者想知道某項服務的收費情況。(A) 回的是「付款」方式，牛頭不對馬嘴；(C) 提到的同樣是「付款」的情況，自然不可選。唯有選項 (B) 正確地回答了問題。

14 正解 A

When can we expect your decision?
(A) Before the end of the week.
(B) I'm looking forward to it too.
(C) I'll inspect them very carefully.

我們什麼時候可以等到妳的決定？
(A) 週末之前。
(B) 我也很期待。
(C) 我會非常仔細地檢查它們。

> 解析 本題同為 "Wh-" 問句，以疑問詞 "When" 起頭，問對方何時能告知決定，選項 (A) 直接將「時間」講出，提供確切資訊，故為正解。(B) 說自己也很期待，不知所云；(C) 的敘述同樣地無厘頭。注意，選項 (C) 的 "inspect" 與問題中的 "expect" 使用了相同的字根 "spect"（意指 look），但字首的邏輯卻剛好相反：in- 是 "in" 的意思，ex- 則是 "out" 的意思。

15 正解 B

Where should we display the sale items?
(A) Everything on this rack is 20% off today.
(B) Let's put them near the front of the store.
(C) This place wasn't here before, was it?

我們該把特賣品陳列在哪裡？
(A) 這個架上的每樣東西今天都打八折。
(B) 我們就把它們擺在靠店鋪前面的地方。
(C) 這裡以前沒有這間店，對吧？

> 解析 本題為 "Wh-" 問句，以疑問詞 "Where" 起頭，問對方特價品應陳列於何處。選項 (A) 回答了某些商品的折扣，並未針對「何處」作出回應；選項 (C) 同樣未提供問話者所需要的資訊，故二者皆不可選。本題應選 (B)。注意，雖然原問句中的 "sale items" 指「特價品」，但不可因選項 (A) 提及折扣商品就因此誤選。

16 正解 A

When does the mail arrive?
(A) Usually not until after lunch.
(B) They're paid every other week.
(C) It's about a ten minute walk from here.

郵件什麼時候會到？
(A) 通常要到午餐過後。
(B) 他們每隔一週會拿到薪資。
(C) 從這裡走過去差不多十分鐘。

> 解析 本題是以 "When" 起始的 "Wh-" 問句，問話者想知道郵件的到達時間，選項 (A) 直接答出了此項資訊，所以是正確回應。選項 (B) 提到的是「發薪」時間，選項 (C) 提到的是「路程」時間，皆與提問風馬牛不相及。

17 正解 B

Can you access the files?
(A) Yes, I could use some accessories.
(B) No, I don't have the password.
(C) I need them right away.

你能夠存取檔案嗎？
(A) 是的，我可以用一些配件。
(B) 不行，我沒有密碼。
(C) 我馬上就需要它們。

> 解析　本題為 "Yes-No" 問句，詢問對方是否能夠存取檔案。選項 (A) 提到的是「配件」，與原問句不相干；選項 (C) 提及「需要它們」亦為答非所問。本題應選 (B)，說話者表示自己沒有密碼，所以無法存取檔案。注意，選項 (A) 的 accessories 與原問句中的 access 雖然為同源字，但用法和意思皆不同：前者為名詞，指「配件」；後者為動詞，指「存取」。

18 正解 B

Could we have all three computers repaired by this Friday?
(A) Sure, it'll just take a couple of weeks.
(B) Maybe, but it would be faster to replace them.
(C) It's a good way to save some money.

三台電腦可不可以在這星期五前全部修好？
(A) 沒問題，只需要幾個星期。
(B) 也許可以，但把它們換掉會比較快。
(C) 這是省一些錢的好辦法。

> 解析　本題亦為 "Yes-No" 問句題，針對提問，選項 (A) 雖然先說了「沒問題」，但之後卻表示需要好幾個禮拜，不知所云；選項 (C) 的敘述亦是令人丈二金剛摸不著頭腦，完全離題。正確答案是 (B)，回話者先以「也許可以」作為回應，但也提出了自己對於修復三台電腦的看法：乾脆換新電腦。

19 正解 A

Would you mind helping out at the meeting tomorrow?
(A) If John doesn't mind, I'd be happy to.
(B) That's OK, I'll just help myself.
(C) Yes, I met them all at the airport.

你介不介意明天開會時來幫忙？
(A) 假如約翰不介意，我會很樂意來。
(B) 沒關係，我自己弄就好。
(C) 是的，我在機場見到了他們所有人。

> 解析　本題同為 "Yes-No" 題型，問話者想知道對方是否介意明日開會時過來幫忙。選項 (A) 雖然未直接回應 "Yes" 或 "No"，但明白表示如果約翰不介意，自己會很樂意幫忙，故為正解。選項 (B) 所提的「自己弄」與原問句毫不相干；選項 (C) 用了 "Yes" 作為回應，不過之後所說的在機場見到某些人同樣與提問不搭軋。

20 正解 B

Would you consider a transfer to the sales department?
(A) About two years ago. I love it.
(B) I would have to think about it.
(C) Yes, I would prefer to stay in HR.

你要不要考慮調到業務部去？
(A) 差不多兩年前。我非常喜歡。
(B) 我得想一想才行。
(C) 是的，我比較想待在人資。

> 解析　本題仍為 "Yes-No" 問句，詢問對方是否願意考慮調到業務部。選項 (A) 提及「時間」與主旨無關；選項 (C) 雖然用了 "Yes" 回答，但卻是說自己比較想待在人資部，邏輯不通。本題應選 (B)，說話者雖然未直接以 "Yes" 或 "No" 作答，但明白表示得先想一想，因此為合理回應。

21 正解 B

What's her new position at the company?
(A) Her office is right next to the meeting room.
(B) She's now in charge of training new hires.
(C) Well, she certainly deserved the promotion.

她在公司的新職位是什麼？
(A) 她的辦公室就在會議室的隔壁。
(B) 她現在負責訓練新聘人員。
(C) 嗯，她確實值得晉升。

> 解析　本題為 "Wh-" 問句，以疑問詞 "What" 起頭，問對方女子在公司擔任什麼新職位。(A) 提到的是辦公室的地點，答非所問；(C) 則說她值得晉升，同樣不知所云。選項 (B) 明確指出女子的新職務，故為正解。

22　正解 C　

Where should we open the first store?
(A) The earliest one opens at nine or nine thirty.
(B) At the end of the month when the design is finished.
(C) Somewhere near the university would be good.

我們該把第一家店開在哪裡？
(A) 最早的一間在九點或九點半開門。
(B) 月底完成設計時。
(C) 大學附近的地點應該會不錯。

解析　本題為 "Wh-" 問句，以疑問詞 "Where" 起頭，問對方他們的第一間店應該開在哪裡。選項 (A) 提到的是某間店的開門時間，與原問句無關；選項 (B) 提到的同樣與「時間」有關，並未針對 "Where" 作出回應。選項 (C) 明確地針對問話者所問指出了地點，故為正解。

23　正解 C　

Do you know where I can park near here?
(A) Yes, there's a very nice park at the end of that street.
(B) There are lots of good restaurants around the corner.
(C) Sorry, I'm not very familiar with this area.

妳知道這附近有哪裡可以停車嗎？
(A) 是的，街尾有座非常好的公園。
(B) 轉角有很多不錯的餐館。
(C) 抱歉，我對這個區域不是很熟。

解析　本題為 "Yes-No" 問句，問對方是否知道附近何處可以停車。選項 (A) 雖用了 "Yes" 作回應，但卻是說街尾有座公園，不知所云；選項 (B) 提及轉角有許多不錯的餐館，同樣與原問句不相干。正確答案是 (C)，回話者表示因為對該區不熟悉，因此無法幫助對方。

24　正解 A　

Does that old fax machine still work?
(A) It did the last time I tried it.
(B) It's between the phone and computer.
(C) Actually, I'm at work right now.

那台舊的傳真機還能用嗎？
(A) 上次我試的時候還行。
(B) 在電話和電腦之間。
(C) 事實上我現在正在工作。

解析　本題亦為 "Yes-No" 問句題型，詢問對方舊的那部傳真機是否仍堪用。選項 (A) 雖然未直接用 "Yes" 或 "No" 回應，但說明了上次她使用時沒有問題，因此為合理答案。選項 (B) 提到的是傳真機所在之處，明顯答非所問；選項 (C) 則是以自己正在工作作為回應，同樣不可選。

25　正解 C　

Will you be able to receive a call during the meeting?
(A) No, I haven't been notified about it.
(B) Just tell her after the meeting is over.
(C) I'm actually going to turn my phone off.

妳開會的時候能夠接電話嗎？
(A) 沒有，我並沒有被通知。
(B) 等會一開完就告訴她。
(C) 其實我會把手機關機。

解析　本題仍為 "Yes-No" 問句，問話者想知道對方開會時是否能接電話。選項 (A) 雖用了 "No" 回答，但卻是說自己沒被通知，牛頭不對馬嘴；選項 (B) 提及開完會後告知某人，同樣答非所問。選項 (C) 明白表示自己會把手機關掉，也就是說，她並不會接電話。

26　正解 A

I'd like to return this jacket.
(A) Sure. May I ask why?
(B) Just go down hall and turn right.
(C) He took it back to the store yesterday.

我想退這件外套。
(A) 沒問題。我可以問一下為什麼嗎？
(B) 走過大廳右轉就到了。
(C) 他昨天把它拿回到店裡。

解析　本句為一平述句，說話者表示想把外套退掉，選項 (A) 的回答即為合理回應。選項 (B) 所言顯然與「退外套」一事不相干；選項 (C) 所說的更是與說話者毫無關係。

27 正解 C

Do you advertise online?
(A) Yes, I definitely think you should.
(B) I purchased a few items last week.
(C) Not currently, but we have in the past.

你（們）有在網路上登廣告嗎？
(A) 是的，我的確認為你應該要。
(B) 我上星期買了幾樣東西。
(C) 目前沒有，但是我們以前登過。

> **解析** 本題為 "Yes-No" 問句，問話者想知道對方是否有在網路上刊登廣告。選項 (A) 雖答了 "Yes"，但之後的句子與原問句無關；選項 (B) 提到的是「購物」，牛頭不對馬嘴。本題應選 (C)，回話者表示雖然目前沒有刊登廣告，但先前曾刊登過。

28 正解 C

Excuse me, where's the concert hall?
(A) Concerts usually start at about eight, I think.
(B) That's OK. No trouble at all.
(C) It's that white building across the street.

不好意思，請問音樂廳在哪裡？
(A) 我想音樂會通常是八點左右開始。
(B) 沒關係。一點都不麻煩。
(C) 就是對街的那棟白色大樓。

> **解析** 本題為 "Wh-" 問句，詢問對方音樂廳之所在地。選項 (A) 答的是「音樂會」("concert") 開始的時間，而非「音樂廳」("concert hall") 之地點；選項 (B) 的回答亦未針對所問作出回應。正確答案是 (C)，回話者明確指出音樂廳即「對街的那棟白色大樓」。注意，勿因問話者在開頭先說了 "Excuse me" 就誤選 (B)，因為在此 "Excuse me" 並不是真正用來道歉，而是用來表達「客氣地請問」之意。

29 正解 A

When is the first payment due?
(A) Not until the end of the month.
(B) Sure, I'll show you how to do it.
(C) We usually meet in the morning.

第一筆付款什麼時候到期？
(A) 月底前才需要付。
(B) 沒問題，我會教你怎麼做。
(C) 我們通常是在早上見面。

> **解析** 本句為 "Wh-" 問句，說話者想知道第一筆付款何時到期。選項 (A) 明確答出時間點，故為正解。選項 (B) 提到的「教你怎麼做」及選項 (C) 提到的「通常是在早上見面」皆答非所問。

30 正解 C

Why was the staff meeting cancelled?
(A) Don't worry. I'm sure John can handle it.
(B) I'll arrange some additional seating for the staff.
(C) It wasn't. It's just been postponed until tomorrow.

員工會議為什麼取消了？
(A) 別擔心。我確信約翰能夠處理。
(B) 我會替員工們安排一些額外的座位。
(C) 並沒有取消。只是延到了明天。

> **解析** 本題亦為 "Wh-" 問句題型，詢問對方員工會議為何被取消。選項 (A) 提及「約翰能處理」與選項 (B) 提及「替員工們安排座位」顯然皆未針對問題作回應。本題應選 (C)，回話者告訴問話者會議並未取消，只是延期。

31 正解 C

Are you familiar with the company's travel policy?
(A) Yes, I have both health and dental insurance through the company.
(B) My supervisor goes to Chicago every three months or so.
(C) A little. It's mostly about how much we're allowed to spend.

你對公司的出差旅行政策熟不熟？
(A) 是的，公司有幫我保健康和牙科險。
(B) 我的上司每三個月左右就會去芝加哥一趟。
(C) 知道一些。它主要是關於我們能夠被允許花費多少錢。

> **解析** 本題為 "Yes-No" 問句，問話者想知道對方是否熟悉公司的差旅政策。選項 (A) 雖用了 "Yes" 作回應，但卻是在敘述公司幫自己保的險，文不對題；選項 (B) 提及其上司每三個月到芝加哥一趟，同樣答非所問。正確答案是 (C)，回話者表示自己略知一二，並告知問話者該政策的重點。注意，原問句中提到的 "policy" 可指「保險單」，但不可因此誤選 (A)。

PART 3

Questions 32-34 refer to the following conversation.

第 32 到 34 題請參照下面這段對話。

M: Hello, I'm calling to book an airport shuttle from Princeton to Newark. I need to be at the airport by noon on Monday.

W: Of course, sir. We can have a shuttle pick you up in Princeton at nine-thirty Monday morning. The weekday fare is sixty-five dollars.

M: OK, that sounds perfect. My address here is 660 Rosedale Road. Also, I'd like to know if there's room in the shuttle for my golf clubs.

W: There is, but we charge a five-dollar fee for oversized luggage.

男：你好，我打電話來是想預訂從普林斯頓到紐華克的機場接駁車。我需要在星期一中午前到機場。

女：好的，先生。我們可以在星期一早上九點半派接駁車去普林斯頓接您。平日的車資是 65 美元。

男：好，聽起來很完美。我的地址是羅斯岱爾路 660 號。還有，我想知道接駁車上有沒有空間擺我的高爾夫球桿。

女：有的，但如果行李過大要收 5 美元的費用。

---

32 正解 C

Where most likely does the woman work?
(A) At an airport
(B) At a golf course
(C) At a shuttle service
(D) At a train station

女子最有可能是在哪裡工作？
(A) 機場
(B) 高爾夫球場
(C) 接駁車服務處
(D) 火車站

解析 本題屬「推論」題，問女子最有可能是在何處工作。由女子第一次回應男子時所說的 "We can have a shuttle pick you up .... The weekday fare is sixty-five dollars." 「我們可以……派接駁車去……接您。平日的車資是 65 美元。」即可合理推斷，女子應該是在「接駁車服務處」工作。正確答案是 (C)。

---

33 正解 C

Why is the man calling?
(A) To book a flight
(B) To inquire about a room
(C) To arrange transportation
(D) To schedule a delivery

男子為什麼打電話？
(A) 為了預訂航班
(B) 為了查詢客房
(C) 為了安排交通工具
(D) 為了預訂送貨時間

解析 本題屬「細節」題，問男子為何要打電話。由男子一開頭就直接提到的 "... I'm calling to book an airport shuttle from Princeton to Newark." 「我打電話來是想預訂從普林斯頓到紐華克的機場接駁車。」即可知，他是「為了安排交通工具」而來電。正確答案是 (C)。

---

34 正解 D

What does the woman say will cost extra?
(A) Changing the pick-up time
(B) Traveling on a weekday
(C) Using a credit card
(D) Transporting oversized luggage

女子說什麼須額外收費？
(A) 更改接送時間
(B) 平日旅遊
(C) 使用信用卡
(D) 載運過大的行李

解析 由女子回應男子詢問接駁車上是否有空間放高爾夫球桿時所說的 "There is, but we charge a five-dollar fee for oversized luggage." 「有的，但如果行李過大要收 5 美元的費用。」即可知，選項 (D) 為正解。注意，"transport" 指「運輸」，其名詞 "transportation" 則除了指「運輸」外，還有「交通工具」的意思。

Vocabulary
☐ **airport shuttle** 機場接送車　☐ **fare**（交通工具的）票價　☐ **oversized** 過大的

Questions 35-37 refer to the following conversation.

W: I really like this suitcase. Do you have any others like it?

M: Just one. It's a smaller size, but the color is the same. Would you like to see it?

W: No, the size of this one is perfect. I'm just concerned about this wheel. It seems to be cracked.

M: Well, if you don't mind waiting a few minutes, I can replace it right now. How does that sound?

第 35 到 37 題請參照下面這段對話。

女：我非常喜歡這個手提箱。你們有沒有其他任何類似的？

男：只有一個。尺寸比較小，可是顏色一樣。您想要看看嗎？

女：不用了，這個的尺寸很完美。我只是擔心這個輪子。它似乎已經裂了。

男：嗯，如果您不介意等幾分鐘，我可以馬上更換。這樣聽起來如何？

---

35 正解 **D**

Where most likely is this conversation taking place?
(A) In a bicycle shop
(B) In a hotel lobby
(C) In a bus station
(D) In a luggage store

這段對話最有可能發生在哪裡？
(A) 腳踏車店
(B) 飯店大廳
(C) 公車站
(D) 行李箱店

解析　本題為「推論」題。由女子一開始說的 "I really like this suitcase. Do you have any others like it?"「我非常喜歡這個手提箱。你們有沒有其他任何類似的？」及男子回應時所說的 "Just one. ... Would you like to see it?"「只有一個。……您想要看看嗎？」即可合理推斷，這段對話發生的地點最有可能是「行李箱店」，故本題選 (D)。

---

36 正解 **B**

What is the problem?
(A) An order is late.
(B) An item is damaged.
(C) The customer cannot wait.
(D) The merchandise is the wrong size.

發生了什麼問題？
(A) 某項訂貨延遲了。
(B) 某個物件損壞了。
(C) 顧客不能等。
(D) 商品的尺寸錯了。

解析　本題考細節。由女子第二次發言時提到的 "I'm ... concerned about this wheel. It seems to be cracked."「我……擔心這個輪子。它似乎已經裂了。」及男子回應時所說的 "... I can replace it right now."「……我可以馬上更換。」可確定有「某個物件損壞了」，故正解為 (B)。

---

37 正解 **C**

What does the man offer to do?
(A) Lower a price
(B) Offer a refund
(C) Replace a part
(D) Order a replacement

男子提議要做什麼？
(A) 降價
(B) 退款
(C) 更換零件
(D) 訂購替代品

解析　本題考點同樣落在「細節」部分。如上一題的說明，女子一說手提箱有一個輪子裂了，男子立即回應說他可以馬上更換，因此本題選 (C)。

Vocabulary

☐ **cracked** 破裂的

M 🇨🇦 W 🇺🇸

Questions 38-40 refer to the following conversation.

第 38 到 40 題請參照下面這段對話。

M: Excuse me, I want to use the swimming pool, but I don't have my membership card with me.

W: Oh, okay. I can look up your account on the computer. Do you have a driver's license or some other kind of identification with you?

M: I have my student ID card. Is that alright?

W: Umm, sure. That would be fine. Here's a day pass. You can use it to access the pool and the gym until nine o'clock tonight.

男：不好意思，我想使用游泳池，可是我的會員卡沒帶在身上。

女：噢，好。我可以用電腦查一下您的帳號。您身上有沒有帶駕照或其他證件？

男：我有帶學生證。可以嗎？

女：嗯，沒問題。可以的。這是當日通行證。今晚九點之前您可以用它進入泳池和健身房。

---

38 正解 D

What does the man want to do?
(A) Sign up to use the gym
(B) Renew his membership
(C) Get a new card
(D) Use the swimming pool

男子想做什麼？
(A) 登記使用健身房
(B) 更新會員資格
(C) 辦一張新卡
(D) 使用游泳池

解析 本題為「細節」題，問男子想做什麼。男子一開始就明白表示 "... I want to use the swimming pool ...."「我想使用游泳池……。」故正解為 (D)。

---

39 正解 A

Where most likely is the conversation taking place?
(A) At a sports center
(B) At a school
(C) At a computer store
(D) At a car rental company

這段對話最有可能發生在哪裡？
(A) 運動中心
(B) 學校
(C) 電腦店
(D) 租車公司

解析 本題為「推論」題。由女子第二次發言時所說的 "Here's a day pass. You can use it to access the pool and the gym ...."「這是當日通行證。……您可以用它進入泳池和健身房。」即可推斷，兩人應該是在「運動中心」談話。正確答案是 (A)。

---

40 正解 D

What does the woman give the man?
(A) An access code
(B) A student ID card
(C) An application form
(D) A temporary pass

女子給了男子什麼？
(A) 一個存取碼
(B) 一張學生證
(C) 一份申請表
(D) 一張臨時通行證

解析 本題同樣考細節。男子想使用游泳池，但沒有帶 "membership card"「會員卡」，不過因為他有 "student ID card"「學生證」可證明他的身分，所以女子給了他一張 "day pass"「當日通行證」，而由於 "day pass" 僅供一日使用，因此屬於「臨時性」的通行證，故本題選 (D)。

Vocabulary

☐ **day pass** 一日通行票券 ☐ **access** 使用（權）；進入

第1回完全解析

PART 3

Questions 41-43 refer to the following conversation.

W: Hello, Newvis Electronics customer service. How may I help you?

M: Um, yeah, hi. I just bought a Newvis television. The instructions said I should mail in a "registration card," but I don't see anything like that in the box.

W: You must have purchased the Newvis Clearset. Is that right?

M: Yes, how did you know?

W: I'm afraid some outdated instruction manuals were shipped with that model. It's been selling well, and we've experienced some difficulty trying to meet the demand.

M: So, can you send me the updated manual?

W: Actually, the latest version of the Clearset manual is available for download on our website. You can register your product there as well. Would you like me to email a link to you?

第 41 到 43 題請參照下面這段對話。

女：您好，這裡是紐維斯電子客服。有什麼可以效勞的嗎？

男：嗯，是的，妳好。我剛買了一台紐維斯的電視。說明書上說我應該要郵寄「登錄卡」，可是我在箱子裡並沒有看到任何類似的東西。

女：您一定是買了紐維斯高清組，對不對？

男：對，妳怎麼知道？

女：那一款恐怕是附上了過時的說明手冊。它賣得不錯，所以我們在試圖因應需求上碰到了一些困難。

男：那妳能不能把更新過的手冊寄給我？

女：事實上，最新版的高清組手冊上我們的網站就可以下載。您也可以在上面登錄您購買的產品。您要不要我把連結用電郵寄給您？

---

41 正解 A

What does the woman say about the Newvis Clearset?
(A) It is very popular.
(B) It is somewhat outdated.
(C) It is difficult to use.
(D) It is no longer for sale.

女子提到了紐維斯高清組的什麼事？
(A) 它非常暢銷。
(B) 它有點過時。
(C) 它很難用。
(D) 它已經不再販售。

> 解析　本題考點落在「細節」部分。女子在第三次發言時提到 "It's been selling well ...."「它賣得不錯……。」而句中的 "It" 指的正是她第二次發言時所說的 "Newvis Clearset"「紐維斯高清組」。換句話說，女子就是在告訴男子該款電視機相當暢銷，因此本題選 (A)。

---

42 正解 B

What does the man request?
(A) A registration card
(B) An updated manual
(C) A new warranty
(D) A full refund

男子要索取什麼？
(A) 登錄卡
(B) 更新過的手冊
(C) 新的保固
(D) 全額退費

> 解析　男子在第一次發言時提到，他買的新電視所附的說明書上說他必須郵寄「登錄卡」，但箱子裡並沒有任何「登錄卡」；而女子則告訴他，他拿到的應該是已過時的說明書，男子因而詢問 "So, can you send me the updated manual?"「那妳能不能把更新過的手冊寄給我？」因此本題正解為 (B)。

---

43 正解 C

What does the woman suggest the man do?
(A) Call a customer service number
(B) Email a company
(C) Visit a website
(D) Purchase a television

女子建議男子做什麼？
(A) 撥打一個客服號碼
(B) 寄電郵到一家公司
(C) 上一個網站
(D) 買一台電視

> 解析　針對男子對於更新手冊的詢問，女子的回應是 "... the latest version of the Clearset manual is available for download on our website. ... Would you like me to email a link to you?"「……最新版的高清組手冊上我們的網站就可以下載。……您要不要我把連結用電郵寄給您？」換言之，女子建議男子做的是 (C) Visit a website「上一個網站」。

Vocabulary

☐ **outdated** 過時的　　☐ **registration** 註冊；登錄　　☐ **updated** 更新的

M 🍁 W 🇺🇸

Questions 44-46 refer to the following conversation.

W: You're going to the regional sales conference this week, aren't you?

M: Yes, I have to. I'm giving a presentation Wednesday afternoon.

W: Well, some of us are planning to stay an extra day. We'll go shopping or to an art museum during the day on Thursday, have dinner together, and then see a play that night. Would you like to join us?

M: That sounds great, but isn't it too late to get theater tickets?

W: Well, my sister works at a theater. She told me as long I tell her how many tickets we need by six o'clock tonight, she can definitely get them. I know that's not a lot of time, but think about it and let me know.

M: I don't need to think about it. I'll be there!

第 44 到 46 題請參照下面這段對話。

女：你這星期要去參加區域業務大會，對吧？

男：是的，我非去不可。我星期三下午要做簡報。

女：嗯，我們有些人打算多待一天。我們在星期四白天會去逛街或到美術館，接著一起吃晚餐，然後當晚再去看戲劇。你要不要跟我們一道去？

男：聽起來很棒，可是買戲票不會太遲了嗎？

女：嗯，我姊姊在戲院上班。她跟我說只要我在今天晚上六點前告訴她需要幾張票，她就肯定能弄到手。我知道時間不是很多，但你考慮一下再跟我說。

男：不用考慮了。我一定到！

---

44 正解 D

Why does the woman talk to the man?
(A) To ask him to attend a conference
(B) To persuade him to give a presentation
(C) To discuss his plans for the weekend
(D) To invite him to an event

女子為什麼跟男子交談？
(A) 為了要求他出席一場會議
(B) 為了說服他做簡報
(C) 為了討論他的週末計畫
(D) 為了邀請他參加一項活動

解析 本題為「推論」題。在女子確定男子也要去參加區域業務大會之後便告訴他說，她和幾個同事打算多待一天，到處逛逛、一起吃晚餐，再去看戲劇表演。接著她就問男子 "Would you like to join us?"「你要不要跟我們一道去？」而男子最後的回答是 "I'll be there!"「我一定到！」由此可推斷，女子與男子交談的原因是 (D) To invite him to an event「為了邀請他參加一項活動」。

---

45 正解 C

What does the woman say is important?
(A) Visiting an art museum
(B) Booking a hotel room
(C) Making a quick decision
(D) Arranging transportation

女子說什麼事很重要？
(A) 參觀美術館
(B) 預訂飯店房間
(C) 趕緊作決定
(D) 安排交通工具

解析 本題屬「細節」題。女子在第三次發言時提到，如果要去看戲劇表演就必須在當晚六點之前確定需要幾張票，並且還跟男子說 "I know that's not a lot of time, but think about it and let me know."「我知道時間不是很多，但你考慮一下再跟我說。」因此本題選 (C)。

---

46 正解 A

What does the man agree to do?
(A) Join a group of coworkers
(B) Help the woman get tickets
(C) Reserve seats for the conference
(D) Consider the woman's suggestion

男子同意做什麼事？
(A) 加入一群同事的行列
(B) 幫忙女子弄到票
(C) 保留會議席位
(D) 考慮女子的建議

解析 本題亦屬「細節」題，問男子同意做何事。由男子最後所說的 "I don't need to think about it. I'll be there!"「不用考慮了。我一定到！」即可知，男子願意加入同事的行列。正確答案是 (A)。

Vocabulary
□ **conference**（大型）會議

第 1 回完全解析

PART 3

101

Questions 47-49 refer to the following conversation.   第 47 到 49 題請參照下面這段對話。

M: Thanks for taking the time to meet with me, Julia. I know you have a busy schedule.

W: It's no problem at all. Is your proposal for the new IT budget ready yet?

M: Almost. I'm still thinking about how to lower our software costs.

W: That was our biggest IT expense last year.

M: Right—even more than the new computers we bought. I've been researching how much it would cost to develop our own software. It would be more expensive at first, but save money over time.

W: That sounds like an investment that management would at least consider.

M: I think I will suggest it at the next board meeting.

男：謝謝妳抽空見我，茱莉亞。我知道妳的行程很忙。

女：完全不成問題。針對資訊科技新預算的提案你準備好了嗎？

男：差不多了。我還在思考要怎麼降低軟體成本。

女：那是我們去年在資訊科技上的最大一筆開銷。

男：沒錯，甚至超過了我們所買的新電腦。我一直在研究自行開發軟體要花多少錢。一開始會比較貴，可是時間久了就會省錢。

女：這聽起來像是管理階層起碼會考慮一下的投資。

男：我想在下次的董事會上我會這樣建議。

---

47 正解 C

What are the speakers discussing?   說話者在討論什麼？

(A) A department meeting   (A) 一個部門會議
(B) A new schedule   (B) 一個新時程
(C) A budget proposal   (C) 一個預算提案
(D) A computer purchase   (D) 一個電腦採購案

解析 女子第一次發言時即問男子 "Is your proposal for the new IT budget ready yet?"「針對資訊科技新預算的提案你準備好了嗎？」男子則回應說 "Almost. I'm still thinking about how to lower our software costs."「差不多了。我還在思考要怎麼降低軟體成本。」而接下來的談論仍以此預算提案為重心。由此確定本題應選 (C)。

---

48 正解 A

What does the woman say about the software?   女子提及軟體的什麼事？

(A) It is expensive.   (A) 它很昂貴。
(B) It is outdated.   (B) 它過時了。
(C) It is too slow.   (C) 它太慢了。
(D) It is overpriced.   (D) 它的定價過高。

解析 本題考的是細節。在男子提到降低軟體成本之後，女子即說 "That was our biggest IT expense last year."「那是我們去年在資訊科技上的最大一筆開銷。」換言之，女子顯然認為軟體相當昂貴。因此，答案是 (A) It is expensive.。

---

49 正解 C

What does the man decide to do?   男子決定要做什麼？

(A) Research a product   (A) 研究一項產品
(B) Support a proposal   (B) 支持一個提案
(C) Make a recommendation   (C) 提出一個建議
(D) Explain a policy   (D) 解釋一項政策

解析 本題亦考細節。女子在第三次發言時表示 "That sounds like an investment that management would at least consider."「這聽起來像是管理階層起碼會考慮一下的投資。」而由男子的回應 "I think I will suggest it at the next board meeting."「我想在下次的董事會上我會這樣建議。」即可知，正解為 (C) Make a recommendation。

Vocabulary

☐ **IT** (information technology) 資訊科技   ☐ **expense** 開支；費用   ☐ **over time** 隨著時間

🎵 MP3 01-41

Questions 50-52 refer to the following conversation.

M: Hello, my name is Eric Costas. I'm a third year biology major here and I'm looking for a summer internship. I read on the department website that your lab will be starting three new experiments soon. Do you have any openings for a lab assistant?

W: Actually, we are a little understaffed at the moment. What kind of lab experience do you have?

M: Well, last year I worked in Professor Jensen's lab in the chemistry department. I'm sure that she would give me a good recommendation.

W: Oh, okay. I'll give Professor Jensen a call. In the meantime, why don't you email your resume to me?

第 50 到 52 題請參照下面這段對話。

男：你好，我叫艾瑞克‧柯斯塔斯。我是本校生物系三年級生，正在尋找暑期實習機會。我在系網站上看到說你們的實驗室即將展開三項新實驗。請問你們有任何實驗室助理的缺嗎？

女：事實上我們目前有點缺人。你具備哪種實驗室的經驗？

男：嗯，去年我在化學系簡森教授的實驗室工作過。我確信她對我會有相當正面的推薦。

女：噢，好的。我會打通電話給簡森教授。在此同時，你何不用電郵把履歷寄來給我？

50 正解 A

Why did the man call the woman?
(A) To look for work
(B) To ask about an experiment
(C) To arrange a tour
(D) To introduce a professor

男子為什麼打電話給女子？
(A) 為了找工作
(B) 為了詢問有關一項實驗的事
(C) 為了安排一趟參訪
(D) 為了介紹一位教授

解析 男子在第一次發言時就提到 "... I'm looking for a summer internship. ... Do you have any openings for a lab assistant?" 「……我正在尋找暑期實習機會。……請問你們有任何實驗室助理的缺嗎？」由此即可確定男子是「為了找工作」而打這通電話。正確答案是 (A)。

51 正解 B

What does the woman mean when she says, "we are a little understaffed at the moment"?
(A) The lab doesn't currently have any workers.
(B) She may have a position for the man.
(C) The staff require additional training.
(D) She doesn't have time to talk with the man.

女子所說的 "we are a little understaffed at the moment" 是什麼意思？
(A) 實驗室目前沒有任何工作人員。
(B) 她也許有一個適合男子的職位。
(C) 工作人員需要額外的訓練。
(D) 她沒有時間跟男子多談。

解析 本題考詞句解釋，問女子說的 "we are a little understaffed at the moment" 所指為何。就字面上而言，此句應譯為「目前我們有一點人手不足」，而依女子說這句話時的語境來推斷，她的意思應該是選項 (B) She may have a position for the man.「她也許有一個適合男子的職位」。

52 正解 C

What will the woman do next?
(A) Schedule an interview
(B) Write a recommendation
(C) Call a colleague
(D) Email a resume

女子接下來會做什麼？
(A) 排定一個面試時間
(B) 寫一封推薦信
(C) 打電話給一位同仁
(D) 用電郵寄履歷

解析 本題考點落在「細節」部分。在男子告訴女子他相信簡森教授會願意推薦他之後，女子即回應說 "Oh, okay. I'll give Professor Jensen a call."「噢，好的。我會打通電話給簡森教授。」而由於簡森教授與女子皆為該校教職員，因此本題選 (C) Call a colleague「打電話給一位同仁」。

第 1 回完全解析

PART 3

Vocabulary
☐ **opening** 職缺　☐ **understaffed** 人手不足的　☐ **staff** 職員；工作人員　☐ **colleague** 同事

Questions 53-55 refer to the following conversation.　　　第 53 到 55 題請參照下面這段對話。

M: Hi, I'm Jerome Selwin. I'm moving my accounting practice to a different location, and I'm looking for someone to design the new office.

W: Thank you for getting in touch with us, Mr. Selwin. We have extensive experience designing interiors for all kinds of professionals—lawyers, financial advisors, and of course accountants.

M: Great. I'd like to meet with a designer to discuss the details as soon as possible. We're planning to sign the lease later today and move next month. I know that's not a lot of time.

W: That should be no problem. We can have someone meet with you at your convenience any time next week. Could you first give me a little information now about the size and location of the space?

男：嗨，我叫傑若米‧瑟文。我即將把我的會計業務搬到另外一個地方，正在找人設計新的辦公室。

女：感謝您與我們聯絡，瑟文先生。在為各種專業人士做室內設計方面，我們有廣泛的經驗，這些人士包括律師、理財顧問，當然還有會計師。

男：好極了。我想盡快跟設計師見面討論細節。我們打算在今天稍後簽訂租約，下個月就搬過去。我知道時間不是很多。

女：那應該不成問題。看您什麼時候方便，我們下週就能派人跟您見面。您現在能不能先跟我稍微說明一下空間的大小和地點？

---

53 正解 **A**

What type of service does the woman's company provide?
(A) Interior design
(B) Accounting services
(C) Legal advice
(D) Office management

女子的公司提供的是什麼類型的服務？
(A) 室內設計
(B) 會計服務
(C) 法律諮詢
(D) 辦公室管理

解析　由男子第一次發言時說的 "... I'm looking for someone to design the new office." 「……我正在找人設計新的辦公室。」及女子的回應 "Thank you for getting in touch with us .... We have extensive experience designing interiors ..." 「感謝您與我們聯絡，……做室內設計方面，我們有廣泛的經驗……。」即可合理推斷，女子公司所提供的應該是「室內設計」的服務。正解為 (A)。另注意，選項 (D) 的 "management" 除了一般作「管理」解之外，在多益考試中也常用來指「管理階層」。

---

54 正解 **D**

What does the man say he wants to do?
(A) Open a new accounting practice
(B) Consult with a financial advisor
(C) Hire a moving company
(D) Meet with a designer

男子說他想做什麼？
(A) 開啟新的會計業務
(B) 與理財顧問商議
(C) 雇用搬家公司
(D) 與設計師見面

解析　本題考的是細節。由男子第二次發言時所說的 "I'd like to meet with a designer to discuss the details as soon as possible." 「我想盡快跟設計師見面討論細節。」即可確定 (D) 為正解。

---

55 正解 **A**

When will the man sign the lease?
(A) Later that day
(B) The next week
(C) The next month
(D) Whenever it is convenient

男子會在什麼時候簽訂租約？
(A) 當天稍後
(B) 下一週
(C) 下一個月
(D) 任何方便的時候

解析　本題亦考細節，問男子會在何時簽約。由男子第二次發言時所說的 "We're planning to sign the lease later today ..." 「我們打算在今天稍後簽訂租約……。」即可知，男子會在「當日稍後」簽約。正確答案是 (A)。

Vocabulary

☐ **practice** 業務；工作

Questions 56-58 refer to the following conversation. | 第 56 到 58 題請參照下面這段對話。

W: Hi, Ted. I just got off the phone with Rexroth Lighting. They're wondering why we haven't shipped their order yet.

M: Well, we manufactured the desk lamps according to their new specifications, but the larger lamps didn't fit inside the old packaging. I ordered new boxes this morning, but they won't get here until Friday.

W: What should I tell Rexroth?

M: If there are no other problems, we're looking at next week.

W: Okay. I'll send them an email and let them know what's happening.

女：嗨，泰德。我剛跟力士樂照明通過電話。他們想知道我們為什麼還沒把他們訂的貨送出去。

男：嗯，我們依照了他們的新規格來製作桌燈，可是因為燈比較大裝不進舊的包裝裡。我今天早上訂了新的箱子，不過要等星期五才會送到。

女：我該怎麼跟力士樂說？

男：假如沒有別的問題，我們就看下星期吧。

女：好。我會寄電郵給他們，讓他們知道是怎麼回事。

---

56 正解 B

Where do the speakers most likely work? | 說話者最有可能是在哪裡工作？
(A) At a shipping company | (A) 貨運公司
(B) At a factory | (B) 工廠
(C) At a store | (C) 商店
(D) At a warehouse | (D) 倉庫

> 解析 本題屬「推論」題，問說話者最有可能是在何處工作。由女子第一次發言時說的 "I just got off the phone with Rexroth Lighting. They're wondering why we haven't shipped their order yet." 「我剛跟力士樂照明通過電話。他們想知道我們為什麼還沒把他們訂的貨送出去。」及男子的回應 "Well, we manufactured the desk lamps according to their new specifications, but ...." 「嗯，我們依照了他們的新規格來製作桌燈，可是……。」即可合理推斷，兩人最有可能是在一家「工廠」工作。

---

57 正解 B

What does the man mean when he says, "we're looking at next week"? | 男子所說的 "we're looking at next week" 是什麼意思？
(A) It will take several days to make the packaging. | (A) 包材要花上好幾天製作。
(B) The order can't be shipped this week. | (B) 訂的貨這星期無法送出去。
(C) He will arrange a meeting in the near future. | (C) 他在不久的將來會安排會面。
(D) They will start manufacturing the order next week. | (D) 他們會在下星期開始製造預訂之貨品。

> 解析 本題考詞句解釋。若將 "we're looking at next week" 直譯的結果會是「我們正在看著下星期」，不知所云；但若加上男子整句話的前半 "If there are no other problems" 「假如沒有別的問題」，合理的翻譯應該是「我們就看下星期吧。」而由男子先前提到的 "... but the larger lamps didn't fit inside the old packaging. ... new boxes ... won't get here until Friday." 「……可是因為燈比較大裝不進舊的包裝裡。……新的箱子……要等星期五才會送到。」即可斷定，他所說的「我們就看下星期吧。」意思應該就是「訂的貨這星期無法出貨。」正解為 (B)。注意，"order" 此字可指「訂購」、「訂貨」、「訂單」，在此則指「訂的貨品」。

---

58 正解 D

What will the woman include in her email? | 女子的電郵裡會包含什麼內容？
(A) A design idea for the new packaging | (A) 新包裝的設計構想
(B) A document with the latest specifications | (B) 含最新規格的文件
(C) A revised manufacturing schedule | (C) 修訂過的製造時程
(D) An explanation for the delay in shipping | (D) 出貨延誤的解釋

> 解析 本題考細節。女子在對話末尾表示 "I'll send them an email and let them what's happening."，而她所謂的 "what's happening" 指的當然就是之前男子對於無法及時出貨所做的解釋，因此本題選 (D) An explanation for the delay in shipping。

Vocabulary

☐ **specification** 規格　☐ **packaging** 包裝

Questions 59-61 refer to the following conversation with three speakers.

M1: I didn't know the sales conference this weekend was such a big deal. People are flying in from all over the country! Arranging the airport transportation has been a lot more work than I expected.

W: It's actually a really fun event—a lot of meetings, but, as you know, also a lot of fun social events. Are we ready?

M2: I think so. I've confirmed everyone's hotel reservations and arranged everything for the welcome luncheon. And you've booked a restaurant for the big farewell dinner—right, Frank?

M1: Oh, no! I've been so busy dealing with the airport transportation that I forgot to look for a good location for the dinner.

M2: That could be a problem. I think we may have trouble finding a large enough space on such short notice.

W: You're probably right. Let's get in touch with some catering companies. We may have to have the dinner served at the conference center.

第 59 到 61 題請參照下面這段三人對話。

男1：我不曉得本週末的業務大會竟然這麼盛大。全國各地都有人飛過來！安排機場交通比我預期的要費事得多。

女：其實這是個相當有趣的活動──是有很多會要開，可是你知道的，也會有很多有趣的社交活動。我們準備就緒了嗎？

男2：我想是吧。我確認過每個人的飯店訂房，也把歡迎午餐會的一切都安排好了。你訂好惜別晚宴的餐廳了──對吧，法蘭克？

男1：噢，糟糕！我一直忙著處理機場交通的問題，忘了去找晚宴的合適地點。

男2：這可能會是個問題。這麼臨時通知，我想要找到夠大的場地也許不容易。

女：你說得沒錯。我們跟幾家外燴公司聯絡一下。我們可能必須在會議中心辦晚宴了。

59 正解 D

What are the speakers mainly discussing?
(A) Places to take visitors to their city
(B) Ways to get from the airport to the hotel
(C) Possible locations for a welcome luncheon
(D) Plans for an upcoming sales conference

說話者主要是在討論什麼？
(A) 可以帶造訪他們城市之遊客去的地方
(B) 從機場到飯店的方式
(C) 歡迎午餐會的可能地點
(D) 即將舉行之業務大會的規畫

解析 第一名男子一開始就提到由於有許多人會搭飛機前來參加業務大會，因此他必須安排機場交通。接著女子提到會有很多會議和社交活動，並詢問 "Are we ready?"。第二名男子則回應說 "I think so."，並表示他已確認了每個人的飯店訂房，也已安排好歡迎午餐會。而在對話的後半段三人則是在討論惜別晚宴的相關事宜。綜合以上各點可推定本題正解為 (D)。

60 正解 B

What problem do the speakers have?
(A) They are unable to confirm some hotel reservations.
(B) They haven't found a location for an important event.
(C) They can't find a large enough space for a conference.
(D) They don't have time to arrange airport transportation.

說話者遇到了什麼問題？
(A) 他們無法確認某些飯店的訂房。
(B) 他們尚未為一項重要的活動找到地點。
(C) 他們無法為會議找到一個夠大的地方。
(D) 他們沒有時間安排機場交通。

解析 第一名男子 (Frank) 在第二次發言時提到，自己因為忙著處理機場交通的問題所以忘了找晚宴的地點。第二名男子則回應說 "That could be a problem. I think we may have trouble finding a large enough space on such short notice." 「這可能會是個問題。這麼臨時通知，我想要找到夠大的場地也許不容易。」而女子也同意這個說法。因此可確定，三人遇到的問題應該是選項 (B) 所述。

61 正解 C

What does the woman suggest they do?
(A) Book a restaurant for a farewell dinner
(B) Get in touch with a hotel
(C) Use a catering company
(D) Reschedule a social event

女子建議該怎麼做？
(A) 為惜別晚宴預訂餐廳
(B) 聯絡飯店
(C) 雇用外燴公司
(D) 重新安排社交活動的時間

解析 本題考細節，問女子的建議為何。由女子所說的 "Let's get in touch with some catering companies. We may have to have the dinner served at the conference center." 「我們跟幾家外燴公司聯絡一下。我們可能必須在會議中心辦晚宴了。」即可知，正確答案是 (C) Use a catering company。

Vocabulary

☐ **luncheon** 午餐 ☐ **upcoming** 即將來臨的 ☐ **get in touch with** 與～聯絡 ☐ **catering** 承辦酒席

Questions 62-64 refer to the following conversation and office plan. 第 62 到 64 題請參照下列對話和辦公室位置圖。

W: How's it going, Glen? Have you moved everything into the sales office yet?

M: No, I'm still dealing with the IT area. I don't know how they're going to install all that equipment in that tiny space. And that stuff is heavy, too.

W: Yeah, it was a lot of work to load it all into the truck. Anyway, when you're done with IT, can you come down and give me a hand in the kitchen? I could use a hand moving the refrigerator.

M: Okay, I'll be down in just a minute.

女：情況怎樣，葛藍？你把所有東西都搬到業務辦公室了嗎？

男：還沒，我還在打理資訊科技區。我不曉得他們要怎麼把那些設備全部安裝在那麼狹小的空間裡，而且那些東西還很重。

女：是啊，要把它們全部裝進卡車裡可是件大工程。不管怎樣，你資訊科技部分搞定之後，能不能下來到廚房幫我個忙？我需要人手幫忙搬冰箱。

男：好，我等會兒就下去。

West Wing		East Wing
Conference Room	4th FL.	Management Offices
Accounting	3rd FL.	Sales / Marketing / IT
Cafeteria / Break Room	2nd FL.	Kitchen
Reception	1st FL.	Meeting Rooms

西翼		東翼
大會議室	四樓	管理階層辦公室
會計	三樓	業務 / 行銷 / 資訊科技
自助餐廳 / 休息室	二樓	廚房
接待處	一樓	小會議室

62 正解 A

Who most likely are the speakers?
(A) Office movers
(B) Truck drivers
(C) Computer installers
(D) Cafeteria workers

說話者最有可能是什麼人？
(A) 幫辦公室搬家的工人
(B) 卡車司機
(C) 電腦安裝人員
(D) 自助餐廳工作人員

解析 由兩人在對話中提到的搬動某家企業不同部門的物品，以及女子第二次發言時所說的 "... it was a lot of work to load it all into the truck"「……要把它們全部裝進卡車裡可是件大工程。」即可合理推斷，他們是「搬家工人」，故本題選 (A)。

63 正解 C

Look at the graphic. Where is the man currently working?
(A) On the first floor
(B) On the second floor
(C) On the third floor
(D) On the fourth floor

請看圖表。男子目前在哪裡作業？
(A) 一樓
(B) 二樓
(C) 三樓
(D) 四樓

解析 本題屬「細節」題，問男子目前人在何處。男子在第一次發言時明確表示 "... I'm still dealing with the IT area."「……我還在打理資訊科技區。」而依辦公室位置圖所示，資訊科技部位於該公司的「三樓」，因此答案就是 (C)。

64 正解 D

What are the speakers probably going to do next?
(A) Load up a truck
(B) Meet in the sales office
(C) Install some equipment
(D) Move a refrigerator

說話者接下來大概會做什麼？
(A) 把東西搬上卡車
(B) 在業務辦公室碰面
(C) 安裝一些設備
(D) 搬冰箱

解析 本題屬「推論」題，問說話者接下來的行動。女子在第二次發言時要求男子到廚房幫忙她搬冰箱，而由男子的回應 "Okay, I'll be down in just a minute."「好，我等會兒就下去。」即可推斷，兩人接下來應該是會 (D) Move a refrigerator。

Questions 65-67 refer to the following conversation and receipt.　　第 65 到 67 題請參照下列對話和收據。

W: Hi, excuse me, I bought this backpack last year and I'd like to return it and get a refund. I haven't used it.

M: Is there something wrong with it? If a product isn't defective, we don't offer refunds after fourteen days—only exchanges.

W: Oh, I'm sure there's nothing wrong with it. It's just a really dark color, and I realized that I needed something brighter. I just started bicycling to work, and I want to be a little more visible.

M: Well, we do have that design in orange. I could simply exchange it for you, but there would be a small restocking fee.

W: Okay. Let's do that.

女：嗨，請問一下，我去年買了這個背包，我想把它退掉，拿回退款。我還沒用過。

男：背包是有什麼問題嗎？假如產品沒有瑕疵，我們在十四天後就不提供退款——只能換貨。

女：噢，我確信它完全沒問題。只是它的顏色真的很暗，而我意識到我需要的是比較亮的顏色。我剛開始騎腳踏車上班，想要稍微顯眼一點。

男：嗯，我們那款設計倒是有橘色的。我可以直接幫您更換，但要酌收些許手續費。

女：好，就這樣辦。

```
         ||||| |||| |||||
         0 123456 789012

        Jeb's Sporting Goods
        1121 Kingstone Pl., Newcastle

           Exchange Receipt
          February 12 16:28 pm

RETURNED
25L Highlander Backpack, Purple      $20.00
Tax                                  $ 2.00
 . . . . .
Total                                $22.00
 . . . . .

EXCHANGED
25L Highlander Backpack, Orange      $20.00
Tax                                  $ 2.00
 . . . . .
Total                                $22.00
 . . . . .

Restocking Fee                       $ 5.00
 . . . . .
Total                                $ 5.00
 . . . . .

      Thank you for shopping with us.
No refunds or exchanges without a receipt.
```

```
              傑布氏運動用品
        1121 Kingstone Pl., Newcastle

              換貨收據
           2 月 12 日 16:28 pm

退貨
25 公升高地人背包，紫色               $20.00
稅金                                 $ 2.00

總額                                 $22.00

換貨
25 公升高地人背包，橘色               $20.00
稅金                                 $ 2.00

總額                                 $22.00

手續費                               $ 5.00

總額                                 $ 5.00
              銘謝惠顧
         無收據不得退款或換貨
```

65 　正解 A

What problem does the woman mention?
(A) She purchased the wrong color item.
(B) The product is defective.
(C) She already used the product.
(D) The store doesn't offer exchanges.

女子提到了什麼問題？
(A) 她買到顏色錯誤的品項。
(B) 產品有瑕疵。
(C) 她已經使用了該產品。
(D) 該店不提供換貨。

解析　女子在第二次發言時跟男子說明了她之所以要退貨的原因："It's ... a really dark color, and I realized that I needed something brighter."「……它的顏色真的很暗，而我意識到我需要的是比較亮的顏色。」換句話說，她買了一個顏色不對的背包，因此本題選 (A)。

66 　正解 D

What does the woman say recently happened?
(A) She started a new job.
(B) She exchanged some currency.
(C) She purchased a bicycle.
(D) She changed her method of commuting.

女子說最近發生了什麼事？
(A) 她開始了新工作。
(B) 她兌換了一些貨幣。
(C) 她買了一輛腳踏車。
(D) 她改變了通勤方式。

解析　本題須從細節理解來作答。女子在第二次發言時也解釋了為什麼她需要顏色較亮的背包："I just started bicycling to work, and I want to be a little more visible."「我剛開始騎腳踏車上班，想要稍微顯眼一點。」言下之意就是她先前用別的方式通勤，故正解為 (D)。

67 　正解 B

Look at the graphic. How much additional money will the woman be asked to pay?
(A) $2
(B) $5
(C) $20
(D) $22

請看圖表。女子會被要求支付多少額外金額？
(A) $2
(B) $5
(C) $20
(D) $22

解析　男子在第二次發言時表示 "I could simply exchange it for you, but there would be a small restocking fee."「我可以直接幫您更換，但要酌收些許手續費。」而該商店的換貨收據上明確顯示手續費的金額為 $5，所以答案是 (B)。

Vocabulary

☐ **defective** 有缺陷的　☐ **restocking fee** 退貨手續費（重新包裝入庫等費用）

Questions 68-70 refer to the following conversation and report.

W: I just got an email from a rather unhappy customer.

M: Was it a complaint about one of our products, or was it the website again?

W: The website. She wanted to purchase a jacket, but her credit card information disappeared when she clicked on the confirmation button.

M: That's a software problem, but it sounds like we should simplify the entire check-out process.

W: Actually, check-out issues are not even the most common type of problem. I've made a report categorizing all the complaints we've received about our website this year. To be honest, we may have to consider rebuilding the entire site.

M: You may be right. Let's go over the data you've collected and develop a proposal for management that addresses the issues.

Category	Issue	Number of Complaints
1	Registration	66
2	Passwords	132
3	Navigation	23
4	Purchasing	71

第 68 到 70 題請參照下列對話和報告。

女：我剛收到了一位相當不滿的顧客寄來的 email。

男：是在投訴我們的某一樣產品，或者又是網站？

女：是網站。她想購買一件外套，可是一點選確認鍵，她的信用卡資訊就消失了。

男：那是軟體的問題，可是聽起來好像我們應該把整個結帳流程簡化。

女：事實上結帳的問題甚至不算是最常見的問題類型。我已經寫了一個報告把我們今年所收到的所有關於網站的投訴全部歸類。老實說，我們也許必須考慮重建整個網站。

男：妳或許說對了。我們來檢視一下妳所蒐集到的資料，並幫管理層擬出一個處裡這些問題的提案。

類別	問題	投訴次數
1	登錄	66
2	密碼	132
3	導覽	23
4	購買	71

68 正解 C

Where do the speakers most likely work?
(A) At a credit card company
(B) At an architecture firm
(C) At an online store
(D) At a data management company

說話者最有可能是在哪裡工作？
(A) 信用卡公司
(B) 建築事務所
(C) 網路商城
(D) 資料管理公司

解析 本題屬「推論」題，問說話者最有可能是在哪裡工作。由兩人在對話中不斷提到的「網站」(website) 以及「購買」(purchase)、「點選」(click)、「結帳流程」等即可推斷，他們應該是在一家「網路商城」工作。

69 正解 D

Look at the graphic. What category of complaint are the speakers discussing?
(A) Category 1   (C) Category 3
(B) Category 2   (D) Category 4

請看圖表。說話者在討論的是第幾類投訴？
(A) 第 1 類   (C) 第 3 類
(B) 第 2 類   (D) 第 4 類

解析 女子第一次發言時說她收到一封客訴 email，而在第二次發言時則說明了該顧客所遭遇到的狀況："She wanted to purchase a jacket, but her credit card information disappeared when she clicked on the confirmation button."「她想購買一件外套，可是一點選確認鍵，她的信用卡資訊就消失了。」換言之，該顧客之所以會投訴是因為她在網上購物時碰到了問題。依該公司的客訴分類這明顯屬「第 4 類」，故本題選 (D)。

70 正解 D

What will the speakers do next?
(A) Contact affected users
(B) Start collecting data
(C) Simplify the registration process
(D) Review customer complaints

說話者接下來會做什麼？
(A) 聯繫受影響的用戶
(B) 開始蒐集資料
(C) 簡化登錄流程
(D) 審視顧客的投訴

解析 女子在第三次發言時提到 "I've made a report categorizing all the complaints we've received ...."「我已經寫了一個報告把我們……收到的所有……投訴全部加以歸類。」而由男子的最後一句話 "Let's go over the data you've collected ...."「我們來檢視一下妳所蒐集到的資料……。」即可知，兩人接下來應該會做的事為 (D)。注意，原文中的 "go over" 與選項 (D) 的 "review" 為同義字詞。

Vocabulary
☐ **rather** 相當；有點　☐ **categorize** 將……加以分類　☐ **affect** 影響

## PART 4

01-48 | 01-49

Questions 71-73 refer to the following telephone message.

Hello, Mr. Klein, this is Jill Ashby calling from Three Gals' Garage. We changed the oil and did a full inspection. Everything is in good working order. While working on the car, I did notice that the two front tires are ready to be replaced. We have those at sixty-five dollars each, I thought you'd like to know that there's a special sale this week—four tires for two hundred dollars, including labor. You won't find them for less than that. We're expecting you to pick up the car when we close at six tonight, but if you'd like me to go ahead and change some or all of the tires, just give me a call any time before five. It takes about an hour.

第 71 到 73 題請參照下面這段電話留言。

您好,克萊恩先生,我是吉兒·艾許比,我從三妞車庫打來。我們換了油,也做了完整的檢測。一切情況都很好。在打理車子時,我留意到兩個前輪差不多該換了。我們的輪胎每個賣 65 美元,我想您會想知道,本週有特惠,四個輪胎加人工只收 200 美元。您不會找到比這要低的價錢了。我們今晚六點打烊時會恭候您來取車,但如果您想要我把一些或全部的輪胎換掉的話,五點前隨時打電話給我。換輪胎差不多要一個小時。

71 正解 D

What type of service does the speaker provide?
(A) Vehicle storage
(B) Car rental
(C) Order processing
(D) Automobile repair

說話者提供的是什麼類型的服務?
(A) 車輛存放
(B) 汽車租賃
(C) 訂單處理
(D) 汽車修理

解析 本題屬「推論」題。說話者一開始就說她是從「三妞車庫」(Three Gals' Garage) 打電話過來的,接著又提到「換油」(changed the oil)、「換……輪胎」(change ... the tires) 等。合理的推斷是,她的工作應該與汽車維修相關,故正解為 (D)。

72 正解 A

What does the woman mean when she says, "You won't find them for less than that"?
(A) She is offering the lowest price.
(B) She is trying to find a smaller size.
(C) She is willing to help him look.
(D) She is expecting the man to call.

女子所說的 "You won't find them for less than that." 是什麼意思?
(A) 她提供最低價格。
(B) 她在想辦法找較小的尺寸。
(C) 她願意幫他找。
(D) 她期待男子來電。

解析 女子在說題目這句話之前提及 "... there's a special sale this week—four tires for two hundred dollars, including labor." 「……本週有特惠,四個輪胎加人工只收 200 美元。」因此,當她接著說 "You won't find them for less than that" 時意思應該就是,沒有比這優惠更低的價格了。正確答案是 (A)。

73 正解 B

If the listener wants the service, when should he return the call?
(A) Within the hour
(B) By five o'clock
(C) Before closing time
(D) Any time this week

如果聽者想要該項服務,他應該要在什麼時候回電?
(A) 在該個鐘頭內
(B) 五點前
(C) 打烊時間前
(D) 本週任何時候

解析 本題考細節,問如果聽者想要該項服務,他應該在何時回電。女子在留言末尾明白表示 "... if you'd like me to ... change ... the tires, just give me a call any time before five." 「……如果您想要我把……輪胎換掉的話,五點前隨時打電話給我。」因此本題選 (B)。

Vocabulary

☐ **inspection** 檢查;視察 ☐ **in good working order** 運作狀態良好 ☐ **replace** 取代;更換

Hi, this is Darrel Dixon from the planning department. I've been informed that you'll be representing the company at a trade show next month in São Paulo. I'm calling because I've been asked to assist you with all of the travel arrangements. The first thing I'll do is apply for your visa, so I'll need a copy of your passport and a recent passport-size photo. I'll also be making your flight and hotel reservations, so if you plan to extend your visit in order to meet with clients or sightsee in the area, I'll need to confirm that as soon as possible. We have enough time, but it's always best to get these details taken care of quickly.

嗨，我是企畫部的達爾瑞・狄克森。我接到通知說，你將代表公司到聖保羅參加一個在下個月舉辦的貿易展。我打來是因為上面要我協助你處理所有的差旅安排。我第一件要做的事就是幫你辦簽證，所以我需要你的護照副本和近期的護照格式大頭照。我還會幫你預約班機和飯店，所以如果你打算將參訪延長以便拜會客戶或者在當地觀光的話，我就必須盡快做確認。我們有足夠的時間，但趕緊把這些細節都處理好總是不會錯。

74　正解 C

Why is the listener going to travel?
(A) To meet some clients
(B) To go sightseeing
(C) To attend a trade show
(D) To visit a branch office

聽者為什麼會要去旅行？
(A) 為了會見客戶
(B) 為了去觀光
(C) 為了參加貿易展
(D) 為了參訪分公司

解析　本題考細節，問聽者為何要去旅行。由留言的第二句話 "I've been informed that you'll be representing the company at a trade show next month in São Paulo."「我接到通知說，你將代表公司到聖保羅參加一個在下個月舉辦的貿易展。」即可知，正確答案是 (C)。

75　正解 A

What does the speaker plan to do first?
(A) Apply for a visa
(B) Book airline tickets
(C) Reserve a hotel room
(D) Arrange a tour

說話者打算首先要做什麼？
(A) 辦簽證
(B) 訂機票
(C) 訂飯店房間
(D) 安排參訪

解析　本題亦考細節，問說話者打算首先做何事。由留言第四句話中提到的 "The first thing I'll do is apply for your visa ...."「我第一件要做的事就是幫你辦簽證……。」即可知，答案就是 (A) Apply for a visa。

76　正解 A

What does the speaker have to confirm?
(A) Travel dates
(B) Hotel requirements
(C) A passport number
(D) Frequent flyer miles

說話者必須確認什麼？
(A) 旅程日期
(B) 飯店規定
(C) 護照號碼
(D) 常客里程數

解析　由留言的倒數第二句話中提到的 "I'll ... be making your flight and hotel reservations, so if you plan to extend your visit ... I'll need to confirm that ...."「我……會幫你預約班機和飯店，所以如果你打算將參訪延長……我就必須……做確認。」可知，說話者必須確認的是聽者的「旅程日期」。選項 (A) 為正解。

Vocabulary
□ **apply for** 申請　　□ **extend** 延長；延伸　　□ **branch office** 分支機構；分公司

第 1 回完全解析

PART 4

Questions 77-79 refer to the following announcement.　第 77 到 79 題請參照下面這段宣告。

Good evening everyone, and welcome to tonight's gala dinner. Every year, the Edgewood Culinary Institute holds this event to feature the fabulous foods created by our graduating students. Our instructors train aspiring chefs in the basics, but also encourage them to bring their creativity to the table. The dishes you will taste tonight are accented with flavors from around the world, but all were created with fresh, local produce. In the program, you can read about those ingredients and the cooperation we've developed over the years with farmers in the area, a few of whom are here tonight. During the meal, there will be several cooking demonstrations on the stage. After the dessert course, the students will come out of the kitchen and you're invited to stay and ask them any questions you may have. But for now, bon appétit.

大家晚安，歡迎蒞臨今晚的慶祝晚宴。每年埃奇伍德烹飪學院都會舉辦這項活動以展示由我們應屆畢業生所創作出的絕妙美食。我們的講師在基本功上訓練有志於此的主廚，同時也鼓勵他們把創意端上桌。各位今晚將品嚐的菜餚突顯的是來自世界各地的特色風味，但全都是以新鮮、在地的農產品來料理。在節目單裡，各位可以看到那些食材的相關資料，以及多年來我們如何與本地農民培養出合作關係，而今晚就有幾位農民來到了現場。在用餐期間，台上會有多場烹調示範。在用過甜點之後，學生們會走出廚房，請各位留步，看看您有什麼問題都可以問他們。但現在先請飽餐一頓。

77　正解 B

What is the purpose of this event?
(A) To promote a new restaurant
(B) To showcase student achievements
(C) To celebrate a talented chef
(D) To thank local food producers

這場活動的目的是什麼？
(A) 宣傳新餐廳
(B) 展現學生的成就
(C) 表揚有才華的主廚
(D) 感謝在地的食物生產者

解析　本題屬「細節」題，問活動的目的為何。說話者的第二句話 "Every year, the Edgewood Culinary Institute holds this event to feature the fabulous foods created by our graduating students."「每年埃奇伍德烹飪學院都會舉辦這項活動以展示由我們應屆畢業生所創作出的絕妙美食。」直接表明舉辦本活動的目的就是要展現該校學生的成果，故本題選 (B)。

78　正解 D

According to the speaker, what can be found in the program?
(A) Names of the instructors
(B) A description of the institute
(C) Profiles of the chefs
(D) Information about the ingredients

根據說話者所言，在節目單裡可以看到什麼？
(A) 講師的名字
(B) 對學院的描述
(C) 主廚的簡介
(D) 食材的相關資訊

解析　說話者在第四句中提到 "The dishes you will taste tonight are accented with flavors ...."「各位今晚將品嚐的菜餚突顯的是……的風味……。」接著就提到 "In the program, you can read about those ingredients ...."「在節目單裡，各位可以看到那些食材的相關資料……。」由此可斷定，本題正解為 (D)。

79　正解 D

What will happen at the end of the event?
(A) Instructors will hold a cooking demonstration.
(B) Farmers will talk about locally grown food.
(C) Guests will attend a dessert reception in the kitchen.
(D) Students will answer guests' questions.

在活動的尾聲會發生什麼事？
(A) 講師會進行烹調示範。
(B) 農民會談論在地出產的食物。
(C) 賓客會出席廚房的甜點招待會。
(D) 學生會回答賓客的問題。

解析　本題亦為「細節」題。由宣告的倒數第二句 "After the dessert course, the students will come out of the kitchen and you're invited to stay and ask them any questions you may have."「在用過甜點之後，學生們會走出廚房，請各位留步，看看您有什麼問題都可以問他們。」即可知，正確答案是 (D) Students will answer guests' questions.。

Vocabulary

- **gala dinner**（著盛裝出席的）慶祝晚宴　 **culinary** 烹飪的　 **institute**（專科性的）學校　 **feature** 以……為特色
- **fabulous** 極好的；絕妙的　 **aspiring** 有抱負的　 **chef** 主廚　 **accent** 強調　 **produce** 農產品　 **program** 節目（單）
- **ingredient**（烹調的）原料；材料　 **demonstration** 示範　 **promote** 宣傳；推銷　 **showcase** 展示　 **profile** 人物簡介

Questions 80-82 refer to the following announcement.

第 80 到 82 題請參照下面這段宣告。

Welcome to this special all-hands meeting. As some of you know, we've been in talks to acquire the California-based marketing firm Mighty Mite. I'm pleased to announce those discussions were successful and Mighty Mite is now a valued member of Sufficient Inc. This is both our first large-scale acquisition and our first international subsidiary. Don't say we're not ambitious. Mighty Mite is a leader in mobile marketing, and we believe their location-based ad serving platform is where the market is heading. Victor Chang, a senior manager at Mighty Mite, will post a report today on our internal website explaining how their system works. I would like everyone at Sufficient to read it. Our company has just gained a lot of mobile marketing expertise, and all of us should take advantage of it.

歡迎參加這場特別的全體會議。誠如在座某些人所知，我們一直在洽談收購位於加州的行銷公司「大不點」。我很高興地宣布這些討論很成功，大不點現在已是豐實公司的一個寶貴成員。這既是我們首次的大規模收購，也是我們第一家國際子公司。不要說我們沒有企圖心。大不點是行動行銷的領導者，我們相信他們的定位式廣告服務平台就是市場的走向。張維多，一位大不點的資深經理，今天會把一份解釋他們的系統是如何運作的報告貼在我們內部的網站上，我希望豐實的每個人都去看看。我們公司剛獲得大量行動行銷的專業知識，大家都應該善加利用。

80 正解 C

What is the purpose of the announcement?
(A) To explain an upcoming merger
(B) To introduce a new manager
(C) To discuss a recent acquisition
(D) To report on a business competitor

這段宣告的目的是什麼？
(A) 解釋即將到來的一件合併案
(B) 介紹一位新任經理
(C) 討論最近的一件收購案
(D) 針對一個商業競爭對手做報告

解析 本題屬「推論」題，問本宣告的目的為何。由宣告第三、四句中所提到的 "I'm pleased to announce ... Mighty Mite is now a valued member of Sufficient Inc. This is ... our first large-scale acquisition ...."「我很高興地宣布……大不點現在已是豐實公司的一個寶貴成員。這……是我們首次的大規模收購……。」以及之後針對大不點這家公司所做的相關敘述可推斷，正解為 (C)「討論最近的一件收購案」。

81 正解 B

What does the man mean when he says, "Don't say we're not ambitious"?
(A) He wants listeners to wait until he has finished.
(B) He feels his company has an aggressive strategy.
(C) He takes a conservative approach to business.
(D) He hopes employees will support the decision.

男子所說的 "Don't say we're not ambitious." 是什麼意思？
(A) 他要聽者等他把話說完。
(B) 他覺得他的公司有積極的策略。
(C) 他在商業上採取保守的態度。
(D) 他希望員工支持該決定。

解析 本題考詞句解釋。男子說 "Don't say we're not ambitious." 言下之意當然就是指 "We are ambitious."。而說自己公司有企圖心當然就表示他認為他的公司是有積極策略的。正確答案是 (B)。

82 正解 C

What does the man ask listeners to do?
(A) Print out a marketing report
(B) Attend a training session
(C) Review an online document
(D) Take advantage of Mr. Chang's visit

男子要求聽者做什麼？
(A) 把一份行銷報告列印出來
(B) 參加一個訓練課程
(C) 檢視一份線上文件
(D) 善加利用張先生的到訪

解析 本題考的是細節。由男子在宣告第七、八句中提到的 "Victor Chang ... will post a report today on our internal website .... I would like everyone ... to read it."「張維多……今天會把一份……報告貼在我們內部的網站上，我希望……每個人都去看看。」即可知，本題應選 (C) Review an online document「檢視一份線上文件」。

Vocabulary

- **all-hands meeting** 全員出席的會議　□ **acquire** 獲得；取得　□ **mighty mite** 形體微小但力量巨大的事物　□ **large-scale** 大規模的
- **acquisition** 獲得；收購　□ **subsidiary** 子公司　□ **mobile marketing** 行動行銷　□ **location-based** 定位式的　□ **head** 朝特定方向前進
- **expertise** 專門技術；專業知識　□ **take advantage of** 利用　□ **merger** 合併　□ **aggressive** 侵略的；積極進取的　□ **strategy** 策略
- **conservative** 保守的　□ **training session** 訓練課程

Questions 83-85 refer to the following advertisement.　　第 83 到 85 題請參照下面這則廣告。

If you've been thinking about learning a musical instrument, the Sebastiani School may be just what you've been looking for. No matter your current skill level—from absolute beginner to professional musician—we have courses that are just right for you. Local students can study at any of our three Melbourne-area campuses, and all students can take advantage of our private online classes. Our always available reference library of nearly one thousand master class videos is ranked by students as their favorite part of the Sebastiani experience. Come to the annual Sebastiani Street Fair on July 1 to learn more. Current instructors and students will be performing and they will be happy to answer all your questions. And if you can't make it, visit us at sebastianischool. edu, where the entire event will be streamed live.

如果您一直在考慮學樂器，謝巴斯提亞尼學校可能就是您要找尋的目標。不論您目前的技巧程度為何——從完完全全的初學者到職業樂手——我們都有恰恰適合您的課程。本地學生可以在我們設於墨爾本地區的三個校區中的任何一處上課，而且所有的學生都可以利用我們的私人線上課程。我們隨時可供使用、含近千部大師授課影片的參考資料庫被學生們列為謝巴斯提亞尼體驗中他們最喜愛的部分。欲知詳情，請於七月一日蒞臨一年一度的謝巴斯提亞尼街展覽會。我們現有的講師和學生會在現場表演，他們也會非常樂意回答您所有的問題。假如您無法到場，請上我們的網站：sebastianischool. edu，整場活動會用網路直播。

83　正解 A

What does the Sebastiani School specialize in?
(A) Music education
(B) Online marketing
(C) Computer programming
(D) Library science

謝巴斯提亞尼學校專門從事什麼？
(A) 音樂教育
(B) 線上行銷
(C) 電腦編程
(D) 圖書館學

> **解析** 本題屬「推論」題。由廣告的第一句 "If you've been thinking about learning a musical instrument, the Sebastiani School may be just what you've been looking for."「如果您一直在考慮學樂器，謝巴斯提亞尼學校可能就是您要找尋的目標。」以及之後提到的各種學習課程與教學影片等來推斷，該校專門從事的應該是 (A)「音樂教育」。

84　正解 D

According to the advertisement, what do students like most about the Sebastiani School?
(A) Flexible schedules
(B) Low prices
(C) Excellent instruction
(D) Online resources

根據廣告，學生最喜歡謝巴斯提亞尼學校的什麼東西？
(A) 有彈性的課程
(B) 低廉的價格
(C) 一流的教學
(D) 線上資源

> **解析** 本題屬「細節」題。由廣告的第四句 "Our always available reference library of nearly one thousand master class videos is ranked by students as their favorite part of the Sebastiani experience."「我們隨時可供使用、含近千部大師授課影片的參考資料庫被學生們列為謝巴斯提亞尼體驗中他們最喜愛的部分。」即可知，學生們最喜歡的是該校「隨時可取得」的 (D)「線上資源」。

85　正解 C

What is scheduled to happen on July 1?
(A) Alumni will perform for the students.
(B) A graduation ceremony will be held.
(C) Faculty and students will be available to talk.
(D) Registration for the next term will begin.

七月一日預定會發生什麼事？
(A) 校友會為學生表演。
(B) 會舉行畢業典禮。
(C) 教師和學生會現身談話。
(D) 下學期的註冊會開始。

> **解析** 由廣告第五、六句中提到的 "Come to the annual Sebastiani Street Fair on July 1 .... Current instructors and students ... will be happy to answer all your questions."「……請於七月一日蒞臨一年一度的謝巴斯提亞尼街展覽會。我們現有的講師和學生……會非常樂意回答您所有的問題。」即可知，正解為 (C)「教師和學生會現身談話。」

Vocabulary

☐ **absolute** 絕對的；完全的　☐ **reference** 參考　☐ **annual** 一年一次的　☐ **stream live** 用網路直播　☐ **specialize in** 專門從事；專攻
☐ **flexible** 有彈性的　☐ **resource** 資源　☐ **alumni** 校友（為 "alumnus" 之複數形）　☐ **graduation ceremony** 畢業典禮　☐ **faculty** 全體教師

01-54

第 86 到 88 題請參照下面這段電話留言。

Hi, Beth! I really need your help with something. I was supposed to get everything set up for the party after the softball game on Friday, but I'm afraid I won't be able to make it. Remember how I twisted my ankle rounding third yesterday? Well, my doctor's appointment is Friday. Perfect timing, I know. I realize that you've handled the last two parties, but if you could cover for me Friday, I'd definitely make it up to you next season. And if you can't, don't worry. I'll work something out. Anyway, I'm looking forward to seeing everyone play in the season finale next week! It's a big game! Too bad I'll have to watch it from the bleachers.

嗨，貝絲！有件事我非常需要妳幫忙。星期五壘球賽後的派對本來一切都該由我來安排，但我恐怕是無能為力了。還記得我昨天在繞過三壘時，是怎麼把腳踝給扭到了嗎？嗯，我跟醫生約了星期五。我知道，時間就是這麼湊巧。我明白前兩場派對都是由妳主辦，但假如妳星期五能幫我頂一下，我下一季一定會補償妳。如果妳不行的話，也不用擔心。我會想辦法把事情搞定。不管怎樣，我很期待在下週的季決賽時看到每個人都上場！這可是場大賽！而我卻必須在看台上觀賽，太慘了。

86 正解 A

Why is the woman calling?
(A) To ask for a favor
(B) To announce some good news
(C) To express her gratitude
(D) To change her appointment

女子為什麼打電話？
(A) 為了請求幫忙
(B) 為了宣布好消息
(C) 為了表示感謝
(D) 為了更改約診時間

解析 本題考細節。女子在打完招呼之後就開門見山跟對方說：“I really need your help with something.”「有件事我非常需要妳幫忙。」接著便說明她為何需要幫忙。由此可確定，她來電的目的是 (A) To ask for a favor「為了請求幫忙」。

87 正解 C

What does the woman imply when she says, "Perfect timing, I know"?
(A) She thinks the party was scheduled at the right time.
(B) She believes all the guests will arrive on time.
(C) She feels the appointment is inconveniently scheduled.
(D) She doesn't want to change the time of the game.

當女子說 "Perfect timing, I know." 時是在暗示什麼？
(A) 她認為聚會排對了時間。
(B) 她相信所有的客人都會準時到達。
(C) 她覺得約診時間排得不是時候。
(D) 她不想更換比賽的時間。

解析 "Perfect timing" 的原意是「時間恰恰好」，而由於「好巧不巧」原本應由她主辦的派對與她的就醫門診時間剛好都是禮拜五，所以當她說 "Perfect timing, I know." 時應該是在告訴對方她也知道約診時間安排得並不是時候，因此本題選 (C)。

88 正解 B

Why is the woman looking forward to next week?
(A) Her ankle will be healed by then.
(B) An important game will be played.
(C) It is her turn to organize the party.
(D) She plans to give Beth a gift.

女子為什麼期待下週？
(A) 她的腳踝到時候就會痊癒。
(B) 有一場重要的比賽要開打。
(C) 輪到她主辦聚會。
(D) 她打算送一份禮物給貝絲。

解析 本題屬「細節」題，問女子為何會期待下週。女子在留言的倒數第三句中提及 "... I'm looking forward to seeing everyone play in the season finale next week!"「……我很期待在下週的季決賽時看到每個人都上場！」接著又說 "It's a big game!"「這可是場大賽！」很明顯地，女子之所以會期待下週是因為到時候「有一場重要的比賽要開打。」正確答案是 (B)。

第 1 回完全解析

PART 4

Vocabulary

☐ **be supposed to** 應該～　☐ **set up** 安排；設立　☐ **softball** 壘球　☐ **make it** 完成（某事）　☐ **twist** 扭傷　☐ **round** 繞過
☐ **appointment** 約診　☐ **cover for** 代理；頂替　☐ **definitely** 一定　☐ **make it up to** 補償（某人）　☐ **work out** 解決
☐ **season finale** 季決賽　☐ **bleachers**（運動場的）看台　☐ **gratitude** 感激；謝意　☐ **inconveniently** 不方便地　☐ **heal** 使痊癒

Questions 89-91 refer to the following news report.

第 89 到 91 題請參照下面這則新聞報導。

This is Jenny Thunder from WCOL radio news. I'm standing near the Barton Street Bridge, which has just been closed by authorities. Water levels in the rushing Pieman River below have reached unprecedented heights, and may rise further as the storm continues to hammer the area. Weather forecasters did not expect a storm of this intensity—not only the massive rainfall, but also the violent gusts of wind, some of which have reached one hundred kilometers per hour. It's really something else. All residents are encouraged to stay indoors and avoid unnecessary journeys. There are currently no plans to evacuate people from homes in low-lying areas, but local authorities are closely monitoring the situation and are expected to make an announcement at 9:30 tonight. We'll be covering that live, so please do tune in for that.

我是 WCOL 廣播電台新聞的珍妮‧桑德。我正站在剛被主管機關封閉的巴頓街橋附近。下方水流湍急的派曼河之水位已經來到前所未有的高度，而且隨著暴風雨持續肆虐本區，水位或許還會再上升。氣象預報人員並沒有預料到暴風雨會這麼強，不但雨量龐大，而且風勢猛烈，有些已達每小時一百公里。真的相當驚人。所有的居民被要求待在室內，避免不必要的外出。目前並沒有計畫要低窪地區的民眾從家中撤離，但地方主管機關正密切監控情勢，預計今晚 9:30 會有消息宣布。屆時我們會做現場報導，請務必收聽。

89 正解 C

According to the speaker, what is happening today?
(A) A new bridge is being opened.
(B) A lightning strike is being reported.
(C) A storm is passing through the area.
(D) A river is flooding its banks.

根據說話者所言，今天發生了什麼事？
(A) 有一座新橋開通。
(B) 正有人通報雷擊。
(C) 有場暴風雨正通過當地。
(D) 有一條河溢堤。

解析 本題屬「推論」題。由報導一開始提到的 Barton Street Bridge 之封閉和接著提到的 Pieman River 水位上漲可合理推斷，該區域正受到暴風雨的侵襲。而若加上在第三句話中所提及的 "... as the storm continues to hammer the area."「……隨著暴風雨持續肆虐本區……。」即可確定，本題正解為 (C)「有場暴風雨正通過當地。」

90 正解 A

What does the speaker mean when she says, "It's really something else"?
(A) The storm is quite extraordinary.
(B) The wind is more dangerous than the rain.
(C) The forecast was for sunny skies.
(D) The situation is being closely monitored.

說話者所說的 "It's really something else." 是什麼意思？
(A) 暴風雨相當不尋常。
(B) 風比雨危險。
(C) 天氣預報說會是晴天。
(D) 情勢正受到密切監控。

解析 本題考詞句解釋。"something else" 除了一般用來指「別的東西」之外，還有一個俚語的用法，表示「不尋常的人事物」。而依前後文意來判斷，說話者說 "It's really something else." 時，她想表達的應該是「此次暴風雨的強度驚人，十分不尋常。」因此本題選 (A)。

91 正解 D

What are listeners advised to do at 9:30?
(A) Evacuate their homes
(B) Avoid unnecessary journeys
(C) Contact local authorities
(D) Listen to a broadcast

報導中建議聽眾在 9:30 時做什麼？
(A) 撤離家園
(B) 避免不必要的外出
(C) 與當地的主管機關聯繫
(D) 收聽廣播

解析 本題考的是細節。由報導末尾提到的 "... local authorities ... are expected to make an announcement at 9:30 tonight. We'll be covering that live, so please do tune in for that."「……地方主管機關……預計今晚 9:30 會有消息宣布。屆時我們會做現場報導，請務必收聽。」即可知，正確答案是 (D)「收聽廣播」。

Vocabulary

☐ **authority** 主管機關　☐ **water level** 水位　☐ **rushing** 水流湍急的　☐ **unprecedented** 前所未有的　☐ **hammer** 重擊
☐ **weather forecaster** 氣象預報員　☐ **intensity** 強度　☐ **massive** 巨大的；大量的　☐ **gust**（一陣）強風　☐ **resident** 居民　☐ **evacuate** 撤離
☐ **low-lying** 低窪的　☐ **closely** 嚴密地；仔細地　☐ **monitor** 監測；監控　☐ **cover** 採訪；報導　☐ **lightning strike** 雷擊　☐ **flood** 溢出；氾濫
☐ **bank** 堤；岸　☐ **extraordinary** 異常的；令人驚奇的　☐ **forecast**（天氣）預報；預測　☐ **broadcast** 廣播

Questions 92-94 refer to the following excerpt from a meeting.

As you know, the company will be opening two new offices and making other capital-intensive investments in the coming months. To maintain a positive cash flow, each department is being asked to reduce its annual operating budget by eight percent. This is the main goal I'd like everyone to work toward this year. To help with this, I'm asking all department heads to review their budgets for the previous ten years, identify ways we can cut costs, and report those back to the group. I've already done this for the operations department, and I've written a report detailing which measures were effective and which were not. I'll email that report to everyone here so you can use it as a template. It'll be easier for us to analyze the data if we all use the same format.

第 92 到 94 題請參照下面這段會議摘錄。

誠如各位所知,公司將在未來的幾個月開設兩個新的營業處,並從事其他的資本密集投資。為了維持正現金流,每一個部門都會被要求減少年度營運預算 8%。這是我今年要大家努力的主要目標。為了有助於做到這點,我要求各部門主管檢視之前十年的預算,找出可以削減成本的方式,並把這些事回報給集團。我已經幫營運部做了這件事,並寫了一份報告詳述哪些措施有效、哪些沒效。我會把那份報告用電郵寄給在座的每個人,各位可以用它來作範本。如果我們全都用一樣的格式,分析資料時就會比較容易。

92　正解 A

What does the speaker want to focus on this year?
(A) Lowering operating expenses
(B) Writing accurate reports
(C) Increasing sales revenue
(D) Cutting capital-intensive investments

說話者今年想聚焦於什麼?
(A) 降低營運開銷
(B) 撰寫精確的報告
(C) 增加銷售營收
(D) 削減資本密集投資

解析 由會議節錄第二、三句中所提到的 "... each department is being asked to reduce its annual operating budget .... This is the main goal I'd like everyone to work toward this year." 「……每一個部門都會被要求減少年度營運預算……。這是我今年要大家努力的主要目標。」即可知,本題應選 (A)。注意,原文中的 "budget" 被代換成 "expenses"。

93　正解 B

What does the speaker request help with?
(A) Opening offices
(B) Collecting data
(C) Emailing information
(D) Operating equipment

說話者要求幫忙做什麼?
(A) 開設營業處
(B) 蒐集資料
(C) 用電郵寄資訊
(D) 操作器材

解析 節錄的第四句提到 "To help with this, I'm asking all department heads to review their budgets for the previous ten years ...." 「為了有助於做到這點,我要求各部門主管檢視之前十年的預算……。」而為了檢視前十年的預算,主管們當然必須先蒐集一些相關資料,因此本題選 (B) Collecting data。

94　正解 D

What will the listeners receive by email?
(A) A blank template
(B) A detailed spreadsheet
(C) A formatted budget
(D) A completed report

聽者會經由電郵收到什麼?
(A) 一份空白範本
(B) 一份詳細的試算表
(C) 一份格式化的預算
(D) 一份已完成的報告

解析 與前兩題相同,本題亦為「細節」題。說話者在末尾提及 "... I've written a report .... I'll email that report to everyone ...." 「我已經……寫了一份報告……。我會把那份報告用電郵寄給……每個人……。」由此即可知,正確答案是 (D) A completed report「一份已完成的報告」。

Vocabulary

- **capital-intensive** 資本密集的　□ **investment** 投資　□ **cash flow** 現金流　□ **operating** 營運的;操作的　□ **budget** 預算　□ **previous** 先前的
- □ **detail** 詳細說明　□ **measure** 手段;措施　□ **template**【電腦】範本　□ **analyze** 分析　□ **format** 格式　□ **accurate** 準確的;精確的
- □ **revenue** 收益;(國家的) 歲收　□ **blank** 空白的　□ **detailed** 詳細的　□ **spreadsheet** 試算表　□ **formatted** 格式化了的

Questions 95-97 refer to the following talk and map. 第 95 到 97 題請參照下列談話和地圖。

Everyone! May I please have your attention. I've just been informed that part of Concourse One—the stretch between the Information Desk and Luxury Lane—has been closed temporarily for renovations. That means all passengers—even those like our group who are departing from Terminal One—must make a short detour. After passing through the security checkpoint, walk up Concourse Two. Terminal One is accessible via a shopping area with a lot of small boutiques called the Luxury Lane. Our departure time remains unchanged, so we won't have time for a meal, but I do encourage you to check out the gift shop, which has a great selection of local products and souvenirs. Okay, I'll see you all at Gate one-oh-four in forty-five minutes.

各位請注意。我剛接到通知，第一大廳有部分因整修而暫時封閉，也就是詢問台與奢華道之間的那段。這表示所有的旅客都必須繞一小段路，甚至連要從第一航站出發的人，就像我們這一團，也不例外。通過安檢站後，往第二大廳走。經過有著很多小型精品店、被稱為奢華道的購物區就能到第一航站。我們的出發時間依舊不變，所以我們不會有用餐的時間，但我倒是很鼓勵各位到禮品店瞧瞧，裡面有很不錯的精選在地產品和伴手禮。好了，那我們就 45 分鐘後在 104 號登機門見。

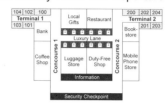

95　正解 A

Who most likely are the listeners?
(A) Tour group members
(B) Construction crew workers
(C) Airport employees
(D) Flight attendants

聽者最有可能是什麼人？
(A) 旅行團團員
(B) 建築工班工人
(C) 機場員工
(D) 空服員

解析 首先，由談話中提到的 "Concourse One"「第一大廳」、"Terminal One"「第一航站」、"Gate one-oh-four"「104 號登機門」等可斷定，說話者與聽者此刻是在飛機場。而由談話第三句中提到的 "That means all passengers ... like our group ...."「這表示所有的旅客……就像我們這一團……。」即可推知，聽者為 (A)「旅行團團員」。

96　正解 B

Look at the graphic. Where will the listeners be unable to go?
(A) Terminal 1
(B) The coffee shop
(C) The bookstore
(D) The duty-free shop

請看圖表。聽者無法走到哪裡？
(A) 第一航站
(B) 咖啡館
(C) 書店
(D) 免稅店

解析 談話的第二句中提到 "... part of Concourse One—the stretch between the Information Desk and Luxury Lane—has been closed ...."「……第一大廳有部分……暫時封閉，也就是詢問台與奢華道之間的那段。」而依圖示，「咖啡館」即位於第一大廳被封閉之處，因此本題選 (B)。

97　正解 D

What does the woman advise the listeners to do?
(A) Walk up Terminal 2
(B) Go immediately to the gate
(C) Relax at the restaurant
(D) Browse the gift store

女子建議聽者做什麼？
(A) 往第二航站走
(B) 立刻到登機門
(C) 到餐廳放鬆一下
(D) 逛逛禮品店

解析 女子在談話的倒數第二句中明確表示 "... I do encourage you to check out the gift shop ...."「……我……很鼓勵各位到禮品店瞧瞧……。」故正解為 (D)。注意，"check out" 與 "browse" 屬同義字詞。

Vocabulary

- **concourse**（機場或火車站內的）大廳　□ **stretch**（土地的）一段　□ **information desk** 詢問台；服務台　□ **luxury** 奢華　□ **temporarily** 暫時地
- **renovation** 整修　□ **depart** 離開；出發　□ **terminal** 終點站；航站（大廈）　□ **detour** 繞道　□ **checkpoint** 檢查站
- **accessible** 可到達的；易使用的　□ **via** 經由　□ **boutique** 精品店　□ **departure** 離開；出發　□ **check out** 看看　□ **selection** 精選品
- **souvenir** 紀念品　□ **crew** 一組工作人員　□ **flight attendant** 空服員　□ **duty-free** 免稅的　□ **browse** 瀏覽；逛（商店、書店等）

Questions 98-100 refer to the following telephone message and form.

Hi, Kayla—it's Jay. I got the equipment request form you sent, and I think there may be some missing information. There isn't a start day listed for the new designer. I'll have everything ready for her by June 4, but if it's earlier than that please let me know. Also, there seems to be a missing note. I assume that she'll need design software installed, so I'll go ahead and do that. I interviewed Dex Findler, so I know she's planning on using her own laptop and phone for work. I guess that's it. I heard from Tim that you're traveling, so I won't expect a call, but text me if there's anything I've missed. Thanks.

第 98 到 100 題請參照下列電話留言和表單。

嗨，凱拉，我是傑伊。我收到妳寄來的器材申請表了，我想有些資訊或許漏掉了。裡面並沒有列出那位新進設計人員的報到日。我會在六月四日前替她把一切準備好，但如果是早於這一天，請通知我一聲。還有，附註似乎是漏寫了。我假定她會需要安裝設計軟體，所以我就直接這麼做了。黛克斯‧芬德勒是由我面試的，所以我知道她打算用自己的筆電和手機來工作。我想就這樣了。我聽提姆說妳在出差，所以我就不等妳的電話了，但假如我有什麼疏漏的話，就傳個簡訊給我。謝謝。

IT Equipment Request -- New Employee					
Name	Department	Start Day	Desktop	Laptop	Mobile Phone
Jason Yee	Sales	June 4		✓	✓
Dex Findler	IT	June 4			
Ben Kim	Marketing	June 4		✓	✓
Pam Bundy	Design		✓*		✓
* Notes:					
				Authorization: Kayla Sayers	

資訊科技器材申請表 — 新進員工					
姓名	部門	報到日	桌電	筆電	手機
易傑森	業務	6 月 4 日		✓	✓
黛克斯‧芬德勒	資訊科技	6 月 4 日			
金班恩	行銷	6 月 4 日		✓	✓
潘邦迪	設計		✓*		✓
*附註：					
				審核：凱拉‧賽爾斯	

98 正解 D

Look at the graphic. Which employee does the speaker need more information about?
(A) Jason Yee
(B) Dex Findler
(C) Ben Kim
(D) Pam Bundy

請看圖表。說話者需要的是關於哪位員工的更多資訊？
(A) 易傑森
(B) 黛克斯‧芬德勒
(C) 金班恩
(D) 潘邦迪

解析 本題屬「細節」題。留言的第二、三句話中提到 "... I think there may be some missing information. There isn't a start day listed for the new designer."「……我想有些資訊或許漏掉了。裡面並沒有列出那位新進設計人員的報到日。」而依新進員工之器材申請表所示，報到日期未被列出的是設計部門的潘邦迪，故本題選 (D)。

99 正解 B

What does the speaker assume will happen?
(A) The listener will revise the document.
(B) The designer will require special software.
(C) Dex Findler will request a mobile phone.
(D) Kayla Sayers will return his call.

說話者假定會發生什麼事？
(A) 聽者會修訂文件。
(B) 該設計人員會需要特殊軟體。
(C) 黛克斯‧芬德勒會申請手機。
(D) 凱拉‧賽爾斯會回他電話。

解析 雖然器材申請表上顯示潘邦迪需要使用桌電（該欄位打了勾），但同時也顯示須進一步看附註之說明（以星號標示），不過下方附註一欄中卻是空白的。針對這一點說話者表示 "... there seems to be a missing note. I assume that she'll need design software installed ...."「……附註似乎是漏寫了。我假定她會需要安裝設計軟體……。」由此即可知，正確答案是 (B)。注意，原文中的 "design software" 被以 "special software" 取代。

100 正解 D

What is the listener asked to do if there is a problem?
(A) Install some software
(B) Submit a form
(C) Contact a manager
(D) Send a text message

如果有問題的話，聽者被要求做什麼？
(A) 安裝某個軟體
(B) 提交一份表格
(C) 與一位經理聯繫
(D) 發一則簡訊

解析 由說話者在留言末尾所說的 "... text me if there's anything I've missed."「……假如我有什麼疏漏的話，就傳個簡訊給我。」可知，選項 (D) Send a text message 即為正解。

Vocabulary
☐ **equipment** 器材；設備　☐ **request form** 申請表　☐ **missing** 失蹤的；缺漏的　☐ **assume** 假定　☐ **install** 安裝；設置
☐ **interview** 面試；面談　☐ **revise** 修訂　☐ **submit** 提交；呈送

PART 5

101 正解 B

Grassley Audio is excited to ------- the release of the DJ500 line of headphones.

(A) announcing   (B) announce   (C) announced   (D) announces

葛雷斯利音響非常高興宣布推出 DJ500 款的耳機。

> **解析** 本題考正確之動詞型態。由空格前出現的 "to" 可知，空格內應填入「原形動詞」，故 (B) announce 為正確答案。注意，空格前的 "to" 並非「介系詞」的 "to"，而是構成「不定詞」的 "to"。另，若本句中的 "is excited" 之後為介系詞 "about"，則其後應選擇使用「動名詞」作為其「受詞」，也就是，(A) announcing。

102 正解 D

The lecture will be followed ------- a question and answer session.

(A) after   (B) then   (C) as   (D) by

演講之後接著會有問答時段。

> **解析** 本題考正確之介系詞。由空格前出現的句子結構為 "S + be + V-pp" 可知，本句為一「被動句」，因此空格內適合填入的介系詞應為 (D) by。注意，不可因 "follow" 有「跟隨」之意，就誤選 (A) after。另，選項 (C) then 實為「副詞」，但因其義可為「然後」、「接著」，故亦應小心，不可誤選。

103 正解 B

The IT department will require employees to ------- change their password.

(A) formerly   (B) regularly   (C) previously   (D) recently

資訊科技部門會要求員工們定期更換密碼。

> **解析** 本題為「單字」考題，須選出正確之副詞。由句構可知，該副詞必須用來修飾空格後的原形動詞 "change"，而由前後文意推斷，最合理的用字應為 (B) regularly，也就是說，密碼應該要「定期地」更換。選項 (A) formerly 指「從前」、「以前」，選項 (C) previously 指「原先」、「先前」，選項 (D) recently 指「最近」、「近來」，三者明顯皆與句意不符。

104 正解 D

All employees who sign up for the training session will receive an email confirming their ------- for the event.

(A) register   (B) registers   (C) registered   (D) registration

所有報名參加訓練課程的員工都會收到一封確認已登記參加該項活動的電子郵件。

> **解析** 本題考正確之字詞變化。由空格前的代名詞之所有格 "their" 即可知，空格內應填入的是「名詞」，因此本題應選 (D) registration。須注意的是選項 (A) register 有時亦作「名詞」用，但意思是「登記簿」、「註冊表」，與句意並不相符，故不可選。

105 正解 C

Snyder Inc.'s annual 5K Fun Run is this Saturday, and all employees and their families are welcome to -------.

(A) challenge   (B) accompany   (C) participate   (D) adjoin

史奈德公司一年一度的 5 公里樂跑就在本週六舉行，歡迎全體員工與家人一同參加。

> **解析** 本題為「單字」考題，須選出符合前後文意的原形動詞。由句子前半提到的由公司主辦的樂跑活動來推斷，當然是歡迎所有員工與家人都來「參加」，因此本題選 (C) participate。選項 (A) challenge「挑戰」、(B) accompany「伴隨」及 (D) adjoin「鄰接」皆不可選。注意，不可誤選 (A)，因為 "challenge" 本身為「及物動詞」，也就是說，其後須接一名詞作為其「受詞」。

Vocabulary

☐ **line**（產品等的）種類

106 正解 C

To schedule an appointment with Ms. Jackson, either call her assistant ------- fill out the online form on her website.

(A) and   (B) if   (C) or   (D) but

要和傑克森小姐預約，可打電話給她的助理，或是上她的網站填寫線上表格。

> **解析** 本題考正確之連接詞組。由句中的 "either" 即可知，與其搭配的連接詞應為 (C) or。其餘選項雖皆為「連接詞」，但都無法與 "either" 組合。

107 正解 D

Please transfer all calls to Ms. Ginsberg, who can assist Mr. Chen's clients while ------- is unavailable.

(A) his   (B) himself   (C) him   (D) he

陳先生沒空時，請把來電全部轉給金斯柏格小姐，她能夠協助陳先生的客戶。

> **解析** 本題考正確之代名詞。由空格前的從屬連接詞 "while" 可知，其後應為一完整子句，也就是，必須為一具有「主詞＋動詞」之結構，而空格後的 "is" 為「動詞」，因此空格內應填入可作為「主詞」的主格代名詞 (D) he。

108 正解 A

The ------- policy is just one part of the sales agreement.

(A) return   (B) returnable   (C) returned   (D) returning

退貨政策只是銷售協議的一部分。

> **解析** 本題考正確之複合名詞。雖然由空格前的定冠詞 "The" 與空格後的名詞 "policy" 來推斷，空格內應填入一「形容詞」，但形容詞 (B) returnable（指「可退還的」）及可作形容詞用的過去分詞 (C) returned 與現在分詞 (D) returning 皆無法與 "policy" 構成合理的組合，因此本題選可作「名詞」使用的 (A) return，也就是說，由 "return" 加上 "policy" 構成一「複合名詞」："return policy"「退貨政策」。

109 正解 C

Guests of the CEO will be seated ------- the long table near the window.

(A) among   (B) in   (C) at   (D) on

執行長的客人會被安排坐在窗子旁的長桌。

> **解析** 本題考正確之介系詞。由前後文意可推知，空格後的 "the long table" 應該是客人被安排的座位之處，而四選項中最能清楚表達「所在處」的介系詞為 (C) at。

110 正解 B

The restaurant they took us to had some of the most ------- dishes I've ever had.

(A) memorial   (B) memorable   (C) memorizing   (D) memorized

他們帶我們去的餐廳提供了一些我所吃過最難忘的料理。

> **解析** 本題考正確之形容詞。四選項中最適合用來修飾空格後之 "dishes" 的應該是 (B) memorable「難忘的」。選項 (A) memorial 指「紀念的」，用來形容 "dishes" 並不恰當。選項 (C) memorizing 為動詞 "memorize"「熟記」的現在分詞，選項 (D) memorized 則為 "memorize" 的過去分詞，而雖然分詞可作形容詞用，但二者明顯皆不適合用來修飾 "dishes"。

111 正解 A

All musical instruments must be promptly returned to the band manager ------- the scheduled practice has been completed.

(A) once   (B) soon   (C) immediately   (D) often

預定的練習一完成，所有的樂器就必須馬上歸還給樂團經理。

> **解析** 本題考正確之連接詞。由空格前後皆為完整之子句可知，空格內須填入一「連接詞」，而四選項中唯一能作連接詞用的是 (A) once「一……就……」。選項 (B) soon「很快地」、(C) immediately「立即」與 (D) often「時常」三者皆為「副詞」，故不可選。注意，選項 (A) once 亦可作副詞用，意思是「一次」、「曾經」。

112 正解 C

To avoid damaging the equipment, it is important to follow the instructions ------- when cleaning the device.

(A) care   (B) careful   (C) carefully   (D) caring

為了避免損及設備，在清理裝置時，仔細地遵照指令很重要。

> **解析** 本題考正確之字詞變化。由空格前為一完整之子句而空格後為一完整之「省略式」子句可推知，空格內應填入一不致影響原句結構的「副詞」，故本題正解為 (C) carefully。選項 (A) care 可作「名詞」或「動詞」，選項 (B) careful 為「形容詞」，選項 (D) caring 則為現在分詞，三者皆無法被置於空格之中。

113 正解 B

Mr. Burroughs was hired to ------- the writers and artists who design our greeting cards.

(A) explain   (B) supervise   (C) order   (D) create

巴勒斯先生受雇來指導為我們設計賀卡的撰寫人和畫家。

> **解析** 本題為「單字」考題，須選出適合以空格後之 "the writers and artists ..." 作為其受詞之原形動詞。選項 (A) explain「解釋」與選項 (D) create「創造」明顯不應以「人」作為其「受詞」，故不選。選項 (C) order「命令」雖可以「人」作為其「受詞」，但若填入空格內全句形成的意思並不明確。正確答案是 (B) supervise「監督」、「指導」。

114 正解 C

Gooseberry Inc. will open an office in Paris in preparation for an ------- into the European market.

(A) expanding   (B) expanse   (C) expansion   (D) expand

古斯貝瑞公司會在巴黎開設辦事處，以準備擴展進入歐洲市場。

> **解析** 本題考正確之字詞變化。由出現在空格前的不定冠詞 "an" 可知，空格內應填入一「名詞」，因此「動詞」選項 (D) expand 可先排除。另，選項 (A) expanding 雖可視為「動名詞」，但其前並不適合使用不定冠詞，故亦可排除。而選項 (B) expanse 雖為「名詞」，但意思是「廣闊之區域」，與前後句意不相符。本題正解為 (C)「擴展」。

115 正解 B

The Instagoo mobile device is ------- quick in opening most apps.

(A) remarkable   (B) remarkably   (C) remarked   (D) remarks

英斯塔果品牌的行動裝置在開啓大部分的應用程式方面都相當快速。

> **解析** 本題測驗的是正確之字詞變化。由空格後的形容詞 "quick" 即可推知，空格內應填入可作為其修飾語的「副詞」，而四選項中只有 (B) remarkably 為副詞，故為正解。選項 (A) remarkable 為「形容詞」、(C) 為動詞 "remark" 之「過去分詞」、(D) 為動詞 "remark" 之「第三人稱單數形」。注意，"remark" 指「評論」，但 "remarkable" 用來表示「顯著的」、「不凡的」，而 "remarkably" 則指「顯著地」、「非常地」。

Vocabulary

☐ **promptly** 迅速地；立即　　☐ **expand** 擴大；拓展

116 正解 A

Mr. Baxter is proposing a ------- strategy for increasing our market share among teenagers.

(A) different   (B) various   (C) furious   (D) insistent

貝克斯特先生將提出一個不同的策略以增加我們青少年中的市占率。

> **解析** 本題為「單字」考題，須選出適合用來修飾空格後名詞 "strategy"「策略」之「形容詞」。由於 "strategy" 為「單數」形，因此可先排除須接「複數」名詞的 (B) various。另，選項 (C) furious「暴怒的」與 (D) insistent「堅持的」明顯皆不適合，故亦不選。正確答案是 (A) different「不同的」。

117 正解 D

Enter your email address below if you would like to receive regular updates ------- our products and services.

(A) regard   (B) regards   (C) regarded   (D) regarding

如果您想收到有關我們產品與服務的定期更新，請於下方輸入您的電郵地址。

> **解析** 本題考正確之字詞變化。由於本句中 "if-" 子句內的及物動詞 "would like" 已有明確的受詞 (to receive regular updates)，因此空格內應填入的是一可以其後之 "our products and services" 為受詞的「介系詞」。而四選項中唯一的介系詞為 (D) regarding「關於」。注意，"regarding" 原為動詞 "regard" 之現在分詞，如今已作「介系詞」用。另，"regard" 除了有「和……有關」之意外，更常用來指「視為」、「注視」。順帶一提，"regard" 亦可作「名詞」用，指「重視」、「關心」、「敬意」，其複數形 "regards" 則為「問候」之意。

118 正解 D

------- the sales team and the technical staff are available to reply to customer inquiries.

(A) Because   (B) While   (C) Either   (D) Both

業務團隊和技術人員都有空可回覆顧客的詢問。

> **解析** 本題考正確之連接詞組。由句中用來連接 "the sales team" 與 "the technical staff" 的連接詞 "and" 即可知，與其搭配的字詞為 (D) Both。選項 (A) Because 與 (B) While 皆為「從屬連接詞」，無法與本身屬「對等連接詞」的 "and" 連用。另，選項 (C) Either 應搭配另一「對等連接詞」"or"。

119 正解 B

During the remodeling, the copy machine will be ------- located in the hallway near the meeting rooms.

(A) partially   (B) temporarily   (C) normally   (D) permanently

整修期間，影印機將暫時擺在會議室旁的走道上。

> **解析** 本題為「單字」考題，須選出適合用來修飾句中被動結構中之過去分詞 "located" 的「副詞」。由前後文意可推知，在整修期間，影印機應該是「暫時地」被置於走道上，正確答案是 (B)。選項 (A) partially「部分地」、(C) normally「正常地」及 (D) permanently「永久地」明顯皆不符句意。

120 正解 C

We were not immediately able to offer a complete ------- of what went wrong.

(A) explain   (B) explainable   (C) explanation   (D) explained

出了什麼差錯，我們並無法立刻提供完整的解釋。

> **解析** 本題測驗的是正確之字詞變化。由空格前的形容詞即可推知，空格內應填入一「名詞」，而四選項中唯一的名詞是 (C) explanation，故為正解。「動詞」選項 (A) explain、「形容詞」選項 (B) explainable 與「過去分詞」選項 (D) explained 明顯皆為誤。

Vocabulary

☐ **market share** 市場占有率   ☐ **remodel** 翻修；整修

121 正解 A

The location of Ms. Chee's retirement party ------- to the Balboa Grill.

(A) has been moved   (B) to be moving   (C) being moved   (D) has been moving

齊女士退休宴的地點已經改到了巴布亞燒烤。

> **解析** 本題考正確之動詞型態。由於本句缺乏的是「動詞」,因此屬「不定詞」結構的 (B) to be moving 和屬「分詞」結構的 (C) being moved 可先排除。而因為「地點」是「被」更改的,所以本題應選屬「現在完成被動式」的 (A) has been moved。選項 (D) has been moving 則為「現在完成主動式」,不可選。

122 正解 D

Only managers are required to attend the sales workshop, but ------- in the customer service seminar is mandatory for all employees.

(A) consistency   (B) arrival   (C) improvement   (D) participation

只有經理人員必須出席業務工作坊,但客服研討會全體員工都必須參加。

> **解析** 本題為「單字」考題,須選出可作為本句中對等連接詞 "but" 後之第二個對等子句之「主詞」的名詞。由前後文意來推斷,本句要表達的應該是,雖然業務工作坊只要求經理人員出席,但客服研討會則規定所有員工都必須「參加」,正確答案是 (D)。選項 (A) consistency「一致」、(B) arrival「抵達」與 (C) improvement「改善」明顯皆非句意所需。注意,題目當中的 "mandatory"「強制性的」為一重要多益單字,不可不知。

123 正解 D

The redesign of the website ------- to increase user interaction, but actually it had no measurable effect.

(A) intend   (B) intended   (C) intending   (D) was intended

網站的重新設計旨在增進使用者的互動,但實際上並沒有明顯的效果。

> **解析** 本題考正確之動詞型態。與前句相同,本句以對等連接詞 "but" 連接前後兩個對等子句;與前句不同的是,在本句中第一個子句缺乏「動詞」。選項 (C) intending 為「現在分詞」,可先排除。選項 (A) intend 雖為動詞,但既非「第三人稱單數形」亦非「過去式」,因此無法與主詞 "The redesign of the website" 相對應,故亦不可選。選項 (B) intended 可視為「過去式動詞」(或「過去分詞」),但因為主詞 "The redesign ..." 為「事物」,無法「意圖」做任何事,所以也不正確。本題應選屬「過去被動式」的 (D) was intended。

124 正解 B

Over half of all new hires this year were made ------- referrals from current employees.

(A) because   (B) through   (C) since   (D) though

今年所有的新聘人員中有超過半數是透過現有員工所轉介的。

> **解析** 本題考正確之介系詞。由於本句屬「簡單句」,因此可先排除用來引導「從屬子句」的「從屬連接詞」選項 (A) because 與 (D) though。而選項 (C) since 雖然除了作「從屬連接詞」用之外也可當「介系詞」,但其後必須接一「過去時間」(如 "yesterday"、"last year" 等),故不可選。正確答案是 (B) through。注意,本句中的 "referral"「轉介」由動詞 "refer" 變化而來,不可與另一同源名詞 "reference"「介紹信」、「推薦人」混淆。

125 正解 A

Free product training, follow-up calls, and similar ------- ensure better customer retention.

(A) practices   (B) practiced   (C) practical   (D) practically

免費的產品訓練、後續的跟進電話以及類似的做法能夠確保較好的顧客維繫率。

> **解析** 本題考正確之字詞變化。由空格前的形容詞 "similar" 即可推斷,空格內應填入一「名詞」,而四選項中只有 (A) practices「(慣常)做法」為名詞,故為正解。不過請注意,"practice" 亦常作動詞用,指「練習」、「實行」、「從事」,而選項 (B) practiced 即為其過去式(或「過去分詞」)。另,選項 (C) practical 為形容詞,指「實際的」,選項 (D) practically 則為副詞,指「實際上」。

126 正解 B

Shipping costs are ------- calculated based on the weight of the order and the desired speed of delivery.

(A) competitively   (B) automatically   (C) similarly   (D) significantly

運費是依照訂貨的重量和要求的交件速度自動計算出來的。

> **解析** 本題為「單字」考題，必須選出適合用來修飾被動結構中之過去分詞 "calculated" 的副詞。選項 (A) competitively 指「競爭地」、(B) automatically 指「自動地」、(C) similarly 指「相似地」、(D) significantly 指「意味深長地」。選項 (A)、(C)、(D) 顯然都很難與 "calculated" 搭上關係，唯有選項 (B) 可為其合理的修飾語。

127 正解 B

The purpose of the meeting is to decide ------- the department can reduce costs in the coming year.

(A) only   (B) how   (C) even   (D) so that

開會的目的是要決定該部門能夠如何降低來年的成本。

> **解析** 本題考正確之從屬連接詞。由空格前的及物動詞 "decide" 及空格後的完整子句可推知，空格內應填入一可引導「名詞子句」的從屬連接詞。由於選項 (A) only 與選項 (C) even 皆為「副詞」，因此可先排除。選項 (D) so that 雖為從屬連接詞，但引導的應是「副詞子句」，故不選。正確答案是 (B) how。注意，在本句中由 "how" 所引導、作為 "decide" 之「受詞」的名詞子句屬所謂的「間接問句」。

128 正解 D

When opening a new retail outlet, location is always the most important -------.

(A) consequence   (B) movement   (C) reduction   (D) consideration

在開設新的零售店時，地點向來都是最重要的考量。

> **解析** 本題為「單字」考題。由前後文意可推斷，在開設商店時，地點應該是極重要的「考量」，因此本題選 (D) consideration。選項 (A) consequence「後果」、(B) movement「移動」和 (C) reduction「減少」明顯皆與句意不搭軋。

129 正解 B

Rather than purchasing new computer equipment, the consulting company recommended upgrading our software -------.

(A) enough   (B) instead   (C) otherwise   (D) either

該顧問公司建議我們把軟體升級，而不是購買新的電腦設備。

> **解析** 本題考正確之副詞。由句首的片語連接詞 "rather than"「而不是」即可知，於句尾處應使用具「取而代之」含意的副詞 (B) instead。選項 (A) enough 表「足夠」、選項 (C) otherwise 指「否則」、選項 (D) either 則可用於否定句中表「也（不）」，三者明顯皆非句意所需。

130 正解 C

Several restaurants near the office offer a discount to those with a ------- employee ID card.

(A) mutual   (B) accountable   (C) valid   (D) prudent

辦公室附近有幾家餐廳對那些持有有效員工證的人都會給予折扣。

> **解析** 本題為「單字」考題，須選出適合修飾空格後之複合名詞 "employee ID card" 的形容詞。首先可排除選項 (B) accountable「應負責任的」，因為空格前的不定冠詞並非 "an"，而是 "a"。而選項 (A) mutual「相互的」與 (D) prudent「謹慎的」明顯皆不適合用來作 "employee ID card" 之修飾語。正確答案是 (C) valid「有效的」。

Vocabulary

☐ **outlet** 商店

## PART 6

Questions 131-134 refer to the following email.

From: Joe Shlabotnik, Director of Water Safety, Green Valley Lake
To: All Lifeguards and Junior Lifeguards
Subject: Water Safety Training
Date: Thursday, April 22

The bathing beach at Green Valley Lake will open for the summer ------- on June 1. To prepare for the season, weekly
131.
training sessions will be offered at the Boathouse each Saturday afternoon in May. Junior lifeguards ------- to attend all four
132.
sessions. -------, we also encourage senior lifeguards to come by to refresh their skills and share their knowledge with less
133.
experienced staff. At Green Valley Lake, we believe that learning together leads to better working relationships, and those

relationships help create a safer environment for our community. -------.
134.

Best regards,
Joe Shlabotnik

131. (A) this month
(B) as usual
(C) recently
(D) at first

132. (A) expects
(B) expected
(C) expecting
(D) are expected

133. (A) At once
(B) Therefore
(C) Of course
(D) Especially

134. (A) We hope all Green Valley lifeguards take advantage of this opportunity.
(B) Thank you all for organizing such a memorable event.
(C) We look forward to having another successful school year.
(D) The next training session will be emailed to you on Saturday.

第 131 到 134 題請參照下面這封電子郵件。

寄件者：綠谷湖水上安全主任喬‧史拉波尼克
收件者：全體救生員和初級救生員
主　旨：水上安全訓練
日　期：4 月 22 日星期四

今夏綠谷湖海濱浴場將一如往常於 6 月 1 日開放。為了替本季做準備，五月的每週六下午將在船庫舉行週訓課。初級救生員四堂課全都要出席。當然，我們也鼓勵資深救生員前來溫習技能，並與經驗較少的人員分享他們的知識。在綠谷湖，我們相信一起學習會帶來更好的工作關係，而且這些關係有助於為我們社區創造出更安全的環境。希望綠谷的全體救生員都能善加利用這次的機會。

喬‧史拉波尼克上

131 正解 B

解析 由於本句已明確提及海濱浴場將於六月一日開放，因此選項 (A) this month「這個月」、(C) recently「最近」與 (D) at first「最初」皆不合理。本題應選 (B) as usual「照常」，表示該海濱浴場每年都於同一時間對外開放。

133 正解 C

解析 前一句提到初級救生員都必須參加訓練課程，而本句則說他們「也」鼓勵資深救生員前往溫習技能。由此可推斷，兩句之間最合理的起承轉合用詞應該是 (C) Of course「當然」。選項 (A) At once「立刻」、(B) Therefore「因此」與 (D) Especially「尤其」皆非前後文意所需。

132 正解 D

解析 本句缺乏動詞，因此非屬動詞的選項 (C) 可立即排除。而由於主詞 "Junior lifeguards" 為複數，故選項 (A) 也可排除。另，因為浴場「將」於六月開放，所以「過去式」選項 (B) 亦不可選。正確答案是 (D) are expected。注意，在此屬「被動式」的 "are expected" 真正的意思是「必須要」，而非表面上的「被期待」之意。

134 正解 A

解析 本句為信末最後一句話，理當針對信中內容做一總結，而四選項中，唯有選項 (A) 符合此目的。選項 (B) 提到的「感謝主辦活動」、選項 (C) 提到的「期待另一學年」與 (D) 提到的「用電郵寄送下次課程」明顯皆與此信內容不相干。

Vocabulary
☐ **session** 講習班　☐ **lifeguard** 救生員　☐ **refresh** 恢復（精神、記憶等）　☐ **lead to** 導致

Zeblen Consulting regularly surveys our clients to research how we can improve the ------- we offer them. To make working
135.
at Zeblen as fulfilling as possible, we're now asking our own employees those questions. The responses you provide will
help us improve ------- company culture and work environment. -------.
136.   137.

The survey was designed by Mittleman Research, and it is available at mittlemanresearch.com/zeblen. Please visit that
------- and complete the survey by Friday. You will not be asked for any personally identifying information and all responses
138.
will be completely anonymous.

135. (A) serve
(B) services
(C) serving
(D) servicing

136. (A) its
(B) their
(C) our
(D) that

137. (A) To give just one example, we could provide more trees and plants in the office.
(B) We hope that all employees will find time to attend the workshop.
(C) Clients will be asked how Zeblen can better meet their professional needs.
(D) Topics include advancement opportunities, compensation, and workplace support.

138. (A) company
(B) site
(C) evaluation
(D) report

第 135 到 138 題請參照下面這則公告。

澤布蘭顧問公司定期對我們的客戶進行調查,以研究我們能如何改善對他們所提供的服務。為了使澤布蘭的作業盡可能圓滿,我們現在將問自家的員工那些問題。各位提供的回覆將有助於改善公司的文化與工作環境,主題包括升遷機會、薪酬和職場支援。

本調查由密托曼研究設計,並登載在 mittlemanresearch.com/zeblen 上,請在週五前上該網站完成填寫。本調查不會索取任何個人識別資訊,所有的回覆也將完全匿名。

135 正解 B

解析 由空格前的定冠詞 "the" 即可知,空格內應填入一「名詞」,因此動詞選項 (A) serve「服侍」、「服務」可先排除。而選項 (C) serving 雖可作普通名詞用,但指的是「一人份的食物」,與句意無關;選項 (D) servicing 雖可視為作「動詞」用的 "service" 之動名詞,但意思是「從事服務性之工作」或「維修」、「檢修」,同樣與句意不符。本題應選 (B) services「服務」。注意,事實上 (A) serve 有時可作名詞用,但意思是「發球」,與本文主題毫不相干。

137 正解 D

解析 本句為本文第一段的最後一句話,而本段主旨在於說明該公司將對員工所做之調查。列出該調查之主要內容的 (D) Topics include advancement opportunities, compensation, and workplace support. 為最合理選項。至於選項 (A) 提到的「在辦公室增加植栽」、選項 (B) 提到的「請員工參加工作坊」,以及選項 (C) 提到的「詢問客戶該如何滿足他們的需求」皆與本段主旨無關。

136 正解 C

解析 一般在提及自己所服務的公司時,多以第一人稱複數代名詞 "we" 來表示,這點可從第一句話中連續出現的兩個 "we" 得到驗證。而在本題中為了表達「本」公司之意,自然應該選擇使用 "we" 的所有格 "our"。選項 (C) 為正解。

138 正解 B

解析 由前後文意可知,發文者是要受文者前往設計該調查的密托曼公司之「網站」填寫資料,因此本題選 (B) site。選項 (A) company「公司」、(C) evaluation「評估」與 (D) report「報告」明顯皆非句意所需。注意,「上……網站」應用 "visit" 此動詞表示。

Vocabulary

☐ **fulfilling** 令人滿足的　　☐ **anonymous** 匿名的　　☐ **compensation** 補償(金);(工作的)報酬

-------. The north elevator will be closed during the month of October and the south elevator will be closed all of November.
139.

These closures are annoying, but necessary to ensure the safety of everyone in the building.

Let's work together to minimize the disruption. First, try to avoid using the working elevator in the morning and evening when it is most in demand. Large items, ------- bicycles, should only be transported when there is no one else waiting. If
140.
you live on one of the lower floors, take the stairs whenever possible. Most importantly, please be ------- of others. Lines
141.
will be long, and we should be especially mindful of the needs of older residents and those with young children.

Thank you for your -------. If you have any questions or concerns, please contact the property manager.
142.

139. (A) All tenants are kindly asked to take the stairs until further notice.
(B) Be advised that bicycles are not allowed to be transported in the elevators.
(C) Please note that elevator maintenance this fall will cause some inconvenience.
(D) Building management would like to remind everyone to remain calm.

140. (A) example of
(B) include
(C) unlike
(D) such as

141. (A) considerate
(B) prominent
(C) familiar
(D) magnificent

142. (A) proposal
(B) cooperation
(C) advice
(D) suggestion

第 139 到 142 題請參照下面這則公告。

請注意，今年秋季的電梯維修將造成一些不便。北側電梯將於十月間關閉，南側電梯則將於十一月時整月關閉。關閉這些電梯會令人覺得困惱，但為了確保大家在大樓裡的安全有其必要性。

讓我們一起努力將干擾減到最低。首先，試著避免在需求最大的早上和傍晚使用工作電梯。如腳踏車等的大型物件只應在沒有別人等候時載運。假如您住在較低的樓層，可能的話請走樓梯。最重要的是，請體貼他人。隊伍將會很長，我們應該要格外顧及年長居民和攜有年幼子女者的需要。

感謝各位的合作。若有任何問題或疑慮，請聯絡物業管理人。

---

139 正解 C

解析 本句為本公告的第一句話，理當開宗明義表達出公告的主旨。而由其後各段落，甚至各句話，皆與「電梯維修」有關的情況來推斷，選項 (C) 即為正解。選項 (A) 雖與電梯維修有關，但要求住戶走樓梯應屬公告之「細節」，而非主旨，故不可選。同樣地，提及腳踏車不可用電梯載運的選項 (B) 和提及管理部要大家保持冷靜的選項 (D) 皆屬「細節」，故皆為誤。

141 正解 A

解析 由下一句話提到的「顧及年長居民和攜有年幼子女者的需要」反推即可知，空格內應填入的是 (A) considerate「體貼的」。選項 (B) prominent「突出的」、(C) familiar「熟悉的」與 (D) magnificent「壯麗的」明顯皆與前後文意無關。

140 正解 D

解析 由空格前後的字詞和標點符號 "Large items," 及 "bicycles," 可推知，腳踏車乃所謂大型物件之「一例」，因此答案是 (D) such as。選項 (A) example of 為錯誤之表達方式，若改成 "for example" 即為正解。選項(B) include「包括」為動詞，不可選，若改成分詞形式的介系詞 "including"，即可選擇。選項 (C) unlike「不像」為介系詞，文法正確但意思不通，若改成肯定的 "like"，即可為正確答案。

142 正解 B

解析 本句為本公告結尾的第一句話。由第一段對住戶的提醒及第二段對住戶的要求可推知，在公告最後應該先對住戶們的「合作」表示感謝，因此本題選 (B) cooperation。選項 (A) proposal「提案」、(C) advice「忠告」與 (D) suggestion「建議」三者則與本文之內容主旨毫不相干。

Vocabulary
☐ **annoying** 困惱的　☐ **ensure** 確保　☐ **minimize** 減到最小　☐ **disruption** 中斷；擾亂

Dr. Sembla Nyad
Templeton University
872 Skylab Rd.
Austin, Texas

Dear Professor Nyad,

It is my distinct pleasure to invite you to be a featured speaker at the Sunnyvale Technology Summit this year. Your research on the history of social media is essential to the discussion of this year's theme, which is "The future of online communities." If you are -------, perhaps we could discuss topics for a possible talk over the phone.
143.

Speakers are not directly compensated, but we will gladly ------- travel and hotel expenses. More importantly, the summit
144.
is a place to meet people. Our ------- is to bring together leaders from the academy, business, and government for far-
145.
reaching discussions on the interplay of technology and society.

-------. Details about the summit are available at our website: sunnyvaletech.com. Please feel free to call me anytime if you
146.
have any questions.

Sincerely,

Timothy Jessup
Director, Sunnyvale Technology Summit
t.jessup@sunnyvaletech.com
(512) 555-3667

143. (A) interest
(B) interested
(C) interesting
(D) interestingly

144. (A) receive
(B) require
(C) restrict
(D) reimburse

145. (A) mission
(B) sponsor
(C) experiment
(D) dilemma

146. (A) I have included a check to cover your expenses.
(B) I am sure you will enjoy working at Sunnyvale.
(C) I do hope that you are able to join us this year.
(D) I encourage you to decide on the theme as soon as possible.

Vocabulary
☐ **featured speaker** 主要演講人 ☐ **summit** 高峰（會） ☐ **essential** 不可或缺的 ☐ **far-reaching** 影響深遠的；廣泛的 ☐ **interplay** 交互作用

森布拉‧尼亞德博士
坦普頓大學
德州奧斯丁天空實驗室路 872 號

尼亞德教授鈞鑑：

非常高興邀請您在今年的桑尼韋爾科技高峰會中擔任主講人。對於今年的主題「線上社群之未來」的討論而言，您對社群媒體史所做的研究是不可或缺的。假如您有興趣的話，我們容或能透過電話討論一下可能的發言題目。

演講人並不會直接領取酬勞，但我們很樂意補償差旅和住宿費。更重要的是，此高峰會是結識朋友的好地方。我們的任務是將學界、商界和政府方面的領導人湊在一起，以針對科技與社會的交互作用做深而廣的討論。

非常希望您今年能夠加入我們的行列。此次高峰會的細節公布於我們的網站 sunnyvaletech.com 上。如果您有任何問題，請隨時來電。

順頌　時綏

提摩西‧傑瑟普
桑尼韋爾科技高峰會主任
t.jessup@sunnyvaletech.com
(512) 555-3667

143 正解 B

解析 由空格前的主詞與動詞結構來推斷，空格內可填入名詞或形容詞，因此可先排除副詞選項 (D) interestingly「有趣地」。其次，就語意邏輯來看，說某人是「興趣」是不通的，因此名詞選項 (A) interest 亦可排除。最後，因為寫信者是要邀請對方參與活動，應該是問對方是否「感興趣」，所以答案是 (B) interested，而非指「有趣的」之選項 (C) interesting。

144 正解 D

解析 由前半句提到的「演講人不會直接領取酬勞」及句中的對等連接詞 "but"「但」可推知，主辦方（即句中之 "we"）應該是會「補償」對方的差旅和住宿費，因此本題選 (D) reimburse。選項 (A) receive「收到」邏輯不通，選項 (B) require「需要」與 (C) restrict「限制」亦不知所云，故三者皆不可選。

145 正解 A

解析 由動詞 "is" 之後所提到的「將學界、商界和政府方面的領導人湊在一起……做深而廣的討論」可推知，此乃主辦方之「任務」，因此正解為 (A) mission。選項 (B) sponsor「贊助商」與句意完全不搭軋；選項 (C) experiment「實驗」與 (D) dilemma「困境」則同樣與句意有相當大的距離。

146 正解 C

解析 本句為此邀請函最後一個段落的第一句話。在提出邀請（第一段）並說明細節（第二段）之後，最合理的接續應該就是表達出邀請人誠摯歡迎對方前來參與活動的希望，因此本題選 (C)。至於選項 (A) 所提到的「附上支票以支付對方的花費」、選項 (B) 所提到的「對方到桑尼韋爾工作會很愉快」，以及選項 (D) 提到的「希望對方儘早決定主題」皆與信中內容有所扞格，故皆不可選。

Questions 147-148 refer to the following job announcement.

~~ IT Analyst Wanted ~~

Tenz Personal Help Desk is seeking a motivated IT professional with excellent interpersonal skills for a full-time off-site position. Tenz delivers personalized on-demand IT support via online chat and video conferencing to residential customers and small businesses. In addition to having comprehensive, up-to-date technical knowledge of the hardware and software our customers use, the successful candidate must be able to communicate patiently and effectively with customers who may not have technical knowledge. To be considered, you must have a computer with a video camera and a reliable Internet connection. Tenz analysts work from home, but this is not a flexible or freelance position. Working hours are 8 AM to 5 PM Interested applicants should complete the online form at tenzpersonalhd.com/careers by May 15.

第 147 到 148 題請參照下面這則徵才通告。

~~ 誠徵資訊科技分析師 ~~

坦茲個人服務台將徵聘一位有幹勁、人際技能一流的資訊科技專業人士,擔任全職的外部職位。經由線上聊天和視訊會議,坦茲為住家顧客和小型企業提供個人化的按需資料支援。除了對顧客所使用的軟硬體須具備全面、最新的技術知識外,對於不一定具備科技知識的顧客,錄取人選還必須能耐心、有效地與其溝通。欲獲考量者須自備附攝影機的電腦及可靠的網路連線。坦茲分析師一職為在家工作但並非彈性或自由接案之職位。工時為上午八點至下午五點。有興趣的應徵者請於 5 月 15 日前至 tenzpersonalhd.com/careers 填寫線上表格。

147 正解 B

What is stated as a requirement for the job?
(A) Visiting customer homes and small businesses
(B) Ownership of the proper equipment
(C) The ability to repair computer hardware
(D) Experience working as an off-site employee

關於此職務,文中提到的條件是什麼?
(A) 拜訪顧客住家和小型企業
(B) 擁有適當的裝置設備
(C) 修復電腦硬體的能力
(D) 當過外部員工的經驗

解析 本題考細節,問應徵此職務的必備條件。由文中第四句提到的 "... you must have a computer with a video camera and a reliable Internet connection." 可知,正確答案是 (B)。選項 (A) 所說的「拜訪住家與企業」、選項 (C) 所說的「修復電腦硬體的能力」和 (D) 所說的「當過外部員工的經驗」則皆未在文中提及。

148 正解 D

What does the announcement indicate about Tenz?
(A) It is a successful and growing business.
(B) It mainly employs freelance workers.
(C) It will make a hiring decision by mid-May.
(D) It expects employees to be sociable.

通告中指出了坦茲的什麼事?
(A) 它是持續成長中的成功事業。
(B) 它主要是聘用自由接案的工作者。
(C) 它會在五月中決定錄取與否。
(D) 它期待員工懂得交際。

解析 本題亦考細節,問通告中指出該公司何事。由通告的第一句話 "Tenz Personal Help Desk is seeking a motivated IT professional with excellent interpersonal skills ..." 即可知,本題應選 (D)。至於選項 (A) 所說的該公司為「持續成長的成功事業」、(B) 所說的該公司「主要聘用自由接案者」和 (C) 所說的該公司「將於五月中決定錄取與否」在文中皆未提及。

Vocabulary

- [ ] **motivated** 積極性高的　[ ] **interpersonal** 人與人之間的　[ ] **off-site** 異地的;公司外部的　[ ] **on-demand** 按需的;隨選的
- [ ] **video conference** 視訊會議　[ ] **comprehensive** 綜合的　[ ] **hardware** 硬體　[ ] **software** 軟體　[ ] **freelance** 自由接案的　[ ] **sociable** 善交際的

Olivia Su 2:25
My train was delayed, so I won't get to Waterford station until about 2:50.

Jason Marcus 2:27
That's cutting it close. I'll call Mr. Kotter and ask if we can push back the meeting to 3:15.

Olivia Su 2:28
I don't think that's necessary. There's an underground walkway between the station and the basement of Mr. Kotter's office building.

Jason Marcus 2:33
I didn't know that.

Olivia Su 2:36
It's near Exit 4.

Olivia Su 2:37
I'm sure I can make it to the office by 3:00.

Jason Marcus 2:39
OK. I'll wait for you outside Exit 4 then.

Olivia Su 2:41
Actually, why don't you go directly to Mr. Kotter's office and get the computer set up.

Jason Marcus 2:45
You got it.

奧麗薇亞·蘇 2:25
我的班車誤點了,所以我 2:50 左右才能到沃特福站。

傑森·馬庫斯 2:27
那有點緊迫。我會打電話給寇特先生,問他能不能把會議延後到 3:15。

奧麗薇亞·蘇 2:28
我認為沒那個必要。車站和寇特先生辦公大樓的地下室之間有地下走道。

傑森·馬庫斯 2:33
這我倒不曉得。

奧麗薇亞·蘇 2:36
它就鄰近四號出口。

奧麗薇亞·蘇 2:37
我確信能在 3:00 前趕到辦公室。

傑森·馬庫斯 2:39
好。到時候我會在四號出口外等妳。

奧麗薇亞·蘇 2:41
其實你何不乾脆直接去寇特先生的辦公室把電腦準備好?

傑森·馬庫斯 2:45
沒問題。

---

149 正解 A

What is suggested about Ms. Su?
(A) She is familiar with Waterford Station.
(B) She works for Mr. Kotter.
(C) She wants to postpone the meeting.
(D) She prefers to meet with Mr. Kotter alone.

訊息中暗示了蘇小姐的什麼事?
(A) 她對沃特福站很熟。
(B) 她替寇特先生工作。
(C) 她想把會議往後延。
(D) 她偏好與寇特先生單獨見面。

> **解析** 本題為「推論」題,問文中暗示了蘇小姐的什麼事。由奧麗薇亞·蘇的第二次發言中的第二句話 "There's an underground walkway between the station and the basement of Mr. Kotter's office building." 及傑森·馬庫斯的反應 "I didn't know that." 可推斷,前者對該車站算是相當熟悉,因此本題選 (A)。至於選項 (B)、(C) 和 (D) 則皆無法由二人的對話中推論出。

150 正解 C

At 2:45, what does Mr. Marcus mean when he writes, "You got it"?
(A) He believes Ms. Su will arrive on time.
(B) He knows Ms. Su will bring her computer.
(C) He will follow Ms. Su's suggestion.
(D) He thinks Ms. Su should contact Mr. Kotter.

二點四十五分時,馬庫斯先生打的 "You got it." 是什麼意思?
(A) 他相信蘇小姐會準時抵達。
(B) 他知道蘇小姐會把電腦帶來。
(C) 他會聽從蘇小姐的建議。
(D) 他認為蘇小姐應該會聯絡寇特先生。

> **解析** 本題考詞句解釋,問馬庫斯先生回應蘇小姐所說的 "... why don't you go directly to Mr. Kotter's office and get the computer set up." 之用語含意。"You got it." 在一般日常對話中常被用來表達「同意對方」之意,例如在此處就指「好的」、「沒問題」,換言之,馬庫斯先生的意思就是「他會聽從蘇小姐的建議。」正解為 (C)。

Vocabulary
- [ ] **cut it close** 時間卡太緊　　[ ] **push back** 延後　　[ ] **make it to** 到場;及時抵達

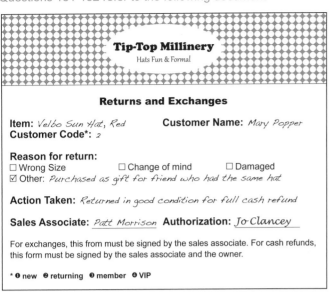

Tip-Top Millinery
Hats Fun & Formal

Returns and Exchanges

Item: Velbo Sun Hat, Red   **Customer Name:** Mary Popper
Customer Code*: 2

Reason for return:
☐ Wrong Size   ☐ Change of mind   ☐ Damaged
☑ Other: Purchased as gift for friend who had the same hat

Action Taken: Returned in good condition for full cash refund

Sales Associate: Patt Morrison   **Authorization:** Jo Clancey

For exchanges, this from must be signed by the sales associate. For cash refunds, this form must be signed by the sales associate and the owner.

* ❶ new   ❷ returning   ❸ member   ❹ VIP

頂尖女帽
休閒與正式頂戴

退　換　貨

品項：美而棒遮陽帽，紅色　　顧客姓名：瑪莉・帕波

顧客代碼*：2

退貨原因：
☐ 尺寸有誤   ☐ 改變心意   ☐ 受損
☑ 其他：買來當禮物，朋友卻有相同的帽子

所採行動：退貨狀態良好，退還全額現金

銷售同仁：佩特・莫里森　　授權：喬・柯藍希

如為換貨，本單須經銷售同仁簽名；如為退現金，本單須經銷售同仁及店主簽名。

* ❶ 新   ❷ 回頭   ❸ 會員   ❹ 貴賓

---

151 正解 C

Who most likely is Jo Clancey?
(A) Ms. Morrison's friend
(B) A salesperson at the store
(C) The owner of Tip-Top Millinery
(D) The designer of the Velbo Sun Hat

喬・柯藍希最有可能是什麼人？
(A) 莫里森小姐的朋友
(B) 店內的銷售人員
(C) 頂尖女帽的店主
(D) 美而棒遮陽帽的設計師

解析 本題屬「細節」題，但必須做一些小小的推論。由文件中「所採行動」之項目可知，顧客帕波女士要求的是「退還全額現金」，而根據文件下方提到的規定 "For cash refunds, this form must be signed by the sales associate and the owner." 可知，此單據除了銷售同仁的簽名之外，還需要「店主」簽字。由於單據上已顯示出 Patt Morrison 為「銷售同仁」，因此另一位簽名者 Jo Clancey 自然為「店主」。注意，事實上此單據並未明示 Jo Clancey 為該店之「店主」，但依常理判斷，只有「店主」才有「授權」(authorization) 的資格，因此本題選 (C)。

152 正解 D

What does the document indicate about the customer?
(A) She will purchase a different hat.
(B) She often returns items to the store.
(C) She exchanged the hat for one of equal value.
(D) She has been to the store before.

文件中指出了顧客的什麼事？
(A) 她會購買一頂不同的帽子。
(B) 她常到此店退貨。
(C) 她換了一頂等值的帽子。
(D) 她之前曾經到過店裡。

解析 本題亦屬「細節」題，但同樣地必須做一點推論。由文件中的「顧客代碼」項目可知，帕波女士為第二類顧客；由文件最下方列出的顧客代碼說明可知，第二類顧客為「回頭客」。而既然帕波女士屬「回頭客」，也就表示「她之前曾經到過店裡。」正解為 (D)。

Vocabulary
☐ **millinery** 女帽（業）   ☐ **refund** 退款   ☐ **associate** 同事；（生意上的）夥伴

From:	Charles Nelson
To:	Kumiko Eden
Subject:	New Employee Sales Performance

Dear Ms. Eden,

I did a quick evaluation of the monthly sales revenue generated by new hires, which you can see below. The data seems to support your speculation that the training program is not functioning effectively. After six months, new staff are still far from reaching the company average of €5,625. Equally concerning is the flat sales performance during their first three months of employment.

There are some limitations to the data. I haven't accounted for seasonal sales fluctuations or employees who left the company during their first six months. Nevertheless, it does suggest that management may want to make some changes. It would be premature to recommend a particular course of action, such as outsourcing the training program or replacing it with a mentoring system.

We might even consider eliminating it, but those decisions will require further research. Let me know how I can help.

Best regards,
Charlie

New Employee Average Monthly Sales Volume							
Sales Revenue (Euros)	5,001-6,000						
	4,001-5,000						
	3,001-4,000						
	2,001-3,000						
	1,001-2,000						
	501-1,000						
	0-500						
		Month 1	Month 2	Month 3	Month 4	Month 5	Month 6

寄件者：查爾斯‧尼爾森
收件者：久美子‧艾登
主　旨：新進員工銷售表現

艾登女士鈞鑑：

我很快地評估了新人所帶進的月銷售營收，結果您可在底下看到。資料似乎支持您認為訓練課程並未有效發揮作用的推測。在六個月後，新進人員還是遠遠未達到公司平均的 5,625 歐元。同樣令人擔憂的是，在雇用的頭三個月期間他們貧乏的銷售表現。

這些資料並不完整。我還沒有計入季度銷售波動，或是在頭六個月期間就離開公司之員工的表現。儘管如此，它們卻顯示管理階層也許會想做些改變。要建議採取特定的行動策略，例如把訓練課程外包，或是以輔導制度來取代它，則言之過早。

我們甚至可能考慮把它淘汰掉，但這些決定有賴進一步的研究。讓我知道我能怎麼幫上忙。

查理敬上

新進員工月平均銷售量							
銷售營收（歐元）	5,001-6,000						
	4,001-5,000						
	3,001-4,000						
	2,001-3,000						
	1,001-2,000						
	501-1,000						
	0-500						
		第 1 個月	第 2 個月	第 3 個月	第 4 個月	第 5 個月	第 6 個月

153 正解 C

Why is Mr. Nelson writing the email?
(A) To brainstorm new marketing strategies
(B) To gather data about sales performance
(C) To report a preliminary analysis
(D) To recommend a solution to a problem

尼爾森先生為何寫這封電子郵件？
(A) 為了新的行銷策略進行腦力激盪
(B) 為了蒐集銷售表現的資料
(C) 為了報告一項初步的分析
(D) 為了推薦一個解決問題的方法

解析 本題為「推論」題，問尼爾森先生寫這封電子郵件的目的。由信件第一段的第一句 "I did a quick evaluation ...." 及第二段的第一句和第二句 "There are some limitations to the data. I haven't accounted for seasonal sales fluctuations or ...." 可推知，尼爾森所做的分析報告並不完整，因此本題選 (C)。選項 (A) 提到的「為新行銷策略進行腦力激盪」、選項 (B) 提到的「蒐集銷售表現資料」及選項 (D) 提到的「推薦解決問題的方法」皆非尼爾森信中所要表達的意思。

154 正解 A

What is indicated about the training program?
(A) It is not meeting management's expectations.
(B) It will be replaced with a mentoring system.
(C) It should be outsourced to a consulting company.
(D) It will be eliminated if performance does not improve.

文中指出了訓練課程的什麼事？
(A) 它沒有達到管理階層的期望。
(B) 它將會被監督制度取代。
(C) 它應該被外包給顧問公司。
(D) 假如表現沒有改善，它就會被淘汰掉。

解析 本題考細節，問關於訓練課程的正確敘述。由信件第一段的第二句 "The data seems to support your speculation that the training program is not functioning effectively." 可知，公司的訓練課程並不成功。而由寄信者尼爾森先生信中的語氣與態度來推斷，對方（艾登女士）應為公司高層，因此本題選 (A)。另，由第二段的最後一句話 "It would be premature to recommend a particular course of action, such as outsourcing the training program or replacing it with a mentoring system." 及第三段的第一句話 "We might even consider eliminating it, but those decisions will require further research." 可知，選項 (B)、(C) 與 (D) 所提目前尚無定論，故皆不可選。

Vocabulary

☐ **speculation** 臆測　☐ **account for** 計算　☐ **fluctuation** 波動　☐ **premature** 過早的　☐ **mentoring** 輔導　☐ **eliminate** 排除；淘汰
☐ **brainstorm** 集思廣益

All the Buzz about the New Hornet
By Mika Sanchez

SAN JOSE, CA (July 26) – After months of rumors, eBe Mobile Solutions announced this morning that its flagship smartphone, the Hornet 1, is now available for purchase. The Hornet represents a major gamble for the company—not only did eBe completely redesign the phone, they reimagined the purchasing process as well. — [1] —.

The phone's six-inch screen covers the entire front side, except for a small speaker and camera at the top. It is a stunning technical achievement, but perhaps even more innovative is what lies—or doesn't lie—beneath the screen. When ordering their Hornet 1, users can save money by removing features that they don't need, for example the fingerprint scanner or the headphone jack. At the same time, they can pay to upgrade their phone with components they want, such as a better camera, a larger battery, or more memory. — [2] —.

Once a global leader in smartphone sales, eBe has been struggling to maintain market share in recent years. Some analysts have expressed concern about whether eBe can deliver its customized phones in a timely manner. They warn that eBe may have rushed the Hornet 1 to market in order to beat competitors, who generally release new models in August and September. — [3] —.

Jenny Yu, spokesperson for eBe, said, "We believe the Hornet 1 is an unprecedented achievement not just for eBe, but for the entire mobile communications industry." — [4] —.

第 155 到 157 題請參照下面這則報導。

關於新黃蜂沸沸揚揚的傳聞

美加‧桑契斯報導

加州聖荷西（七月二十六日）——在謠傳數月後，eBe 行動解方今早宣布，旗下的旗艦智慧手機黃蜂一號現已上市。黃蜂這款手機代表了該企業的一場豪賭，eBe 不但將手機完全重新設計，並設想出未曾想像過的購買流程。— [1] —

除了頂端的小型喇叭和鏡頭外，六吋螢幕便涵蓋了整個機身正面。這是令人驚豔的技術成就，但容或更為創新的則是螢幕底下有裝——或沒裝——什麼。在訂購黃蜂一號時，把不需要的性能去掉，例如指紋掃描或耳機孔，使用者就能省錢。在此同時，只要付費便能以想要的組件來為手機升級，諸如較好的鏡頭、較大的電池或更多的記憶體。— [2] —

eBe 曾經是智慧手機銷售的全球領導者，近年來卻跌跌撞撞地試圖維持市占率。對於 eBe 能否及時交付客製化手機，有些分析師表達了憂慮。他們警告，eBe 急著將黃蜂一號推上市面，或許是為了打敗通常在八、九月推出新款的競爭對手。— [3] —

eBe 的發言人于珍妮表示：「我們相信黃蜂一號是前所未見的成就，不僅僅對於 eBe 而言是如此，對整個行動通訊業而言也是。」— [4] —

Vocabulary
☐ **flagship** 旗艦 ☐ **stunning** 絕妙的；驚人的 ☐ **innovative** 創新的 ☐ **feature** 特點；具特色的功能 ☐ **jack** 插座 ☐ **component** 組件
☐ **customized** 客製化的 ☐ **timely** 適時的 ☐ **rush** 趕緊做

What is indicated about the Hornet 1?
(A) Its components have all been upgraded.
(B) Its screen covers the entire front side.
(C) Some of its features are optional.
(D) Most of its users will save money.

文中指出了黃蜂一號的什麼事？
(A) 它的組件全都已經升級。
(B) 它的螢幕涵蓋了整個正面。
(C) 它的某些特殊功能可自由選配。
(D) 它的使用者大部分都會省到錢。

解析　本題屬「細節」題，但必須做些許推論。針對黃蜂一號的特殊功能，文章第二段第三句中提到 "... users can save money by removing features that they don't need ...."，第四句則提到 "... they can pay to upgrade their phone with components they want ...."，也就是說，使用者可依自己的需求、喜好移除或增添某些功能。換言之，這些功能對購買者而言是可自由選擇的，因此本題選 (C)。而報導中並未說該手機的全部零件都已升級，也沒有說它的螢幕完全涵蓋了整個正面（因為還有喇叭和鏡頭），更未提及大部分的使用者都可省到錢，故選項 (A)、(B) 與 (D) 皆為誤。

What is reported about eBe Mobile Solutions?
(A) It has chosen a risky strategy.
(B) It can deliver its phones quickly.
(C) It is a global leader in smartphone sales.
(D) It will release its flagship product soon.

文中報導了 eBe 行動解方的什麼事？
(A) 它選擇了一個有風險的策略。
(B) 它很快就能交付手機。
(C) 它是現今智慧手機銷售的全球領導者。
(D) 它很快就會推出旗艦產品。

解析　本題亦考細節，問此篇文章是關於 eBe 公司何事的報導。由文章第一段第二句提到的 "The Hornet represents a major gamble for the company ...." 「黃蜂這款手機代表了該企業的一場豪賭……」可知，推出黃蜂手機對 eBe 而言是一個頗具風險的策略，因此正解為 (A)。另，因為文中提及有些分析師擔心 eBe 無法及時交付客製化手機，所以選項 (B) 不正確。而報導中的確提到 eBe 是智慧手機銷售的全球領導者，但「曾經是」而非「現在是」，因此選項 (C) 亦為誤。最後，由於 eBe 的旗艦智慧手機黃蜂一號「已經」推出，因此選項 (D) 同樣不可選。

In which of the positions marked [1], [2], [3], and [4] does the following sentence best belong?

"All told, the Hornet 1 comes in more than one hundred configurations."

(A) [1]
(B) [2]
(C) [3]
(D) [4]

下面這個句子插入文中標示的 [1]、[2]、[3]、[4] 四處當中的何處最符合文意？

「黃蜂一號總共有上百種組搭。」

(A) [1]
(B) [2]
(C) [3]
(D) [4]

解析　本題為「插入句」題。由於插入句的重點是黃蜂一號各種特殊功能的組搭，因此最合理的位置應該是第二段末尾，也就是，緊接在針對該手機可自由增減功能的舉例說明之後。正確答案是 (B)。

Vocabulary
☐ **optional** 可任意選擇的　☐ **all told** 總計　☐ **configuration** 配置；組態

Memo

DATE: February 2

We are excited to announce the hiring of Janice Kropotkin, who will serve as our new director of communications. Ms. Kropotkin comes to us with twenty years of experience in public relations, most recently a five-year appointment as press secretary for Mayor Quinn. Before her public service, Ms. Kropotkin worked for a decade as a spokesperson for Charmine Industries, and before that as an ombudswoman for the Daily Pilot newspaper.

Ms. Kropotkin will give a short talk on Friday afternoon at 4:30 in the employee cafeteria. She plans to discuss her experiences as well as outline her plans for the future. If you have questions about the direction of the department, she would be happy to address them. Ms. Kropotkin also plans to use the meeting as an opportunity to solicit feedback on the company website, a redesign of which will be her first major project. Members of the marketing and sales departments are strongly urged to attend.

第 158 到 160 題請參照下面這則備忘錄。

備忘錄

日期：二月二日

我們很高興地宣布聘請了珍妮絲・克魯波特金來擔任我們的新通訊主任。在加入我們的行列之前，克魯波特金女士就已經有二十年的公關經驗，最近的五年間她擔任的是昆恩市長所派任的新聞秘書。在任公職前，克魯波特金女士曾在夏民工業當過十年的發言人，而在此之前則是《領航日報》的申訴專員。

週五下午 4:30，克魯波特金女士將在員工餐廳發表簡短的談話。她預計要談談本身的經驗，並概述對未來的計畫。假如各位對部門的走向有什麼問題，她會很樂意回答。克魯波特金女士還打算利用會面的機會就公司的網站徵求回饋，重新設計該網站將會是她的第一件重大工程。我們強力敦促行銷和銷售部門的成員出席。

第 1 回完全解析

PART 7

Vocabulary

□ **press secretary** 新聞秘書　□ **spokesperson** 發言人　□ **ombudswoman** 女申訴專員　□ **address**（針對問題）回答　□ **solicit** 請求；懇求
□ **feedback** 回饋；反饋　□ **urge** 敦促

158 正解 B

In what field does Ms. Kropotkin specialize?
(A) Online communication
(B) Public relations
(C) Industrial planning
(D) News reporting

克魯波特金女士專攻哪個領域？
(A) 網路通訊
(B) 公關
(C) 產業規劃
(D) 新聞報導

> 解析　本題考細節，問克魯波特金女士專攻的領域為何。由第一段第二句話的前半 "Ms. Kropotkin comes to us with twenty years of experience in public relations" 可推知，克魯波特金女士是「公關」方面的專家，因此本題選 (B)。而雖然文中提到克魯波特金女士將擔任通訊主任，但並沒有說她擅長網路通訊，因此 (A) 不可選。另，文中雖提到她曾在夏民工業做過發言人，但這與產業規劃並無直接關聯，故 (C) 亦不可選。最後，文中提及她曾在《領航日報》工作過，但擔任的是申訴專員而非記者，所以 (D) 同樣為錯誤選項。

159 正解 B

For how many years did Ms. Kropotkin work for Charmine Industries?
(A) 5
(B) 10
(C) 15
(D) 20

克魯波特金女士在夏民工業服務了幾年？
(A) 五年
(B) 十年
(C) 十五年
(D) 二十年

> 解析　本題考的同樣是細節問題。備忘錄第一段第三句明白指出 "... Ms. Kropotkin worked for a decade ... for Charmine Industries ..."，而因 "a decade" 指的是「十年」，因此本題選 (B)。注意，"decade" 為常考單字，"a decade" 是「十年」，"two decades" 則為「二十年」，依此類推。

160 正解 A

What is NOT scheduled to happen at the gathering?
(A) Food and drinks will be served.
(B) Opinions will be collected.
(C) A brief presentation will be made.
(D) A question and answer session will be held.

下列何者「未」預定會發生於集會？
(A) 會供應吃的和喝的。
(B) 會蒐集意見。
(C) 會有簡短的報告。
(D) 會有問答時段。

> 解析　本題考文中「未」提及的細節。由第二段第一句提到的 "Ms. Kropotkin will give a short talk ..."「克魯波特金女士將發表簡短談話」、第三句提到的 "If you have questions ... she would be happy to address them."「假如各位有什麼問題……她會很樂意回答」及第四句提到的 "Ms. Kropotkin also plans ... to solicit feedback ..."「克魯波特金女士還打算……徵求回饋」可知，選項 (B)、(C)、(D) 皆為此次集會預定會發生的事，因此皆為誤。本題應選文中未提及的 (A)。注意，不要被文中的 "the employee cafeteria"「員工餐廳」誤導，而以為當天會有餐飲供應。

Vocabulary

☐ **question and answer session** 問答時段

Vacarro, Kristen [2:02 PM]
So, it's already Wednesday. We need to figure out if we can get the prototype quadcopter up and running before Stan and I leave for the toy show on Friday.

Vacarro, Kristen [2:03 PM]
I promised Toy Star I'd show them something special. They have over 200 stores now—I'd hate to disappoint them.

Henderson, Stan [2:05 PM]
The hardware is ready. I modified the body of the drone to accept the new camera. It's not perfect, but it should be good enough for a few demonstrations.

Jin, Alpha [2:18 PM]
The software is a work in progress. The camera has a lot of new functionality that I'm trying to make accessible with our current hand controller.

Vacarro, Kristen [2:20 PM]
Our flight departs at noon. Is that going to be enough time?

Jin, Alpha [2:22 PM]
I'll have the coding done by Thursday night, but I'll need at least one day for testing. A failed demonstration is worse than no demonstration.

Vacarro, Kristen [2:24 PM]
OK, it looks like we're going to have a non-functional prototype. We'll just have to make do.

Henderson, Stan [2:29 PM]
Hang on. We're meeting with Toy Star Saturday afternoon, right? What if I postpone my flight by a day?

Vacarro, Kristen [2:31 PM]
You'd have to make it to the conference center before 4:30.

Henderson, Stan [2:31 PM]
It's worth a shot. If Alpha is in, I'll get my flight changed.

Jin, Alpha [2:32 PM]
Let's do it.

第 161 到 164 題請參照下面這段線上聊天討論。

Vacarro, Kristen [2:02 PM]
那麼,已經星期三了。我們需要搞清楚,在我和史丹星期五前往玩具展前,能不能讓四旋翼機原型正常運作。

Vacarro, Kristen [2:03 PM]
我向玩具之星保證過,我會秀特別的東西給他們看。他們現在有超過兩百間店,我可不想讓他們失望。

Henderson, Stan [2:05 PM]
硬體就緒了。我修改了無人機的機體好裝上新的相機。它不算完美,但只是要示範幾次的話應該夠好了。

Jin, Alpha [2:18 PM]
軟體部分正在努力中。這個相機有很多新功能,我正試著讓現有的手控器可用來操控它們。

Vacarro, Kristen [2:20 PM]
我們的班機中午出發。這樣時間夠嗎?

Jin, Alpha [2:22 PM]
我星期四晚上前會把編碼搞定,但至少需要一天來測試。示範失敗比不示範還糟。

Vacarro, Kristen [2:24 PM]
好,看起來我們的原型機似乎沒辦法正常運作。我們也只好將就應付過去了。

Henderson, Stan [2:29 PM]
等等。我們是在星期六下午拜會玩具之星,對吧?要是把我的班機延後一天呢?

Vacarro, Kristen [2:31 PM]
你必須在 4:30 前趕到會議中心。

Henderson, Stan [2:31 PM]
值得一試。假如艾法可配合,我就把班機改掉。

Jin, Alpha [2:32 PM]
就這麼辦。

• **Vocabulary** 見下頁

161 正解 B

What kind of business do the chat participants likely work for?
(A) A camera maker
(B) A toy manufacturer
(C) A software firm
(D) A toy store

聊天成員可能是哪一種行業的員工？
(A) 相機廠商
(B) 玩具製造商
(C) 軟體公司
(D) 玩具店

> **解析** 本題屬「推論」題，問此段線上聊天的成員可能的行業。由克麗絲汀‧瓦卡羅第一與第二次發言時提到的 "toy show" 和 "Toy Star" 以及之後三人針對他們的無人機產品 "the prototype quadcopter" 之軟硬體所做的討論可推知，他們三個人應該是某玩具製造廠商的員工。正確答案是 (B) A toy manufacturer。

162 正解 D

When will Stan Henderson travel to the show?
(A) Wednesday
(B) Thursday
(C) Friday
(D) Saturday

史丹‧亨德森會在什麼時候動身去展覽？
(A) 星期三
(B) 星期四
(C) 星期五
(D) 星期六

> **解析** 本題屬「細節」題，但必須做一點推論。由克麗絲汀第一次發言時提到的 "... Stan and I leave for the toy show on Friday." 可知，二人原訂於週五前往玩具展。但由之後三人的對話可知，因為艾法負責的軟體部分要到週四晚上才能完全搞定，而且需要一天做測試，所以史丹提議 "What if I postpone my flight by a day?"，也就是，他可改到週六再出發。而由艾法最後所說的 "Let's do it." 可確定，史丹會於 (D) Saturday「星期六」動身前往玩具展。

163 正解 C

What will Ms. Jin most likely do next?
(A) Change her flight time
(B) Repair a camera
(C) Work on some software
(D) Perform some tests

靳小姐接下來最有可能會做什麼？
(A) 更改班機時間
(B) 修復相機
(C) 處理一些軟體
(D) 做一些測試

> **解析** 本題考推論，問靳小姐接下來最有可能會做什麼。由靳小姐第一次發言時說的 "The software is a work in progress." 和第二次發言時說的 "I'll have the coding done by Thursday night ...."，以及她最後說的 "Let's do it." 可推知，接下來她應該會針對產品的軟體做一些處理。正解為 (C) Work on some software。

164 正解 D

At 2:24 PM, what does Kristen Vacarro mean when she writes, "We'll just have to make do"?
(A) They are determined to finish the project on time.
(B) They must immediately make another prototype.
(C) They have just enough work for each of them to do.
(D) They will manage despite imperfect circumstances.

二點二十四分時，克麗絲汀‧瓦卡羅打的 "We'll just have to make do." 是什麼意思？
(A) 他們決心要準時把案子完成。
(B) 他們必須立刻做另一個原型。
(C) 他們每個人都有不少工作要做。
(D) 他們會應付過去，儘管情況並不完美。

> **解析** 本題考點為詞句解釋。由瓦卡羅小姐此次發言的第一句話 "OK, it looks like we're going to have a non-functional prototype." 可知，她認為他們的產品其實未盡完善。但由於玩具展已迫在眉睫，他們也只好「勇往直前」了，因此本題選 (D)。注意，"make do" 為慣用語，有「湊和」、「將就」的意涵。

Vocabulary

- □ **figure out** 想出；搞懂 □ **prototype** 原型 □ **quadcopter** 四旋翼機 □ **up and running** 有效運作的 □ **leave for** 出發前往 □ **modify** 修改
- □ **drone** 無人機 □ **in progress** 進行中 □ **functionality** 功能性；機能 □ **coding**【電腦】程式編碼 □ **non-functional** 非正常運作的
- □ **make do** 設法應付 □ **hang on**（要對方）等一下 □ **shot** 嘗試 □ **be in** 願意參與或貢獻 □ **manage** 能夠應付

The South Coast Gardening Cooperative
Give Your New Lemon Tree a Healthy Start!

Congratulations! With proper care, the lemon tree you have just purchased will bring you joy for decades to come. Take a moment to familiarize yourself with this amazing plant.

Overview
◆ This three-to-four-year-old tree is ready to be removed from its container and planted in the ground.
◆ Select a sunny spot at least two meters away from buildings, fences, or other trees.
◆ Make sure the place you choose has good drainage—wet soil can damage the roots.
◆ Analyze the soil. Lemons are acidic, but the trees grow best in neutral soil.
◆ After you have found the perfect location, dig a wide, shallow hole. Carefully remove the tree from its container and plant it together with the potting soil.

Care
◆ For the first several weeks, water thoroughly every other day. After the adjustment period, water weekly: more in summer, less in winter.
◆ If the tree does not bear fruit or otherwise appears unhealthy, call us. Our experts can suggest a suitable fertilizer as a first step.
◆ If problems persist, we can arrange to visit your tree to observe the soil conditions, root system, and other factors, such as pests and diseases, that may be affecting its health. Current fees for these and other services are available at southcoastgardeningcoop.org/services.

第 1 回 完全解析

PART 7

第 165 到 167 題請參照下面這篇指示。

南岸園藝合作社

為新的檸檬樹帶來健康的起步！

恭喜！在適當照料下，您剛才購買的檸檬樹將在往後數十年為您帶來喜悅。請花點時間讓自己熟悉這株美妙的植物。

概述

◆ 這棵三、四歲的樹隨時可移出容器種在地上。
◆ 挑選離建物、圍籬或其他樹木至少兩公尺遠且有日照的位置。
◆ 您所選的地點務必要排水良好，土壤潮濕可能會使根部受損。
◆ 分析土壤。檸檬為酸性，但樹卻是在中性的土壤裡長得最好。
◆ 找到完美的地點後，挖個寬淺的洞。小心地把樹移出容器，並把它跟盆栽的土壤一起種下去。

照料

◆ 頭幾週時，每隔一天就徹底澆一次水。在調整期之後，則每週澆水：夏天多、冬天少。
◆ 假如樹不結果，或顯得不健康，請打電話給我們。我們的專家能夠建議合適的肥料作為第一步。
◆ 假如問題不止，我們則能安排訪視您的樹，以觀察土況、根系和其他或許會影響到健康的因素，諸如蟲害和疾病。這些服務以及其他服務的現行費用登載於 southcoastgardeningcoop.org/services。

Vocabulary

☐ **cooperative** 合作社 ☐ **proper** 適當的 ☐ **familiarize** 使熟悉 ☐ **amazing** 驚人的；美妙的 ☐ **container** 容器 ☐ **fence** 圍籬
☐ **drainage** 排水（系統） ☐ **acidic** 酸性的 ☐ **neutral** 中性的 ☐ **potting soil** 盆栽用土 ☐ **thoroughly** 完全地；徹底地 ☐ **adjustment** 調整
☐ **bear fruit** 結果實 ☐ **fertilizer** 肥料 ☐ **persist** 持續 ☐ **factor** 因素 ☐ **pest** 害蟲

What is described in the Overview section?　　　　概述部分描述了什麼？
(A) How to choose a suitable plant for the soil　　(A) 如何針對土壤選擇合適的植物
(B) How to care for the tree in its container　　　(B) 如何照料在容器裡的樹
(C) How to select and prepare an area for planting　(C) 如何挑選和準備種植區
(D) How to provide the optimal amount of watering　(D) 如何提供最適切的澆水量

解析　本題考細節。概述部分的第二、三點提及「種植地點的選擇」，第三、四點則與「分析土壤及挖洞」有關，由此可知選項 (C) 為正解。選項 (A) 說的「針對土壤選擇植物」之邏輯與事實恰恰相反，因為概述中提到的是須選擇中性土壤，也就是說，應該是「針對植物選擇土壤」。至於選項 (B) 提到的「照料在容器裡的樹」這一點在文中並未觸及。而選項 (D) 提到的「澆水量」則列於文中「照料」的部分，不屬「概述」，故不可選。

According to the instructions, what should people do　根據指示，在展開作業前民眾該做什麼？
before beginning to work?　　　　　　　　　　(A) 替區塊排水
(A) Drain the area　　　　　　　　　　　　　(B) 檢測土壤
(B) Test the soil　　　　　　　　　　　　　　(C) 挖一個洞
(C) Dig a hole　　　　　　　　　　　　　　　(D) 移除容器
(D) Remove the container

解析　本題考點同樣為細節理解。由概述部分的第四、五點可知，在民眾把樹移出容器種在土壤中之前必須先「分析土壤」，因此正解為 (B)。（注意，原文中用的 "analyze" 被以同義的 "test" 取代。）而因文中並未提及「替區塊排水」，所以選項 (A) 為誤。至於選項 (C) 提到的「挖洞」與 (D)「移除容器」則應屬「展開作業」的一部分，故亦不可選。

Why are people advised to visit the cooperative's website?　民眾為什麼被建議去上合作社的網站？
(A) To receive a fertilizer recommendation　　　(A) 以取得肥料相關的推薦
(B) To view the prices for inspections　　　　　(B) 以查閱診察的價格
(C) To schedule a visit to the cooperative　　　(C) 以預約參訪該合作社
(D) To request an expert phone consultation　　(D) 以索取專家的電話諮詢

解析　本題亦屬「細節」題。文中「照料」部分第三點的最後明白表示 "Current fees for these and other services are available at southcoastgardeningcoop.org/services."，也就是說，想知道該合作社所提供服務之費用的民眾可以上他們的網站查詢。本題選 (B) To view the prices for inspections。（注意，原文中所使用的 "fees" 以 "prices" 取代。）

Vocabulary
☐ **optimal** 最佳的　☐ **drain** 排水　☐ **consultation** 諮詢

From:	afithian@ppleup.com
To:	\<All Employees\>
Subject:	Plans for February
Date:	January 14

Everyone at headquarters is looking forward to welcoming the 64 colleagues from across town who will be working here in February while the midtown office is being renovated. It'll be a tight squeeze, but we've found space for everyone.

The Market Research and Communications teams will appropriate all five meeting rooms on the second floor. Everyone will have to be creative about finding meeting space—or finding reasons not to have meetings.

Customer Service and Technical Support team members will be using spare desks downstairs in the IT, Operations, and Purchasing departments.

Because members of the Sales and Business Development teams are issued laptops, we're asking you to work remotely. If you're in the area, we've reserved the meeting room at Phil's Coffee all month. Phil's is in the Packer Building across the street from HQ. The meeting room is in the basement and it seats 12.

As a reminder, the company is still offering two additional days off for every three days of vacation taken in February. It's a great time for a holiday!

Finally, no additional parking can be made available. Paid parking in the area is not cheap, so please consider bicycling to work, using public transportation, or carpooling. If you need a ride or can offer a ride, click here to be taken to the company's ride-sharing board. Help out if you can.

There will undoubtedly be some inconveniences, but this will also be a wonderful opportunity to get to know our colleagues better. Let's make the most of it.

Sincerely,
Alissa Fithian

第 168 到 171 題請參照下面這封電子郵件。

寄件者：afithian@ppleup.com
收件者：＜全體員工＞
主　旨：二月份計畫
日　期：1 月 14 日

總部的同仁們都很期待歡迎 64 位同事於二月份城中辦公室整修期間跨城來此上班。屆時總部會很擠，但我們已經為大家都找好了空間。

市場研究和通訊團隊將占用二樓的全部五間會議室。每個人都必須發揮創意為開會找空間——或為不開會找理由。

客服和技術支援團隊的成員將使用樓下資訊科技、營運和採購部門的空桌。

由於業務和事業發展團隊的成員都配有筆電，所以請各位遠距上班。假如你在區內，我們已經在菲爾咖啡包了整月的會議室。菲爾位在總部對街的派克大樓，會議室在地下室，可容納十二個人。

提醒各位，二月份每請休三天，公司仍會提供兩天額外的假。這可是休假的大好時機！

最後，這裡沒有額外的停車位可釋出。區內的付費停車位並不便宜，所以請考慮騎腳踏車上班、搭乘大眾運輸，或是共乘汽車。假如你需要搭便車或是能夠提供便車，請按此以進入公司的共乘佈告欄。可以的話請助一臂之力。

當然肯定會有一些不便，但這也是一個可以更加認識同事的絕佳機會。讓我們好好利用它吧。

艾莉莎・費斯安敬上

Vocabulary
☐ **squeeze** 擁擠　☐ **appropriate** 適當的　☐ **issue** 發行；配給　☐ **remotely** 遠距離地　☐ **seat** 坐得下；容納　☐ **reminder** 提醒記憶之物
☐ **public transportation** 大眾運輸　☐ **carpooling** 汽車共乘　☐ **undoubtedly** 無疑地　☐ **inconvenience** 不方便（之處）

168 正解 C

What is the purpose of this email?
(A) To welcome a group of new workers
(B) To announce the opening of a new office
(C) To assign work spaces to employees
(D) To explain a remodeling project

這封電子郵件的目的是什麼？
(A) 歡迎一群新進員工
(B) 宣布新辦公室的開張
(C) 為員工分配工作空間
(D) 解釋一項翻修計畫

> **解析** 本題屬「推論」題。文中第一段首先提到公司總部會增加 64 位員工，因此辦公室會很擁擠，而接下來的第二、三、四段立刻說明辦公室空間的分配。由此可推知，這封電子郵件的目的就是 (C) To assign work spaces to employees。至於選項 (A) 提到的「新進員工」、(B) 提到的「新辦公室」及 (D) 提到的「整修計畫」皆與本文無關。

169 正解 B

The word "appropriate" in paragraph 2, line 1, is closest in meaning to
(A) correct
(B) take control of
(C) look out for
(D) allocate

第二段第一行的 "appropriate" 這個字的意思最接近
(A) 改正
(B) 支配
(C) 找出
(D) 分派

> **解析** 本題考單字的含意。一般而言，"appropriate" 多作「形容詞」，指「恰當的」，但在本文中為「及物動詞」（受詞是 "all five meeting rooms on the second floor"），意思是「占用」，而四選項中意思與其最接近的應該是具「支配」、「控制」之意的 (B) take control of。

170 正解 C

Where is the Operations Department located?
(A) On the third floor
(B) On the second floor
(C) On the first floor
(D) In the basement

營運部位於何處？
(A) 三樓
(B) 二樓
(C) 一樓
(D) 地下室

> **解析** 本題屬「細節」題。本文第二段提及市場研究與通訊團隊將占用「二樓」的會議室，而第三段則提到客服和技術支援團隊將使用「樓下」資訊科技、營運和採購部門的空桌。由此可知，營運部應該是在「一樓」。(C) 為正解。

171 正解 D

According to the email, what are employees discouraged from doing?
(A) Using a laptop
(B) Meeting in a coffee shop
(C) Taking a vacation
(D) Paying for parking

根據電子郵件，員工不被鼓勵做什麼？
(A) 使用筆電
(B) 在咖啡館見面
(C) 休假
(D) 付費停車

> **解析** 本題屬「推論」題。由本文第六段第二句 "Paid parking in the area is not cheap, so please consider bicycling to work, using public transportation, or carpooling."「區內的付費停車位並不便宜，所以請考慮騎腳踏車上班、搭乘大眾運輸，或是共乘汽車。」可推知，該公司並不鼓勵員工做的事應為 (D) Paying for parking「付費停車」。而選項 (A)、(B)、(C) 則剛好相反，是公司希望員工做的事。

Vocabulary

☐ **allocate** 分配；分派

Burnett Investment Research

476 5th Avenue
New York, NY 10018
burnettresearch.com

November 18
Mr. Tajima Hideki
Health Insights International
5-7-13 Minami-Azabu
Minato-ku, Tokyo 106-8575

Dear Mr. Tajima:

We were very pleased to learn that you have agreed to transfer your referral agreement from TPR to Burnett Investment Research. When Burnett acquired TPR, we made a commitment to honor all existing contracts and agreements, but of course agents such as yourself maintained the option of upgrading. We think you made the right choice. — [1] —.

Please review the Burnett referral agreement, which I have signed and enclosed. The commission rate and payment schedule we offer are identical to those in the TPR agreement. Also unchanged are the global pharmaceutical industry reports, which will continue to be produced by TPR and marketed under the name "Burnett-TPR." — [2] —. The new agreement makes available to you Burnett's extensive list of research reports. Our focus on medical services and equipment has in recent years been expanded to include consumer-facing companies, especially those specializing in fitness-tracking, digital records management, and nutritional supplements. We believe these additional resources will be of interest to your existing clients, and will allow you to expand your current client base. — [3] —.

As for the TPR agreement, I have signed two copies of a Mutual Termination letter. Please sign one and return it to us together with a signed copy of the Burnett agreement. Both documents should reach us before December 31. I am looking forward to working with you as we embark on this promising new endeavor. If you have any questions or concerns, please do not hesitate to contact me. — [4] —.

Sincerely,

John Most

John Most
Business Development Manager, Burnett Investment Research

Enclosures

柏奈特投資研究
紐約州 10018 紐約市第五大街 476 號
burnettresearch.com

十一月十八日
田島英樹先生
國際健康透視
東京 106-8575 港區南麻布 5-7-13

田島先生鈞鑑：

我們非常高興得知，您同意將您的轉介協議由 TPR 轉到柏奈特投資研究。柏奈特收購 TPR 時，承諾會履行所有既存的合約與協議，但如您這樣的代理商當然保有升等的選擇權。我們認為，您做了對的選擇。— [1] —

請審閱我已簽名並隨附的柏奈特轉介協議。我們所開出的佣金比率和付款時程一如 TPR 的協議。同樣沒有改變的是，全球製藥業報告將繼續由 TPR 製作，並以「柏奈特－TPR」的名義來行銷。— [2] — 新協議將使您可取得柏奈特廣泛的研究報告清單。我們對醫療服務與設備的關注近年來已擴大範圍，我們納入了面對消費者的公司，尤其是那些專攻健康追蹤、數位紀錄管理和營養補給品的企業。我們相信這些額外的資源會令您現有的客戶感興趣，並能讓您擴大目前的客群。— [3] —

至於 TPR 的協議，我簽了兩份相互終止函。請在其中一份上簽名，並連同一份已簽署的柏奈特協議寄回給我們。兩份文件應於十二月三十一日前寄達。隨著我們即將開展這項前景看好的新作為，非常期待與您共事。如有任何疑問或憂慮，請隨時與我聯絡。— [4] —

謹啓

約翰・莫斯特
柏奈特投資研究事業發展經理
附件

172 正解 C

Why did Mr. Most send this letter to Mr. Tajima?
(A) To announce an acquisition
(B) To suggest an investment strategy
(C) To describe the terms of an agreement
(D) To inquire about a contract

莫斯特先生為什麼寄這封信給田島先生？
(A) 為了宣布一項收購
(B) 為了建議一個投資策略
(C) 為了描述一項協議的條款
(D) 為了洽詢一份合約

解析 本題屬「推論」題。由信件的第一段可知，田島先生已同意將轉介協議轉到柏奈特。因而在第二段中莫斯特先生就說明了新協議的一些條款，包括佣金比率、付款時程，以及全球製藥業報告的製作與柏奈特的研究報告清單之取得等相關處理方式。由此可推斷，莫斯特先生寫這封信的目的應該是 (C) To describe the terms of an agreement。選項 (A)、(B)、(D) 所言明顯皆非此信之要旨。

Vocabulary

☐ **insight** 洞悉；洞察力　☐ **transfer** 轉移；轉讓　☐ **referral** 轉介　☐ **commitment** 承諾　☐ **honor** 履行　☐ **enclose** 隨函附寄
☐ **commission** 佣金　☐ **pharmaceutical** 製藥的　☐ **extensive** 廣泛的　☐ **fitness-tracking** 健康追蹤　☐ **supplement** 補充物；補給品
☐ **mutual** 相互的　☐ **termination** 終止　☐ **promising** 有前途的　☐ **endeavor** 努力　☐ **hesitate** 遲疑　☐ **inquire** 詢問

173 正解 C

What did Mr. Most send with the letter?
(A) A research report
(B) An investment guide
(C) A referral agreement
(D) A client list

莫斯特先生連同信件寄了什麼？
(A) 研究報告
(B) 投資指南
(C) 轉介協議
(D) 客戶名單

解析	本題考的是「細節」問題。在信中第二段的第一句 "Please review the Burnett referral agreement, which I have signed and enclosed." 莫斯特先生明白表示他附寄了「柏奈特轉介協議」，因此答案是 (C)。注意，事實上根據第三段之內容所述，莫斯特先生還附寄了兩份「相互終止函」，但這並不影響作答，因為其他選項皆與此無關。

174 正解 A

The phrase "embark on" in paragraph 3, line 4, is closest in meaning to
(A) commence
(B) agree with
(C) invest in
(D) cooperate

第三段第四行的 "embark on" 這個片語的意思最接近
(A) 開始
(B) 同意
(C) 投資
(D) 合作

解析	"embark on" 此片語指「著手（做）」，通常用於困難或費時的新計畫或活動之前，而四選項中以 (A) commence「開始」與其意思最相近。

175 正解 C

In which of the positions marked [1], [2], [3], and [4] does the following sentence best belong?

"Fund managers and financial advisers will benefit from research conducted by our global network of investment strategists."

(A) [1]
(B) [2]
(C) [3]
(D) [4]

下面這個句子插入文中標示的 [1]、[2]、[3]、[4] 四處當中的何處最符合文意？

「基金經理人和理財顧問將會受惠於我們的投資策略師全球網所做的研究。」

(A) [1]
(B) [2]
(C) [3]
(D) [4]

解析	題目插入句的重點在於告知對方 Burnett Investment Research 的投資策略師針對全球市場所做的研究對於對方企業的發展是很有助益的，因此最合理的出現位置應為第二段末尾 "We believe these additional resources will be of interest to your existing clients, and will allow you to expand your current client base." 此句之後。亦即，莫斯特先生用後一個句子來強化他的前一個句子，故本題選 (C)。

From: June Wai

To: stanley.roper@rivercityrentals.com

Subject: Four apartments in June

Date: April 17

Dear Mr. Roper:

I spoke with you earlier on the phone about possibly renting apartments for the four researchers who will be visiting Renjex's River City laboratory this June. As requested, I've noted the names and requirements of each of our visiting colleagues.

- Janet Wood: requires access to public transportation and nearby amenities
- Cindy Snow: prefers a simple, inexpensive option
- Jack Tripper: will be living with his wife
- Lana Shields: would like a quiet neighborhood

Our campus is located in the Arts District, so apartments in that area would be ideal, but Forrest Hills, where I reside, is a lovely, peaceful area. And I suppose Ms. Wood would prefer something more centrally located.

We'll need the apartments from June 1 to June 30. Ms. Snow will be staying until July 5, but can stay in a hotel for the final few days, unless special accommodations can be made. I'm eager to have this taken care of, so I'd appreciate it if you could let me know what you have available by April 20. I look forward to hearing from you soon.

Best regards,
June Wai
Administration Supervisor, Renjex Labs

第 176 到 180 題請參照下列電子郵件和文件。

寄件者：June Wai
收件者：stanley.roper@rivercityrentals.com
主　旨：六月份四間公寓
日　期：4 月 17 日

羅伯先生鈞鑑：

我先前在電話裡和您談到，今年六月有四位研究人員將造訪蘭傑克斯的河市實驗室，我們可能會為他們租用公寓。依照您的要求，以下註明各個到訪同仁的姓名和需求。

－珍妮・伍德：須使用大眾運輸和鄰近的公共設施
－辛蒂・史諾：偏好簡單、不貴的選項
－傑克・崔波：將與妻子同住
－拉娜・席爾茲：想住安靜的地段

我們的校區位於藝術區，因此當地的公寓應該都挺理想的，但我住的佛瑞斯丘是個宜人、寧靜的地方。我想伍德小姐會偏好較接近市中心的地點。

我們需要公寓的時間是從六月一日到六月三十日。史諾小姐會待到七月五日，但最後幾天她可以住旅館，除非我們能安排特別的住宿。我很想把這件事搞定，所以如果您能在四月二十日前讓我知道您手上有什麼適合的待租物件的話，我會非常感激。期待很快得到您的回音。

魏君恩　上
蘭傑克斯實驗室行政主管

Vocabulary

☐ **researcher** 研究人員　☐ **laboratory** 實驗室　☐ **amenities** 便利設施（複數形）　☐ **option** 供選擇之事物　☐ **ideal** 理想的　☐ **reside** 居住
☐ **accommodations** 住宿之處（複數形）　☐ **available** 可利用的；現成的　☐ **administration** 行政；管理　☐ **supervisor** 監督者；督導者

River City Short-Term Apartment Rentals
List of Apartments

Location ▾	Apartment ▾	Type* ▾	Rent ▾	June ▾
Forrest Hills	Shadow Point Apartments #111	Studio	$590	Available
Arts District	Topanga Suites #206	Studio	$680	Available
Town Center	City Garden #912	Studio	$975	Unavailable
Waterfront	Vista Tangento #306	1 Bedroom	$825	Unavailable
Town Center	City Garden #1401	1 Bedroom	$1,115	Available

* Studio apartments are single-occupancy only. One-bedroom apartments may have up to two residents, but in that case a monthly $50 service fee is added to the rent to cover the increase in utilities.

河市短期公寓出租
公寓名單

地點 ▾	公寓 ▾	類型* ▾	租金 ▾	六月 ▾
佛瑞斯丘	影點公寓 111 號	套房	$590	待租
藝術區	托龐卡套房 206 號	套房	$680	待租
市中心	城市花園 912 號	套房	$975	已租
濱水區	唐珍托景 306 號	一房一廳	$825	已租
市中心	城市花園 1401 號	一房一廳	$1,115	待租

* 套房公寓只容單人入住。一房一廳房型最多可容兩人入住，但若二人入住，每月租金須加 $50 的服務費，以支應所增加的水電瓦斯費。

---

176 正解 C

Why did Ms. Wai send the email?
(A) To request materials for a laboratory
(B) To promote her company in the city
(C) To inquire about available apartments
(D) To get information about visiting researchers

魏小姐為什麼寄這封電子郵件？
(A) 為了替實驗室索取材料
(B) 為了替她的公司在城裡做宣傳
(C) 為了詢問是否有待租的公寓
(D) 為了打聽來訪研究人員的資訊

> 解析
> 本題屬「推論」題。由第一段第一句中提到的 "renting apartments for the four researchers"「為四位研究員租用公寓」，和最後一段中提到的 "let me know what you have available"「讓我知道您手上有什麼待租物件」可知，魏小姐寫這封信的目的應該是 (C)。其他選項皆與信中內容不相干。

Vocabulary

☐ **short-term** 短期的　☐ **rental** 出租；租用　☐ **studio** 工作室；攝影棚；（出租）套房　☐ **suite**（飯店之）套房　☐ **waterfront** 濱水地區
☐ **vista** 景色；美景　☐ **occupancy** 占用；居住　☐ **in that case** 如果是那樣　☐ **utility**（水、電、瓦斯等）公共事業（常用複數）

What is suggested about Janet Wood?
(A) She intends to get a driver's license.
(B) She has recently moved to River City.
(C) She currently commutes by subway or bus.
(D) She will not have access to a car in June.

文中暗示了珍妮‧伍德的什麼事？
(A) 她有意考駕照。
(B) 她最近搬到了河市。
(C) 她目前靠地鐵或公車通勤。
(D) 她在六月份不會有車可開。

解析 本題同樣為「推論」題。由魏小姐針對珍妮‧伍德之需求所提到的 "requires access to public transportation" 可知，她「必須使用大眾運輸工具」，換句話說，她屆時不會有自己的車可開，因此本題選 (D)。至於選項 (A)「她有意考駕照」與 (C)「她目前靠地鐵或公車通勤」皆無法由信中資訊推論而得。而選項 (B)「她最近搬到了河市」則與事實不符，因為信中表明包括珍妮等四位研究人員是六月時才會造訪河市實驗室。

What area of the city would Lana Shields likely prefer?
(A) Forrest Hills
(B) Arts District
(C) Town Center
(D) Waterfront

拉娜‧席爾茲可能會偏好市內的什麼區？
(A) 佛瑞斯丘
(B) 藝術區
(C) 市中心
(D) 濱水區

解析 本題亦屬「細節」題，但必須做些許推論。依照魏小姐對於拉娜‧席爾茲之需求所提到的 "would like a quiet neighborhood" 可知，拉娜希望住的地方比較安靜；魏小姐在信中也提及她自己住的佛瑞斯丘就是一個宜人、寧靜之所 (... Forrest Hills, where I reside, is a lovely, peaceful area.)。由此可推斷，在四個選項地區中拉娜應該會比較喜歡 (A) Forrest Hills。

When is Mr. Tripper expected to move out?
(A) April 20
(B) June 1
(C) June 30
(D) July 5

崔波先生預計什麼時候會搬走？
(A) 四月二十日
(B) 六月一日
(C) 六月三十日
(D) 七月五日

解析 本題考細節，問崔波先生預計何時搬出公寓。魏小姐於信中第三段明白表示 "We'll need the apartments from June 1 to June 30."，由此可推知，崔波先生會在六月三十日搬出，所以答案是 (C)。注意，七月五日是史諾小姐離開的時間，與其他三位研究人員無關，不可誤選。

What is indicated about one-bedroom apartments?
(A) They are more expensive than studios.
(B) The cost of utilities is not included in the rent.
(C) They are more expensive if there are two residents.
(D) They are more likely to be available than studio apartments.

文中指出了一房一廳房型的什麼事？
(A) 它們比套房貴。
(B) 水電瓦斯費不包含在租金內。
(C) 如果有兩個房客，就會比較貴。
(D) 它們比套房公寓更可能租得。

解析 本題考點同樣為細節理解。由表單末尾的注意事項可知，一房一廳房型可住兩個人，但必須加付 50 美元的水電、瓦斯等相關服務費 (One-bedroom apartments may have up to two residents, but ... a monthly $50 service fee is added ... to cover the increase in utilities.)，因此本題選 (C)。另，依表單所列出之價格相互比較，選項 (A) 明顯為誤。至於「水電瓦斯費包不包括在租金內」或「一房一廳房型是否比套房公寓更可能租得」則無法由文中所提供之資訊得知，故選項 (B) 與 (D) 亦皆不可選。

Vocabulary

☐ **commute** 通勤

第 1 回完全解析

PART 7

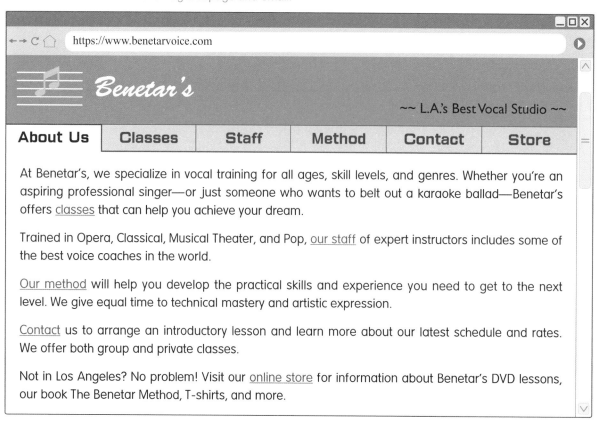

第 181 到 185 題請參照下列網頁和電子郵件。

~~~洛杉磯最好的聲樂工作室~~~

關於我們	課程	人員	方法	聯絡我們	店鋪

班尼塔專精各年齡、技巧水準和類型的發聲訓練。無論您是胸懷大志的職業歌手，或者只是想高唱一曲卡拉 OK 流行情歌的人，我們都能提供能夠幫助您達成夢想的課程。

我們的專家教師人員受過歌劇、古典、音樂劇和流行樂的訓練，其中不乏一些世界最好的聲樂教練。

我們使用的方法能幫助您發展您所需要的實用技巧與經驗以更上一層樓。對於精進技術和藝術表達我們投入等量的時間。

請跟我們聯絡以便安排一堂入門課，並獲取更多與最新課程表及收費相關的資訊。我們提供團體與個人課程。

不在洛杉磯嗎？沒問題！您可以上網瀏覽我們的線上店鋪以了解與班尼塔的 DVD 課程、用書《班尼塔方法》、T 恤相關以及其他更多的資訊。

From:	Jan Kilmister
To:	info@benetarvoice.com
Subject:	Possible Cooperation
Date:	December 28

To Whom It May Concern:

I recently moved to the Los Angeles area and was quite excited when I came across your website. If possible, I would like to set up a time to come by and discuss a few areas of possible cooperation.

I have a Master of Arts in Vocal Performance from Northern University in Chicago. I was active in the musical theater community there as a performer and as a singing instructor for nearly ten years. I was also the lead singer of The Pink Sky Monkeys, a rock band.

During that time I created an online scheduling and billing system that allowed me to teach students remotely via video. I believe there is a growing need for this kind of service, and I would welcome the chance to discuss how this software could be used at Benetar's. Also, I noticed that you don't have instructors who specialize in rock and roll. If you were looking to expand in that direction, I would be happy to offer a few free demonstration classes for you and your students.

Sincerely,
Jan Kilmister

寄件者：Jan Kilmister
收件者：info@benetarvoice.com
主　旨：可能的合作
日　期：12 月 28 日

敬啓者：

我近來搬到了洛杉磯地區，在無意間看到貴網站時相當興奮。如果可能的話，我想約個時間過去一趟，並討論幾個可能的合作面向。

我擁有芝加哥北方大學聲樂演唱的藝術碩士學位。我在當地的音樂劇社群活躍了近十年，擔任演出者和歌唱教師。我也是搖滾樂團粉紅天猴的主唱。

在那段期間，我創立了一個線上排程和計費系統，這使得我可靠視訊來遠距教導學生。我相信這種服務會有擴增的需求，希望有機會可以討論一下這樣的軟體能如何運用在班尼塔。另外，我留意到貴公司並沒有專攻搖滾樂的教師。假如貴公司著眼於往這個方向擴展，我很樂意為貴公司和學生上幾堂免費的示範教學課。

謹啓

珍・基爾米斯特

181 正解 A

What is NOT suggested about Benetar's?
(A) It has teachers from all over the world.
(B) It trains singers in several styles of music.
(C) It focuses on technical mastery.
(D) It offers singing classes for children.

關於班尼塔，文中「未」暗示什麼？
(A) 它有來自世界各地的老師。
(B) 它訓練數種音樂風格的歌手。
(C) 它聚焦於精進技術。
(D) 它有提供兒童歌唱課程。

解析　本題為「推論」題。由網頁上的第一句話 "At Benetar's, we specialize in vocal training for all ages, skill levels, and genres." 「班尼塔專精各年齡、技巧水準和類型的發聲訓練。」可推知，班尼塔「有」訓練不同音樂風格的歌手，也「有」提供兒童歌唱課程，因此 (B) 和 (D) 皆為誤。而由第三段第二句 "We give equal time to technical mastery and artistic expression." 「對於精進技術和藝術表達我們投入等量的時間。」則可推知，班尼塔「有」將焦點擺在精進技術，因此 (C) 亦不可選。由文中資訊無法推論出來的應該是選項 (A)，故為正解。

Vocabulary
□ **come across** 偶然遇見；偶然發現　□ **come by**（短時間）拜訪　□ **billing** 開帳單

182 正解 C

What is indicated about Benetar's?
(A) It has recently relocated from Chicago.
(B) It offers private classes on the Internet.
(C) It sells merchandise on its website.
(D) It posts its most recent schedule online.

文中指出了班尼塔的什麼事？
(A) 它在近期由芝加哥搬遷過來。
(B) 它有提供線上個人課程。
(C) 它在網站上有賣商品。
(D) 它會把最近期的課程表貼上網。

> 解析 由網頁上的最後一段最後一句話 "Visit our online store for information about Benetar's DVD lessons, our book The Benetar Method, T-shirts, and more." 可知，班尼塔的網站除了提供資訊外，還販售如 T 恤等商品，因此本題選 (C)。而由於文中並未提及班尼塔近期由芝加哥搬遷過來，故 (A) 為誤。另，雖然班尼塔有提供個人課程，但文中並未表示是「線上課程」，因此 (B) 亦為誤。最後，依照網頁上的訊息，欲取得最新課程表，必須直接與班尼塔聯絡，他們的網站上只提供 DVD 課程的相關資訊，因此 (D) 同樣不可選。

183 正解 C

What style of singing offered by Benetar's is Ms. Kilmister most qualified to teach?
(A) Classical
(B) Pop
(C) Musical Theater
(D) Rock

基爾米斯特小姐最有資格來教班尼塔所提供的哪一類歌唱？
(A) 古典
(B) 流行
(C) 音樂劇
(D) 搖滾

> 解析 依電子郵件中基爾米斯特小姐的自述，她擁有聲樂演唱的藝術碩士學位，且曾在音樂劇社群擔任演出者和歌唱教師長達十年，由此可推斷，她最有資格教的歌唱類型應為 (C)「音樂劇」。注意，雖然基爾米斯特小姐有提到曾經擔任過搖滾樂團的主唱，也提及她可以示範幾堂搖滾樂的演唱教學，但這些都不能代表她最具教人演唱搖滾樂的資格，因此不可誤選 (D)。

184 正解 D

What is suggested about Ms. Kilmister?
(A) She has a degree in software development.
(B) She prefers to teach group classes.
(C) She plays guitar in a music group.
(D) She would like to work at Benetar's.

文中暗示了基爾米斯特小姐的什麼事？
(A) 她有軟體開發的學位。
(B) 她偏好教團體課程。
(C) 她在樂團裡彈吉他。
(D) 她想在班尼塔工作。

> 解析 基爾米斯特小姐在電子郵件的第一與第三段中都表示了希望與班尼塔合作的意願，由此可推斷，她應該是想到班尼塔工作，因此本題選 (D)。而因為基爾米斯特小姐擁有的是藝術碩士的學位，並非軟體開發的學位，所以 (A) 不正確。另，基爾米斯特小姐在信中只提到她可以靠視訊遠距教導學生，並不能因此而推斷她偏好教團體課程，所以 (B) 亦不正確。最後，基爾米斯特小姐在樂團擔任過的是主唱，無法由此推論她有彈吉他，因此 (C) 同樣不可選。

185 正解 D

What does Ms. Kilmister ask about?
(A) The procedure for registering for classes
(B) The rates for online instruction
(C) The software used by Benetar's
(D) The future plans of the studio

基爾米斯特小姐詢問什麼事？
(A) 報名課程的手續
(B) 線上教學的收費
(C) 班尼塔所用的軟體
(D) 歌唱教室的未來計畫

> 解析 基爾米斯特小姐在信中的第三段提及希望與對方討論可以如何運用她所開發的軟體，並表示如果對方有意往搖滾樂方面擴展，她願意做示範教學。由此可推知，她想知道班尼塔是否有什麼未來計畫。正確答案是 (D)。另，由於信中並無任何資訊顯示基爾米斯特小姐想知道對方報名課程的手續、線上教學的收費，或是所使用的軟體，因此其他選項皆為誤。

Vocabulary
□ **relocate** 重新安置；（使）遷徙　□ **merchandise** 商品　□ **procedure** 手續；程序　□ **register** 登記；註冊

Keynote Speaker Profile

Penny Rosemont has been involved in the creation of over a dozen video games in her long and storied career. Below are a few highlights.

Vegetable Mayhem
As lead game designer, Ms. Rosemont was responsible for creating the unique social aspects of this communal farming game, which are generally credited with sparking its world-wide success.

Diamond Moonshot
The game pairs two players from different countries who must work together to build a spaceship and fly it to a diamond-shaped moon. It was Ms. Rosemont's first time serving in the role of creative director.

Birdie Derby
To develop this racing game, Ms. Rosemont started her own company—Massive Penny Gaming. The new CEO scored a huge global hit with this game that pits large "flocks" (actually teams of up to 1,000 players) against each other in massive round-the-world races.

Rainbow Dream
More a critical success than a commercial one, this educational game teaches players the skills they need to make their own video game. To progress to the highest levels, advanced players need to show beginners how to accomplish various technical tasks.

第 186 到 190 題請參照下列簡介、時程和電子郵件。

專題講者簡介

在她長期且著名的職涯中,潘妮‧羅斯蒙特曾參與創作過十幾款電玩遊戲。以下是她的幾個亮點之作。

青菜之亂
身為首席遊戲設計師,羅斯蒙特女士負責為這款公共農場遊戲創造出獨特的社群面向,而一般認為這款遊戲能在世界各地受到歡迎應歸功於這些獨特的面向。

奔向鑽石衛星
這款遊戲將來自不同國家的兩個玩家配對,這兩個人必須一起動手建造一艘太空船,並駕著它飛到一個鑽石型的衛星上。這是羅斯蒙特女士第一次擔當創意總監的角色。

小鳥大賽
為了開發這款賽車遊戲,羅斯蒙特女士自創了一家公司——大潘妮遊戲。這款遊戲讓龐大的「鳥群」(實際上是達上千位玩家的隊伍)在遍及世界各地的大型競賽中相互比拚,而這位新任執行長也藉此在全球造成了大轟動。

彩虹之夢
與其說它是商業上的成功,不如說是受到評論界的肯定。這款具教育功能的遊戲教導玩家自行打造電玩遊戲所需的技巧。要晉升到最高等級,進階玩家必須教初學者如何達成各種技術上的任務。

Vocabulary
□ **be involved** 參與;與……有關 □ **storied** 著名的 □ **highlight** 最精彩的部分 □ **mayhem** 大混亂 □ **unique** 獨特的 □ **communal** 公共的
□ **credit** 歸功(常用被動) □ **spark** 觸發;引起 □ **moonshot**(火箭、太空船等的)向月球發射
□ **moon**(地球的衛星)月球;(其他行星的)衛星 □ **creative director** 創意總監 □ **racing** 賽車 □ **CEO**(= Chief Executive Officer)執行長
□ **score**(在運動比賽中)得分;贏得 □ **hit** 成功、受歡迎之事物 □ **pit** 使競爭;使相鬥 □ **flock**(鳥、羊等的)群
□ **up to** 達到(數量、標準等) □ **critical** 批判的;危急的;評論界的 □ **progress** 前進;進步 □ **advanced** 先進的;高階的
□ **accomplish** 完成(任務) □ **various** 各式各樣的 □ **task** 差事;工作;任務

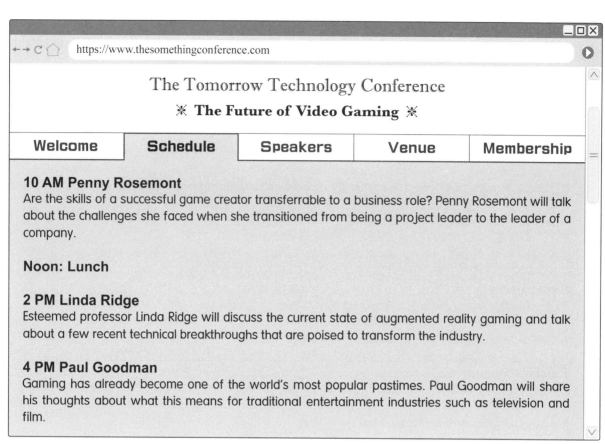

The Tomorrow Technology Conference

※ The Future of Video Gaming ※

| Welcome | Schedule | Speakers | Venue | Membership |

10 AM Penny Rosemont

Are the skills of a successful game creator transferrable to a business role? Penny Rosemont will talk about the challenges she faced when she transitioned from being a project leader to the leader of a company.

Noon: Lunch

2 PM Linda Ridge

Esteemed professor Linda Ridge will discuss the current state of augmented reality gaming and talk about a few recent technical breakthroughs that are poised to transform the industry.

4 PM Paul Goodman

Gaming has already become one of the world's most popular pastimes. Paul Goodman will share his thoughts about what this means for traditional entertainment industries such as television and film.

明日科技大會

※ 電玩遊戲的未來 ※

| 歡迎 | 時程 | 講者 | 地點 | 會員 |

上午十點　潘妮‧羅斯蒙特

成功遊戲創作者的本領能否轉換到經營企業的角色上？潘妮‧羅斯蒙特將暢談從擔任專案領導人轉變為公司領導人時所面臨的挑戰。

中午：午餐

下午兩點　琳達‧李季

備受敬重的教授琳達‧李季將討論擴增實境遊戲的現況，並暢談近來幾項可望翻轉產業的技術性突破。

下午四點　保羅‧古德曼

玩電玩已成為世上最風行的消遣之一。對諸如電視和電影等傳統娛樂產業來說，這意謂著什麼？保羅‧古德曼將分享他的想法。

Vocabulary

☐ **venue**（事件）發生地點；（活動）場所　☐ **transferrable** 可轉移的　☐ **challenge** 挑戰　☐ **transition** 過渡；轉變　☐ **esteemed** 受人尊敬的　☐ **current** 目前的　☐ **augmented reality gaming**（AR gaming）擴增實境遊戲　☐ **recent** 最近的　☐ **breakthrough** 突破　☐ **poised** 準備就緒的　☐ **transform** 徹底改變　☐ **gaming** 玩電玩　☐ **pastime** 娛樂；消遣　☐ **entertainment industry** 娛樂產業

From:	rgruder@tttc.com
To:	penny.rosemont@mail.mpg.com
Subject:	Many thanks!
Date:	October 1

Dear Ms. Rosemont,

I would like to thank you for your compelling presentation. Everyone at the Tomorrow Technology Foundation was impressed by your ability to weave your personal story into a larger discussion of the evolution of the business side of gaming. It was truly inspirational.

And thank you also for your patience as we dealt with the microphone issue. I'm not sure I would have been so gracious had it been me up there on the stage. If we are fortunate enough to have you back to speak next year, rest assured that we'll change the batteries before your talk, not during it!

Thank you again, and please do keep in touch.

Roberta Gruder

寄件者：rgruder@tttc.com
收件者：penny.rosemont@mail.mpg.com
主　旨：多謝！
日　期：10 月 1 日

羅斯蒙特女士鈞鑑：

我想謝謝您引人入勝的演說。對於您能將個人的故事融入電玩商業面之演進這樣大面向的討論之中，明日科技基金會的每個人都印象深刻。真的是深具啓發。

在我們處理麥克風的問題之際，也感謝您的耐心。要是當場換成是我在台上，我不確定自己會不會這麼能夠體諒。如果我們明年能有幸再請到您來演講，請放心，我們會在您發言前就把電池換好，而不是在您發言時更換！

再次謝謝您，請務必保持聯絡。

羅貝塔‧葛魯德

---

186 正解 D

What is one common feature in all of Ms. Rosemont's games?
(A) They connect players from different countries.
(B) They focus on teaching technical skills.
(C) They have generated significant revenue.
(D) They require players to work together.

在羅斯蒙特女士所有的遊戲中，一個共同的特性是什麼？
(A) 它們連結不同國家的玩家。
(B) 它們聚焦於教導技術本領。
(C) 它們賺進相當多的營收。
(D) 它們需要玩家們共同合作。

解析 本題考點為細節理解。由簡介裡「青菜之亂」中提到的 "this communal farming game"「這款公共農場遊戲」、「奔向鑽石衛星」中提到的 "players ... must work together"「玩家……必須一起動手」、「小鳥大賽」中提到的 "teams of up to 1,000 players"「達上千位玩家的隊伍」及「彩虹之夢」一項中提到的 "advanced players need to show beginners how ..."「進階玩家必須教初學者如何……」可知，羅斯蒙特女士的遊戲之共同特色為「都需要玩家們合作」。答案是 (D)。至於其他選項只是其中一款或數款的情況，故皆非正解。

Vocabulary
☐ **impressed** 印象深刻的　☐ **weave** 編織　☐ **evolution** 演變；進化　☐ **inspirational** 有啓發性的；激勵人心的　☐ **gracious** 親切的；寬恕的
☐ **had it been** (= if it had been) 假如是　☐ **rest assured** 放心

187 正解 C

Which game did Ms. Rosemont discuss at the conference?
(A) Vegetable Mayhem
(B) Diamond Moonshot
(C) Birdie Derby
(D) Rainbow Dream

羅斯蒙特女士在大會上討論的是哪一款遊戲？
(A) 青菜之亂
(B) 奔向鑽石衛星
(C) 小鳥大賽
(D) 彩虹之夢

解析 本題亦考細節。在大會時程「上午十點」一項中提到 "Penny Rosemont will talk about the challenges she faced when she transitioned from being a project leader to the leader of a company."「潘妮·羅斯蒙特將暢談從擔任專案領導人轉變為公司領導人時所面臨的挑戰。」換句話說，羅斯蒙特女士在大會上會討論到的應該是她自己當老闆時所製作的遊戲。而在遊戲簡介中唯一提到相關資訊的是「小鳥大賽」一項："To develop this racing game, Ms. Rosemont started her own company ...."「為了開發這款賽車遊戲，羅斯蒙特女士自創了一家公司……。」因此本題選 (C)。

188 正解 A

What is indicated about the keynote speech?
(A) It was interrupted by a technical problem.
(B) It was scheduled for the end of the day.
(C) It was recently added to the schedule.
(D) It was delivered by a respected professor.

文中指出了專題演講的什麼事？
(A) 它被一個技術問題打斷。
(B) 它被安排在當天的最後一段時間。
(C) 它近期才被加進時程裡。
(D) 它是由一位受敬重的教授所發表。

解析 本題同屬「細節」題。在羅貝塔·葛魯德寫給潘妮·羅斯蒙特的電子郵件中（第二段第一句）提到 "... thank you ... for your patience as we dealt with the microphone issue."「在我們處理麥克風的問題之際，……感謝您的耐心。」由此可推斷，羅斯蒙特女士的演講曾因麥克風出了問題而被中斷，故本題選 (A)。至於 (B) 所言與事實並不相符，因為該演講是被安排在上午十點，也就是當天的第一場。而選項 (C) 則更是無中生有。最後，(D) 中所提到的「受敬重的教授」應該是指琳達·李季，但李季教授並非當日的專題講者。

189 正解 B

In the email, the word "compelling" in paragraph 1, line 1, is closes in meaning to
(A) required
(B) forceful
(C) reasonable
(D) practical

電子郵件第一段第一行的 "compelling" 這個字的意思最接近
(A) 必需的
(B) 有說服力的
(C) 合理的
(D) 務實的

解析 本題考點為單字的含意。"compelling" 這個字原是動詞 "compel"「強迫」的現在分詞，轉作形容詞用後，被用來指「令人信服的」、「引人入勝的」，而與它意思最相近的單字應為 (B) forceful「強而有力的」、「有說服力的」。

190 正解 C

What is probably true about Ms. Gruder?
(A) She is employed by a video game company.
(B) She will give a presentation the following year.
(C) She is the organizer of the conference.
(D) She had a problem with the microphone.

關於葛魯德小姐的敘述，下列何者可能為真？
(A) 她受雇於一家電玩遊戲公司。
(B) 她明年將發表演說。
(C) 她是大會的籌辦人。
(D) 她的麥克風出了問題。

解析 本題為「推論」題。由電子郵件的「寄件者」部分及最後的簽名可知，葛魯德小姐為該信的寫作者。她在信中代表 "Tomorrow Technology Foundation"「明日科技基金會」感謝羅斯蒙特女士的演說，並表示明年想再度邀請她，而很明顯地，「明日科技基金會」正是主辦「明日科技大會」的單位。由此可合理推論，葛魯德小姐極可能就是大會的籌辦人，故本題選 (C)。至於選項 (A) 和 (B) 的敘述皆無法由文中資訊得到論證。而 (D) 則為「張冠李戴」，因為麥克風出問題的是羅斯蒙特而非葛魯德。

Vocabulary

☐ **generate** 產出（電、熱等）；賺（錢） ☐ **significant** 意義重大的；相當數量的 ☐ **interrupt** 打斷；使中斷 ☐ **deliver** 交付；遞送；演講
☐ **presentation** 簡報；演說 ☐ **organizer** 主辦人；籌辦者

Questions 191-195 refer to the following product information, online review, and response.

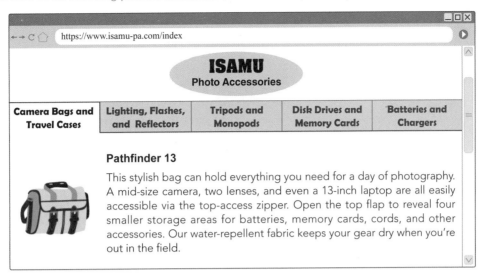

Pathfinder 13

This stylish bag can hold everything you need for a day of photography. A mid-size camera, two lenses, and even a 13-inch laptop are all easily accessible via the top-access zipper. Open the top flap to reveal four smaller storage areas for batteries, memory cards, cords, and other accessories. Our water-repellent fabric keeps your gear dry when you're out in the field.

第 191 到 195 題請參照下列產品資訊、線上評論和回應。

	伊薩姆 攝影配件			
相機包和旅行箱	照明、閃光燈和反光板	三腳架和單腳架	磁碟機和記憶卡	電池和充電器

Pathfinder 13

一日攝影所需要的一切本款流行包都裝得下。頂部開口的拉鏈設計可讓中型相機、兩個鏡頭，甚至於 13 吋的筆電全都輕鬆好拿。打開頂蓋就會看到四個較小的置物區塊，可以用來放電池、記憶卡、電線和其他配件。當您人在野外時，防水材質則能保持裝備的乾燥。

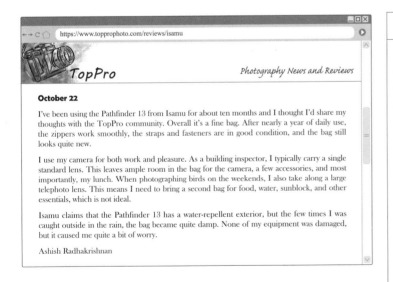

TopPro — *Photography News and Reviews*

October 22

I've been using the Pathfinder 13 from Isamu for about ten months and I thought I'd share my thoughts with the TopPro community. Overall it's a fine bag. After nearly a year of daily use, the zippers work smoothly, the straps and fasteners are in good condition, and the bag still looks quite new.

I use my camera for both work and pleasure. As a building inspector, I typically carry a single standard lens. This leaves ample room in the bag for the camera, a few accessories, and most importantly, my lunch. When photographing birds on the weekends, I also take along a large telephoto lens. This means I need to bring a second bag for food, water, sunblock, and other essentials, which is not ideal.

Isamu claims that the Pathfinder 13 has a water-repellent exterior, but the few times I was caught outside in the rain, the bag became quite damp. None of my equipment was damaged, but it caused me quite a bit of worry.

Ashish Radhakrishnan

攝影快報與評比

十月二十二日

我已經使用伊薩姆的 Pathfinder 13 差不多十個月了，我想在 TopPro 社群分享我的想法。整體來說，它是個蠻不錯的包包。在我天天使用將近一年後，拉鏈操作仍然順暢，帶子和釦件的狀態也都良好，整個包包看起來還是相當新。

我的相機兼用在工作和消遣上。身為建築檢查員，我通常都會攜帶單一標準鏡頭。這使得包包裡有充裕的空間放相機、一些配件，以及最重要的——我的午餐。在週末拍攝鳥類時，我還會帶上大型的望遠鏡頭。這意味我需要為了食物、水、防曬乳和其他的必備品而攜帶第二個包包。

伊薩姆宣稱 Pathfinder 13 有防水的外層，但有幾次我在外面碰到下雨，包包卻變得相當潮濕。我的器材並沒有任何一樣受損，但還是讓我頗為擔心。

阿席史‧拉哈克里史南

Vocabulary

- **accessory** 配件
- **lighting** 照明
- **flash** 閃光燈
- **reflector** 反光板
- **tripod** 三腳架
- **monopod** 單腳架
- **disk drive** 磁碟機
- **battery** 電池
- **charger** 充電器
- **stylish** 時髦的；流行的
- **photography** 攝影（術）
- **lens** 鏡片；鏡頭
- **top-access** 頂部開口的
- **zipper** 拉鏈
- **flap**（衣袋、包包等的）蓋
- **reveal** 顯現；揭露
- **storage** 貯藏；儲存
- **cord** 繩索；電線
- **water-repellent** 防水的
- **fabric** 紡織品；布料
- **gear** 排檔；裝備；服裝
- **review** 審核；評論；寫評論
- **community** 社區；社群
- **overall** 整體而言；大致上
- **strap** 帶子；吊環
- **fastener** 釦件
- **inspector** 督察者；檢查員
- **typically** 典型地；通常
- **ample** 寬闊的；充足的
- **photograph** 拍攝；照片
- **telephoto** 遠距照相的
- **sunblock** 防曬乳
- **essential** 必需品
- **exterior** 外部
- **damage** 損壞

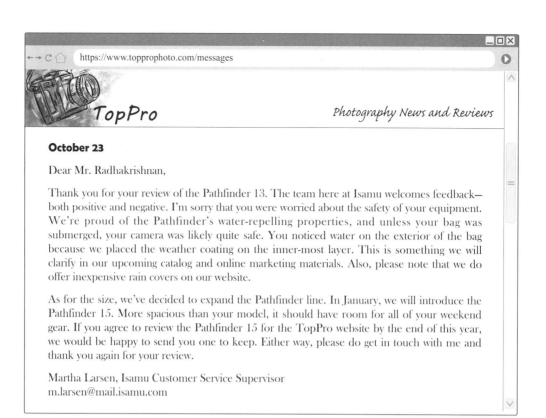

攝影快報與評比

十月二十三日

拉哈克里史南先生鈞鑒：

感謝您對 Pathfinder 13 的評論。我們伊薩姆團隊歡迎反饋，正負面的皆然。很抱歉讓您對器材的安全擔心了。我們對 Pathfinder 的防水性能很自豪，除非您是把包包浸在水裡，否則相機十之八九是相當安全的。您之所以會發現包包外層上有水，是因為我們在最內層上了防水塗料。這是我們會在即將發布的目錄和線上行銷內容中加以澄清的事。另外，請鑒察我們在網站上其實有販售便宜的遮雨罩。

至於大小，我們決定將 Pathfinder 系列加以擴充。一月時我們會推出 Pathfinder 15。它比您的型號要寬敞，應該有空間收納您所有的週末裝備。假如您願意在今年底前在 TopPro 網站評論 Pathfinder 15，我們很樂意寄一組給您留用。無論如何，請務必與我聯繫，並再次感謝您的評論。

伊薩姆客服督導
瑪莎·拉爾森
m.larsen@mail.isamu.com

191 正解 A

What does Mr. Radhakrishnan write about his Pathfinder 13?
(A) It is large enough to use for work.
(B) It was purchased recently.
(C) It caused his camera to get wet.
(D) It is stylish and spacious.

拉哈克里史南先生針對他的 Pathfinder 13 寫了什麼？
(A) 它夠大，足以在工作上使用。
(B) 它是在近期購買的。
(C) 它使他的相機弄濕了。
(D) 它時髦又寬敞。

解析 在評論的第二段中拉哈克里史南先生提到 "As a building inspector, I typically carry a single standard lens. This leaves ample room in the bag for the camera, a few accessories ...."「身為建築檢查員，我通常都會攜帶單一標準鏡頭。這使得包包裡有充裕的空間放相機、一些配件……。」換言之，他認為 Pathfinder 13 夠大，在工作上使用沒有問題，因此本題選 (A)。至於 (B) 說它是最近才買的並不正確，因為拉哈克里史南先生說他的包包已經用了十個月；(C) 說的它讓他的相機弄濕了亦非事實，因為根據拉哈克里史南先生的說法，「器材並未受損」。最後，(D) 中提到的 "spacious"「寬敞的」（與 "ample" 同義）雖屬正確，但 "stylish"「時髦的」則非拉哈克里史南先生之意，而是伊薩姆產品資訊上的用字，因此亦為誤。

• Vocabulary 見下頁

In the review, the word "claims" in paragraph 3, line 1, is closest in meaning to
(A) asserts
(B) admits
(C) demands
(D) realizes

評論第三段第一行的 "claims" 這個字的意思最接近
(A) 堅稱
(B) 承認
(C) 要求
(D) 了解

> 解析 "claim" 指「聲稱」、「宣稱」，很明顯地，與文中 "claims" 意思最相近的應該是選項 (A) asserts「堅稱」。

What does Ms. Larsen offer to Mr. Radhakrishnan?
(A) An inexpensive rain cover
(B) A free catalog
(C) A new camera
(D) A larger bag

拉爾森小姐要提供什麼給拉哈克里史南先生？
(A) 一個便宜的遮雨罩
(B) 一份免費的目錄
(C) 一個新相機
(D) 一只更大的包包

> 解析 在拉爾森小姐之回應的第二段中提到，伊薩姆公司在一月時會推出比 Pathfinder 13 具更大收納空間的 Pathfinder 15。她表示，如果拉哈克里史南先生年底前願意在 TopPro 網站評論 Pathfinder 15 的話，他們公司願意送一組給他留用 (If you agree to review the Pathfinder 15 for the TopPro website by the end of this year, we would be happy to send you one to keep.)，因此正解為 (D)。注意，文中第一段末尾提到的「便宜的遮雨罩」是伊薩姆的販售商品，拉爾森小姐並沒有說要贈送，故不可誤選 (A)。

What must Mr. Radhakrishnan do in order to receive a gift from Ms. Larsen?
(A) Visit a website
(B) Write a review
(C) Call customer service
(D) Return a product

拉哈克里史南先生必須做什麼才會收到拉爾森小姐的贈禮？
(A) 上一個網站
(B) 寫一篇評論
(C) 致電客服
(D) 把一項產品退掉

> 解析 本題考與上一題相關的細節，問拉哈克里史南先生必須做何事才能得到拉爾森小姐的贈禮。由上一題的討論可推知，題目中所提到的 "gift"「禮物」指的就是 Pathfinder 15 包包，而拉爾森小姐也說得非常清楚 "If you agree to review the Pathfinder 15 ... we would ... send you one ...."，所以答案是選項 (B) Write a review。

What does Ms. Larsen indicate about the water-repellent coating?
(A) It is quite safe for customers to use.
(B) It allows a camera to be safely submerged.
(C) It is located on the inside of the bag.
(D) It will be introduced in the coming year.

拉爾森小姐指出了防水塗料的什麼事？
(A) 對顧客而言它在使用上相當安全。
(B) 它可以讓相機安全地浸在水裡。
(C) 它位在包包的內部。
(D) 它將在明年推出。

> 解析 由拉爾森小姐所寫之回應的第一段第五句話 "You noticed water on the exterior of the bag because we placed the weather coating on the inner-most layer."「您之所以會發現包包外層上有水，是因為我們在最內層上了防水塗料。」即可知，正確答案是 (C)。注意，句子裡提到的 "weather coating" 指的就是題目中的 "water-repellent coating"。另，由於文中並無任何與塗料是否安全的相關資訊，因此 (A) 不可選。至於 (B) 說的該塗料「可以讓相機安全地浸在水裡」、(D) 說的該塗料「將在明年推出」二者皆明顯與文中資訊不符，故亦不可選。

Vocabulary

- ☐ **positive** 肯定的；正面的；陽性的　☐ **negative** 否定的；負面的；陰性的　☐ **property** 特性；資產　☐ **submerge** 使沒入水中
- ☐ **inner-most** 最裡面的　☐ **layer** 層　☐ **clarify** 澄清　☐ **spacious** 寬敞的　☐ **room** 房間（可數）；空間（不可數）

Attention All Orchestra Members

I'm thrilled to announce that Fontella Fox will be joining us on stage for our concert on Saturday! The current plan is for Ms. Fox to close the concert with two songs—her recent hit "Look Out" and another song to be announced. I'll work out the song arrangements with Ms. Fox's music director before our rehearsal on Friday. We'll only have that one chance to practice, so be prepared to stay as long as it takes.

This is a wonderful opportunity for us to perform with a talented and versatile pop singer. Let's make the most out of it. In the meantime, please listen to "Look Out" and be ready for anything!

第 196 到 200 題請參照下列公告、電子郵件和文章。

管弦樂團全體團員請注意

我非常高興地宣布,馮泰拉・福克斯將在星期六的音樂會登上舞台加入我們!目前的計畫是,福克斯小姐會以兩首歌(她近期的大作〈當心〉,另一首待宣布)來為音樂會壓軸。在週五的排練之前,我會和福克斯小姐的音樂總監把歌的編曲搞定。我們就只有這一次的機會練習,所以以需要待多久就得待多久,大家都要做好心理準備。

對我們而言,能夠跟一位具有天賦且多才多藝的流行歌手一起演出實在是一個大好機會。我們要充分把握。在此同時,請大家去聽一下〈當心〉並做好萬全的準備!

From:	Gozen Steimer <g.steimer@ffenterprises.com>
To:	Sally Tase <sallytase@greensboroughorch.org>
Subject:	Saturday concert
Date:	Thursday, July 2

Dear Ms. Tase,

It was great talking with you. I just wanted to confirm what we discussed on the phone. Ms. Fox will take the stage after the "William Tell Overture" and immediately perform "Look Out." After the song, you will introduce her, she will greet the audience, and then the show will end with Ms. Fox's performance of "My Oh My."

I've attached sheet music for both songs. You'll probably have to make some adjustments, but I'm sure we can work out any issues when we meet on Friday. Ms. Fox is really looking forward to this event! If you have any questions, please give me a call.

Gozen Steimer
FF Enterprises, Music Director

寄件者:Gozen Steimer <g.steimer@ffenterprises.com>
收件者:Sally Tase <sallytase@greensboroughorch.org>
主 旨:星期六的音樂會
日 期:7 月 2 日星期四

塔瑟女士鈞鑑:

上次與您相談甚歡。我只是想要確認我們在電話中所討論的事。福克斯小姐會在〈威廉泰爾序曲〉後上台,並立刻演出〈當心〉。曲畢之後,您將介紹她,她也會向觀眾致意,然後節目就在福克斯小姐演出〈我的老天〉中畫下句點。

我附上了兩首歌的樂譜。您可能必須做些調整,但我確信我們週五碰面時可以把任何問題都搞定。福克斯小姐十分期待這場盛會!如有任何疑問,煩請來電。

FF 企業音樂總監
葛琴・史泰默

Vocabulary

☐ **orchestra** 管弦樂團　☐ **thrilled** 非常興奮的　☐ **arrangement** 安排;協定;編曲　☐ **rehearsal** 排演;排練　☐ **talented** 有天分的;才華洋溢的
☐ **versatile** 多才多藝的;多功能的　☐ **in the meantime** 在此同時　☐ **confirm** 證實;確認　☐ **take the stage** 登上舞台　☐ **overture** 序曲
☐ **look out** 小心　☐ **sheet music** 樂譜　☐ **issue** 發行;(刊物的)期號;問題　☐ **event** 事件;活動

Surprise Guest at the Bijou

The Greensborough Orchestra ended its season on a high note at the Bijou Concert Hall last night. After a lively two-hour program of French and Italian opera favorites, pop star Fontella Fox took the stage and charmed the audience with a couple of songs from her latest album, *Too Few*. Backed by lush layers of strings, Ms. Fox's voice took on a warmth that is sometimes missing from her studio productions.

The enthusiastic crowd demanded an encore, and Fox returned to the stage with conductor Sally Tase. After a few words with the musicians, Fox and the orchestra launched into "Habanera," the famous aria from Bizet's opera *Carmen*. The crowd responded to Ms. Fox's operatic debut with a standing ovation.

Ms. Tase later confirmed that Saturday was the first time the orchestra played "Habanera" with Ms. Fox. "I knew that Fontella had some classical training, but until that moment on stage, I had no idea she sang opera!" Tase said. "I think the concertgoers really appreciated the spontaneity and sense of adventure she brought to the evening."

—By Marcel Dubois, Music Criti

「珠寶」的驚喜嘉賓

昨晚在珠寶音樂廳，格林斯伯勒管弦樂團精采的演出為本季畫下了完美的句點。在兩個小時動聽的法國和義大利歌劇名曲的演唱之後，流行歌星馮泰拉‧福克斯登上舞台，以她最新專輯《太少》裡的幾首歌擄獲了觀眾們的心。在層層豐沛弦樂的襯托下，福克斯小姐的歌聲展現出在她的錄音製作中有時所欠缺的暖度。

熱情的群眾要求安可曲，福克斯便和指揮莎莉‧塔瑟回到了台上。在跟樂手們說了幾句話後，福克斯和管弦樂團突然端出了比才歌劇《卡門》裡著名的詠嘆調〈哈巴奈拉〉。對於福克斯小姐的歌劇初登場，群眾則以起立鼓掌作為回應。

塔瑟女士事後證實，週六是管弦樂團首次與福克斯小姐演出〈哈巴奈拉〉。「我知道馮泰拉受過一些古典訓練，但直到在台上的那一刻，我都不曉得她會唱歌劇！」塔瑟說。「我想樂迷們都非常欣賞她為當晚所帶來的自發性與冒險感。」

——馬賽爾‧杜柏瓦，樂評

PART 7

196 正解 B

Who most likely posted the notice?
(A) Fontella Fox
(B) Sally Tase
(C) Gozen Steimer
(D) Marcel Dubois

公告最有可能是誰貼出的？
(A) 馮泰拉‧福克斯
(B) 莎莉‧塔瑟
(C) 葛琴‧史泰默
(D) 馬賽爾‧杜柏瓦

解析 公告第一段中提到 "The current plan is for Ms. Fox to close the concert with two songs—her recent hit "Look Out" and another song .... I'll work out the song arrangements with Ms. Fox's music director before ... Friday." 「目前的計畫是，福克斯小姐會以兩首歌……來為音樂會壓軸。在週五……前，我會和福克斯小姐的音樂總監把歌的編曲搞定。」將這些資訊與葛琴‧史泰默寫給莎莉‧塔瑟之電子郵件中第二段提到的 "I've attached sheet music for both songs. You'll probably have to make some adjustments ... we can work out any issues when we meet on Friday." 「我附上了兩首歌的樂譜。您可能必須做些調整……我們週五碰面時可以把任何問題都搞定。」作個對照，不難推斷 (B) 莎莉‧塔瑟即為公告的貼出者。

Vocabulary

☐ **bijou** 珠寶   ☐ **on a high note** 非常成功地（多與 "end"、"begin" 連用）   ☐ **favorite** 最喜愛的人事物   ☐ **lush** 繁茂的；豐富的
☐ **strings** 弦樂器（複數形）   ☐ **take on** 呈現；承擔   ☐ **enthusiastic** 極有興趣的；熱情的   ☐ **demand** 要求   ☐ **encore** 安可曲
☐ **conductor** 指揮；導體   ☐ **launch into** （積極地）展開   ☐ **aria** 詠嘆調   ☐ **operatic** 歌劇的   ☐ **debut** 首次登台   ☐ **ovation** 熱烈鼓掌
☐ **classical** 古典（音樂）的   ☐ **concertgoer** 常參加音樂會者   ☐ **spontaneity** 自發性   ☐ **adventure** 冒險   ☐ **critic** 批評者；評論家

What are orchestra members instructed to do on Friday?
(A) Attend a rehearsal
(B) Announce a new song
(C) Meet with a music critic
(D) Arrive earlier than usual

管弦樂團的團員受指示要在星期五做什麼？
(A) 參加排練
(B) 宣布一首新歌
(C) 與一位樂評見面
(D) 比平常早到

解析　本題考的是「細節」問題。由公告第一段最後兩句話中提到的 "I'll work out the song arrangements ... before our rehearsal on Friday. We'll only have ... one chance to practice, so be prepared to stay as long as it takes."「在週五的排練之前，我會……把歌的編曲搞定。我們就只有……一次的機會練習，所以需要待多久就得待多久，大家都要做好心理準備。」即可知，該管弦樂團的團員星期五必須「參加排練」。選項 (A) 為正解。

What is indicated about the orchestra members?
(A) They are accomplished singers.
(B) They performed an unrehearsed song.
(C) They are fans of Fontella Fox.
(D) They publicized the concert.

文中指出了管弦樂團團員的什麼事？
(A) 他們是有造詣的歌手。
(B) 他們演奏了一首沒有排練過的歌。
(C) 他們是馮泰拉・福克斯的粉絲。
(D) 他們為該場音樂會做了宣傳。

解析　由公告與電子郵件中的資訊可知，在正式演出前該樂團曾演練過〈當心〉和〈我的老天〉這兩首歌。但依照樂評馬賽爾・杜柏瓦的文章，在音樂會中福克斯小姐除了這兩首歌之外，還應觀眾要求唱了一首安可曲──歌劇《卡門》裡的詠嘆調〈哈巴奈拉〉。而杜柏瓦在文章的第三段還提到經樂團指揮塔瑟女士證實，這是該樂團首次與福克斯小姐演出該首歌曲 (Ms. Tase later confirmed that Saturday was the first time the orchestra played "Habanera" with Ms. Fox.)。由此可知，選項 (B) 即為正解。至於其他選項之內容皆無法由文中資訊得到佐證。

What is true about Fontella Fox?
(A) She is a professional opera singer.
(B) She teaches the audience to sing in a variety of styles.
(C) She sang three songs at the concert.
(D) She asked the audience to sing with her.

關於馮泰拉・福克斯的敘述，下列何者為真？
(A) 她是專業的歌劇演唱家。
(B) 她教觀眾以各式各樣的風格來演唱。
(C) 她在音樂會上演唱了三首歌曲。
(D) 她要求觀眾與她同唱。

解析　本題亦為「細節」題。由公告中讚馮泰拉・福克斯是 "talented and versatile pop singer"「具有天賦且多才多藝的流行歌手」及樂評文章中稱她為 "pop star"「流行歌星」來看，選項 (A) 並不正確。而選項 (B) 和 (D) 二者則更明顯為無中生有。正確答案是 (C) She sang three songs at the concert.「她在音樂會上演唱了三首歌曲。」（這三首歌分別是流行曲〈當心〉與〈我的老天〉，以及詠嘆調〈哈巴奈拉〉。）

What does Mr. Dubois indicate about the concert?
(A) The orchestra mostly played unfamiliar songs.
(B) It was the conductor's debut performance.
(C) The audience joined in singing the final song.
(D) It was the first time Fontella Fox sang opera publicly.

杜柏瓦先生指出了音樂會的什麼事？
(A) 該管弦樂團大多演奏不熟悉的歌曲。
(B) 這是該指揮的初登場演出。
(C) 觀眾加入合唱了最後一首歌。
(D) 這是馮泰拉・福克斯首次公開演唱歌劇。

解析　根據杜柏瓦先生在文章第二段最後一句話中提到的 "Ms. Fox's operatic debut"「福克斯小姐的歌劇初登場」可知，福克斯小姐應該是第一次公開演唱歌劇，因此本題選 (D)。而由於杜柏瓦先生的文章中並未提及任何與選項 (A)、(B)、(C) 相關的資訊，故三者皆不可選。

解答總覽

題號	正解	題號	正解	題號	正解	題號	正解	題號	正解
1	B	41	A	81	A	121	A	161	D
2	D	42	B	82	C	122	C	162	C
3	C	43	D	83	A	123	A	163	B
4	A	44	B	84	C	124	D	164	A
5	D	45	C	85	C	125	D	165	C
6	A	46	A	86	C	126	B	166	D
7	C	47	C	87	A	127	A	167	C
8	C	48	A	88	D	128	D	168	B
9	B	49	C	89	B	129	A	169	C
10	A	50	A	90	B	130	C	170	D
11	B	51	B	91	C	131	C	171	C
12	C	52	C	92	C	132	B	172	D
13	B	53	A	93	C	133	D	173	A
14	A	54	D	94	A	134	A	174	C
15	B	55	A	95	A	135	D	175	C
16	A	56	B	96	B	136	A	176	D
17	C	57	B	97	A	137	C	177	D
18	B	58	D	98	D	138	B	178	A
19	A	59	C	99	D	139	D	179	C
20	B	60	B	100	B	140	C	180	B
21	B	61	D	101	B	141	D	181	A
22	C	62	A	102	D	142	A	182	B
23	B	63	C	103	B	143	D	183	D
24	A	64	D	104	B	144	A	184	B
25	C	65	A	105	D	145	C	185	B
26	A	66	D	106	A	146	B	186	B
27	C	67	D	107	C	147	B	187	A
28	C	68	C	108	A	148	D	188	B
29	A	69	D	109	D	149	A	189	D
30	C	70	D	110	C	150	D	190	B
31	C	71	B	111	C	151	B	191	D
32	C	72	B	112	B	152	D	192	A
33	C	73	C	113	D	153	D	193	A
34	D	74	C	114	A	154	C	194	B
35	A	75	B	115	C	155	A	195	C
36	B	76	D	116	A	156	C	196	B
37	A	77	B	117	B	157	A	197	B
38	D	78	D	118	D	158	C	198	C
39	C	79	D	119	B	159	B	199	D
40	C	80	C	120	B	160	C	200	A

1 　正解 B

(A) He's wearing glasses.
(B) He's typing on a keyboard.
(C) He's moving a computer.
(D) He's checking his watch.

(A) 他戴著眼鏡。
(B) 他正在鍵盤上打字。
(C) 他正在搬電腦。
(D) 他正在看手錶。

解析

照片顯示一名男子坐在電腦前工作。由於他並沒有戴眼鏡，因此 (A) 不正確。而因為他是在打字而非搬動電腦，所以 (C) 亦不正確。另，男子雖然戴著手錶，但眼睛是看著螢幕的，因此 (D) 同樣為誤。本題正確答案是 (B)。

2 　正解 D

(A) Pedestrians are crossing the street.
(B) Chairs are stacked up inside the stores.
(C) Bicyclists are riding on the sidewalk.
(D) Trees are growing along the walkway.

(A) 行人正在過街。
(B) 商店裡堆了椅子。
(C) 腳踏車騎士正騎在人行道上。
(D) 樹木沿著走道生長。

解析

照片顯示街道的一邊有些商店，另一邊則種有一些樹，而街道上除了看得到一些行人外，也有一些人坐在一旁戶外的桌椅處。由於行人並不是在過街，因此 (A) 不正確。而照片中看得到的椅子皆置於戶外，故 (B) 為誤。另，照片中的腳踏車全都停放在一旁，因此 (C) 同樣不可選。本題唯一的正確描述為 (D)。

Vocabulary
☐ **stack up** 堆疊

3 　正解 C

(A) She's planting a tree.
(B) She's sweeping the grass.
(C) She's raking the leaves.
(D) She's mowing the lawn.

(A) 她正在種一棵樹。
(B) 她正在把草掃起來。
(C) 她正在耙葉子。
(D) 她正在修剪草坪。

解析

照片顯示一名女子正在用耙子整理落葉。女子明顯並非在種樹，故 (A) 為誤。而女子雖然是站在草地上，可是既不是在掃草，也不是在剪草，所以選項 (B) 與 (D) 皆不正確。正確答案是 (C)。

Vocabulary
☐ **rake** 把⋯⋯耙在一起　☐ **mow** 刈（草坪等的）草

4　正解 A

(A) The doctor is showing someone a brochure.
(B) The doctor is pointing at the woman.
(C) The doctor is signing a piece of paper.
(D) The doctor is drawing a small diagram.

(A) 醫生正拿著一本小冊子給某個人看。
(B) 醫生正指著女子。
(C) 醫生正在一張紙上簽字。
(D) 醫生正在畫一個小型圖解。

照片顯示一位醫師正拿著一本小冊子並指著冊子上的一張圖片給另外一個人看。因為這位醫師並未指著女子，也沒有在簽字，也不是在畫任何東西，所以選項 (B)、(C)、(D) 皆為誤。唯有 (A) 為正確描述。

Vocabulary
☐ **brochure**（資料或廣告）手冊　☐ **diagram** 圖表；圖解

5　正解 D

(A) They're crossing the street.
(B) They're stepping onto the sidewalk.
(C) They're walking on the grass.
(D) They're walking two by two.

(A) 他們正在過街。
(B) 他們正踏上人行道。
(C) 他們正走在草地上。
(D) 他們正兩個兩個地走著。

照片顯示有一群人正以「成雙」的方式走在一條步道上。因為這些人並不是在過街，所以 (A) 不正確。而這些人既非正踏上人行道亦非走在草地上，因此 (B) 與 (C) 同樣為誤。本題應選 (D)。

6　正解 A

(A) There is some equipment on the shelves.
(B) There is a technician next to the sink.
(C) A number of drawers have been left open.
(D) The research area has several small stools.

(A) 架子上有一些器材。
(B) 水槽旁邊有一位技師。
(C) 有幾個抽屜被開著沒關。
(D) 研究區有幾張小凳子。

照片顯示的是一個放了許多電子器材的房間。由於照片中並沒有人，也看不出有水槽，故 (B) 為誤。而房間內所有的抽屜都是關閉的，所以 (C) 亦不正確。另，房間內只看到一張高腳凳，所以 (D) 也不對。四選項中唯一正確的描述為 (A)，因為照片中在架子上的確放了一些器材。

Vocabulary
☐ **technician** 技術人員；技師　☐ **drawer** 抽屜

PART 2

7 正解 C

Are you planning to attend the conference?
(A) Yes, it was well worth the time.
(B) I intend to complete it soon.
(C) I'm not, but Sally will go.

你是否打算參加會議？
(A) 是的，時間花得很值得。
(B) 我想趕快把它弄完。
(C) 我並不打算去，但莎莉會去。

> **解析** 本題為 "Yes-No" 問句，說話者想知道對方是否打算出席會議。選項 (A) 雖然用了 "Yes" 回應，但之後說的 "it was well worth the time"「時間花得很值得」卻答非所問。選項 (B) 同樣不知所云。正確答案是 (C)。注意，回話者雖未直接用 "No" 來回應，但說 "I'm not" 同樣也清楚表明態度。

8 正解 C

Would you rather meet at the warehouse or the factory?
(A) My home is quite close to the office.
(B) They're both fairly new facilities.
(C) It's more convenient for me to visit you.

你寧可在倉庫或是工廠見面？
(A) 我家離辦公室蠻近的。
(B) 這兩個都是相當新的設施。
(C) 我去拜訪你比較方便。

> **解析** 本句雖以助動詞 "Would" 起頭，但在句中卻出現對等連接詞 "or"，也就是說，本句並非 "Yes-No" 問句，而是要聽者做選擇的「二選一」問題。說話者想知道的是對方想在倉庫或是工廠見面。選項 (A) 明顯與原問句不搭軋。選項 (B) 仍是答非所問。至於 (C) 雖然同樣未做出選擇，但回話者卻表示可以去拜訪對方，因此也算是一種合理的回應，故為本題正解。

9 正解 B

Who's in charge of ordering supplies?
(A) Just use the company credit card.
(B) Probably Jeff or Sharon.
(C) I need a new keyboard.

誰負責訂購日常用品？
(A) 用公司的信用卡就行了。
(B) 大概是傑夫或雪倫。
(C) 我需要一個新的鍵盤。

> **解析** 本句是以疑問詞 "Who" 起頭的 "Wh-" 問句，問對方負責採購用品的是誰。選項 (A) 明顯答非所問。選項 (C) 更是不知所云。本題應選 (B)。

10 正解 A

We haven't updated our website in years.
(A) It's not a priority.
(B) I'll download the app.
(C) Probably next January.

我們已經多年沒有更新網站了。
(A) 這並不是優先事項。
(B) 我會下載應用程式。
(C) 很可能是明年一月。

> **解析** 本句為平述句，說話者表示他們已多年未更新網站。針對這樣的說法，選項 (A) 應為最合理的回應。(B) 提到的「下載應用程式」(download the app) 與 (C) 提到的「明年一月」(next January) 明顯與原句內容風馬牛不相及。注意，"app" 應唸成 [æp]，而非 [e]‧[pi]‧[pi]。

11 正解 B

Where does Akiko keep the projector?
(A) She bought it online.
(B) It's next to the printer.
(C) Actually, James took over the project.

亞希子把投影機收在哪？
(A) 她是上網買的。
(B) 在印表機旁邊。
(C) 實際上案子由詹姆斯接手了。

> **解析** 本題是以疑問詞 "Where" 起頭的 "Wh-" 問句，說話者想知道亞希子把投影機收在何處。三選項中只有 (B) 針對問題回答出投影機被置放之處，故為正解。選項 (A) 與 (C) 明顯皆答非所問。注意，"projector"「投影機」與 "project"「企畫案」雖為同源字，但意思相去甚遠。

12 正解 C

Why don't we offer to take Mr. Belzer to lunch?
(A) That's an excellent restaurant.
(B) He appreciated the invitation.
(C) OK, I'll make a reservation.

我們何不請貝澤先生去吃午餐？
(A) 那是家一流的餐館。
(B) 他感謝受邀。
(C) 好，我會去訂位。

 本題表面上是以疑問詞 "Why" 起頭的 "Wh-" 問句，但其實屬於以 "Why don't we" 起始、用來表達委婉建議的一種慣用句法。說話者「提議」邀請貝澤先生吃午餐，選項 (C) 所言顯然為針對此提議唯一合理的回應，選項 (A) 與 (B) 則皆牛頭不對馬嘴。

13 正解 B

Are you responsible for approving the budget?
(A) Yes, moving was significant cost.
(B) No, that's part of Kevin's job.
(C) It was inexpensive and worked very well.

是妳負責審核預算嗎？
(A) 是的，搬遷要耗費可觀的成本。
(B) 不是，那是凱文職務的一部分。
(C) 它不貴而且運作得非常好。

本題為 "Yes-No" 問句，說話者問對方是否負責審核預算。選項 (A) 雖然用了 "Yes" 來回應，但接下來說的 "moving was significant cost"「搬遷要耗費可觀的成本」卻不知所云。選項 (B) 先用 "No" 作回應，跟著則說明「那是凱文職務的一部分」合情合理，故為正解。選項 (C) 則不知所指為何，自然不可選。

14 正解 A

Didn't you lead the sales seminar last May?
(A) I do it every year.
(B) Please, go right ahead.
(C) It was a great bargain.

去年五月的業務研討會不是由妳帶領的嗎？
(A) 每年都是我在帶。
(B) 請自便。
(C) 它非常地划算。

本題以 "Didn't" 起頭，為一否定 "Yes-No" 問句。針對說話者的提問「去年五月的業務研討會是否由對方帶領」，選項 (A) 雖未直接用 "Yes" 來作答，但說 "I do it every year."「每年都是我在帶」當然包括了去年，屬合理回應，故為正解。至於 (B) 與 (C) 則明顯與原問句內容毫不相干。

15 正解 B

What will the training consist of?
(A) It'll be on Monday at nine o'clock.
(B) It's mostly about how to use the new software.
(C) I made a list of all our current customers.

培訓會包含些什麼？
(A) 會在星期一九點的時候。
(B) 主要是關於新的軟體要怎麼用。
(C) 我列出了一份目前我們所有顧客的名單。

本句為以疑問詞 "What" 起頭的 "Wh-" 問句，問培訓會的「內容」。選項 (A) 答的是「時間」，與原問句不搭軋。選項 (C) 亦是牛頭不對馬嘴。正確答案是 (B)。

16 正解 A

I haven't heard back from Harold yet.
(A) Did you ask him to call you?
(B) I'll introduce you to him.
(C) He usually speaks quite loudly.

我還沒收到哈洛德的回覆。
(A) 妳有要他打電話給妳嗎？
(B) 我會把妳介紹給他。
(C) 他講話通常相當大聲。

本題為平述句，說話者表示尚未收到哈洛德的回覆。選項 (A) 所言為合理的回應：因為說話者說哈洛德還沒有給她一個答覆，所以回話者很自然地想知道對方是否有要求哈洛德打電話給她。選項 (B) 則明顯與原句不搭軋，而選項 (C) 同樣不知所云。

17 正解 C

Do you know if Naomi will join the hiring committee?
(A) She would make an excellent employee.
(B) I would if I had a little more time.
(C) She has already declined the offer.

你知不知道直美是否會加入徵才委員會？
(A) 她會是個優秀的員工。
(B) 假如我有多一點的時間，我就會。
(C) 她已經婉拒了邀約。

> 解析 本句為 "Yes-No" 問句，說話者問對方知不知道直美會否加入徵才委員會。選項 (A) 明顯角色錯亂。選項 (B) 亦是「竹蒿套菜刀」，弄錯了主角。本題應選 (C)，回話者間接表達直美並不會加入該委員會。

18 正解 B

Will you have to reschedule your trip?
(A) I would love to visit Hawaii.
(B) That won't be necessary.
(C) I don't have any appointments today.

妳會不會必須重新排定行程？
(A) 我很樂意參訪夏威夷。
(B) 不會有那個必要。
(C) 我今天沒有任何約見。

> 解析 本句亦為 "Yes-No" 問句，說話者問對方是否必須重排行程。選項 (A) 明顯答非所問，選項 (C) 亦未針對提問作回應。正確答案是 (B)，回話者雖未直接說 "No"，但明確表示沒有必要重做安排。

19 正解 A

When is the new Osaka office expected to open?
(A) Sometime in late May or early June.
(B) There's always someone there before nine.
(C) Their original proposal was not accepted.

新的大阪辦事處預計什麼時候開張？
(A) 五月底或六月初的某個時候。
(B) 九點前那裡向來都會有人。
(C) 他們原本的提案未被採納。

> 解析 本句為以疑問詞 "When" 起頭的 "Wh-" 問句，說話者想知道新辦事處預定何時開張。明白指出「何時」的 (A) 即為正解。選項 (B) There's always someone there before nine. 中雖然出現了「九點前」此時間點，但與原問句問的 "When" 毫不相干。選項 (C) 所言則更是不知所云。

20 正解 B

Are we supposed to change our password every month?
(A) I haven't applied.
(B) Not anymore.
(C) It wasn't enclosed.

我們是不是每個月都應該換密碼？
(A) 我尚未申請。
(B) 再也不用了。
(C) 它並沒有被附上。

> 解析 本題同樣為 "Yes-No" 問句，說話者想知道是否該每個月更換密碼。選項 (A) 與 (C) 明顯皆與原問句中提到的「換密碼」扯不上關係，故皆不可選。選項 (B) Not anymore. 雖未直接答 "No"，但說「再也不用了」亦等於告訴對方答案是否定的，故為正解。

21 正解 B

Is it too late to change my reservation?
(A) I'm afraid we only accept cash.
(B) It depends on what we have available.
(C) Yes, I can confirm your booking.

要改訂位是不是太遲了？
(A) 抱歉，我們只接受現金。
(B) 那要看我們還有沒有其他的位子。
(C) 是的，我可以確認您的預約。

> 解析 本題亦為 "Yes-No" 題型。針對說話者的提問，選項 (A) 明顯答非所問。選項 (C) 雖然用了 "Yes" 回應，但接下來說的「我可以確認您的預約」同樣與原問句不搭軋。本題應選 (B) It depends on what we have available.，回話者表示能否改訂位要看還有沒有其他的位子。

22 正解 C

Didn't Martin used to work for that company?
(A) I became accustomed to it eventually.
(B) He graduated four years ago.
(C) No, I think it was Kevin.

馬丁以前不是在那家公司上班嗎？
(A) 我最終變得習慣了。
(B) 他是四年前畢業的。
(C) 不，我想那是凱文。

解析 本句以 "Didn't" 起頭，為一否定 "Yes-No" 問句。針對說話者的提問「馬丁以前是否在那家公司上班」，選項 (A) 說的是自己的情況，與馬丁不相干，自不可選。選項 (B) 中的主詞 "He" 雖可指馬丁，但說他「四年前畢業」與問話者想知道的資訊扯不上關係。正確答案是 (C) No, I think it was Kevin.，回話者除了告訴對方他弄錯了之外，還提供了額外的資訊：以前在那家公司上班的應該是凱文。

23 正解 B

Australia / USA

When do we have to submit the final report?
(A) The first draft is nearly complete.
(B) I'll have to confirm that with Mandy.
(C) Email it to the CEO and cc the general manager.

我們必須在什麼時候交總結報告？
(A) 初稿快要完成了。
(B) 我必須跟曼蒂確認這點。
(C) 用電郵把它寄給執行長，並把副本寄給總經理。

解析 本句為以疑問詞 "When" 起頭的 "Wh-" 問句，說話者想知道何時須交報告。選項 (A) 答的是「初稿」的情況，而問話者問的是「總結報告」的期限，二者毫無交集。(C) 亦未針對報告之期限作出回應。本題應選 (B) I'll have to confirm that with Mandy.，回話者表示時間尚待確認。注意，選項 (C) 中的 "cc" 為 "carbon copy" 之縮寫，意思是「副本」，亦可作動詞用，指「寄副本給（某人）」。

24 正解 A

Where can we set up our equipment?
(A) On the table next to the stage.
(B) Whenever it's convenient for you.
(C) It only takes about an hour.

我們可以把器材架設在哪裡？
(A) 舞台旁邊的桌子上。
(B) 只要你們方便隨時都可以。
(C) 只要花一小時左右。

解析 本題為以疑問詞 "Where" 起頭的 "Wh-" 問句，說話者想知道器材可架設於何處。選項 (A)「舞台旁邊的桌子上」清楚地指出地點，故為正解。選項 (B) 與 (C) 則皆與「時間」有關，明顯未搔到癢處，因此皆不可選。

25 正解 C

Jack inquired about joining the sales team.
(A) I didn't know he played baseball.
(B) He's quite good at finding bargains.
(C) We would be lucky to have him.

傑克詢問了加入業務團隊的事。
(A) 我並不知道他打棒球。
(B) 他很擅長找到便宜貨。
(C) 有他加入的話算我們走運。

解析 本題為一平述句，說話者告知對方傑克曾詢問加入業務團隊一事。(A) 提到的「打棒球」明顯與「加入業務團隊」八竿子打不著。(B) 提到的「擅長找到便宜貨」(good at finding bargains) 也與「加入團隊」扯不上邊。正確答案是 (C)，回話者想表達的是：如果傑克真的能夠加入他們的行列的話就萬幸了。注意，選項 (B) 中的 "bargain" 為名詞，指「便宜貨」；"bargain" 亦可作動詞用，指「討價還價」。

26 正解 A

The vendor wants to renegotiate the contract.
(A) That's not an option.
(B) I'll sign it right now.
(C) They can borrow one from us.

賣方想重新談合約。
(A) 那不是個選項。
(B) 我馬上就簽字。
(C) 他們可以向我們借一個。

解析 本題為平述句，說話者表示賣方欲重新談合約。選項 (B) 所言明顯不合理，因為合約尚未重談，何來簽署的問題。選項 (C) 則完全不知所云，對方要的是重新談判，與借東西毫不相干。正確答案是 (A)，回話者的意思是：重談合約是不可能的事。

第2回完全解析

PART 2

27 正解 C

How often does the copier need servicing?
(A) It makes up to 10,000 copies per day.
(B) The technician will be here this afternoon.
(C) About three or four times a year.

影印機需要多常維修保養？
(A) 它每天能複印多達一萬份。
(B) 技師今天下午會來這兒。
(C) 一年三、四次左右。

> **解析** 本句為以疑問詞 "How" 起始的 "Wh-" 問句，說話者想知道影印機做維修保養的頻率為何。選項 (A) 答的是影印機的「產能」，與原問句不搭軋。選項 (B) 回的是技師來的時間，同樣答非所問。選項 (C) About three or four times a year. 清楚指出影印機維修保養的頻率，故為正解。

28 正解 C

Is Karen still managing the Sleg Gallery?
(A) They're open until seven, I think.
(B) I picked up a few items there last week.
(C) I haven't heard otherwise.

凱倫還在負責管理史雷格畫廊嗎？
(A) 我想他們開到七點。
(B) 我上星期在那裡買了幾件。
(C) 我沒聽說有異。

> **解析** 本題屬 "Yes-No" 題型，說話者問凱倫是否仍在負責管理畫廊。選項 (A) 說的是畫廊的關門時間，答非所問。選項 (B) 所言同樣牛頭不對馬嘴。正確答案是 (C) I haven't heard otherwise.「我沒聽說有異。」回話者的意思當然就是：凱倫仍是該畫廊的管理人。

29 正解 A

Do you know why the package didn't arrive?
(A) We asked the shipping company to investigate.
(B) Because it took almost a week to get here.
(C) For a little more, you can choose express shipping.

你知道包裹為什麼沒送到嗎？
(A) 我們要求貨運公司去調查了。
(B) 因為它過了快一個禮拜才送到這裡。
(C) 多加一點錢，您就能夠選擇快捷貨運。

> **解析** 本句亦為 "Yes-No" 題型。說話者問對方是否知道包裹為何未送到。選項 (B) 所言與原問句完全對不上，因為問話者欲得知的是包裹為什麼「沒」送到，但回話者說的重點卻是它「晚」送到。選項 (C)「多加一點錢，您就能夠選擇快捷貨運。」為尚未發生之事，與未收到包裹扯不上邊。正解為 (A)，回話者雖然沒有直接表示不知道原因，但明確告知問話者他們已經請貨運公司進行調查。

30 正解 C

Could I borrow a power cord for my laptop?
(A) There's an outlet right behind you.
(B) Have you tried turning it off and on again?
(C) Let me see if I can find one.

我能不能借一下筆電的電源線？
(A) 你後面就有個插座。
(B) 你有沒有試試關機重開？
(C) 我來看看是不是能夠找到一條。

> **解析** 同樣也是 "Yes-No" 題。說話者問是否能借用筆電的電源線。選項 (A) 答非所問，而選項 (B) 亦不知所云。本題應選 (C) Let me see if I can find one.「我來看看是不是能夠找到一條。」回話者的意思當然就是：如果找得到電源線便會出借給對方。

31 正解 C

How did you meet Ms. Dubois?
(A) Yes, I'd be happy to introduce you.
(B) We're having lunch together later.
(C) She used to work here.

你是怎麼結識杜布瓦小姐的？
(A) 是的，我很樂意介紹您。
(B) 我們稍後會共進午餐。
(C) 她以前曾在這裡上班。

> **解析** 本題為以疑問詞 "How" 起頭的 "Wh-" 問句，說話者想得知對方是如何結識杜布瓦小姐的。選項 (A) 用了 "Yes" 回應 "Wh-" 問句，明顯為誤。選項 (B) 說的是「稍後」之事，而與杜布瓦小姐結識則「先前」就已發生，時間邏輯不符。正確答案是 (C)「她以前曾在這裡上班。」回話者的意思是，因為兩人曾經一起工作過，所以互相認識。

PART 3

 02-34 ▶ 02-35

M 🇬🇧 W 🇺🇸

Questions 32-34 refer to the following conversation.

第 32 到 34 題請參照下面這段對話。

M: Hi, Terry. Did I miss anything at the meeting this morning?

W: Yes, we got some big news! Starting next month, the hotel is going to start using the guest shuttle to pick up employees at the train station. It's going to make four runs every morning with pick up times at seven, seven-thirty, eight, and eight-thirty.

M: That's great. But what about guests who need to get to the airport then?

W: They'll be given vouchers for a taxi service.

M: Sounds good. I'm definitely going to do that. The city bus is too infrequent.

W: Yeah, they hope this will shorten commute times for everyone. Oh, there are only eight seats, so you have to sign up to reserve the run you want.

男：嗨，特麗。今早的會議上我是不是錯過了什麼？

女：是的，我們獲知一些重大消息！從下個月起，飯店會開始用賓客接駁車在火車站載送員工。接駁車每天早上會跑四趟，載送時間是七點、七點半、八點和八點半。

男：那太好了。可是，需要去機場的賓客呢？

女：他們會得到計程車行抵用券。

男：聽起來不錯。我肯定會去搭。市公車太不密集了。

女：對啊，他們希望這樣能縮短大家的通勤時間。噢，因為只有八個座位，所以你必須去登記才可以預訂你想要的趟次。

---

32 正解 C

Where do the speakers most likely work?
(A) A taxi service
(B) An airport
(C) A hotel
(D) A train station

說話者最有可能是在哪裡工作？
(A) 計程車行
(B) 機場
(C) 飯店
(D) 火車站

解析 本題屬「推論」題。由女子第一次發言時提到的 "... the hotel is going to start using the guest shuttle to pick up employees at the train station."「……飯店會開始用賓客接駁車在火車站載送員工。」以及第三次發言時說的 "... they hope this will shorten commute times for everyone."「……他們希望這樣能縮短大家的通勤時間。」即可推斷，說話者應該是某飯店的員工。

---

33 正解 C

What change does the woman mention?
(A) Employees will start work earlier next month.
(B) Visitors will be met when their flight arrives.
(C) Staff can be picked up at the train station.
(D) The city bus will run more frequently.

女子提到的改變是什麼？
(A) 員工下個月將開始提早上班。
(B) 訪客在班機抵達時會有人接機。
(C) 員工可以在火車站獲得載送。
(D) 市公車會開得更密集。

解析 本題考細節。女子在第一次發言時先告訴男子 "... we got some big news!"「……我們獲知一些重大消息！」接著就提到 "Starting next month, the hotel is going to ... pick up employees at the train station."「從下個月起，飯店會……在火車站載送員工。」由此可確定正解為 (C)。注意，原文中的 "employees" 被以 "staff" 取代。

---

34 正解 D

What must the man provide?
(A) A flight schedule
(B) A bus pass
(C) A taxi voucher
(D) A shuttle reservation

男子必須提供什麼？
(A) 班機時刻表
(B) 公車乘車證
(C) 計程車抵用券
(D) 接駁車的預約

解析 本題亦考細節，問男子必須提供什麼。由女子在對話最後所說的 "... there are only eight seats, so you have to sign up to reserve the run you want."「……因為只有八個座位，所以你必須去登記才可以預訂你想要的趟次。」即可知，本題應選 (D) A shuttle reservation「接駁車的預約」。

Vocabulary

☐ **shuttle** 接駁車　☐ **run** 車班；航班　☐ **voucher** 兌換券；代金券

Questions 35-37 refer to the following conversation.　　　第 35 到 37 題請參照下面這段對話。

W: Theo, could you call Ms. Goldfarb at Pinker Cosmetics? I would do it, but I have to present an award at the sales meeting right now.

M: Sure. What would you like me to tell her?

W: I'm scheduled for a video conference with her Monday afternoon, but the IT department will be updating our computers with new software then. Ask her if she can reschedule it for Monday morning. Ten-thirty would be good for me.

M: No problem. I'll let you know what she says.

女：席歐，你可不可以打電話給品客化妝品的葛德法布小姐？我本來要打，可是我現在必須到業務會議去頒一個獎。

男：當然可以。妳要我告訴她什麼？

女：我排定星期一下午要跟她開視訊會議，但資訊科技部那個時候要用新的軟體來更新我們的電腦。你問她能不能改約星期一早上。我十點半有空。

男：沒問題。我會讓妳知道她怎麼說。

35 正解 A

What does the woman ask the man to do?
(A) Make a call
(B) Send an email
(C) Give a presentation
(D) Join a video conference

女子要求男子做什麼？
(A) 打一通電話
(B) 寄一封電郵
(C) 做一個簡報
(D) 加入一場視訊會議

解析 本題為「細節」題，問女子要求男子做什麼事。女子在對話的一開始就問男子 "Theo, could you call Ms. Goldfarb at Pinker Cosmetics?"「席歐，你可不可以打電話給品客化妝品的葛德法布小姐？」故正解為 (A) Make a call。

36 正解 B

Why is the woman unable to complete the task?
(A) She has to call a colleague.
(B) She has to attend a meeting.
(C) She has a computer problem.
(D) She has to travel for business.

女子為什麼無法完成差事？
(A) 她必須打電話給一位同事。
(B) 她必須出席一場會議。
(C) 她有一個電腦的問題。
(D) 她必須出差。

解析 本題仍為「細節」題，問女子為何無法完成差事。女子在要求男子打電話之後立即做了解釋："I would do it, but I have to present an award at the sales meeting right now."「我本來要打，可是我現在必須到業務會議去頒一個獎。」而正因為她是頒獎人，所以一定得出席該場會議，故本題選 (B) She has to attend a meeting.。

37 正解 A

What will happen on Monday afternoon?
(A) Some software will be installed.
(B) Some awards will be given out.
(C) A video conference will take place.
(D) A meeting will be scheduled.

星期一下午會發生什麼事？
(A) 某種軟體將會被安裝。
(B) 一些獎項將會被頒發。
(C) 有一場視訊會議將會舉行。
(D) 有一場會議將會被排定。

解析 由女子第二次發言時說的 "I'm scheduled for a video conference with her Monday afternoon, but the IT department will be updating our computers with new software then."「我排定星期一下午要跟她開視訊會議，但資訊科技部那個時候要用新的軟體來更新我們的電腦。」即可知，正確答案是 (A) Some software will be installed.。

Vocabulary
☐ **take place** 發生；舉行

M 🇨🇦 W 🇺🇸

Questions 38-40 refer to the following conversation. 　第 38 到 40 題請參照下面這段對話。

M: Hi, I'm having difficulty charging this laptop that I bought here. At first, I thought the power cord might be damaged so I bought a new one. It didn't help at all.

W: Has the computer suffered any water damage? Was it dropped?

M: No. It's just been sitting on my desk since I purchased it last year.

W: OK. I'm going to remove the battery and install a new one. I'm fairly confident that will solve the problem.

男：嗨，我在替這台在這裡買的筆電充電的時候，遇到了困難。起初我以為或許是電源線受損，所以就買了一條新的，但絲毫無濟於事。

女：電腦有沒有受到任何水損？有沒有摔到？

男：沒有。自從去年購買以來，它就一直只是擺在我的書桌上。

女：好。我會把電池拿掉，裝一個新的。我相當有把握這樣就可以解決問題。

38 正解 D

What is the man's problem?
(A) He cannot find a place to charge his laptop.
(B) His device suffered some water damage.
(C) He was overcharged for a product.
(D) His computer is not functioning properly.

男子的問題是什麼？
(A) 他找不到地方替筆電充電。
(B) 他的裝置受到一些水損。
(C) 他買的產品被多收了錢。
(D) 他的電腦無法正常運作。

解析 本題屬「細節」題，問男子的問題為何。男子一開頭就告知女子他碰到了什麼問題："... I'm having difficulty charging this laptop that I bought here."「……我在替這台在這裡買的筆電充電的時候，遇到了困難。」選項 (D) 所述即為正解。

39 正解 C

What does the woman ask the man about?
(A) When the computer was purchased
(B) Who most recently used the device
(C) Whether the computer had been damaged
(D) What steps he took to solve the problem

女子詢問了男子什麼事？
(A) 電腦是什麼時候購買的
(B) 最近誰用過該裝置
(C) 電腦是否曾受損
(D) 他採取了什麼步驟以解決問題

解析 本題亦考細節。女子第一次發言時即問男子 "Has the computer suffered any water damage? Was it dropped?"「電腦有沒有受到任何水損？有沒有摔到？」因此本題選 (C) Whether the computer had been damaged。

40 正解 C

What does the woman offer to do?
(A) Refund the purchase
(B) Repair the power cord
(C) Replace a component
(D) Return the device

女子提議要做什麼？
(A) 退回購置物品的款項
(B) 修理電源線
(C) 替換一個零件
(D) 退回該裝置

解析 本題仍為「細節」題。由女子第二次發言時所說的 "I'm going to remove the battery and install a new one."「我會把電池拿掉，裝一個新的。」即可知，正確答案是 (C)「替換一個零件」。

第 2 回完全解析

PART 3

Vocabulary
☐ **confident** 自信的；有信心的

173

Questions 41-43 refer to the following conversation. | 第 41 到 43 題請參照下面這段對話。

W: Good morning, you've reached customer service at the Playa Hospitality Group. How may I help you?

M: Hello. I've just received my credit card bill and I think I've been incorrectly charged for my stay at the Playa Resort in Long Beach last month. I had a reservation for a standard room but because the shower was broken, the manager kindly upgraded me to an ocean-view suite and gave me a coupon for the dinner buffet. She told me there would be no additional charges, but these were added to my bill.

W: I understand. If you give me your name, the dates of your stay, and your contact information, I'll confirm that with the manager and adjust your bill according to our policy. I'll update you with the details as soon as I can.

女：早安，這裡是普拉雅餐旅集團客服部。有什麼可以為您效勞的嗎？

男：妳好。我剛剛收到信用卡帳單；我認為我上個月在長灘普拉雅度假村的住宿收費有誤。我訂的是標準房，但因為淋浴壞了，所以經理好心幫我升級到海景套房，並給了我一張自助晚餐的折價券。她跟我說不會有額外的收費，可是這些卻被加進了我的帳單裡。

女：了解。請告知大名、住宿日期和聯絡資料，我會跟經理確認，並根據我們公司的政策來調整您的帳單。我會盡快向您回報詳情。

41 正解 A

Where does the woman most likely work? | 女子最有可能是在哪裡工作？
(A) At a hotel chain | (A) 連鎖飯店
(B) At a credit card company | (B) 信用卡公司
(C) At a restaurant | (C) 餐館
(D) At a travel agency | (D) 旅行社

解析 本題屬「推論」題。由女子第一次發言時所說的兩句話："Good morning, you've reached customer service at the Playa Hospitality Group. How may I help you?"「早安，這裡是普拉雅餐旅集團客服部。有什麼可以為您效勞的嗎？」即可推斷，女子應該是在一家連鎖飯店服務。正確答案是 (A)。

42 正解 B

Why is the man calling? | 男子為什麼打電話？
(A) To complain about an employee | (A) 為了投訴某位員工
(B) To dispute a charge | (B) 為了收費提出質疑
(C) To request an upgrade | (C) 為了要求升級
(D) To cancel a reservation | (D) 為了取消預約

解析 本題屬「細節」題，問男子為何來電。男子在發言時先是告訴對方 "... I think I've been incorrectly charged for my stay at the Playa Resort ...."「……我認為我……在……普拉雅度假村的住宿收費有誤。」接著便說明他如何地被錯誤收費："I had a reservation for a standard room but because the shower was broken, the manager kindly upgraded me ... and gave me a coupon .... She told me there would be no additional charges, but these were added to my bill."「我訂的是標準房，但因為淋浴壞了，所以經理好心幫我升級……並給了我一張……折價券。她跟我說不會有額外的收費，可是這些卻被加進了我的帳單裡。」由此可知，男子之所以打這通電話是因為收費問題而向對方提出質疑。故本題選 (B)。

43 正解 D

What does the woman say she will do next? | 女子說她接下來會做什麼？
(A) Repair some fixtures | (A) 修理一些固定裝置
(B) Update a policy | (B) 更新某項政策
(C) Provide a full refund | (C) 提供全額退款
(D) Contact the manager | (D) 與經理聯絡

解析 由女子第二次發言時所說的 "If you give me your name, the dates of your stay, and your contact information, I'll confirm that with the manager ...."「請告知大名、住宿日期和聯絡資料，我會跟經理確認……。」即可知，本題應選 (D) Contact the manager。

Vocabulary

□ **dispute** 爭執

Questions 44-46 refer to the following conversation.

W: How's the website redesign going, Kevin?

M: The desktop version looks great, but I'm having trouble making it display correctly on mobile devices. Every time I fix one page, something on a different page breaks.

W: I see. Well, the food and beverage fair is just a month away, and it has to be done before then.

M: I could probably create a separate mobile-only site in time.

W: I don't think we want to be responsible for maintaining two versions of the website. Let's outsource the job to a web design company. That would also give you more time to start planning long-term projects like the database upgrade.

第 44 到 46 題請參照下面這段對話。

女：網站的重新設計進行得如何，凱文？

男：桌面版看起來很棒，但要讓它正確地顯示在行動裝置上卻碰到了麻煩。每次我把一頁修好，不同頁面上的東西就掛掉。

女：了解。嗯，餐飲博覽會再一個月就到了，在那之前必須把它搞定。

男：我大概趕得及另外製作一個只限行動裝置使用的網站。

女：我不認為我們應該負責維護兩個不同版本的網站。我們把工作外包給網頁設計公司吧。這樣你也會有比較多的時間開始規劃像資料庫升級那樣長期的案子。

44　正解 B

What is the company planning to do next month?
(A) Create a mobile-friendly website
(B) Participate in a product expo
(C) Outsource a design project
(D) Upgrade the company database

該公司正在計畫下個月要做什麼？
(A) 製作方便行動裝置使用的網站
(B) 參加一個產品展覽會
(C) 將設計案外包出去
(D) 將公司的資料庫升級

> 解析　女子在第二次發言時提到 "... the food and beverage fair is just a month away, and it has to be done before then." 「……餐飲博覽會再一個月就到了，在那之前必須把它搞定。」（本句中的 "it" 「它」指的是女子先前提到的 "the website redesign" 「網站的重新設計」。）由此可推斷，女子的公司下個月將參加該餐飲博覽會。故本題選 (B)。注意，原文中的 "fair" 被以 "expo" 取代，而 "expo" 實為 "exposition" 「展覽會」、「博覽會」之縮寫。

45　正解 C

What problem does the man mention?
(A) He doesn't have time for long-term projects.
(B) Database queries do not work on mobile devices.
(C) Webpages are not displaying correctly.
(D) There is no time to build a mobile-only website.

男子提及什麼問題？
(A) 他沒時間做長期的案子。
(B) 無法在行動裝置上做資料庫查詢。
(C) 網頁無法正確顯示。
(D) 沒時間建立一個限行動裝置使用的網站。

> 解析　本題考細節，問男子提及什麼問題。男子在回應女子的問題時表示 "... I'm having trouble making it display correctly on mobile devices." 「……要讓它正確地顯示在行動裝置上卻碰到了麻煩。」（本句中的 "it" 「它」指的是女子發問時提到的 "the website redesign" 「網站的重新設計」。）由此即可知，正確答案是 (C) Webpages are not displaying correctly. 「網頁無法正確顯示。」

46　正解 A

What does the woman suggest?
(A) Using a professional designer
(B) Making a mobile-only website
(C) Contracting out website maintenance
(D) Hiring a project manager

女子建議做什麼？
(A) 找個專業設計業者
(B) 做出一個限行動裝置使用的網站
(C) 把網站的維護承包出去
(D) 聘請一位專案經理

> 解析　本題仍考細節，問女子建議做什麼。女子在第三次發言時明白表示 "Let's outsource the job to a web design company." 「我們把工作外包給網頁設計公司吧。」也就是說，她認為公司網站的重新設計應該找外面的專業人士來做，故正解為 (A) Using a professional designer。

Vocabulary

☐ **mobile-friendly** 方便行動裝置使用的

MP3 02-40

Questions 47-49 refer to the following conversation.

第 47 到 49 題請參照下面這段對話。

M: Hello, I read in the newspaper that the team is selling rows of seats before the stadium is demolished next month. Are there any still available?

W: Yeah, are you kidding? There are thousands of them.

M: Great. I'd like to reserve two rows of six seats, please.

W: I'm sorry, that's not how it works. Just show up at the stadium during regular business hours and pick out the seats you want. A supervisor will quote you a price. You can take it or leave it.

M: I see. *(pause)* Can I have the seats delivered?

W: Sir, if you want them, you'll need your own truck to haul them away.

男：妳好，我在報紙上看到說，球隊要在球場下個月拆掉之前把成排座椅賣掉。現在還有剩的可買嗎？

女：有啊，你是在開玩笑嗎？有好幾千排耶。

男：太好了。我想預訂兩排六個座位的，麻煩妳。

女：抱歉，我們的排椅不是這樣賣的。你在平常的營業時間直接過來球場，把想要的排椅挑出來。管理人會跟你報一個價錢。你要就買，不要就算了。

男：了解。那我要的排椅可以幫我送嗎？

女：先生，如果你想要那些座椅，就必須自備卡車來把它們運走。

47 正解 C

What does the woman say about the stadium seats?
(A) There is a waiting list for people wanting to purchase them.
(B) Prices for them are listed in the newspaper.
(C) There are a large number of them available.
(D) They are given away during regular business hours.

關於球場的座椅女子說了什麼？
(A) 有一張欲購人士的等候名單。
(B) 價錢刊登在報紙上。
(C) 有大量的座椅可供購買。
(D) 它們在平常的營業時間會免費贈送。

解析　男子想知道球場的座椅是否還有剩下的可以買。針對此問題女子回應道："... are you kidding? There are thousands of them."「……你是在開玩笑嗎？有好幾千排耶。」言下之意當然就是座椅還多得很，故本題選 (C) There are a large number of them available.。

48 正解 A

What does the woman tell the man to do?
(A) Visit the stadium
(B) Purchase a ticket
(C) Suggest a price
(D) Rent a truck

女子告訴男子要做什麼？
(A) 親自到球場
(B) 購買一張票
(C) 建議一個價錢
(D) 租一輛卡車

解析　在男子知道還有座椅可買之後立即向女子預定兩排，但女子卻跟男子說 "... that's not how it works. Just show up at the stadium ... and pick out the seats you want."「……我們的排椅不是這樣賣的。你……直接過來球場，把想要的排椅挑出來。」換言之，男子必須親自到球場去才能買到排椅。正確答案是 (A) Visit the stadium。

49 正解 C

What does the woman imply when she says, "take it or leave it"?
(A) The stadium closes at the end of the day.
(B) The man needs to arrange delivery.
(C) The price is not negotiable.
(D) The seats can be picked up later.

當女子說 "take it or leave it" 時是在暗示什麼？
(A) 球場會在一天結束的時候關閉。
(B) 男子需要安排送貨。
(C) 價錢沒得商量。
(D) 座椅可以事後領取。

解析　本題考詞句解釋。在對話中，女子先是告訴男子 "A supervisor will quote you a price."「管理人會跟你報一個價錢。」接著便說 "You can take it or leave it."「你要就買，不要就算了。」女子未直接說出口的就是「沒有討價還價的空間」。選項 (C) 敘述正確，故為正解。

Vocabulary

☐ **stadium** 體育場　☐ **quote** 報價　☐ **haul** 拖拉（重物）

M 🇬🇧 W 🇺🇸

Questions 50-52 refer to the following conversation.

W: It's not going to be easy to replace Harry Dent. I mean, there aren't too many people who are willing to cover the evening and weekend shifts.

M: I've been thinking about that. The job can be performed remotely, so we could try to recruit people living in Sydney, Taipei, or Tokyo. For them, it would be a normal daytime shift.

W: I never considered that. How would we go about doing that?

M: Let me talk it over with Jill in HR. I'm sure she would have some ideas.

第 50 到 52 題請參照下面這段對話。

女：哈利‧鄧特將不容易被取代。我的意思是，沒有太多人會願意值晚間和週末班。

男：我一直在想這件事。這個工作能遠距執行，所以我們可以試著招募住在雪梨、台北或東京的人。對他們來說，這算是正常的日班。

女：我從來沒考慮過這點。我們要如何著手進行？

男：讓我跟人資部的吉兒討論一下。我確信她會有一些想法。

50 正解 A

What are the speakers discussing?
(A) Recruiting a new employee
(B) Managing an international project
(C) Preparing for a worldwide expansion
(D) Attracting a global clientele

說話者在討論什麼？
(A) 招募新員工
(B) 管理國際專案
(C) 為向全世界擴展做準備
(D) 吸引全球客戶

> 解析 本題屬「推論」題，問說話者在討論什麼。女子一開始就說 "It's not going to be easy to replace Harry Dent."「哈利‧鄧特將不容易被取代。」男子回應道："... we could try to recruit people living in Sydney, Taipei, or Tokyo."「……我們可以試著招募住在雪梨、台北或東京的人。」對此，女子則詢問 "How would we go about doing that?"「我們要如何著手進行？」由以上的對談可推斷，他們正在討論招聘一位新員工之事，故本題選 (A)。

51 正解 B

What does the man say staff should be able to do?
(A) Speak a foreign language
(B) Work remotely
(C) Handle evening shifts
(D) Travel frequently

男子說員工應該能做什麼？
(A) 說外語
(B) 遠距工作
(C) 應付晚班
(D) 頻繁出差

> 解析 本題考細節。女子認為哈利‧鄧特不易被取代的原因是 "... there aren't too many people who are willing to cover the evening and weekend shifts."「……沒有太多人會願意值晚間和週末班。」針對這點，男子的回應是 "The job can be performed remotely ...."「這個工作能遠距執行……。」換句話說，男子認為員工應該能夠 (B) Work remotely「遠距工作」。

52 正解 C

What does the man suggest?
(A) Hiring Harry Dent
(B) Working on weekends
(C) Consulting a colleague
(D) Traveling to Asia

男子暗示了什麼？
(A) 雇用亨利‧鄧特
(B) 在週末上班
(C) 請教一位同事
(D) 到亞洲出差

> 解析 本題同樣為「推論」題。對於女子所問的「我們要如何著手進行？」此問題，男子並未直接給出答案，而是跟對方說 "Let me talk it over with Jill in HR. I'm sure she would have some ideas."「讓我跟人資部的吉兒討論一下。我確信她會有一些想法。」換言之，男子明顯地在暗示，他會去徵詢一位人資部同仁的意見。因此，正解為 (C)。注意，原文中的 "HR" 為 "human resources" 的縮寫。

Vocabulary
☐ **shift** 輪班　☐ **recruit** 招募　☐ **clientele** 顧客；客戶

Questions 53-55 refer to the following conversation.

第 53 到 55 題請參照下面這段對話。

M: That was an amazing tour. Five restaurants in three hours. I can't believe how much I ate, and how delicious everything was.

W: I'm glad you had a good time. And you know, besides food tours our company also offers architectural tours, historical tours, and there's even a canoe tour through the harbor.

M: I didn't know that. I have friends visiting next weekend. I bet they'd love the history tour. Is there one scheduled for Saturday?

W: Oh, our history expert is out of town for a few weeks. But you know, I've been on that tour a hundred times and I know the route. If you want to book a private tour, I would be happy to show you all around.

M: That sounds great. My friends are going to love it.

男：那真是個令人開心的行程。三小時跑五家餐館。我不敢相信自己吃了那麼多，而每樣東西都那麼好吃。

女：很高興您玩得很愉快。您知道嗎？除了美食行程外，本公司還推出建築行程、歷史行程，甚至是穿越港口的獨木舟行程。

男：這點我倒不知道。我下個週末會有朋友來訪。我打賭他們一定會很喜歡歷史行程。有排在星期六的嗎？

女：噢，我們的歷史專家正好出城幾週。但您知道嗎，我跟過那個行程上百次，而且知道路線。如果您想預訂一個私人行程的話，我很樂意帶你們四處看看。

男：聽起來很棒，我的朋友會很喜歡。

---

53 正解 A

What kind of tour was just completed?
(A) A food tour
(B) An architectural tour
(C) A historical tour
(D) A boat tour

剛被完成的是哪一種行程？
(A) 美食行程
(B) 建築行程
(C) 歷史行程
(D) 遊船行程

解析 本題屬「細節」題，問剛被完成的是哪一種行程。由男子在對話一開始所講的 "That was an amazing tour. Five restaurants in three hours. I can't believe how much I ate, and how delicious everything was."「那真是個令人開心的行程。三小時跑五家餐館。我不敢相信自己吃了那麼多，而每樣東西都那麼好吃。」即可知，正解為 (A)「美食行程」。

---

54 正解 D

What does the man inquire about?
(A) The types of outings offered
(B) The cost of a private tour
(C) The preferences of a friend
(D) The availability of an activity

男子詢問了什麼事？
(A) 被推出的出遊類型
(B) 私人行程的費用
(C) 某位朋友的偏好
(D) 某項活動的檔期

解析 本題考點落在「細節」部分。在男子聽了女子介紹他們公司所推出的各種行程後，隨即告訴女子他下個週末會有朋友來訪，而他認為他的朋友們很喜歡歷史行程，因此便問女子 "Is there one scheduled for Saturday?"「有排在星期六的『歷史行程』嗎？」由此可知，本題應選 (D)「某項活動的檔期」。

---

55 正解 A

What will the woman most likely do on Saturday?
(A) Lead a historical tour
(B) Canoe through the harbor
(C) Learn a new tour route
(D) Travel out of town

女子週六最有可能會做什麼？
(A) 帶領一趟歷史行程
(B) 划獨木舟穿越港口
(C) 認識一個新的行程路線
(D) 出城旅遊

解析 本題屬「推論」題。在女子知道男子想為朋友安排歷史行程之後，便告訴男子他們的歷史專家正好不在城內，但她本身也熟悉該行程之路線，因此自我推薦，表示願意帶男子與其友人四處看看。而由男子對此的回應 "That sounds great. My friends are going to love it."「聽起來很棒，我的朋友會很喜歡。」即可推斷，正確選項是 (A)。

Vocabulary

☐ **canoe** 獨木舟

Questions 56-58 refer to the following conversation.

M: Michelle! You're smiling! You landed the contract, didn't you?

W: We did it! Our company is now responsible for creating the entire Fargo Outfitters brand identity—website, product packaging, even business cards. And it wouldn't have happened without those amazing logo prototypes that you designed.

M: I really appreciate that, but it really was a team effort.

W: You know, this calls for a celebration. Could you ask around and see if everyone is available after work? Maybe we could try that new Japanese restaurant around the corner.

M: I'll do that and let you know.

第 56 到 58 題請參照下面這段對話。

男：蜜雪兒！妳在笑！妳拿到合約了，對吧？

女：我們辦到了！我們公司現在要負責打造法果服裝的整個品牌識別——網站、產品包裝，甚至是名片。而如果沒有你設計的那些令人驚豔的商標原型的話，這一切就不會發生。

男：很感謝妳這麼說，不過這其實是團隊的努力。

女：你知道嗎，這需要慶祝一下。你能不能四處問問，看大家下班後有沒有空？也許我們可以試試轉角附近那家新的日本餐廳。

男：我會問一下大家然後通知妳。

---

56 正解 B

What has the woman recently accomplished?
(A) She was promoted to manager.
(B) She secured a large contract.
(C) She designed a new logo.
(D) She launched a new company.

女子最近達成了什麼？
(A) 她被升為經理了。
(B) 她獲得了一份大合約。
(C) 她設計了一個新商標。
(D) 她成立了一家新公司。

> **解析** 由男子第一次發言時所說的 "Michelle! ... You landed the contract, didn't you?"「蜜雪兒！……妳拿到合約了，對吧？」以及女子的回應 "We did it! Our company is now responsible for creating the entire Fargo Outfitters brand identity ...."「我們辦到了！我們公司現在要負責打造法果服裝的整個品牌識別……。」即可知，本題應選 (B) She secured a large contract.。注意，原文中的 "landed" 與選項 (B) 中的 "secured" 同義，皆指「取得」、「獲得」。

---

57 正解 B

What does the man mean when he says, "I really appreciate that"?
(A) He is glad that Fargo Outfitters likes his design.
(B) He is grateful for the woman's acknowledgement.
(C) He is thankful for the team's hard work.
(D) He enjoys the process of creating logos.

男子所說的 "I really appreciate that" 是什麼意思？
(A) 他很高興法果服裝喜歡他的設計。
(B) 他很感謝女子對他的肯定。
(C) 他很謝謝團隊的努力。
(D) 他很享受創作商標的過程。

> **解析** 本題考點為詞句解釋。一般而言，"appreciate" 這個字可作「欣賞」或「感謝」解。在本對話中，"I really appreciate that" 這句話是男子在聽到女子對他的讚賞（"... it wouldn't have happened without those amazing logo prototypes that you designed."「……如果沒有你設計的那些令人驚豔的商標原型的話，這一切就不會發生。」）之後所說的。由前後文意可知，男子之所以會說這句話應該是想表示 (B) He is grateful for the woman's acknowledgement.「他很感謝女子對他的肯定。」

---

58 正解 D

What does the woman ask the man to do?
(A) Make a reservation
(B) Host a ceremony
(C) Schedule some overtime
(D) Contact some colleagues

女子要求男子做什麼？
(A) 訂位
(B) 主持一場典禮
(C) 排定一些加班時間
(D) 與一些同事聯繫

> **解析** 本題屬「細節」題，問女子要求男子做什麼。女子在第二次發言時說 "... this calls for a celebration. Could you ask around and see if everyone is available after work?"「……這需要慶祝一下。你能不能四處問問，看大家下班後有沒有空？」因此，正確答案是 (D) Contact some colleagues「與一些同事聯繫」。

Vocabulary

☐ **brand identity** 品牌識別   ☐ **secure** 獲得

第 2 回完全解析

PART 3

Questions 59-61 refer to the following conversation with three speakers.

M1: You two remember that our department is responsible for organizing the company picnic this year, right?

W: Yes, but doesn't the sales team usually handle that?

M2: They've done it for the past few years, but Ms. Tenner hasn't been happy with how they managed it. She's noticed that employees aren't very excited about attending.

W: What does she have in mind?

M1: She didn't offer any specific suggestions. She just asked us to come up with some activities by the end of the week. We're scheduled to brief her at three-thirty Friday afternoon.

M2: That's not a lot of time. We'd better get started.

第 59 到 61 題請參照下面這段三人對話。

男1：你們兩個還記得我們部門要負責籌辦公司今年的野餐，對吧？

女：是的，不過這通常不是業務團隊在處理的嗎？

男2：過去幾年都是由他們負責，但他們的表現坦納小姐並不滿意。她發現員工們並沒有非常樂意參加。

女：她有什麼想法？

男1：她並沒有給任何明確的建議。她只是要我們在週末前想出一些活動。我們排定要在星期五下午三點半向她簡報。

男2：這樣我們可沒多少時間。我們最好開始動起來。

59　正解 C

What are the speakers mainly discussing?
(A) A sales seminar
(B) A department merger
(C) A company event
(D) A meeting schedule

說話者主要是在討論什麼？
(A) 一場業務研討會
(B) 一項部門的合併
(C) 一場公司的活動
(D) 一個會議時程

> **解析** 本題屬「推論」題，問說話者主要是在討論什麼。第一名男子一開始就提到 "... our department is responsible for organizing the company picnic this year ..."「……我們部門要負責籌辦公司今年的野餐……」接著三人雖然論及前幾年的狀況，但重點還是在討論今年該如何辦好活動。而由第二名男子最後所說的 "We'd better get started."「我們最好開始動起來。」更可確定，本題應選 (C) A company event。

60　正解 B

Who most likely is Ms. Tenner?
(A) The head of sales
(B) The speakers' supervisor
(C) An event organizer
(D) A corporate caterer

坦納小姐最有可能是什麼人？
(A) 業務部主管
(B) 說話者的上司
(C) 活動的籌辦人
(D) 企業外燴業者

> **解析** 本題亦屬「推論」題，問坦納小姐最有可能是什麼人。第二名男子第一次發言時先是提到坦納小姐對過去幾年所舉辦的野餐並不滿意，於是女子便表示想知道坦納小姐有何想法。第一名男子則回應說坦納小姐並未給明確建議，反倒是要他們自己想出一些活動。而由第一名男子所說的最後一句話 "We're scheduled to brief her at three-thirty Friday afternoon."「我們排定要在星期五下午三點半向她簡報。」可確定，坦納小姐為三人的上司。

61　正解 D

What do the speakers need to do by Friday?
(A) Organize a meeting
(B) Submit a report
(C) Prepare a picnic
(D) Suggest some ideas

說話者在星期五之前需要做什麼？
(A) 籌辦一場會議
(B) 提交一份報告
(C) 準備一場野餐
(D) 建議一些構想

> **解析** 本題仍屬「推論」題，問說話者在週五前需要做什麼。如上題解析中提到的，坦納小姐並未針對今年的野餐給出明確建議，反倒是要求他們想出一些活動 (She didn't offer any specific suggestions. She just asked us to come up with some activities ....)。而由於說話者必須在星期五向坦納小姐簡報，因此可斷定，他們在星期五之前需要先有一些構想，故正解為 (D) Suggest some ideas。

Vocabulary
☐ **brief** 做簡報

Questions 62-64 refer to the following conversation and advertisement.

W: Hi, Benjamin. I'm looking at the ad you just designed for us, and I just have a couple of comments. First of all, there are two t's in Coletta.

M: Oh, how embarrassing. I'll correct that right away. What was the other thing?

W: Well, the image you used is what we call a pedestal fan. Because we specialize in ceiling fans, I'm worried the ad might be misleading.

M: It's no trouble to change the image. I wonder if you could email me a list of the companies you work with. Many manufacturers make images of their products available for marketing purposes.

W: Oh, well, you can find that information on our website. Just click on the "partners" link.

第 62 到 64 題請參照下列對話和廣告。

女：嗨，班傑明。我正在看你剛為我們設計的廣告，我只有兩點評論。首先，"Coletta" 裡面有兩個 "t"。

男：噢，真尷尬。我馬上就把它改過來。另一件事是什麼？

女：嗯，你所用的圖片是我們所謂的落地扇。因為我們專做吊扇，所以我擔心廣告或許會使人誤解。

男：改圖片並不麻煩。不知道妳能不能把跟妳合作的公司名單用電郵寄給我。很多廠商都會為了行銷的目的而把產品的圖片刊登出來。

女：噢，嗯，你在我們的網站上就能找到那些資訊。只要點選 "partners" 的連結就行了。

Coleta 風扇公司
與我們共事輕鬆如風！

五月份來店購買任何產品
皆可獲贈免費的手持式風扇

1435 Ridge Rd., Mountain Gap, CO　(970) 555-6893

62　正解 A

Look at the graphic. According to the woman, which information is incorrect?
(A) The name of the company
(B) The advertising slogan
(C) The terms of the offer
(D) The location of the business

請看圖表。根據女子所言，哪一項資訊不正確？
(A) 公司名稱
(B) 廣告標語
(C) 要約條款
(D) 商號地點

> **解析** 女子在第一次發言時提到 "... there are two t's in Coletta." 「……"Coletta" 裡面有兩個 "t"。」而廣告中在 "Fan Co." 前寫的是 "Coleta"，也就是，明顯少了一個 "t"，因此本題選 (A) The name of the company「公司名稱」。

63　正解 C

What does the woman say she is concerned about?
(A) Misleading manufacturers
(B) Bothering the designer
(C) Confusing customers
(D) Misinforming retailers

女子說她擔憂什麼事？
(A) 誤導廠商
(B) 打擾設計人員
(C) 使顧客困惑
(D) 向零售商提供錯誤訊息

> **解析** 由女子第二次發言時所說的 "... the image you used is what we call a pedestal fan. Because we specialize in ceiling fans, I'm worried the ad might be misleading."「……你所用的圖片是我們所謂的落地扇。因為我們專做吊扇，所以我擔心廣告或許會使人誤解。」即可知，本題應選 (C)。注意，選項 (A) 雖然使用了原文中的 "misleading"「誤導」、「使人誤解」這個字，但對象不對，不可誤選。

64　正解 D

What does the man ask the woman to do?
(A) Visit a website
(B) Contact a manufacturer
(C) Return a call
(D) Email a list

男子要求女子做什麼？
(A) 上一個網站
(B) 聯絡一個廠商
(C) 回一通電話
(D) 用電郵寄一份名單

> **解析** 由男子第二次發言時所說的 "I wonder if you could email me a list of the companies you work with."「不知道妳能不能把跟妳合作的公司名單用電郵寄給我。」可知，選項 (D) 即為正解。

Vocabulary

☐ **pedestal** 底座　☐ **misleading** 使人誤解的

Questions 65-67 refer to the following conversation and floor plan.

W: Excuse me, are you with Ottumwa Technologies?

M: Yes, you're in the right place.

W: I'm glad I was able to find your booth. I can't believe how many different companies are recruiting candidates here today.

M: Well, the newspaper says it's the biggest fair of its kind. What position are you interested in?

W: Your website said you have openings for technical sales engineers.

M: That's right. We've reserved a meeting room where you can have a cup of coffee and fill out an application. Just take the elevator to the fourth floor. It's the first room on the right as you exit the elevator.

W: I'll do that. Thank you very much.

第 65 到 67 題請參照下列對話和樓層圖。

女：不好意思，請問你們是奧塔姆瓦科技嗎？

男：是的，妳來對地方了。

女：真高興能找到你們的攤位。我不敢相信今天有這麼多不同的公司在這裡招募人選。

男：嗯，報紙上說這是此種博覽會中最大的。妳對什麼職位有興趣？

女：你們的網站上說你們有技術業務工程師的職缺。

男：沒錯。我們訂了一間會議室，妳可以去喝杯咖啡並填寫應徵表。只要搭電梯到四樓，出電梯的右邊第一間就是。

女：我會的。非常謝謝你。

---

65 正解 A

Where most likely are the speakers?
(A) At a job fair
(B) At a technology conference
(C) At a sales seminar
(D) At a coffee shop

說話者最有可能在哪裡？
(A) 就業博覽會
(B) 科技大會
(C) 業務研討會
(D) 咖啡館

> 解析　本題屬「推論」題。由女子第二次發言時所說的 "I'm glad I was able to find your booth. I can't believe how many different companies are recruiting candidates here today."「真高興能找到你們的攤位。我不敢相信今天有這麼多不同的公司在這裡招募人選。」及男子的回應 "Well, the newspaper says it's the biggest fair of its kind."「嗯，報紙上說這是此種博覽會中最大的。」即可斷定正解為 (A)。

---

66 正解 D

How did the woman learn about the position?
(A) From a recruiter
(B) From a newspaper ad
(C) From a candidate
(D) From a website

女子是如何得知有職缺的？
(A) 從一位招募人員那兒
(B) 從報紙廣告上
(C) 從一位應徵者那兒
(D) 從一個網站上

> 解析　本題考點落在「細節」部分。男子在第二次發言時問女子 "What position are you interested in?"「妳對什麼職位有興趣？」而由女子的回答 "Your website said you have openings for technical sales engineers."「你們的網站上說你們有技術業務工程師的職缺。」即可知，女子是從網站上獲得職缺訊息的。

---

67 正解 D

Look at the graphic. Which room will the woman go to next?
(A) The Pomelo Room   (C) The Papaya Room
(B) The Guava Room   (D) The Mango Room

請看圖表。女子接下來會去哪個房間？
(A) 柚子室   (C) 木瓜室
(B) 番石榴室   (D) 芒果室

> 解析　男子在第三次發言時先是提到他們公司在四樓訂了一間會議室，女子可前去喝杯咖啡並填寫應徵表格。接著便跟女子說 "Just take the elevator to the fourth floor. It's the first room on the right as you exit the elevator."「只要搭電梯到四樓，出電梯的右邊第一間就是。」而由四樓會議室的圖示可知，出電梯右手邊的第一間會議室為 (D)「芒果室」。

Vocabulary

☐ **booth** 隔間　☐ **candidate** 求職者；候選人

Questions 68-70 refer to the following conversation and graph.

第 68 到 70 題請參照下列對話和圖表。

M: At every annual sales conference, I ask the salesperson of the year to join me on stage to share a few tips with us. This year, it's Kate Stern. Welcome, Kate!

W: Thank you, Mr. Chen.

M: For a long time, your team reported average results. This year we saw a huge improvement. What happened?

W: We changed the way we did things. Every customer who comes in now interacts with at least three people: a greeter, a sales representative, and a manager. Previously, it was just one.

M: And that's all it took?

W: Well, we also decided to split all sales commissions and bonuses equally. It created a wonderful cooperative atmosphere. We don't have the largest volume of sales—I think that's Hamstead—but on a per capita basis, we do better than anyone.

男：在每次的年度銷售大會上，我都會請年度最佳銷售員上台來跟我們分享幾個秘訣。今年的得獎人是凱特・史騰。歡迎妳，凱特！

女：謝謝您，陳先生。

男：很久以來，貴團隊一直都成績平平。今年我們則看到了巨大的進步。發生了什麼事？

女：我們改變了做事的方式。現在每一位來店的顧客至少都會跟三個人互動：接待員、銷售代表和經理。原先則只有一個人。

男：就只是這樣嗎？

女：嗯，我們還決定把所有的銷售佣金和獎金平均分配。如此一來便打造出一個非常棒的合作氣氛。我們的銷售額並不是最大——我想那是漢姆斯特德——但以人均來算，我們的表現比任何人都好。

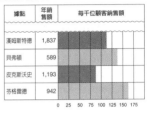

68　正解 C

Why is the woman speaking with the man?
(A) To report some figures
(B) To receive a bonus
(C) To offer some advice
(D) To recruit a salesperson

女子為什麼會在跟男子說話？
(A) 為了報告一些數據
(B) 為了領取一份獎金
(C) 為了提供一些建言
(D) 為了招募一位銷售人員

> 解析　本題屬「推論」題，問女子為何會在跟男子說話。男子在對話的一開始就邀請女子上台分享她的成功秘訣 (... I ask the salesperson of the year to join me on stage to share a few tips with us.)。接著在二人的一問一答中，女子則分析了自己與團隊之所以成功的幾個關鍵。由此可斷定，女子與男子談話的原因是 (C)「為了提供一些建言」。

69　正解 D

What happened recently at Kate Stern's location?
(A) A sales conference was held.
(B) A commission was formed.
(C) Some salespeople were promoted.
(D) Some procedures were improved.

凱特・史騰所服務的據點最近發生了什麼事？
(A) 舉行了一場銷售大會。
(B) 成立了一個委員會。
(C) 晉升了一些銷售人員。
(D) 改善了一些程序。

> 解析　男子在第二次發言時問女子為何她的團隊今年能得到不同以往的好成績，女子回應道："We changed the way we did things. Every customer who comes in now interacts with at least three people: a greeter, a sales representative, and a manager. Previously, it was just one."「我們改變了做事的方式。現在每一位來店的顧客至少都會跟三個人互動：接待員、銷售代表和經理。原先則只有一個人。」換言之，女子（凱特・史騰）所服務的據點最近改善了一些作業上的程序。

70　正解 D

Look at the graphic. Which location does Kate Stern most likely work at?
(A) Hamstead
(B) Beaverton
(C) Picsworth
(D) Fenglade

請看圖表。凱特・史騰最有可能是在哪一個據點服務？
(A) 漢姆斯特德
(B) 貝弗頓
(C) 皮克斯沃史
(D) 芬格雷德

> 解析　女子（凱特・史騰）在對話的最後提及 "We don't have the largest volume of sales ... but on a per capita basis, we do better than anyone."「我們的銷售額並不是最大……但以人均來算，我們的表現比任何人都好。」而依圖表所示，每千位顧客銷售額最高的據點為芬格雷德。若以人均的方式來計算，芬格雷德當然還是銷售額最高的據點，因此本題選 (D)。

Vocabulary
- **greeter** 接待員　- **sales commission** 銷售佣金　- **per capita** 按人計算的

第2回完全解析　PART 3

PART 4

Questions 71-73 refer to the following news report.

第 71 到 73 題請參照下面這則新聞報導。

I'm Heather Poe and you're listening to KQCC radio news. Today I'm reporting from the site of a newly opened wind power project in Murdock City. Because wind turbines can be quite loud, some local residents had opposed the wind farm. In response, city officials required builders to keep turbines at least 2,000 feet from homes, schools, and businesses. The Murdock Power Company estimates that the farm will meet forty percent of the city's energy needs, a figure that could double if a proposed expansion is approved. Those plans are currently available for public review and comment at Murdock Power dot com.

我是希瑟‧波，您現在正在收聽 KQCC 廣播新聞。記者今天是在莫達克市新啓用的風力發電廠為各位做報導。由於風力渦輪時而會發出相當大的噪音，有些本地居民是反對風場的。為了回應反對的聲浪，市府官員要求建商必須將渦輪架設於離住家、學校和商號至少兩千英呎以上的地方。莫達克電力公司估計，該場將能滿足該市四成的電力需求，而如果一項擴張的提案能獲准的話，數字便能翻倍。這些計畫目前已公布在莫達克電力的網站上供大眾審視和評論。

71 正解 B

Where is the speaker reporting from?
(A) A radio station
(B) A wind farm
(C) A government office
(D) A local residence

說話者是在哪裡做報導？
(A) 廣播電台
(B) 風場
(C) 政府機關
(D) 當地的住家

> 解析　本題考細節，問說話者是在何處做報導。由報導的第二句話 "Today I'm reporting from the site of a newly opened wind power project in Murdock City."「記者今天是在莫達克市新啓用的風力發電廠為各位做報導。」即可知，正確答案是 (B)。注意，原文中的 "the site of a ... wind power project" 之字面翻譯為「一個……風力計畫的地點」，而其真正指的即是「風力發電廠」，亦即「風場」。

72 正解 B

What does the speaker imply when she says, "city officials required builders to keep turbines at least 2,000 feet from homes, schools, and businesses"?
(A) A requirement was rescinded.
(B) A concern was addressed.
(C) A project was proposed.
(D) A request was rejected.

當說話者說 "city officials required builders to keep turbines at least 2,000 feet from homes, schools, and businesses" 時是在暗示什麼？
(A) 有一項要求被取消。
(B) 有一個憂慮獲得了因應。
(C) 有一個專案被提出。
(D) 有一項請求遭到駁回。

> 解析　說話者在報導中先提到，因為渦輪時而發出很大的噪音，所以有些居民反對風場 (Because wind turbines can be quite loud, some local residents had opposed the wind farm.)。而由說話者緊接著所使用的轉折詞 "In response"「作為對……的回應」即可斷定，說話者所說的 "city officials required builders to keep turbines at least 2,000 feet from homes, schools, and businesses"「市府官員要求建商必須將渦輪架設於離住家、學校和商號至少兩千英呎以上的地方」就是當地政府針對某些居民的憂慮所做出的因應措施。

73 正解 C

What can listeners do on a website?
(A) Purchase renewable energy
(B) Read a news report
(C) Review a proposal
(D) Sign up for a plan

聽眾可以在某個網站上做什麼？
(A) 購買再生能源
(B) 閱讀新聞報導
(C) 審視一項提案
(D) 連署一項計畫

> 解析　說話者在報導的倒數第二句中提及 "... the farm will meet forty percent of the city's energy needs, a figure that could double if a proposed expansion is approved."「……該〔風〕場將能滿足該市四成的電力需求，而如果一項擴張的提案能獲准的話，數字便能翻倍。」而由報導的最後一句話 "Those plans are currently available for public review and comment at Murdock Power dot com."「這些計畫目前已公布在莫達克電力的網站上供大眾審視和評論。」即可知，正解為 (C)。

Vocabulary

☐ **turbine** 渦輪　☐ **oppose** 反對　☐ **wind farm** 風電廠　☐ **estimate** 估計　☐ **rescind** 取消；撤回　☐ **address** 處理；應對
☐ **renewable** 可再生的　☐ **sign up** 報名參加

Questions 74-76 refer to the following announcement.

第 74 到 76 題請參照下面這段宣告。

OK everyone, if there aren't any other questions, we'll end the training session here. You're now up-to-date on several advanced network security tools and practices, which I hope you will implement at your workplaces. If you want to explore this issue in even greater depth, I encourage you to buy my book. In fact, I brought a few copies with me today. Oh, and please remember that you can now register online for my next seminar, which covers mobile device security. Check out my website for the details.

好了，各位，假如沒有其他任何問題，訓練課程就到此為止。幾項最新的進階網路安全工具和作業各位都已經有所掌握，希望你們能夠確實應用在職場上。如果想對這個課題做更深的探討，建議各位買我的書。事實上，我今天就帶了幾本來。噢，請不要忘記你們現在可以上網報名參加我的下一場研討會了，內容談的是行動裝置的安全。詳情參考我的網站。

74 正解 C

Who most likely are the listeners?
(A) Training professionals
(B) Website developers
(C) Computer security specialists
(D) Publishing company representatives

聽者最有可能是什麼人？
(A) 培訓專業人員
(B) 網站開發人員
(C) 電腦安全專家
(D) 出版公司代表

> 解析 本題屬「推論」題。由宣告的第二句話 "You're now up-to-date on several advanced network security tools and practices, which I hope you will implement at your workplaces."「幾項最新的進階網路安全工具和作業各位都已經有所掌握，希望你們能夠確實應用在職場上。」可推知，聽者應該是一群專門處理電腦安全的人士，因此本題選 (C)。

75 正解 B

What does the speaker imply when he says, "I brought a few copies with me today"?
(A) He prepared copies of his presentation.
(B) A book is available for purchase.
(C) Participants will have to share the materials.
(D) His lecture notes are incomplete.

當說話者說 "I brought a few copies with me today" 時是在暗示什麼？
(A) 他準備了幾份簡報的副本。
(B) 有本書可供購買。
(C) 參加者必須共用素材。
(D) 他上課的講義並不完整。

> 解析 本題考點為詞句含意。說話者在說 "I brought a few copies with me today" 之前先提到 "... I encourage you to buy my book."「……建議各位買我的書。」接著則先使用了 "In fact"「事實上」作為轉折詞，才說 "I brought a few copies with me today"「我今天就帶了幾本來。」說話者明顯是在「暗示」聽者他的書可現場購買，故正解為 (B)。

76 正解 D

What does the speaker remind listeners about?
(A) A book on mobile devices
(B) An implementation strategy
(C) A course on network security
(D) An upcoming seminar

說話者提醒了聽者什麼？
(A) 一本談行動裝置的書
(B) 一個施行策略
(C) 一個網路安全課程
(D) 一場即將到來的研討會

> 解析 本題考細節。由說話者在倒數第二句中提到的 "... please remember that you can now register online for my next seminar ...."「……請不要忘記你們現在可以上網報名參加我的下一場研討會了……。」即可知，正確答案是 (D)。

Vocabulary

□ **implement** 實施；執行 □ **explore** 探索；探究 □ **lecture** 授課；講座 □ **implementation** 施行；實踐

Questions 77-79 refer to the following telephone message.　第 77 到 79 題請參照下面這段電話留言。

Hello, I'm calling from Upper Crust City Tours about the tour itinerary you booked on our website. That would be a really large group, so I wanted to confirm the number with you before organizing the transportation and food. For tours of that size we have to make special arrangements. For example, we would prepurchase tickets for the art museum and arrange for several docents to be available. And because the restaurant you chose cannot accommodate a group of that size, I'd like to suggest a different location. I've already emailed a revised itinerary to you. Please take a look at it, and call me back before four-thirty on May 1 to discuss the details. My name is Victor and the number here is 664-7665.	您好，我是從上流社會都市遊覽打過來的，想跟您討論您在我們的網站上所預約的遊覽行程。那樣的話將會是真的好大一個團，所以我想在籌劃交通和餐飲前跟您確認人數。對於人數這麼多的遊覽行程，我們都必須做特別的安排。例如，我們會預購藝術館的門票，並預先多安排幾位導覽員。而且由於您所選擇的餐廳容納不了這麼多人的團體，我想建議一個不同的地方。我已經把修訂過的行程用電郵寄給您了。麻煩您看一下，並在五月一日四點半前回電給我以便討論細節。我叫維多，這裡的號碼是 664-7665。

77　正解 B

What does the speaker imply when he says, "That would be a really large group"?	當說話者說 "That would be a really large group" 時是在暗示什麼？
(A) The company cannot accommodate so many people.	(A) 該公司容納不了這麼多人。
(B) The number of guests provided may be incorrect.	(B) 所提供的賓客人數或許不正確。
(C) The person booking should choose a different activity.	(C) 做預約的人應選擇不同的活動。
(D) The tour may have to be cancelled or postponed.	(D) 該遊覽行程或許必須取消或延期。

> 解析　本題考詞句含意。由題目句後半部分的 "so I wanted to confirm the number with you ...."「所以我想……跟您確認人數。」可推知，說話者說 "That would be a really large group"「那樣的話將會是真的好大一個團」的時候心裡應該是在懷疑該團的人數是否真的有那麼多。選項 (B)「所提供的賓客人數或許不正確。」故為正解。

78　正解 D

What does the speaker say he has changed?	說話者說他更改了什麼？
(A) The date and time of the tour	(A) 遊覽的日期與時間
(B) The location of departure	(B) 出發地點
(C) The type of museum to be visited	(C) 所要參觀的博物館類型
(D) The place where the guests will dine	(D) 賓客將會用餐的地方

> 解析　本題為「細節」題。說話者在留言的第五句中提到 "... the restaurant you chose cannot accommodate a group of that size, I'd like to suggest a different location."「……您所選擇的餐廳容納不了這麼多人的團體，我想建議一個不同的地方。」接著就說 "I've already emailed a revised itinerary to you."「我已經把修訂過的行程用電郵寄給您了。」換言之，說話者已經更改了 (D)「賓客將會用餐的地方」。

79　正解 D

What did the speaker send to the listener?	說話者寄了什麼給聽者？
(A) A museum catalog	(A) 一份博物館的目錄
(B) A preliminary contract	(B) 一份初步的合約
(C) A restaurant reservation	(C) 一家餐廳的訂位
(D) An alternate itinerary	(D) 一個替換的行程

> 解析　本題同為「細節」題。在上題的解析中已提到，說話者告訴聽者 "I've already emailed a revised itinerary to you."，因此本題選 (D)「一個替換的行程」。注意，由於原本的行程已「被修訂」，故新行程屬「替換」之行程。

Vocabulary

☐ **upper crust** 上流社會　☐ **itinerary** 旅遊行程　☐ **docent**（博物館、藝廊等的）導覽員　☐ **accommodate** 容納；提供（某人）住宿
☐ **dine** 用餐　☐ **alternate** 交替的；供替換的

MP3 02-52

Questions 80-82 refer to the following excerpt from a meeting.　　第 80 到 82 題請參照下面這段會議摘錄。

Good afternoon. I'm glad that both the user experience and the technical communication teams are here. As you know, since the launch of version 3.0 of the app, those of us in customer support have been receiving ten times our normal volume of calls and emails. Users are simply baffled by the new interface. The software engineers have told me that reverting to the previous version is impossible, so we have to educate our users on how to use the new version. We're already updating our documentation, but that's not going to be enough. I want you to come up with a plan for an interactive tutorial—something that guides users step by step through the different features of the app. More and more people are deleting the app every day, so time is of the essence.

午安。很高興用戶體驗和技術通訊的團隊都在場。誠如各位所知，3.0 版的應用程式從推出以來，我們這些顧客支援部的人所接到的電話和電郵量是正常的十倍。用戶簡直被新的介面搞得頭昏腦脹。軟體工程師們告訴我，要回頭使用原先的版本是不可能的，所以我們必須教育用戶，告訴他們新版要怎麼用。我們已經在更新使用說明，但這並不夠。我要各位訂定出一個互動式教學指南的計畫──一個能夠一步一步引導用戶將應用程式的不同性能從頭到尾弄清楚的東西。每天把我們的應用程式刪除的人愈來愈多，所以時間是關鍵。

80　正解 C

What part of the company does the speaker most likely work in?
(A) User experience
(B) Technical communication
(C) Customer support
(D) Software engineering

說話者最有可能是在公司的哪一個部門服務？
(A) 用戶體驗
(B) 技術通訊
(C) 顧客支援
(D) 軟體工程

解析　由摘錄的第二句話 "I'm glad that both the user experience and the technical communication teams are here." 「很高興用戶體驗和技術通訊的團隊都在場。」以及第三句中提到的 "those of us in customer support" 「我們這些顧客支援部的人」與第五句的 "The software engineers have told me" 「軟體工程師們告訴我」可合理推斷，說話者所服務的部門應該是 (C) 「顧客支援」。

81　正解 A

What are the customers' mostly complaining about?
(A) The interface is confusing.
(B) The manual is out of date.
(C) The new version is overpriced.
(D) The app is difficult to delete.

顧客主要在抱怨什麼？
(A) 介面令人困惑。
(B) 手冊已經過時。
(C) 新版定價過高。
(D) 應用程式難以刪除。

解析　由說話者在第三句話中所提到的 "... those of us in customer support have been receiving ten times our normal volume of calls and emails." 「……我們這些顧客支援部的人所接到的電話和電郵量是正常的十倍。」及第四句話 "Users are simply baffled by the new interface." 「用戶簡直被新的介面搞得頭昏腦脹。」即可知，顧客們主要是在抱怨 (A) 「介面令人困惑。」注意，原文中的 "baffled" 可用 "confused" 代換，而選項 (A) 中的 "confusing" 則相當於 "baffling"。

82　正解 C

What task does the speaker assign to the listeners?
(A) Conducting customer research
(B) Writing new product documentation
(C) Developing an interactive tutorial
(D) Adding new features to the app

說話者指派給聽者的工作是什麼？
(A) 做顧客研究
(B) 寫新的產品使用說明
(C) 研究出一個互動式教學指南
(D) 為應用程式增添新功能

解析　本題考細節，問說話者指派給聽者的工作為何。由摘錄的倒數第二句話中提及的 "I want you to come up with a plan for an interactive tutorial ...." 可知，說話者希望聽者想辦法研究出一個互動式的教學指南，故本題選 (C)。

Vocabulary

☐ **launch** 發行；投入市場　☐ **baffle** 使困惑　☐ **revert** 回復（原狀）　☐ **documentation**（電腦設備或軟體的）使用說明
☐ **come up with** 想出；提出（計畫、解決方法等）　☐ **interactive** 互動的　☐ **tutorial** 指導手冊；使用指南　☐ **of the essence** 極為重要的
☐ **manual** 使用手冊　☐ **overpriced** 定價過高的

第 2 回完全解析

PART 4

Questions 83-85 refer to the following telephone message.

第 83 到 85 題請參照下面這段電話留言。

Hi, this is Charlotte. I came across your ad for a laptop and I have a few questions about it. I'm OK with the price you listed, and the specifications seem fine for my needs, but you didn't mention how old it is. If you've had it for more than two or three years, I wouldn't be interested. Also, you said you planned to mail it to the purchaser, but if you're anywhere in the Gold Coast area, I'd rather come and get in person. It would save on the shipping and I'd like to test it out before purchasing. Again, my name is Charlotte and you can reach me at 5579-1969.

嗨,我叫夏洛特。我無意間看到你的筆電廣告,我有幾個相關的疑問。對於你所列的價格我沒意見,而且規格看起來也符合我的需要,但你沒有提到你使用了多久。假如你已經擁有它超過了兩、三年,我就不會有興趣了。另外,你說你打算把它郵寄給買家,但如果你是在黃金海岸地區的任何一處,我寧可親自過來拿。這樣可以省下運費,而且我想在購買前先測試一下。再說一遍,我叫夏洛特,打 5579-1969 就能聯絡到我。

83 正解 A

Why is the speaker calling?
(A) To inquire about an advertisement
(B) To suggest a cheaper shipping method
(C) To negotiate a lower price
(D) To find out the listener's location

說話者為什麼打電話?
(A) 為了詢問與一則廣告相關的問題
(B) 為了建議一個較便宜的運送方法
(C) 為了談出一個較低的價格
(D) 為了查出聽者的所在地點

解析 本題考點落在「細節」部分,問說話者為何致電。由留言的第二句話 "I came across your ad for a laptop and I have a few questions about it."「我無意間看到你的筆電廣告,我有幾個相關的疑問。」即可知,正確答案是 (A) To inquire about an advertisement。

84 正解 C

What does the speaker say she is concerned about?
(A) The selling price
(B) The specifications
(C) The age of the item
(D) The time of delivery

說話者說她擔憂什麼?
(A) 售價
(B) 規格
(C) 物件的機齡
(D) 交貨時間

解析 本題同屬「細節」題,問說話者的擔憂為何。說話者在留言的第三句中先是表示她對於該筆電的價錢與規格都可以接受,但接著卻說 "... but you didn't mention how old it is."「……但你沒有提到你使用了多久。」而由下一句話 "If you've had it for more than two or three years, I wouldn't be interested."「假如你已經擁有它超過了兩、三年,我就不會有興趣了。」則可確定,說話者非常在意該筆電的機齡,故正解為 (C) The age of the item。

85 正解 C

What does the speaker offer to do?
(A) Pay for delivery
(B) Contact the seller
(C) Pick up an item
(D) Take an exam

說話者提議要做什麼?
(A) 支付運費
(B) 聯絡賣家
(C) 提取貨品
(D) 參加考試

解析 說話者在留言的第五句中先是提到賣方打算用郵寄的方式把筆電寄給買家,但說話者卻跟對方表示 "... if you're anywhere in the Gold Coast area, I'd rather come and get in person."「……如果你是在黃金海岸地區的任何一處,我寧可親自過來拿。」由此可知,本題應選 (C) Pick up an item。

Vocabulary

☐ **in person** 親自　☐ **shipping** 運輸　☐ **negotiate** 協商;洽談　☐ **pick up** 提取

Questions 86-88 refer to the following excerpt from a meeting.

第 86 到 88 題請參照下面這段會議摘錄。

Before we end the meeting, I'd like to say a few words about Bob Fletcher. After six years with us at Westington, Bob will be moving to Singapore for his wife's work. Bob was hired to work as an engineer on the Enex Controller but quickly distinguished himself as a team leader. He went on to manage the product engineering department and recruited many of the people sitting here today. He will be sorely missed. Bob has told me he doesn't want a big farewell party, but some of us will get together with him in the break room on Friday at five o'clock for an informal send-off. Drinks and snacks will be provided and everyone is invited.

在我們結束會議之前，我談一談包伯‧弗萊契。在威斯汀頓與我們共處了六年後，包伯即將因為太太的工作而搬去新加坡。包伯當初受雇來擔任伊涅克斯控制器的工程師，但很快地就脫穎而出成了團隊領導人。接著他就執掌了產品製作部，並招聘了許多今天在座的人。他將會備受懷念。包伯跟我說他並不希望有盛大的歡送會，但星期五的五點，我們有些人會跟他在休息室聚一聚，當作非正式的餞別。屆時會提供飲料和點心，歡迎每個人都來參加。

86　正解 C

What is the purpose of the announcement?
(A) To introduce a colleague
(B) To discuss a job opening
(C) To acknowledge a coworker
(D) To plan for a retirement

這段宣告的目的是什麼？
(A) 為了介紹同事
(B) 為了討論職缺
(C) 為了向同仁致意
(D) 為了退休擬定計畫

> 解析　本題屬「推論」題。由第一句話中提到的 "... I'd like to say a few words about Bob Fletcher." 「……我談一談包伯‧弗萊契。」以及接著對此人進公司服務後的優異表現之讚揚來推斷，此段宣告的目的應該是 (C) To acknowledge a coworker「為了向同仁致意」。

87　正解 A

What was Bob Fletcher hired to do?
(A) Engineer a product
(B) Lead a team
(C) Manage a department
(D) Recruit a staff member

包伯‧弗萊契當初受雇來做什麼工作？
(A) 設計製作產品
(B) 帶領團隊
(C) 掌管部門
(D) 招聘職員

> 解析　本題屬「細節」題。由說話者在第三句話中所說的 "Bob was hired to work as an engineer on the Enex Controller ...."「包伯當初受雇來擔任伊涅克斯控制器的工程師……。」即可知，正確答案是 (A) Engineer a product「設計製作產品」。注意，原文中的 "engineer"「工程師」在選項 (A) 中作動詞用，指「設計」、「建造」。

88　正解 D

What does the speaker encourage the listeners to do?
(A) Suggest a replacement
(B) Organize a party
(C) Prepare some snacks
(D) Attend a gathering

說話者鼓勵聽者做什麼？
(A) 建議代替品
(B) 籌辦宴會
(C) 準備一些點心
(D) 出席聚會

> 解析　本題亦屬「細節」題。說話者在談話末尾提及星期五的五點在休息室會有一個非正式的送別會。而由最後一句話 "Drinks and snacks will be provided and everyone is invited."「屆時會提供飲料和點心，歡迎每個人都來參加。」即可知，正解為 (D) Attend a gathering「出席聚會」。

Vocabulary
☐ **distinguish** 使顯出特色；使傑出　☐ **sorely** 非常地　☐ **informal** 非正式的　☐ **send-off** 送別會　☐ **replacement** 替代的人或物

第 2 回完全解析　PART 4

Questions 89-91 refer to the following broadcast.

第 89 到 91 題請參照下面這段廣播。

Thank you for listening to Really Random Radio, the world's most eclectic Internet radio station. From Brazilian bossa nova to zesty Zydeco, we only play what you're not expecting. In fact, for the next twenty-four hours, our entire playlist will be decided by you—our listeners. Visit our website and type an artist and song into the request box. You won't hear the most popular choices. Instead, we'll randomly play songs from among the requests we receive. But first, after this short commercial break, stay tuned for an interview with hip-hop legend Walter Mac. Walt will answer that eternal question: What comes first—the lyrics or the music? Don't miss it.

謝謝收聽真隨機廣播電台——世界上最多元化的網路廣播電台。從巴西的巴薩諾瓦爵士樂到熱情洋溢的柴迪科舞曲，我們只播放各位所料想不到的音樂。事實上，在接下來的二十四小時裡，我們的整個播放曲目將由您——我們的聽眾——來決定。請上我們的網站，在點播框裡輸入藝人和歌曲的名稱。各位不會聽到那些最受歡迎的曲子。各位將聽到的是我們從所收到的點播中隨機播放的歌。但首先，在這段簡短的廣告時間後，請接著收聽嘻哈傳奇瓦特‧麥克的專訪。瓦特將回答這個永遠存在的問題：哪個先有——歌詞還是旋律？別錯過了。

89 正解 B

According to the speaker, what is a special feature of the radio station?
(A) It is commercial free.
(B) It plays many kinds of music.
(C) It is owned by the listeners.
(D) It only plays requests.

根據說話者所言，此廣播電台的特色是什麼？
(A) 它沒有廣告。
(B) 它播放許多種類的音樂。
(C) 它是聽眾所擁有的。
(D) 它只播放點播歌曲。

解析 本題為「細節」題，問根據說話者所言，此廣播電台的特色為何。由廣播的第一句話 "Thank you for listening to Really Random Radio, the world's most eclectic Internet radio station."「謝謝收聽真隨機廣播電台——世界上最多元化的網路廣播電台。」可知，此電台所播放的音樂不拘一格，五花八門。因此本題選 (B) It plays many kinds of music.。

90 正解 B

What does the speaker tell the listeners they can do?
(A) Call the station
(B) Visit a website
(C) Ask a question
(D) Request an interview

說話者告訴聽眾說他們能做什麼？
(A) 打電話到電台
(B) 上一個網站
(C) 發問
(D) 要求做訪談

解析 本題亦考細節。說話者在第三句話中先是提到，在接下來的二十四小時內所播放的曲目將由聽眾來決定。接著便說 "Visit our website and type an artist and song into the request box."「請上我們的網站，在點播框裡輸入藝人和歌曲的名稱。」由此可知，選項 (B) Visit a website 即為正解。

91 正解 C

What will Walter Mac be discussing?
(A) The history of hip-hop
(B) An upcoming concert
(C) His song writing process
(D) The inspiration for a new song

瓦特‧麥克將會討論什麼？
(A) 嘻哈的歷史
(B) 即將到來的演唱會
(C) 他寫歌的過程
(D) 新歌的靈感

解析 本題屬「推論」題。說話者在廣播末尾先是要聽眾收聽瓦特‧麥克的專訪，接著則提到 "Walt will answer that eternal question: What comes first—the lyrics or the music?"「瓦特將回答這個永遠存在的問題：哪個先有——歌詞還是旋律？」換句話說，瓦特‧麥克在專訪中應該會論及他個人創作歌曲的過程。因此本題選 (C) His song writing process.。

Vocabulary

☐ **random** 隨機的　☐ **eclectic** 兼容並蓄的；五花八門的　☐ **zesty** 熱情洋溢的　☐ **request** 點播　☐ **commercial**（電視、廣播中的）廣告　☐ **legend** 傳奇　☐ **eternal** 永恆的；永存的　☐ **lyrics** 歌詞（複數形）　☐ **inspiration** 靈感

Questions 92-94 refer to the following announcement.　　第 92 到 94 題請參照下面這段宣告。

Hello. As the head of the IT department, I'm responsible for the security and stability of the computer systems we use. To that end, we have started to transition the company from computers loaded with various programs to a cloud-based system in which all the software you need can be accessed through a web browser. You are all already accessing your email this way. Next week, we will start supporting text editing, spreadsheet, and presentation software. My staff will be available via instant messaging, email, and phone to help you make the transition. It will take some time to get used to the new software, but you'll soon be able to telecommute from home or wherever you happen to be.

大家好。作為資訊科技部的主管，我必須負責我們所使用的電腦系統之安全與穩定。為了達到這個目標，我們已經開始將公司載滿各種程式的電腦轉換成所需的軟體全都能透過網路瀏覽器來存取的一個以雲端為基礎的系統。各位已經全都是以這種方式在存取電子郵件了。下星期，我們會開始支援文字編輯、試算表和簡報軟體。我的幕僚可以經由即時通訊、電子郵件和電話來協助各位做轉換。習慣新軟體要花一點時間，但各位很快就能在家裡或不論你碰巧在哪裡遠距辦公。

92　正解 C

What is the announcement mainly about?
(A) Updating security procedures
(B) Launching a cloud-based email system
(C) Using new software tools
(D) Improving coworker collaboration

這段宣告主要在講什麼？
(A) 更新安全程序
(B) 推出雲端電子郵件系統
(C) 使用新的軟體工具
(D) 改善同事間的合作

解析　本題須做一點點推論。說話者在前半段表示 "To that end, we have started to transition the company from computers loaded with various programs to a cloud-based system ...."「為了達到這個目標，我們已經開始將公司載滿各種程式的電腦轉換成⋯⋯一個以雲端為基礎的系統。」然後又提到經雲端存取電子郵件及支援文字編輯、簡報軟體等。而由總結部分的 "It will take some time to get used to the new software ...."「習慣新軟體要花一點時間⋯⋯。」則可斷定，此段宣告的主旨應該是在談 (C)「使用新的軟體工具」。

93　正解 C

According to the speaker, how can employees get assistance?
(A) By upgrading their system
(B) By searching online
(C) By contacting IT staff
(D) By reading the manual

根據說話者所言，員工可如何獲得協助？
(A) 把他們的系統升級
(B) 上網搜尋
(C) 與資訊科技人員聯絡
(D) 閱讀手冊

解析　說話者藉談話的倒數第二句明白表示 "My staff will be available via instant messaging, email, and phone to help you make the transition."「我的幕僚可以經由即時通訊、電子郵件和電話來協助各位做轉換。」而因為說話者領導的是資科部，所以他的幕僚當然是該部門的人員，故本題選 (C)「與資訊科技人員聯絡」。

94　正解 A

What is an advantage of the new system?
(A) Some employees may work from home.
(B) Instant messaging is built in.
(C) It is easier for the IT staff to maintain.
(D) It takes little time to get used to.

新系統的優點是什麼？
(A) 有些員工或可在家上班。
(B) 內建了即時通訊。
(C) 資訊科技人員比較容易維護。
(D) 不須花多少時間就會習慣。

解析　本題考細節。由宣告的最後一句話 "It will take some time to get used to the new software, but you'll soon be able to telecommute from home or wherever you happen to be."「習慣新軟體要花一點時間，但各位很快就能在家裡或不論你碰巧在哪裡遠距辦公。」可知，選項 (A)「有些員工或可在家上班」就是新系統的優點。

Vocabulary
☐ **text editing** 文字編輯　☐ **instant messaging** 即時通訊　☐ **telecommute** 遠距辦公　☐ **collaboration** 合作；協作

Questions 95-97 refer to the following voice message and list.

第 95 到 97 題請參照下列語音訊息和清單。

Hi Scott, it's David. Thank you so much for agreeing to clean the office while I'm in Atlanta for the management training seminar. After two years as an office assistant, I'm excited to take the next step in my career. I've emailed a list of tasks to you. It should only take about thirty minutes to finish everything. The most time-consuming thing is the vacuuming because you have to move all the chairs out of the way. I placed a sealed envelope on your desk with the instructions and codes you'll need to set and deactivate the security alarm. Don't forget to lock the doors when you leave. Thanks again and see you next week.

Room	Task
Main Office	- Empty trash cans - Vacuum
Meeting Room	- Wipe the table - Water the plants
Copy Room	- Empty the recycling bin - Fill the copier
Kitchen	- Wash the coffee maker - Clean the sink

嗨，史考特，我是大衛。十分感謝你在我到亞特蘭大參加管理培訓研討會之際答應來清理辦公室。在擔任辦公室助理兩年後，我非常高興在職涯中跨出了下一步。我已經用電子郵件把差事清單寄給你了。一切應該只要三十分鐘左右就可以完成。最耗費時間的事就是吸地，因為你必須把椅子全部搬開。我在你的桌上放了一個封好的信封，裡面有你在設定和解除安全警報時所需要的操作說明和密碼。離開時別忘了鎖門。再次感謝，下星期見。

房間	工作
主辦公室	- 清空垃圾桶 - 吸地
會議室	- 擦桌子 - 為植物澆水
影印室	- 清空回收桶 - 將影印機的紙裝滿
廚房	- 清洗咖啡機 - 清理水槽

95 正解 A

Why is the speaker traveling to Atlanta?
(A) To join a training session
(B) To assist a manager
(C) To organize a seminar
(D) To attend a career fair

說話者為什麼要前往亞特蘭大？
(A) 為了參加一個培訓課程
(B) 為了協助一位經理
(C) 為了籌辦一場研討會
(D) 為了出席一個職涯博覽會

解析 由訊息的第二句話 "Thank you so much for agreeing to clean the office while I'm in Atlanta for the management training seminar."「十分感謝你在我到亞特蘭大參加管理培訓研討會之際答應來清理辦公室。」可知，說話者之所以要去亞特蘭大是 (A) 為了參加一個培訓課程。注意，原文中的 "training seminar"「培訓研討會」在選項 (A) 中被以 "training session"「培訓課程」取代。

96 正解 B

What did the speaker leave on the listener's desk?
(A) The key to the office
(B) A sealed envelope
(C) Cleaning instructions
(D) A list of tasks

說話者留了什麼在聽者的桌上？
(A) 辦公室的鑰匙
(B) 加封的信封
(C) 清理的注意事項
(D) 工作清單

解析 本題須仔細聆聽細節。說話者在訊息的倒數第三句中清楚提到 "I placed a sealed envelope on your desk with the instructions and codes you'll need ...."「我在你的桌上放了一個封好的信封，裡面有你……所需要的操作說明和密碼。」選項 (B) 即為正解。

97 正解 A

Look at the graphic. Which room will take the most time?
(A) Main office
(B) Meeting room
(C) Copy room
(D) Employee lounge

請看圖表。哪一個房間會最花時間？
(A) 主辦公室
(B) 會議室
(C) 影印室
(D) 員工休息室

解析 本題亦屬「細節」題。說話者在第六句話中明白指出 "The most time-consuming thing is the vacuuming ...."「最耗費時間的事就是吸地……。」而圖示中唯一列出需要吸地的房間就是 "Main office"，故本題選 (A)。

Vocabulary

☐ **time-consuming** 耗時的　☐ **vacuum** 用吸塵器清掃　☐ **sealed** 密封的　☐ **deactivate** 解除（警報器、炸彈裝置等）　☐ **lounge** 休息室

Questions 98-100 refer to the following announcement and coupon.　第 98 到 100 題請參照下列宣告和折價券。

There are going to be a lot of people in town this week for the surfing contest. That means we're going to have some busy shifts at Joe's Ice Cream. Because our location here on Olive Street doesn't get a lot of foot traffic, I'll be asking everyone to take turns handing out coupons on Main Street. Most of the customers who come in will just want a cone or a sundae, and that's fine. But remember, our profit margins are much higher on beverages, so be sure to promote those when customers are ordering. This is the last big event of the summer. Students will be going back to school soon and business is going to slow down in September, so let's make the most of this opportunity.

很多人會因為本週的衝浪賽而到城裡來。這意味著我們阿喬冰淇淋有幾個班次會很忙。由於我們在橄欖街的這個點人潮不多，所以我會要求每個人輪流到主街上去發折價券。來店的顧客大部分都會只想要個甜筒或聖代，那無所謂。但要記得，飲料的利潤高很多，所以顧客在點東西的時候，務必要推銷這些。這是暑期最後的大型活動。學生很快就會返回校園，生意到了九月會放緩，所以我們要好好把握這次機會。

Joe's Surf City Ice Cream	
10% Off All	
Ice Cream Cones	Frozen Yogurts
Ice Cream Sundaes	Iced Coffees
810 Olive Street	Valid 8/24–8/31

阿喬衝浪之城冰淇淋	
一律九折	
冰淇淋甜筒	冷凍優格
冰淇淋聖代	冰咖啡
奧立佛街 810 號	8/24-8/31 有效

98　正解 D

What does the speaker ask the listeners to do?
(A) Participate in a contest
(B) Work extra shifts
(C) Help direct traffic
(D) Hand out coupons

說話者要聽者做什麼？
(A) 參加比賽
(B) 額外輪班
(C) 幫忙指揮交通
(D) 分發折價券

> 解析　本題考細節，問說話者要聽者做什麼。由說話者在第三句話中所說的 "... I'll be asking everyone to take turns handing out coupons on Main Street."「……我會要求每個人輪流到主街上去發折價券。」可知，正確答案是 (D)。

99　正解 D

Look at the graphic. Which items does the speaker want to sell more of?
(A) Ice cream cones
(B) Ice cream sundaes
(C) Frozen yogurts
(D) Iced coffees

請看圖表。說話者想要多賣哪些品項？
(A) 冰淇淋甜筒
(B) 冰淇淋聖代
(C) 冷凍優格
(D) 冰咖啡

> 解析　本題亦屬「細節」題。說話者在談話的第五句中提及 "... our profit margins are much higher on beverages, so be sure to promote those when customers are ordering."「……飲料的利潤高很多，所以顧客在點東西的時候，務必要推銷這些。」而按圖示，該店所販賣的飲料為冰咖啡，因此本題選 (D)。

100　正解 B

According to the speaker, what will happen in September?
(A) The last big event of the summer will take place.
(B) The store will have fewer customers.
(C) The employees will go back to school.
(D) The listeners will have new opportunities.

根據說話者所言，九月時會發生什麼事？
(A) 暑期最後的大型活動將會舉行。
(B) 來店的客人會變少。
(C) 員工會回到學校。
(D) 聽者會有新的機會。

> 解析　由說話者的最後一句話 "Students will be going back in school soon and business is going to slow down in September ...."「學生很快就會返回校園，生意到了九月會放緩……。」可知，九月時因為要開學，所以來店客的人數會變少。正解為 (B)。

第 2 回完全解析

PART 4

Vocabulary

☐ **surfing** 衝浪　☐ **foot traffic** 顧客流量　☐ **hand out** 分發　☐ **profit margin** 利潤率　☐ **beverage** 飲料

PART 5

101 正解 B

The warranty is valid for a ------- of two years from the date of purchase.

(A) time   (B) period   (C) guarantee   (D) certificate

保證書的有效期間為購買日期起的兩年。

> **解析** 本題為「單字」考題。由空格後的介系詞片語 "of two years"「兩年的……」可知，空格內應填入一表「時間」或「期間」的詞彙。選項 (A) time 雖為「時間」之意，但 "time" 屬不可數名詞，其前不可使用「不定冠詞」"a"，故本題選 (B) period「期間」。至於選項 (C) guarantee「保證」與 (D) certificate「證書」則皆不符題意要求。

102 正解 D

------- her flight arrives on time, we'll have an hour for lunch before the meeting.

(A) Regardless of   (B) No matter   (C) Most likely   (D) Assuming that

假定她的班機準時抵達，那我們在會面前將有一小時可以吃午餐。

> **解析** 本題考正確之從屬結構。由於空格後的 "her flight arrives on time"「她的班機準時抵達」為一完整子句，而逗號後的 "we'll have an hour for lunch ..."「我們……將有一小時可以吃午餐」亦為完整子句，因此理論上空格內應填入一「從屬連接詞」。選項 (A)「不管」屬「片語介系詞」，不可選。選項 (B)「不論」之後應接一「疑問詞」("what"、"who"、"how" 等) 才可視為「連接詞」，故亦不可選。選項 (C)「最可能」則屬「副詞」結構，更非題意所需。正確答案是 (D) Assuming that「假定……」。注意，其實 "assuming that" 並非「連接詞」而是由「現在分詞」"assuming" 加上「連接詞」"that" 所組成的一個「臨時」之結構。須知，"assume"「假定」為一「及物動詞」，其後以 that 子句作為其受詞完全合理，只是在本句中 "assume" 被「降級」為「分詞」，也就是說，在本句中 "Assuming that ..." 乃一「分詞構句」，從屬於逗號後的主句 "we'll have an hour for lunch ..."。

103 正解 B

Our unusual recruiting system was the ------- of our first HR manager.

(A) create   (B) creation   (C) creative   (D) creatively

我們獨特的徵才制度乃首任人資經理所創。

> **解析** 本題考正確之字詞變化。由空格前的「定冠詞」"the" 及空格後的「介系詞」"of" 即可知，空格內應填入的是一「名詞」，而四選項中只有 (B) creation「創造」為名詞，故為正解。另，(A) create 為 "creation" 的原形動詞、(C) creative「有創意的」為形容詞、(D) creatively 則為 creative 的副詞。

104 正解 B

Books purchased ------- Earword Publishing come with a code that allows readers to download an audio version of the text.

(A) with   (B) from   (C) by   (D) for

向伊爾沃德出版社所購得的書都附有可讓讀者下載語音版內文的編碼。

> **解析** 本題考正確之介系詞。空格後的 "Earword Publishing" 乃一出版社，而書當然是「從」出版社所購買「來」的。選項 (B) from 即為正解。

105 正解 D

To activate the software, ------- your purchase by completing the form on our website.

(A) apply   (B) sign   (C) produce   (D) register

要啟用軟體，請上我們的網站填寫表格做購買登記。

> **解析** 本題亦為「單字」考題。由前後文意來推斷，商家之所以要對方上網填表格，應該是想確定對方是否真正購買了他們的產品；在對方填好表格、做了購買「登記」之後，才能啟用軟體。正確答案是 (D) register。而選項 (A) apply「應用」、(B) sign「簽名」與 (C) produce「生產」明顯皆不適合以 "your purchase"「你的購買」作為受詞。

Mr. Tajima's request is not being considered ------- he submitted it after the deadline.

(A) because   (B) reason   (C) due to   (D) caused by

田島先生的請求未獲考慮，因為他是在截止期限後才提出。

解析 本題考正確之連接詞。由於空格的前後皆為完整的子句，因此空格內須填入一「連接詞」，而四選項中只有 (A) because「因為」是連接詞，故為正解。選項 (B) reason「原因」（名詞）、(C) due to「由於」（片語介系詞）、(D) caused by「由……所引起」（過去分詞＋介系詞）雖然意思都與「原因」相關，但文法皆不正確，故皆不可選。

Rent near the subway line is more than ------- budget allows for.

(A) we   (B) us   (C) our   (D) ours

地鐵線附近的租金超過了我們預算的限額。

解析 本題考正確代名詞的用法。由空格後的名詞 "budget"「預算」可知，空格內應填入的是代名詞之「所有格」，故選 (C) our。選項 (A) we 為「主格」、(B) us 為「受格」，(D) ours 則為「所有代名詞」，三者之後皆不應接名詞。

The entrance is ------- the top of the escalator.

(A) at   (B) up   (C) along   (D) under

入口在電扶梯的頂端。

解析 本題須選出正確之介系詞。由前後文意來推斷，本句要表達的應該是：入口「在」電扶梯的頂端，而四選項介系詞中能用來表示「在……（地點）」的是 (A) at。選項 (B) up 指「在……之上」、(C) along 指「沿著」、(D) under 指「在……下方」，三者明顯皆非句意所需。

A human resources consultant helped us refine our recruiting strategy and hiring -------.

(A) positions   (B) managers   (C) accomplishments   (D) procedures

有位人資顧問幫助我們精進了招募策略和雇用程序。

解析 本題考單字。選項 (A) positions 指「職位」、(B) managers 指「經理」、(C) accomplishments 指「成就」、(D) procedures 指「程序」，而最適合置於句中 "hiring"「雇用」之後並與其前之 "recruiting strategy"「招募策略」相呼應的應為 (D)。

With registered mail, the ------- of the letter has to sign a receipt upon delivery.

(A) reception   (B) receiving   (C) receiver   (D) receptionist

至於掛號郵件，收信者必須在信件送達時於收據上簽名。

解析 本題考正確之字形變化。雖然從空格前的定冠詞 "the" 與空格後的介系詞 "of" 可斷定，空格內應填入一「名詞」，但四選項卻皆為名詞：(A) reception 指「接待」、(B) receiving 指「收到」（注意，"receiving" 實為「動名詞」，但一般而言言「動名詞」的功能與「名詞」相同）、(C) receiver 指「收件人」、(D) receptionist 指「接待員」。而依句意，應該是「收信者」才須在收到掛號信時於收據上簽名，故 (C) 為正解。（原句中的 "receipt"「收據」與四選項單字相同，都源自動詞 "receive"。）

Vocabulary

☐ **refine** 提煉；精製

------ a rather slow start, we've ramped up production and are now on schedule.

(A) Because   (B) However   (C) Despite   (D) Although

儘管起步頗慢，但我們加強生產，現在已經追上了進度。

解析 本題考正確之介系詞。由空格後的 "a rather slow start" 為一「名詞片語」可知，空格內應填入一「介系詞」。選項 (A) Because「因為」與 (D) Although「雖然」皆為「連接詞」，故不選。選項 (B) However「然而」為「連接副詞」，故亦不可選。四選項中唯一的「介系詞」為 (C) Despite，將其填入空格後與其受詞 "a rather slow start" 形成表「讓步」的介系詞片語。

The underlying issue must ------ before the contract is signed.

(A) address   (B) be addressed   (C) addressing   (D) to address

根本的問題必須在合約簽訂前就處理好。

解析 本題考正確之動詞型態。由於句中主詞 "The underlying issue"「根本的問題」屬「事物」，因此動詞須使用「被動式」。四選項中只有 (B) be addressed 為被動形式，故為正解。注意，"address" 在本句中指「處理」、「應對」，此用法相當常見於多益考試中。

------ costs were far lower for the pervious copier.

(A) Maintain   (B) Maintained   (C) Maintaining   (D) Maintenance

前一台影印機的維修成本低得多。

解析 本題須選出正確之字形變化。由空格後的 "costs" 為名詞來看，空格內理當填入一「形容詞」。選項 (A) Maintain 為「動詞」，不予考慮。選項 (B) Maintained 為 (A) 之「過去分詞」、選項 (C) Maintaining 為 (A) 之「現在分詞」，二者皆可作「形容詞」用，但不論是表「被動」的 (A) 或表「主動」的 (C) 明顯都不適合用來「修飾」其後的 "costs"。本題正解為名詞選項 (D)。注意，"Maintenance costs"（指「維修成本」）為一「複合名詞」，就文法功能而言，可將 "Maintenance" 視為 "costs" 的「修飾語」。

All of the technology departments ------ R&D are expected to submit a quarterly budget.

(A) except for   (B) as for   (C) in addition   (D) as well

除了研發部之外，所有的科技部門都必須提交季度預算。

解析 本題考正確的片語介系詞。主詞部分有兩個不同的名詞結構："All of the technology departments"「所有的科技部門」與 "R&D"「研發部」，而由之後的述語部分 "are expected to submit a quarterly budget"「必須提交季度預算」可推知，主詞部分的兩個名詞結構間最合理的關係聯結應為一能表達「除了……之外」的字詞，故正解為 (A) except for。四選項中的另一片語介系詞 (B) as for 表達的是「至於」之意，與句意不符，故不選。另，選項 (C) in addition「此外」與 (D) as well「也」則皆屬「副詞」，不適用於本句。

------ we know, the shipment is still in transit.

(A) In regard to   (B) On account of   (C) As far as   (D) In accordance with

就我們所知，貨物還在運送途中。

解析 本題須選出正確的連接詞。由空格後的 "we know" 可知，空格內應填入的是一個能用來引導子句的「連接詞」，而四選項中只有 (C) As far as 可作連接詞用，故為正解。（"as far as we know" 指「就我們所知」。）選項 (A) In regard to「關於」、(B) On account of「由於」與 (D) In accordance with「依照」則皆為「片語介系詞」，故皆不可選。注意，"as far as" 亦可作「片語介系詞」用，例如："This train only goes as far as Daan Station."「這班列車只到大安站。」

116 正解 A

Mr. Kuzma redesigned the logo to more ------- reflect the organization's mission.
(A) accurately　　　　(B) curiously　　　　(C) temporarily　　　　(D) ordinarily

庫茲瑪先生重新設計了標誌以便能夠更精確地反映該組織的使命。

> **解析** 本題考單字。本句前半提到庫茲瑪先生重新設計了商標 (redesigned the logo)，而合理的推斷他這麼做的目的應該是為了能更「精確地」反映該組織的使命 (reflect the organization's mission)。因此本題選 (A) accurately。選項 (B) curiously「好奇地」、(C) temporarily「暫時地」與 (D) ordinarily「通常地」明顯皆與句意不符。

117 正解 B

Refunds must be requested ------- thirty days of purchase.
(A) before　　　　(B) within　　　　(C) during　　　　(D) while

退款的要求必須在購買後的三十日內提出。

> **解析** 本題須選出正確介系詞。由常理判斷，購物退款應是在商品被購買後的一段期間「之內」辦理，故正解為 (B) within。注意，雖然選項 (C) during 具類似之意，但 "during" 通常用於一「固定」的期間之前（如 "during the day"、"during the winter" 等），而不用於表「期限」長短的字詞之前（如本句中的 "thirty days"、"ten minutes" 等）。另，選項 (A) before 指的是「在……之前」，完全與句意不相符。至於選項 (D) while「當……的時候」乃「連接詞」，不予考慮。

118 正解 D

The source of any data used to ------- your proposal must be clearly cited.
(A) deliver　　　　(B) advise　　　　(C) mention　　　　(D) support

用來支持你的提案的任何資料都必須將出處標示清楚。

> **解析** 本題為「單字」考題。由句子之前後文意可推知，主詞部分中所提到的 "data"「資料」應該是被用來「支持」受詞 "your proposal"「你的提案」的，因此本題選 (D) support。選項 (A) deliver「發表」、(B) advise「勸告」與 (C) mention「提到」明顯皆非句意所需。

119 正解 B

In ------- the total cost, don't forget to include the cost of the packaging.
(A) calculate　　　　(B) calculating　　　　(C) calculation　　　　(D) calculator

在計算總成本時，別忘了將包裝成本納入。

> **解析** 本題考正確之字形變化。由空格前的介系詞 "In" 即可知，空格內應填入一「名詞」以作為其「受詞」，因此可先排除動詞選項 (A) calculate。四選項中 (C) calculation 和 (D) calculator 為名詞，但 (D) 指「計算機」，明顯與句意不符；剩下的 (C) 理應為正確選項，但由於 "calculation" 表達的是計算的「結果」，與句意所需的「做計算」之含意有所差異，故亦不可選。本題正解其實為「動名詞」選項之 (B) calculating。注意，「動名詞」與「純」名詞的差別在於，前者著重「動作」與「過程」，後者則表達「狀態」或「結果」。

120 正解 B

Ms. Gutiérrez has ------- flat sales growth in the coming year.
(A) protested　　　　(B) projected　　　　(C) processed　　　　(D) provided

古提耶瑞茲小姐預估明年的銷售成長將不會有什麼增加。

> **解析** 本題須選出具相同字首之正確動詞。由句中提到的 "sales growth in the coming year"「明年的銷售成長」來推斷，主詞 "Ms. Gutiérrez" 所做的應該是一種「推測」，而符合此句意邏輯的動詞為 (B) projected「預估」。選項 (A) protested 指「抗議」、(C) processed 指「處理」、(D) provided 指「提供」，三者皆與句意相去甚遠。注意，本題四選項單字之字首 "pro-" 是 "forward" 之意。

121 正解 A

Hotel staff are trained to decline some guest requests while also ------- an acceptable alternative.

(A) offering   (B) to offer   (C) has offered   (D) offer

飯店的工作人員都受過訓練，在婉拒客人的某些要求的同時也能夠提出可接受的替代方案。

> **解析** 本句考正確之動詞型態。一般而言，出現在本句中的連接詞 "while" 有兩個用法：一、後接完整子句；二、後接 "V-ing"，而因為四選項中並無「子句」形式之答案，因此本題選 (A) offering。不定詞選項 (B) to offer、完成式選項 (C) has offered 及原形動詞 (D) offer 皆與 "while" 之使用規則不符。

122 正解 C

This ------- event space can host anything from a business conference to a wedding banquet.

(A) influential   (B) articulate   (C) adaptable   (D) thoughtful

從商業會議到婚宴，這個適用面很廣的活動空間什麼都能辦。

> **解析** 本題須選出正確之形容詞。如果一個活動空間既能用來舉辦商業會議又能用來舉辦性能完全不同的婚禮，那就表示這個地方的適用面相當廣。很明顯，正確答案是 (C) adaptable。選項 (A) influential「有影響力的」、(B) articulate「口齒清晰的」與 (D) thoughtful「考慮周到的」則皆與句意不搭軋。

123 正解 A

Ms. Lee ------- to replace the floor in the break room before the new refrigerator is delivered.

(A) intends   (B) extends   (C) contends   (D) pretends

李小姐打算在新冰箱送到之前把休息室的地板換掉。

> **解析** 本題須選出具相同字根之正確動詞。由句子的前後文意來推斷，把休息室的地板換掉應該是 Ms. Lee 在新冰箱送來之前「打算」要做的事。正確答案是 (A) intends。選項 (B) extends 指「延伸」、(C) contends 指「競爭」、(D) pretends 則是「假裝」之意，三者皆無法與句意聯結。注意，字根 "tend" 是 "stretch" 的意思。

124 正解 D

Our study shows that it's ------- common for young professionals to own more than one phone.

(A) increase   (B) increased   (C) increasing   (D) increasingly

我們的研究顯示，年輕的專業人員擁有不只一支手機的現象愈來愈普遍。

> **解析** 本題考正確之字形變化。空格前為「主詞＋動詞」的結構 (it's = it is)，而空格後為「形容詞」"common"「普遍的」。由此即可斷定，空格內應填入的是可用來修飾 "common" 此形容詞的「副詞」。正確答案是 (D) increasingly「愈來愈……地」。原形動詞選項 (A) increase、過去式（或過去分詞）選項 (B) increased 及現在分詞（或動名詞）選項 (C) increasing 皆不適用於本句。注意，"increase" 原為「增加」之意，但在變成副詞 "increasingly" 之後則用來指「日益增加地」、「愈來愈……地」。

125 正解 D

The sales figures just came in and we can congratulate ------- on another excellent quarter.

(A) itself   (B) yourselves   (C) oneself   (D) ourselves

剛收到銷售數字，我們可以為我們再度表現亮麗的一季祝賀自己一下。

> **解析** 本題考正確之反身代名詞。由句意可知，要「祝賀自己」的人應該是句中第二個子句的主詞 "we"，因此正解為 (D) ourselves。其他選項的反身代名詞在句中則皆無明確之指稱對象，因此皆為誤。

Vocabulary

☐ **banquet** 宴會

Employees must submit vacation requests three weeks ------- to ensure that all shifts can be covered.

(A) sooner   (B) in advance   (C) up front   (D) ago

員工的休假請求必須預先於三週前提出以確保所有的班次都有替代人手。

> **解析** 本題須選出與時間相關之正確副詞。由前後文意來推斷，空格內應填入一個能表達「預先」、「事先」之意的字詞，而最符合本句需要的選項為 (B) in advance。不過請注意，事實上選項 (C) up front 也具有「預先」或「事先」這樣的含意，但 "up front" 一般用於指「預付款項」時（例如："The fee must be paid up front."「該筆費用必須預先支付。」）至於選項 (A) sooner 與 (D) ago 則明顯不適用於本句："three weeks sooner" 指「（比預計時間）早三個星期」，而 "three weeks ago" 則指「（已過去的）三個星期之前」，二者皆與句意邏輯相去甚遠。

Customers are given immediate access to the database ------- receipt of payment.

(A) upon   (B) for   (C) until   (D) from

付款一收到，顧客就立即可使用資料庫。

> **解析** 本題考正確之介系詞。由前後文意來推斷，空格內應填入一能表達「一……就……」的介系詞，而四選項中只有 (A) upon 此介系詞有同樣的用法（"upon receipt of payment" 指「一收到付款就……」），故為正解。注意，"upon" 的原意是「在……之上」，例如："She carefully placed the vase upon the table."「她小心地把花瓶放在桌子上。」原則上，"upon" 與 "on" 可互通，但前者較正式。

The app works quite ------- for a beta version.

(A) hardly   (B) primarily   (C) closely   (D) smoothly

就測試版而言，這個應用程式運作起來相當順暢。

> **解析** 本句須選出正確之情態副詞。由出現在動詞 "works"「運作」之後的程度副詞 "quite"「相當」即可知，空格內應填入一適合用來修飾 "works" 的「情態副詞」，故本題選 (D) smoothly「順暢地」。選項 (A) hardly「幾乎不」為另一「程度副詞」，明顯不適用於本句；選項 (B) primarily「主要地」與 (C) closely「密切地」則完全不適合用來修飾 "works"。

Demkay Software sponsors an annual coding contest ------- help recruit potential employees.

(A) to   (B) that   (C) so   (D) can

丹凱軟體藉贊助年度程式設計競賽來幫忙招募潛在員工。

> **解析** 本題考正確之功能詞。本句只有一個主詞："Demkay Software"，但卻有兩個動詞："sponsors"「贊助」與 "help"「幫忙」。由第二個動詞 "help" 與第一個動詞 "sponsors" 不同、並未使用第三人稱單數形來看，應在 "help" 之前加上「功能詞」"to" 使其形成「不定詞」，整個句子才能符合文法。正解為 (A)。而由於本句既非「複雜句」亦非「複合句」，因此「從屬連接詞」選項 (B) that 與「對等連接詞」選項 (C) so 皆為誤。至於「助動詞」選項 (D) can，雖然與 "to" 相同，可用來確保其後動詞為「原形」，但其前不應為「主詞＋動詞」之結構，故亦為錯誤。

I wrote a formal proposal, which helped me ------- my ideas.

(A) clarifying   (B) clarified   (C) clarify   (D) clarity

我寫了一個正式的提案，而這個正式提案幫助我釐清了我的一些構想。

> **解析** 本題考正確之字形變化。本句從屬子句中的動詞 "helped" 屬「使役動詞」，依文法其受詞之後的動詞應使用「原形」，因此本題選 (C) clarify「釐清」。「現在分詞」選項 (A) clarifying 與「過去分詞」選項 (B) clarified 皆不合文法。選項 (D) clarity「清晰」則為「名詞」，同樣為誤。注意，也有在 "help" 之後使用「不定詞」的用法，例如："We helped them to clean the house."「我們幫忙他們打掃房子。」不過較為少見。

## PART 6

Questions 131-134 refer to the following advertisement.

Try the new Ball Awareness System today!

Sports coaches are always looking for ways to help their teams perform better. That's ------- we've created the Ball Awareness
131.

System (BAS). From basketball to volleyball, the Ball Awareness System works with any team sport that takes place within

a defined playing area. Players wear special electronic wristbands that provide location data to sensors ------- around the
132.

playing field or court. Coaches can follow the movements of each player in real time via a mobile device app. -------.
133.

As an added benefit, the BAS wristband also ------- as a fitness tracker. Players can monitor metrics such as heart rate,
134.

calories burned, and distance traveled during the game. To learn about all the ways BAS can help you help your team, visit

www.ballawarenesssystem.com today!

---

131. (A) when
(B) how
(C) why
(D) what

132. (A) place
(B) placed
(C) placing
(D) to place

133. (A) Location data is uploaded as soon as the game has ended.
(B) The BAS app uses GPS to track the location of players.
(C) Fans can stay home and watch the game on television.
(D) After the game, players can access the same information.

134. (A) functions
(B) wears
(C) suggests
(D) uses

第 131 到 134 題請參照下面這則廣告。

今天就來試試新的球感系統！

運動教練們總是在設法幫助他們的團隊以求能夠表現得更好。這就是為什麼我們打造了球感系統 (BAS) 的原因。從籃球到排球，球感系統適用於任何在明確劃定的比賽場域內所舉行的團隊運動。選手們只要戴上特殊的腕套就能將位置資料提供給架設在比賽場地或球場周圍的感測器。教練們可透過行動裝置 app 即時掌握各個選手的移動狀況。比賽之後，選手們也能取得同樣的資訊。

有個附帶的好處是，球感系統腕套還可當作體適能追蹤器來使用。選手在比賽期間能藉此監控諸如心率、燃燒的卡路里數和行經距離等指標。欲了解球感系統能夠幫您協助貴團隊的所有方法，請今天就上 www.ballawarenesssystem.com ！

---

131 正解 C

解析 本題須選出正確之從屬連接詞。由第一句 "Sports coaches are always looking for ways to help their teams perform better." 「教練們總是在設法幫助他們的團隊以求能夠表現得更好。」及第二句空格後的 "we've created the Ball Awareness System (BAS)" 「我們打造了球感系統」可推知，前者乃後者發生之「原因」，因此空格內應填入用來表原因的「疑問詞」 "why" 以作為引導其後表「結果」之子句的「從屬連接詞」。(C) 為正解。

133 正解 D

解析 本題考插入句。由前一句中提到的重點 "Coaches can follow the movements of each player in real time ...." 「教練們可……即時掌握各個選手的移動狀況。」可斷定，最合理的接續為 (D)「比賽之後，選手們（也）能取得同樣的資訊。」這兩句話的關鍵聯結即："the same information = the movements of each player"，前者由選手於賽後取得，後者則由教練於比賽中掌握。至於選項 (A)「比賽一結束位置資料就會上傳。」與 (B)「球感系統這個應用程式利用衛星定位系統來追蹤選手的位置。」則皆與前句內容不甚搭軋。而選項 (C)「球迷可待在家裡看電視轉播該場比賽。」則更顯得突兀。

132 正解 B

解析 本題須選出正確之動狀詞。由於 "sensors" 「感測器」是「被」設置在場地周圍的，因此應選擇具「被動」含意的「過去分詞」 (B) placed。注意，不可誤選表「主動」的「現在分詞」 (C) placing。

134 正解 A

解析 由前一段的內容可知，「球感系統腕套」的主要功能在於提供選手的位置資料，而本句要表達的應該是，除了此功能外，它還可「當作」體適能追蹤器 (fitness tracker) 來「使用」。由空格後的介系詞 "as" 可推知，空格內應填入一「不及物動詞」；也就是說，要正確表示「當作……使用」須採用「不及物動詞＋as」的組合，而四個動詞選項中只有 (A) functions 為「不及物」，故為正解。

Vocabulary

☐ **sensor** 感應器　☐ **metrics** 指標（複數形）

Questions 135-138 refer to the following press release.

Replanter, the office plant provider of choice for businesses throughout the northeast, today announced the Tropicalia package, a collection of attractive tropical plants that will bring life and color to even the drabbest office. These plants were chosen for their beauty, their low-maintenance ------- , as well as their ability to grow well in low-light environments. The ------- of the package can be adjusted to meet the needs of the smallest office suite or the largest corporate headquarters.
135.   **136.**

The Tropicalia package ------- six months of weekly maintenance visits by our specialists. -------. After six months, you can choose to have our specialists train you in the care of the plants, or pay a low monthly fee to maintain our professional servicing.
137.   **138.**

135. (A) requires
(B) required
(C) requiring
(D) requirements

136. (A) size
(B) name
(C) location
(D) performance

137. (A) packs up
(B) looks into
(C) comes with
(D) consists of

138. (A) During this period, you can bring your own plants to the office for display.
(B) They will water and prune your plants, and replace any that are not thriving.
(C) This is the time to consider the benefits of a plant-filled work environment.
(D) A specialist can suggest a package of plants that is just right for your office.

第 135 到 138 題請參照下面這篇新聞稿。

瑞普蘭特——東北各地區商號精選辦公室植栽之供應商——今日宣布推出熱帶風專案,這一系列吸引人的熱帶植栽可為哪怕是最沉悶的辦公室帶來生氣與色彩。這些植栽之所以被選定是因為它們的美觀、維護需求低,以及在低光線的環境裡生長良好的能力。專案的大小可調整,以符合最小的辦公室套房或最大的企業總部之需要。

熱帶風專案附送我們的專家逐週維護訪視六個月。他們會替您的植栽澆水、修剪,並且把長得不茂盛的替換掉。六個月後,您可選擇由我們的專家來訓練指導您照料植栽,或是支付低廉的月費續用我們的專業服務。

135 正解 D

解析 本題須選出正確詞形。由於空格前的 "low-maintenance" 「低維護的」為「形容詞」,因此空格內應填入一「名詞」,而四選項中的唯一名詞是 (D) requirements「要求」、「需求」,故為正解。注意,雖然選項 (C) requiring 可視為「動名詞」,但因為動名詞著重「動作」,所以不適用於本句。

137 正解 C

解析 本題考正確之片語動詞。選項 (A) packs up 指「打包(行李)」、選項 (B) looks into 指「調查」、選項 (C) comes with 指「附有」、選項 (D) consists of 則指「由……組成」。選項 (A) 與 (B) 明顯與句意不搭軋,故不選。若選擇 (D),句意將會是:熱帶風專案由我們的專家逐週維護訪視六個月所組成,不知所云。本題應選 (C),亦即,若購買熱帶風專案,就會「附送」六個月的免費服務。

136 正解 A

解析 由後半提到的 "... to meet the needs of the smallest office suite or the largest corporate headquarters"「……以符合最小的辦公室套房或最大的企業總部之需要。」即可反推,能夠加以調整的應該就是此專案的「大小 (size)」。

138 正解 B

解析 本題考插入句。由於上一句中提到了「專家逐週維護訪視六個月」,因此最合理的接續應該是說明這些維護人員之工作內容的選項 (B)「他們會替您的植栽澆水、修剪,並且把長得不茂盛的替換掉。」相對地,選項 (A)「在這段期間,你可以把自己的植栽帶到辦公室展示。」與 (C)「這是思考擺滿植栽的工作環境有何好處的時機。」就顯得與前後文句格格不入,故不可選。至於選項 (D)「一個專家能建議一組正好適合您辦公室的植栽配套。」雖然也提及「專家」,但他 / 她的「專長」顯然無法與前一句提到的「維護訪視」和後一句所說的「照料植栽」聯結,故亦為誤。

Vocabulary

☐ **drab** 無生氣的;平淡的   ☐ **low-maintenance** 低維護的

From: Jetsuna Sakya <j.sakya@springfieldtimes.com>
To: Ruth Horowitz <ruthphorowitz@musicmail.com>
Subject: Your recent letter to the Springfield Times
Date: November 22

Dear Ms. Horowitz,

Thank you very much for your recent letter to the Times ------- to our November 18 article about the city's plan to renovate
139.
the Springfield Art Museum. You ------- several interesting and I think completely original points in the letter, and I was
140.
wondering if you would be interested in expanding your thoughts on the subject into a longer article for the newspaper.

-------.
141.

If you are interested in writing such a piece, please call me as soon as possible. We would need to ------- it from you by 4
142.
PM on November 24 so that it could be on our website that evening and in the paper on November 25, the day of the next

city council meeting.

I look forward to working with you.

Sincerely,
Jetsuna Sakya, Managing Editor
Springfield Times
(541) 565-3227

139. (A) responds
(B) to respond
(C) responded
(D) responding

140. (A) put
(B) did
(C) made
(D) told

141. (A) Your letter will be published with a minor correction.
(B) I could arrange a discount on a two-year subscription.
(C) Our readers are quite interested in the fashion industry.
(D) The ideal length would be about 750 to 1,000 words.

142. (A) receive
(B) borrow
(C) prevent
(D) distinguish

Vocabulary

☐ **renovate** 翻新；整修

寄件者：傑滋納‧薩迦 <j.sakya@springfieldtimes.com>
收件者：露絲‧賀洛維茲 <ruthphorowitz@musicmail.com>
主　旨：您最近給《春田時報》的來信
日　期：11 月 22 日

賀洛維茲女士鈞鑒：

非常感謝您最近給《春田時報》的來信，您在信中針對本報在十一月十八日對於市府計畫整修春田藝術館的報導做出了回應。您提出了幾個有趣而且我認為是完全獨創的論點，我在想，不知道您是否會有興趣將您對這個主題的想法擴充，幫本報寫成一篇較長的文章。理想的長度約為 750 到 1000 字。

假如您有興趣撰寫這樣的一篇文章，請盡快打電話給我。我們需要在十一月二十四日下午四點前收到您的大作，如此才能在當晚把它放在我們的網站上和十一月二十五日（市議會下次開會的日子）的報紙中。

期待與您合作。

《春田時報》主編
傑滋納‧薩迦敬上
(541) 565-3227

139　正解 D

解析 本題須選出正確的動狀詞。由於句中提到的 "your recent letter"「您最近的來信」本身之目的在於針對《春田時報》的報導做出回應，因此應選擇表「主動」的「現在分詞」"responding" 作為其修飾語。正確答案是 (D)。

140　正解 C

解析 本題考正確之搭配字詞。由前後文意來推斷，傑滋納‧薩迦想說的應該是賀洛維茲女士在她的信中「提出了」幾個有趣且獨創的 "points"「論點」，而可與 "points" 搭配，表達「提出了」之意的動詞為 (C) made。

141　正解 D

解析 本題考插入句。由前一句後半提到的 "... expanding your thoughts ... into a longer article ...."「……將您……的想法擴充……成一篇較長的文章……。」可斷定，最合理的接續句應該是告知對方該文章之理想長度的 (D) The ideal length would be about 750 to 1,000 words.。至於選項 (A)「您的來信將在稍做修改之後刊出。」則明顯偏離了前一句話的重點。而選項 (B)「若訂閱兩年我可以安排打個折扣。」與 (C)「我們的讀者對於時裝業相當感興趣。」更是牛頭不對馬嘴。

142　正解 A

解析 本題須選出正確的動詞。由前後文意可知，因為報社必須及時刊出該文章，所以需要在十一月二十四日下午四點前「收到」它（空格後的 "it" 指的是前一句中提到的 "such a piece"「這樣的一篇文章」）。正解為 (A) receive。注意，其他三個動詞選項也都可以用「代名詞 it」當受詞，再接介系詞 from，但置於本句中意思皆不通：(B) borrow 指「借入」、(C) prevent 指「防止」、(D) distinguish 指「區別」。

(May 23) — In a bid to revitalize business in Alpine City, the heart of downtown will be turned into a pedestrian-only shopping district. ------- on June 15, Market Street between Lake Blvd. and Third Street will be completely closed to cars, bicycles, and other personal vehicles. -------.
143. **144.**

"This is going to make downtown a more attractive place to visit," says Jamie Ashby, mayor of Alpine. "It will be a safer environment for families, and will cut down on pollution." Some business owners are worried the change will hurt business. Stan Willis, owner of Alpine Hardware, noticed a twenty percent drop in ------- when the street was closed for repaving
145.
last year. "If people can't park near my store, they're less likely to purchase large or heavy items," he said. "I do hope this brings more people downtown. If it doesn't, I'll ------- my business elsewhere."
146.

143. (A) From
(B) Begin
(C) First
(D) Starting

144. (A) Commercial vehicles will be allowed on Market between 10 PM and 6 AM.
(B) Anyone driving on Lake Blvd. after June 15 will be issued a traffic ticket.
(C) Cyclists will be allowed to use Market Street during non-business hours.
(D) Drivers can take an alternate route from Lake to Third via Market Street.

145. (A) customer
(B) damage
(C) revenue
(D) production

146. (A) going to move
(B) have to move
(C) must move
(D) be moved

第 143 到 146 題請參照下面這篇報導。

（五月二十三日）──為努力重振阿爾潘市的商業，鬧區中心將轉變成徒步購物區。六月十五日起，湖泊大道與第三街之間的市場街將禁止汽車、腳踏車和其他個人交通工具通行。商用車輛晚間十點至早上六點則可行駛市場街。

「這將使鬧區成為一個更具吸引力的造訪場所，」阿爾潘市長傑米‧艾希比說道。「它會是個更安全、適合全家人的環境，而且可降低污染。」有些業主擔心，這個改變會影響生意。阿爾潘五金行的老闆史丹‧衛理斯發現，街道在去年封閉重鋪時，營收掉了兩成。「如果民眾不能在我的店附近停車，他們就比較不可能購買大型或重的物品，」他說。「我衷心希望這會為鬧區帶來更多的人潮。假如沒有的話，我就必須把生意移往別處了。」

143 正解 D

解析 本題須選出具正確字義與字形的單字。由於空格後的介系詞片語 "on June 15" 已表達一名確之日期，因此空格內只能填入可用來指「由……開始」的選項 (D)「現在分詞」 "Starting"。「介系詞」選項 (A) From、「原形動詞」選項 (B) Begin 及「副詞」選項 (C) First 皆無法使用於 "on June 15" 之前。

145 正解 C

解析 由空格後的 "when the street was closed for repaving last year"「街道在去年封閉重鋪時」可推知，當時該五金行的生意一定受到了影響，因而導致「營收」掉了兩成。正確答案是 (C) revenue。選項 (A) 不可選，因為 "customer" 為「可數」名詞，不可單獨使用，且置於介系詞 in 之後亦毫無意義。選項 (B) damage「損害」則與句意邏輯背道而馳，更不可選。至於選項 (D) production「生產」明顯與句意不相干，不予考慮。

144 正解 A

解析 本題考插入句。雖然市場街為徒步購物區，但仍需要貨車將商品運送到商店以供消費者購買。因此，在前一句 "Starting on June 15, Market Street between Lake Blvd. and Third Street will be completely closed to cars, bicycles, and other personal vehicles."「六月十五日起，湖泊大道與第三街之間的市場街將禁止汽車、腳踏車和其他個人交通工具通行。」之後接上 (A)「商用車輛晚間十點至早晨六點則可行駛市場街。」最合理。選項 (B)「任何於六月十五日之後在湖泊大道上開車者都會被開交通罰單。」與前一句內容無直接關係。選項 (C)「腳踏車騎士將被允許於非營業時間使用市場街。」明顯與前一句內容有所衝突。至於選項 (D)「從湖泊大道到第三街駕駛可經由市場街走替代道路。」則完全背離前一句內容。

146 正解 B

解析 本題考正確之動詞組合。由空格前的 "I'll" 可知，其後須接一「原形」動詞，因此可立即排除 (A) going to move。接著可排除 (C) must move，因為 "must" 為「情態助動詞」，而 "will" (I'll = I will) 亦為「情態助動詞」，依文法不可同時使用兩個情態助動詞。至於選項 (B) 中的 "have to" 與 (D) 中的 "be" 雖皆可置於 I'll 之後（"have to" 為「邊際助動詞」，"be" 則為「功能助動詞」），但因為 "be moved" 為「被動式」，與句意不符，所以不可選。正解為 (B) have to move。注意，指「遷移」之意時，"move" 除了作「及物動詞」使用（如本句）外，也常作為「不及物動詞」，例如："They have moved to Boston." 「他們已經搬到波士頓去了。」

Vocabulary
☐ **repave** 重鋪（路等） ☐ **elsewhere** 在別處；到別處

PART 7

Questions 147-148 refer to the following notice.

Savoy Coding Academy Talent Base

Savoy Coding Academy provides comprehensive training in today's most in-demand digital technologies. Companies from startups to established technology firms are finding the skilled programmers they need on the <u>Savoy Coding Academy Talent Base</u>. Every Savoy graduate in our database is certified by Savoy to be proficient in the technical fields identified in their profile. Each member profile also includes a portfolio of completed projects and code samples. Access to the job board website is free of charge and open to all potential employers. Feel free to contact our <u>Career Services</u> department for more information.

第 147 到 148 題請參照下面這則公告。

薩沃耶編碼學苑人才庫

薩沃耶編碼學苑針對現今需求量最大的數位科技提供全面性的訓練。不論是新創企業或老字號科技公司,全都會到薩沃耶編碼學苑的人才庫尋找他們所需要之熟練的程式設計人員。在我們資料庫裡的每位薩沃耶畢業生都經過薩沃耶的認證,一定都精通在個人檔案中所載明的技術領域。各個成員檔案中還包含已完成之案件和程式碼範例的個人作品集。使用求才版網站免收費,歡迎所有的潛在雇主多加利用。如需更多資訊請隨時與我們的職涯服務部聯繫。

---

147 正解 B

What is the purpose of this notice?
(A) To describe a curriculum
(B) To promote a resource
(C) To initiate a service
(D) To recruit programmers

這則公告的目的是什麼?
(A) 說明課程
(B) 宣傳資源
(C) 啓動服務
(D) 招募程式設計人員

解析 本題屬「推論」題,問本則公告的目的為何。文章一開始就提到薩沃耶編碼學苑提供數位科技 (digital technologies) 方面的訓練;接著就說他們所訓練出來的技術純熟之程式設計師 (skilled programmers) 很受科技業界的青睞;然後又對他們的畢業生能力提出了保證 (Every ... graduate ... is certified ... to be proficient);最後則表示歡迎有招聘需求的業主多加利用求才版網站 (the job board website) 且可隨時與他們的職涯服務部 (Career Services department) 聯繫。由以上幾點可確知,本公告之目的就是在推廣薩沃耶這個培育科技人才的資源,因此本題選 (B) To promote a resource。

---

148 正解 D

What can visitors do on the Talent Base website?
(A) Submit a job application
(B) Request access to a database
(C) Review current job openings
(D) View a potential applicant's work

訪客在人才庫的網站上能做什麼?
(A) 提交求職申請
(B) 要求使用資料庫
(C) 審視現有職缺
(D) 看可能的求職者之作品

解析 本題亦屬「推論」題。由公告的第三句話可知,在薩沃耶的資料庫裡每一位畢業生的個人檔案都必須載明各自的技術領域。而由下一句 "Each member profile also includes a portfolio of completed projects and code samples." 「各個成員檔案中還包含已完成之案件和程式碼範例的個人作品集。」則可推斷,只要上人才庫網站就可以看到每位畢業生的作品,因此本題選 (D) To recruit programmers。注意,從薩沃耶畢業後,就自然成為「可能的求職者」。

Vocabulary

☐ **in-demand** 需求量大的 ☐ **startup** 新創企業 ☐ **certify** 證明合格 ☐ **proficient** 精通的 ☐ **identify** 確認;指認;辨識
☐ **portfolio** 個人作品集 ☐ **free of charge** 免收費的 ☐ **potential** 潛在的;可能的 ☐ **curriculum** 課程 ☐ **initiate** 啓動;發起

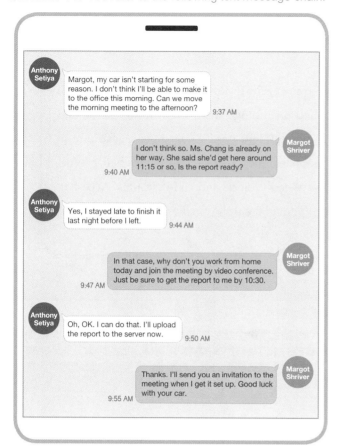

安東尼‧塞迪亞
瑪格，我的車因為某種原因發不動。
我想我今天上午沒辦法進辦公室了。
我們能不能把上午的會議改到下午？ 9:37 AM

瑪格‧施萊弗
我想不行。張小姐已經在路上了。
她說她大概會在 11:15 左右到這裡。
報告準備好了嗎？ 9:40 AM

安東尼‧塞迪亞
是的，我昨天晚上待到很晚，
在離開前把它完成了。9:44 AM

瑪格‧施萊弗
這樣的話，你何不今天就在家上班，
用視訊會議加入開會。只是你務必要
在 10:30 前把報告交給我。9:47 AM

安東尼‧塞迪亞
噢，好。這我辦得到。
我現在就把報告上傳到伺服器。9:50 AM

瑪格‧施萊弗
謝了。等我安排好，
就會把開會邀請傳給你。
希望你能搞定你的車子。9:55 AM

149　正解 A

What is suggested about Anthony Setiya?
(A) He sometimes works overtime.
(B) He usually works from home.
(C) He prefers online meetings.
(D) He works for an auto company.

對話中暗示了安東尼‧塞迪亞如何？
(A) 他有時候會加班。
(B) 他通常在家上班。
(C) 他偏好線上會議。
(D) 他任職於汽車公司。

解析 本題為「推論」題。由安東尼‧塞迪亞回答瑪格‧施萊弗的問題「報告準備好了嗎？」時所說的 "Yes, I stayed late to finish it last night before I left."「是的，我昨天晚上待到很晚，在離開前把它完成了。」可推知，他有時候必須加班。正確答案是 (A) He sometimes works overtime.。

150　正解 D

What does Margot Shriver ask Mr. Setiya to do?
(A) Postpone a meeting
(B) Complete a report
(C) Schedule a video conference
(D) Send a document

瑪格‧施萊弗要塞迪亞先生做什麼？
(A) 將會議延後
(B) 完成報告
(C) 為視訊會議排定時間
(D) 傳送文件

解析 本題屬「細節」題。因為塞迪亞先生（安東尼）已經把報告準備好了，所以瑪格叫他不用親自來開會，但必須在 10:30 之前把報告交到她手中。對此，安東尼回應道："Oh, OK. I can do that. I'll upload the report to the server now."「噢，好。這我辦得到。我現在就把報告上傳到伺服器。」換言之，瑪格要安東尼做的就是將報告傳給她，因此本題選 (D) Send a document。注意，原文中的 "report" 當然是作為「文件」來傳送。

Vocabulary
☐ **satrt** 發動（車子）　☐ **on one's way** （某人）在途中　☐ **work overtime** 加班

Memo

To: All Emerson Employees

From: George Benson

Subject: Policy Changes

Because of the current influenza outbreak, we are implementing several new policies to protect the health and well-being of our staff, customers, and partners. Please be advised of the following changes:

- All visits to the office by non-employees must be pre-approved by a manger. Whenever possible, communicate with vendors and other partners online rather than face-to-face.
- In-person meetings of more than two people are not allowed for any reason. Please coordinate with colleagues by text or phone.
- If you eat lunch at the office, please do so at your desk, not the break room.
- Employees are required to monitor themselves for flu symptoms, including fever, cough, and sore throat. If you feel unwell or exhibit any symptoms, please do not come to work. Supervisors have been asked to grant all reasonable requests for leave and to facilitate work-from-home when appropriate.

These policies will remain in effect until the end of the month, at which point they will be reevaluated and adjusted. I appreciate your cooperation during these difficult times.

Thank you,
G.B.

備忘錄

收件者：艾默森全體員工

寄件者：喬治・班森

主旨：政策變更

由於目前爆發了流感，我們將實施幾項新的政策以保障我們的員工、顧客和生意夥伴之健康與福祉。請留意以下變更：

- 非公司員工到辦公室參訪一律必須經過一位經理事先核准。盡可能在線上，而不要面對面，與賣家和其他生意夥伴聯繫。
- 不論有任何理由都不允許兩個人以上的面對面會議。請以簡訊或電話與同事做協調。
- 如在辦公室用餐，請待在自己的座位上，不要到休息室去。
- 員工必須自我監測流感症狀，包括發燒、咳嗽和喉嚨痛。如果感到不適或出現任何症狀，請勿到班。公司已明令各主管批准所有合理的請假要求，並在適當時協助在家工作。

上列政策將持續生效到月底，屆時將重新評估並做調整。感謝各位在這段困難期間的合作。

謝謝各位

G.B.

---

151 正解 B

What is the purpose of this memo?
(A) To ask for donations
(B) To announce new policies
(C) To warn the employees of a disease
(D) To remind all supervisors of a meeting

這則備忘錄的目的是什麼？
(A) 要求捐款
(B) 宣布新的政策
(C) 提醒員工留意一種疾病
(D) 提醒所有的主管參加一場會議

解析　本題為「推論」題，問備忘錄之目的為何。備忘錄一開頭就提到，由於爆發流感，因此該公司將會實施新政策 (Because of the current influenza outbreak, we are implementing several new policies ....)。接著就列出了四項新政策的內容。發文者還表示這些新政策到月底之前都有效 (These policies will remain in effect until the end of the month ....)。最後則是感謝員工們的合作。由以上幾點可斷定，本則備忘錄的目的為 (B) To announce new policies「宣布新的政策」。

---

152 正解 D

What must a vendor do if he/she wants to visit the company?
(A) Pay an entrance fee
(B) Make an appointment beforehand
(C) Call a supervisor first
(D) Get approval from a manager

若有廠商想參訪該公司必須做什麼？
(A) 支付入場費
(B) 事先預約
(C) 先打電話給一位主管
(D) 取得一位經理的核准

解析　本題屬「細節」題。由第一項新政策中提到的 "All visits to the office by non-employees must be pre-approved by a manger." 「非公司員工到辦公室參訪一律必須經過一位經理事先核准。」即可知，正解為 (D) Get approval from a manager「取得一位經理的核准」。

Vocabulary

☐ **influenza** 流行性感冒（一般簡稱 "flu"）　☐ **outbreak** 爆發　☐ **well-being** 福祉　☐ **pre-approve** 事先核准　☐ **vendor** 小販；銷售廠商
☐ **in-person meeting** 面對面會議　☐ **coordinate** 協調　☐ **break room** 休息室　☐ **symptom** 症狀　☐ **exhibit** 顯示；展現　☐ **grant** 准許
☐ **facilitate** 使便利　☐ **in effect** 生效　☐ **reevaluate** 重新評估　☐ **adjust** 調整　☐ **donation** 捐贈；捐款　☐ **entrance fee** 入場費

Library Book Sale

WHEN

March 5 10:00 AM – 5:00 PM *
March 6 10:00 AM – 1:00 PM

WHERE

Central Library Balboa Room
(Across from the Circulation Desk)

Every year, patrons donate thousands of used books to be sold at the Central Library book sale. Revenue from the sale is used to support the library's general fund.

This event is organized by the Friends of Central Library (FOCL), an independent volunteer group. Join FOCL and your $10 membership fee will entitle you to numerous benefits such as a 10% discount at the library gift shop and reduced-price tickets for the library lecture series. Free bookmarks and snacks will be provided by the head librarian throughout the sale.

* FOCL members are invited to attend the Preview Night on March 4 to get first pick of the books offered during the sale.

時間	地點
3 月 5 日 10:00 AM – 5:00 PM *	央圖巴波亞室
3 月 6 日 10:00 AM – 1:00 PM	（借還書櫃檯對面）

每一年館友都會捐贈成千上萬冊的二手書在央圖的圖書拍賣會上出售，拍賣的營收則用來資助圖書館的綜合基金。

本活動是由獨立的志工團體央圖之友 (FOCL) 所籌辦。加入 FOCL，您的十美元會費就會讓您有資格享受諸多優惠，例如圖書館禮品店可打九折，購買圖書館講座系列門票亦有折價。在整個拍賣期間圖書館長將提供免費的書籤和點心。

＊ 敬邀 FOCL 的會員出席三月四日的預覽之夜，以便優先挑選拍賣期間所提供的書籍。

153　正解 D

What is suggested about the sale?
(A) It will benefit a volunteer group.
(B) The books come from the library.
(C) It is run by the head librarian.
(D) The proceeds will go to the library.

公告中暗示了拍賣的什麼事？
(A) 它將使志工團體受惠。
(B) 書籍來自圖書館。
(C) 它由圖書館長主辦。
(D) 收益將歸圖書館。

解析　本題屬「推論」題。由公告的第一段第二句 "Revenue from the sale is used to support the library's general fund." 可知，拍賣所得將作為圖書館的綜合基金。換言之，實質受益者乃圖書館本身，因此本題選 (D) The proceeds will go to the library.「收益將歸圖書館。」其他選項則皆無法由公告內容推知。

154　正解 C

What is NOT suggested as a reason to join the Friends of Central Library?
(A) Reduced gift shop prices
(B) Discounted lecture tickets
(C) Free gifts and snacks
(D) Early entry to the sale

公告中「未」暗示哪一點是應該加入央圖之友的理由？
(A) 禮品店折價
(B) 講座門票打折
(C) 免費的贈品和點心
(D) 優先進入拍賣會

解析　本題亦為「推論」題。公告中提到，若加入央圖之友將可享受諸多優惠，包括 "a 10% discount at the library gift shop"「圖書館禮品店打九折」、"reduced-price tickets for the library lecture series"「圖書館講座系列門票折價」等。另，在公告的補充說明中則提到，央圖之友若參加三月四日的 "Preview Night"「預覽之夜」，則可 "get first pick of the books offered during the sale"「優先挑選拍賣期間提供的書籍」。以上幾個「好處」應該都屬加入央圖之友的好理由，因此選項 (A)、(B) 與 (D) 皆不可選。正確答案是 (C) Free gifts and snacks，因為文中提到的 "Free bookmarks and snacks will be provided by the head librarian throughout the sale."「在整個拍賣期間圖書館長將提供免費的書籤和點心。」乃針對所有的參與者而言，與加入央圖之友並無直接關聯。

Vocabulary

☐ **circulation desk**（圖書館）借還書櫃檯　☐ **patron** 資助者（本文中指使用圖書館的人）；主顧　☐ **donate** 捐贈　☐ **fund** 基金
☐ **volunteer** 志工　☐ **membership fee** 會費　☐ **entitle** 使有資格　☐ **series** 系列（單複數同形）　☐ **bookmark** 書籤
☐ **head librarian** 圖書館館長　☐ **preview** 預覽　☐ **run** 主辦；經營　☐ **proceeds** 收益（複數形）

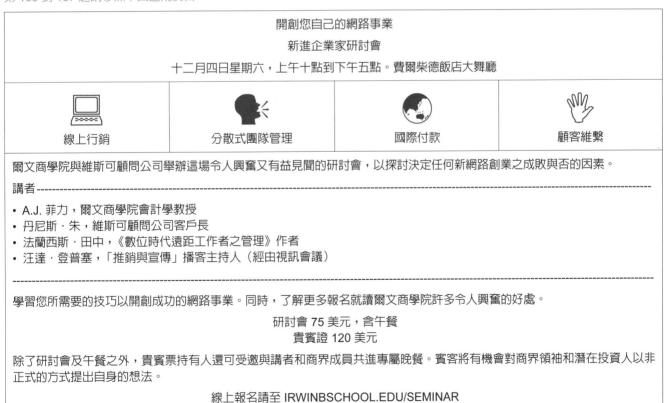

START YOUR OWN ONLINE BUSINESS

A SEMINAR FOR NEW ENTREPRENEURS

Saturday, December 4, 10AM–5PM • Fairchild Hotel Grand Ballroom

ONLINE MARKETING	DISTRIBUTED TEAM MANAGEMENT	INTERNATIONAL PAYMENTS	CUSTOMER RETENTION

The Irwin School of Business and Vestco Consulting present this exciting and informative seminar on the factors that determine the success of any new online business venture.

SPEAKERS
- A.J. Freely, Professor of Accounting at the Irwin School of Business
- Denise Chu, Chief Customer Officer at Vestco Consulting
- Francis Tanaka, Author of *Supervising Remote Workers in the Digital Age*
- Wanda Dempsey, Host of the Promotion and Publicity Podcast (via video conference)

Learn the skills you need to launch a successful Internet business. At the same time, learn more about the many exciting benefits of enrolling at the Irwin School of Business.

SEMINAR $75 *Includes lunch*
VIP PASS $120

In addition to the seminar and lunch, VIP Passholders are invited to an exclusive dinner with the speakers and members of the business community. Guests will have the chance to informally present their ideas to business leaders and potential investors.

REGISTER ONLINE at IRWINBSCHOOL.EDU/SEMINAR

第 155 到 157 題請參照下面這則廣告。

開創您自己的網路事業

新進企業家研討會

十二月四日星期六,上午十點到下午五點。費爾柴德飯店大舞廳

線上行銷	分散式團隊管理	國際付款	顧客維繫

爾文商學院與維斯可顧問公司舉辦這場令人興奮又有益見聞的研討會,以探討決定任何新網路創業之成敗與否的因素。

講者

- A.J. 菲力,爾文商學院會計學教授
- 丹尼斯・朱,維斯可顧問公司客戶長
- 法蘭西斯・田中,《數位時代遠距工作者之管理》作者
- 汪達・登普塞,「推銷與宣傳」播客主持人(經由視訊會議)

學習您所需要的技巧以開創成功的網路事業。同時,了解更多報名就讀爾文商學院許多令人興奮的好處。

研討會 75 美元,含午餐
貴賓證 120 美元

除了研討會及午餐之外,貴賓票持有人還可受邀與講者和商界成員共進專屬晚餐。賓客將有機會對商界領袖和潛在投資人以非正式的方式提出自身的想法。

線上報名請至 IRWINBSCHOOL.EDU/SEMINAR

Vocabulary

- **entrepreneur** 企業家　□ **ballroom** 舞廳　□ **consulting** 諮詢業;顧問業　□ **business venture** 創業　□ **accounting** 會計
- **remote** 遠距的;遠端的　□ **promotion** 推銷;推廣　□ **publicity** 宣傳　□ **enroll** 登記入學、入會等　□ **exclusive** 專用的;獨享的

What is suggested about the seminar?
(A) It is for prospective business owners.
(B) It will primarily be conducted online.
(C) Course credit is available to participants.
(D) Hotel accommodation is included in the fee.

廣告中暗示了研討會如何？
(A) 它是為可能成為企業主的人士而舉辦的。
(B) 它主要會是在線上舉行。
(C) 參加者可取得學分。
(D) 費用含飯店住宿。

解析 本題屬「推論」題，問此廣告暗示了研討會的什麼事。由廣告的大標 "START YOUR OWN ONLINE BUSINESS"「開創您自己的網路事業」以及小標 "A SEMINAR FOR NEW ENTREPRENEURS"「新進企業家研討會」即可斷定，此研討會的對象為可能成為企業主的人士，故正解為 (A)。至於其他選項則皆無法由廣告的任何一部分推知。

Which speaker would most likely discuss distributed team management?
(A) A.J. Freely
(B) Denise Chu
(C) Francis Tanaka
(D) Wanda Dempsey

哪一位講者最有可能討論分散式團隊管理？
(A) A.J. 菲力
(B) 丹尼斯‧朱
(C) 法蘭西斯‧田中
(D) 汪達‧登普塞

解析 本題亦屬「推論」題，問哪一位講者最有可能討論分散式團隊管理。在講者介紹中提到法蘭西斯‧田中是 *Supervising Remote Workers in the Digital Age*《數位時代遠距工作者之管理》一書的作者，換言之，他就是所謂「分散式團隊管理」的專家，因此由他來談這個主題再恰當不過，故正解為 (C)。其他講者的專長明顯皆與此主題無直接關係，因此應該不會是此主題的講者。

What is mentioned as a reason for purchasing a VIP ticket?
(A) Networking opportunities
(B) A complimentary dinner
(C) Preferential seating
(D) An investment seminar

廣告中提到了哪一點是購買貴賓票的理由？
(A) 人脈拓展機會
(B) 免費晚餐
(C) 優先座位
(D) 投資研討會

解析 本題屬「細節」題。由廣告最後一段中提到的 "... VIP Passholders are invited to an exclusive dinner with the speakers and members of the business community."「……貴賓票持有人還可受邀與講者和商界成員共進專屬晚餐。」可知，只要持有貴賓票就有機會認識一些學界與商界的相關人士，以拓展自己的人脈，故正解為 (A)。

Vocabulary

☐ **prospective** 可能的；有希望的　☐ **primarily** 主要地　☐ **course credit** 學分　☐ **participant** 參加者　☐ **networking** 人脈拓展
☐ **complimentary** 免費的　☐ **preferential** 優先的

Twin Lakes City Swimming Pool

The Twin Lakes City Parks and Recreation Department has established these rules for the safety and enjoyment of everyone using the pool. Our aim is to create a wholesome and welcoming environment for all our guests.

Overview

Pool hours are 7 AM to 10 PM Lifeguard hours are 2 PM to 8 PM on weekdays and 9 AM to 9 PM on weekends.

Admission fee: $2 for adults. $1 for children 12 and under.

Exercise lanes may be reserved in 30-minute blocks. No more than two consecutive blocks may be registered. Notify a lifeguard or administrator if a lane you reserved is occupied.

Rules

- No running, diving, or horseplay in or around the pool.
- The following items are not allowed in the pool or on the pool deck: glass containers of any kind, pool toys or flotation devices, food and drinks (except water).
- Children under 12 are not allowed in the pool or on the deck when a lifeguard is not on duty.
- Proper swimming attire is required. Shorts and T-shirts are not permitted in the water. Suitable swimwear items are available for sale at the Twin Lakes Mall across the street from the pool. Towels may be purchased at the pool office.
- Do not use the pool if you feel unwell, exhibit cold or flu symptoms, or have a cut or wound.
- Please use the showers provided before and after entering the pool.
- No more than 25 people may use the pool simultaneously. Exit the pool immediately upon lifeguard request.

第 158 到 160 題請參照下面這則公告。

雙湖市游泳池

雙湖市公園休閒部為了每一位泳池使用者之安全與樂趣而訂定下列規則。我們的目的是為全體來客打造一個有益身心健康且友善宜人的環境。

概述

泳池開放時間為上午七點至晚上十點。救生員值班時間為平日下午兩點至晚上八點，週末上午九點至晚上九點。

入場費：成人 2 美元，十二歲以下兒童 1 美元。

訓練水道以三十分鐘為時段預約，一次不得登記超過連續兩個時段。您所預約之水道如遭占用，請通知救生員或管理人員。

規則

- 泳池中或周圍禁止奔跑、潛水或打鬧。
- 泳池中或泳池畔禁止下列物品：任何一種玻璃容器、泳池玩具或漂浮裝置、飲食（水除外）。
- 救生員未執勤時，十二歲以下兒童禁至泳池中或泳池畔。
- 須著合宜之泳裝，穿短褲、T 恤者不得入水，適當之泳衣品項於泳池對街之雙湖賣場有售。毛巾可至泳池營業處購買。
- 如感不適、出現感冒或流感症狀，或有割傷或其他傷口，請勿使用泳池。
- 在入池前後請使用本泳池所提供之淋浴設備。
- 不得超過二十五人同時使用泳池，經救生員要求須即刻離池。

第 2 回完全解析

PART 7

Vocabulary

☐ **recreation** 消遣；娛樂 ☐ **wholesome** 有益身心健康的 ☐ **overview** 概述 ☐ **admission fee** 入場費 ☐ **consecutive** 連續的
☐ **notify** 通知 ☐ **administrator** 管理者；行政官員 ☐ **horseplay** 胡鬧 ☐ **pool deck** 游泳池周邊
☐ **flotation device** 漂浮裝置（如游泳圈、救生衣等） ☐ **on duty** 執勤；值班 ☐ **attire** 服裝；衣著 ☐ **simultaneously** 同時地

According to the notice, what should guests do after swimming?
(A) Register for an exercise lane
(B) Notify the lifeguard
(C) Use the shower facilities
(D) Return towels to the office

根據公告，來客在游泳後應該做什麼？
(A) 登記使用訓練水道
(B) 通知救生員
(C) 使用淋浴設施
(D) 將毛巾歸還營業處

> 解析 本題考細節，問根據公告，來客在游泳後該做何事。由規則第六條 "Please use the showers provided before and after entering the pool." 「在入池前後請使用本泳池所提供之淋浴設備。」可清楚知道，泳客在游完泳後應該要使用當地的淋浴設施，因此本題選 (C) Use the shower facilities。

What can be done at the City Swimming Pool?
(A) Using pool toys or inflatable devices
(B) Swimming with no lifeguard on duty
(C) Purchasing the required swimwear
(D) Reserving a swimming lane for 90 minutes

在市立游泳池可以做什麼？
(A) 使用泳池玩具或可充氣裝置
(B) 在救生員未執勤時游泳
(C) 購買合乎規定的泳衣
(D) 預約九十分鐘的游泳水道

> 解析 本題屬「細節」題，但必須做一些延伸。規則第二條明白指出漂浮裝置 (flotation devices) 在雙湖市游泳池是被禁止的，因此選項 (A) 為誤。而規則第四條中也清楚表示合宜之泳裝的販售處是泳池對街的雙湖賣場 (Twin Lakes Mall)，所以選項 (C) 同樣為誤。另，在公告的概述部分中提到，訓練水道 (exercise lane) 以三十分鐘為一時段，最多只能連續預約兩個時段，故選項 (D) 亦為誤。正確答案是 (B)。注意，雖然在規則第三條中有提到，十二歲以下兒童在無救生員的情況下是不准下水的，但並沒有任何一條規定說十二歲以上的人不可以在同樣的情況下游泳，因此選項 (B) 成立。

What information is NOT provided?
(A) The reason the rules were created
(B) The pool's opening and closing times
(C) Recommended reservation times
(D) Details about the necessary attire

公告中「未」提供什麼資訊？
(A) 守則制定的原因
(B) 泳池的開放與關閉時間
(C) 建議的預約時間
(D) 必要泳裝的細節

> 解析 公告一開始就提及制定規則的原因是為了泳池使用者之安全與樂趣 (for the safety and enjoyment of everyone using the pool)，因此 (A) 不可選。接著在概述部分則清楚列出開放與關閉的時間：上午七點與晚上十點，故 (B) 亦不可選。另，在第四條規則中則提到必須穿著合宜的泳裝 (Proper swimming attire is required.) 等，所以 (D) 同樣為誤。公告中完全未觸及的是選項 (C) Recommended reservation times，故為正解。注意，勿將概述部分中提到的水道之預約與選項 (C) 中的「預約時間」混為一談。

Vocabulary

☐ **facilities** 設備；設施（複數形）　☐ **inflatable** 可充氣的

Stardust Regency Hotel

Service Assignment

Assignment No.	JGB8675309
Assigned By	Julia Valenzuela
Assigned To	Ty Fenton
Department	☐ Housekeeping ☐ Groundskeeping ☐ Parking and Transportation ☐ Food & Beverage ☑ Facilities ☐ Other (specify) _____
Location	Room 415
Time	March 2, 11:15 AM
Description	A guest reported a malfunctioning air conditioner at 11 AM. She is currently attending a function and will return to the room after 6 PM. Please report back on progress before 5 PM so I can arrange for an upgraded room for Ms. Nakayama if necessary.

Report

I replaced a faulty wall switch. The air conditioner is in good working order now. While inspecting the main unit I noticed the filter was clogged, though this was unrelated to the switch. I washed and returned the filter. I'm not sure who's responsibility it is to monitor and maintain the AC equipment. I think it would be a good idea to schedule a regular—perhaps monthly—visual inspection as part of normal housekeeping duties. If necessary, I can show everyone how to remove and clean the filters.

T. Fenton
March 2, 4:40 PM

第 161 到 163 題請參照下面這個文件。

星塵帝豪飯店
服務工作派遣

派遣編號	JGB8675309
派遣者	茉莉亞‧瓦倫祖拉
受派遣人	泰‧芬頓
部門	☐ 房務 ☐ 場地維護 ☐ 停車與交通 ☐ 餐飲 ☑ 設備 ☐ 其他（確切指明）_____
地點	415 號房
時間	三月二日上午 11:15
說明	來客於上午十一點通報空調故障。她目前正在出席一場聚會，下午六點後會回房。請在下午五點前回報進度，以便我能在必要時為中山女士安排客房升等。

報告

我換掉了一個有問題的牆面開關。空調現在運轉良好。在檢測主機時，我留意到濾網阻塞，雖然這跟開關並不相干。我清洗了濾網並裝了回去。我不確定空調設備是由誰負責監控和維修。我認為排時間定期目視檢測（或許可以每個月一次）以作為正常房務職責的一部分會是好主意。如果有必要，我可以示範給大家看該如何把濾網拿下來清理。

T. 芬頓
三月二日下午 4:40

Vocabulary

☐ **housekeeping** 家務；（旅館的）房務 ☐ **groundskeeping** 場地維護 ☐ **malfunctioning** 出現故障的 ☐ **function**（盛大的）社交活動；聚會
☐ **faulty** 有瑕疵的；有錯誤的 ☐ **switch** 開關 ☐ **inspect** 檢視；勘查 ☐ **filter** 過濾器 ☐ **clog** 阻塞 ☐ **maintain** 保養；維修
☐ **AC** (= air conditioning) 冷氣 ☐ **visual** 視覺的

Who most likely is Mr. Fenton?　　芬頓先生最有可能是什麼人？
(A) A guest of the hotel　　(A) 飯店的客人
(B) A housekeeper　　(B) 房務人員
(C) A hotel supervisor　　(C) 飯店督導
(D) A maintenance worker　　(D) 維修工

解析	本題屬「推論」題。由服務工作派遣單上「部門」一欄中所勾選的 "Facilities" 可知，芬頓先生負責的是各種設備方面的服務。由於 415 號房的冷氣出了問題，因此芬頓先生前往檢視。而由他的工作報告內容可知，他曾換掉一個開關 (I replaced a faulty wall switch.)，也清洗了冷氣機的濾網 (I washed and returned the filter.)。由以上幾點來推斷，芬頓先生應該是一位維修人員。正確答案是 (D) A maintenance worker。

What does the document indicate about Ms. Nakayama?　　文件中指出了中山女士如何？
(A) She requested an upgraded room.　　(A) 她要求客房升等。
(B) She will attend a function when she returns.　　(B) 她回來時會去參加一場聚會。
(C) She will stay in Room 415 that evening.　　(C) 她當晚會住在 415 號房。
(D) She is expecting a report by 5 PM.　　(D) 她在等一份下午五點前會完成的報告。

解析	本題考細節。在派遣單上的「說明」一欄中提到 "She ... will return to the room after 6 PM."「她（指中山女士）……下午六點後會回房（即 415 號房）。」也就是說，中山女士當天晚上會住在 415 號房，因此本題選 (C) She will stay in Room 415 that evening.。

What does Mr. Fenton offer to do?　　芬頓先生表示願意做什麼？
(A) Replace a broken part　　(A) 更換壞掉的零件
(B) Provide supplemental training　　(B) 提供輔充訓練
(C) Make a maintenance schedule　　(C) 排定維修時間表
(D) Perform a monthly inspection　　(D) 執行每月檢測

解析	本題亦為「細節」題。由芬頓先生工作報告的最後一句話 "If necessary, I can show everyone how to remove and clean the filters."「如果有必要，我可以示範給大家看該如何把濾網拿下來清理。」即可知，正解為 (B) Provide supplemental training，亦即，芬頓先生願意提供一些補充訓練。

Vocabulary

□ **housekeeper** 管家；(旅館的) 房務人員　　□ **maintenance** 養護；維修　　□ **supplemental** 補充的

Questions 164-167 refer to the following online chat discussion.

Alice Chen	4:42 PM	OK, we're launching six websites in four weeks, so it's going to be a busy month. Let's start with the Mexican restaurant. Any updates?
Ben Wright	4:44 PM	I finally got the images from the photographer and finished the design on Monday. I'm just waiting for the text now.
Alice Chen	4:45 PM	I thought the website copy had already been edited and approved.
Yusef Khan	4:49 PM	That's true for the English text. The translation company's deadline for the Spanish text is Wednesday.
Alice Chen	5:53 PM	OK. Please follow up on that Yusef. And please ask Ms. Lopez if she wants to check the translation. That's the client's responsibility. Anything else?
Daniela Goldblatt	5:56 PM	Well, Ms. Lopez asked me to use a different online reservation system. I spent the morning working on that.
Alice Chen	6:01 PM	Hmm. You know that things like that can significantly affect the cost of the project. In the future, please discuss major changes with the team before starting work on them.
Daniela Goldblatt	6:05 PM	Fair enough, but it was easy to install, and it has some great features. For example, you can also use it to order to-go meals for pickup.
Alice Chen	6:09 PM	I'll take a look at it. I hope we can use this project as an example for other potential clients. New restaurants are always opening up, so they're a great source of new business for us.

第 164 到 167 題請參照下面這段線上聊天討論。

愛麗絲・陳	4:42 PM	好,我們在四週內要推出六個網站,所以這將是忙碌的一個月。我們從墨西哥餐館開始。有任何更新嗎?
班・萊特	4:44 PM	我總算跟攝影師拿到了圖片,並在星期一完成了設計。我現在正在等內文。
愛麗絲・陳	4:45 PM	我以為網站的副本已經編輯好並且核准了。
尤瑟夫・汗	4:49 PM	英文的內文是這樣沒錯。翻譯公司西班牙文內文的截止期限則是星期三。
愛麗絲・陳	5:53 PM	好。尤瑟夫,這個部分請你跟進。還有,請去問一下羅培茲小姐看她想不想檢查翻譯。那是客戶的責任。還有什麼嗎?
丹妮拉・戈德布拉特	5:56 PM	嗯,羅培茲小姐要我用一個不同的線上預約系統。我一早上都在做這件事情。
愛麗絲・陳	6:01 PM	嗯,妳知道像這樣的事可能會大大影響到案子的成本。未來,在開始做重大的變動之前,請先跟團隊討論。
丹妮拉・戈德布拉特	6:05 PM	有道理,但它安裝容易,而且有些性能很棒。比如說,它還能用來點自取的外賣餐點。
愛麗絲・陳	6:09 PM	我會去看一下。我希望我們可以用這個案子作為其他潛在客戶的範例。新餐館一直不斷地在開,所以對我們來說,它們是一個很不錯的新生意來源。

Vocabulary
☐ **follow up on** 跟進　☐ **work on** 致力於;從事　☐ **significantly** 相當程度地　☐ **to-go** 外帶的　☐ **pickup** 領取

164 正解 A

What kind of business do the chat discussion participants most likely work for?
(A) A web design firm
(B) A Mexican restaurant
(C) A photography studio
(D) A translation company

參與聊天討論者最有可能是在哪種公司行號上班？
(A) 網頁設計公司
(B) 墨西哥餐館
(C) 攝影工作室
(D) 翻譯公司

> **解析** 本題為「推論」題。在討論的一開始愛麗絲‧陳就說 "OK, we're launching six websites in four weeks ...."「好，我們在四週內要推出六個網站⋯⋯。」而接下來四個人談話的主題都圍繞在幫一家墨西哥餐館設計網站的事情上。最後愛麗絲‧陳還明白表示 "New restaurants are always opening up so, they're a great source of new business for us."「新餐館一直不斷地在開，所以對我們來說，它們是一個很不錯的新生意來源。」因此，最合理的推斷是，參與聊天的這四個人應該是在一家網頁設計公司工作。正解為 (A) A web design firm。

165 正解 C

What will Yusef Khan likely do next?
(A) Edit a document
(B) Check a translation
(C) Contact a customer
(D) Set up a system

尤瑟夫‧汗接下來可能會做什麼？
(A) 編輯文件
(B) 檢查翻譯
(C) 聯繫顧客
(D) 設定系統

> **解析** 本題屬「細節」題。由愛麗絲‧陳於五點五十三分時對尤瑟夫‧汗所說的 "... please ask Ms. Lopez if she wants to check the translation."「⋯⋯請去問一下羅培茲小姐看她想不想檢查翻譯。」即可知，尤瑟夫‧汗接下來應該是會與羅培茲小姐聯繫，因此本題選 (C) Contact a customer。

166 正解 D

What did the client request?
(A) An online meeting
(B) A phone call
(C) A revised deadline
(D) A new system

客戶要求了什麼？
(A) 一場線上會議
(B) 一通電話
(C) 修訂過的截止期限
(D) 一個新系統

> **解析** 本題同樣考細節，問客戶要求了什麼。由丹妮拉‧戈德布拉特於五點五十六分時所說的 "... Ms. Lopez asked me to use a different online reservation system."「⋯⋯羅培茲小姐要我用一個不同的線上預約系統。」即可知，本題應選 (D) A new system。

167 正解 C

At 6:05 PM, what does Daniela Goldblatt mean when she writes, "Fair enough"?
(A) She thinks that Ms. Chen is being impartial.
(B) She is pleased the quality of the work is adequate.
(C) She believes that Ms. Chen made a good point.
(D) She is sure the cost of the change is reasonable.

六點五分時，丹妮拉‧戈德布拉特打的 "Fair enough" 是什麼意思？
(A) 她認為陳小姐沒有偏見。
(B) 她很高興工作的品質適切。
(C) 她認為陳小姐言之有理。
(D) 她確信變動的成本合理。

> **解析** 本題考的是詞句解釋。"Fair enough" 字面上的意思是「夠公平」，但在丹妮拉‧戈德布拉特回應愛麗絲‧陳的說話時，她的意思是：妳說得對、妳說得有道理。正確答案是 (C)「她認為陳小姐言之有理。」注意，"fair enough" 實為一慣用語，在一般日常對話中常用來表達「對方的說法合理，可以接受。」

Vocabulary

- [ ] **impartial** 不偏袒的；公正的　　[ ] **adequate** 恰當的；適切的

From:	Emilio Negroni
To:	Janice Hamidou
Subject:	Volunteer Orientation
Date:	June 4

Dear Ms. Hamidou,

I am pleased to offer you a volunteer position at the Yonkers Art Museum. Every year, the Museum is fortunate to welcome an exceptional cohort of forty student volunteers from art history departments at universities in the Hudson Valley and beyond. I myself am a graduate of the YAM internship program and hope that you benefit from it as much as I have.

All new volunteers are required to attend a Volunteer Orientation on June 16. Please see the schedule below for details. And please stop by the museum's information desk any time before the orientation to pick up your official volunteer badge. It allows you free access to the museum and will give you the chance to meet other volunteers and become more familiar with the collection.

Please notify us of your participation by registering at the YAM Volunteer website before June 8. If you are unable to serve as a volunteer or if you cannot attend the orientation, please contact me as soon as possible.

Best regards,
Emilio Negroni
Volunteer Supervisor, Yonkers Art Museum

June 16	VOLUNTEER	ORIENTATION
9:00–10:00	Hudson Auditorium	Overview of the Volunteer Handbook
10:00–12:00	Hudson Auditorium	Introduction to the Collection
12:00–2:00	Atrium Café	Lunch
2:00–4:00	Empire Room	Education Training: School Visits and Guided Tours
4:00–6:00	Nordine Hall	Skills Training: Office Support and Patron Outreach

第 168 到 171 題請參照下面這封電子郵件。

寄件者：埃米里歐・內葛羅尼
收件者：珍妮絲・哈米多
主　旨：志工職前訓練
日　期：6 月 4 日

哈米多小姐您好：

很高興能提供您一個揚克斯藝術博物館的志工職位。本館每年都有幸從哈德遜谷及更遠的地方的大學藝術史系迎來四十位優秀的學生志工大軍。我本身就是揚克斯藝術博物館實習計畫的畢業生，希望您可以跟我一樣從中受益良多。

所有的新志工全都必須參與六月十六日的志工職前訓練。詳情請見下方時程表。在職前訓練前，請隨時抽空到博物館的服務台領取您的正式志工證。憑證可自由出入本館，使您有機會結識其他志工並對館藏更加熟悉。

請在六月八日前上揚克斯藝術博物館志工網站登記，讓我們知道您確定要參加。如果您無法擔任志工或不克參加職前訓練，請盡快與我們聯絡。

埃米里歐・內葛羅尼敬上
揚克斯藝術館志工督導

六月十六日	志工	職前訓練
9:00–10:00	哈德遜廳	《志工手冊》概述
10:00–12:00	哈德遜廳	介紹館藏
12:00–2:00	中庭咖啡館	午餐
2:00–4:00	帝國室	教育訓練：學校參訪與導覽
4:00–6:00	諾丁館	技能訓練：辦公室支援與贊助人拓展

Vocabulary
☐ **exceptional** 優異的　☐ **internship** 實習　☐ **orientation** 職前訓練　☐ **badge** 識別證　☐ **auditorium** 禮堂　☐ **outreach** 拓廣；外展

第 2 回完全解析

PART 7

What is the purpose of this email?
(A) To announce a program
(B) To offer a position
(C) To welcome a visitor
(D) To delegate a responsibility

這封電子郵件的目的是什麼？
(A) 宣布一項計畫
(B) 提供一個職位
(C) 歡迎一位訪客
(D) 委託一項責任

解析 本題屬「推論」題，問電子郵件的目的為何。寄件者埃米里歐·內葛羅尼一開頭就提及 "I am pleased to offer you a volunteer position at the Yonkers Art Museum." 「很高興能提供您一個揚克斯藝術博物館的志工職位。」接著在第二段中他則告知對方新志工皆須參加志工職前訓練 (Volunteer Orientation)。最後他還不忘提醒對方，若無法擔任志工或不克參加職前訓練 (If you are unable to serve as a volunteer or if you cannot attend the orientation)，必須及早通知。由以上幾點可確定，此封電子郵件的目的即 (B) To offer a position。

The word "cohort" in paragraph 1, line 2, is closes in meaning to
(A) apprentice
(B) companion
(C) group
(D) category

第一段第二行的 "cohort" 這個字的意思最接近
(A) 學徒
(B) 同伴
(C) 團體
(D) 類別

解析 本題考單字的含意，問第一段第二行的 "cohort" 這個字與何字意思最相近。"a cohort of" 指的是「一隊……」、「一群……」，因此與 "cohort" 意思最接近的字是 (C) group。

Where can Ms. Hamidou get her volunteer badge?
(A) The Hudson Auditorium
(B) The Empire Room
(C) Nordine Hall
(D) The Information Desk

哈米多小姐可以去哪裡取得志工證？
(A) 哈德遜廳
(B) 帝國室
(C) 諾丁館
(D) 服務台

解析 本題為「細節」題。由電子郵件第二段第三句所提到的 "... please stop by the museum's information desk ... to pick up your official volunteer badge." 「……請……到博物館的服務台領取您的正式志工證。」即可知，正解為 (D) The Information Desk。

According to the email, what must all volunteers do before June 8?
(A) Graduating from an art history department
(B) Organizing an orientation session
(C) Confirming their attendance
(D) Contacting the volunteer supervisor

根據電子郵件，六月八日前所有的志工都必須做什麼？
(A) 畢業於藝術史系
(B) 籌辦職前訓練講習
(C) 確認會參與
(D) 與志工督導聯絡

解析 本題亦考細節。由第三段第一句 "Please notify us of your participation by registering at the YAM Volunteer website before June 8." 「請在六月八日前上揚克斯藝術博物館志工網站登記，讓我們知道您確定要參加。」可知，本題應選 (C) Confirming their attendance。

Vocabulary

☐ **delegate** 委託　☐ **apprentice** 學徒　☐ **category** 類別；範疇

New Confuso Device to Launch?

By Martha Wells

TOKYO (July 21) — Analysts predict popular handheld gaming device manufacturer Confuso Industries is preparing to launch a new device sometime this fall. Analyst Dinesh Crampton has been tracking the sales and inventory of Confuso's latest device across several distribution networks and has identified diminishing supplies of the EBOT 5 in North America, Africa, and Europe. — [1] —. It appears that the company is intentionally reducing its stock.

In a research note published by Drummond Securities, Mr. Crampton argues that that the forthcoming device is likely not the EBOT 6 but rather an entirely new device. — [2] —. Another analyst, Maria Puente of Anticip Research, agrees. "Confuso received several large shipments of Isottech's TR50 microchips," Puente said in an interview. "The use of such powerful chips is a clear indication that Confuso is making a significant change."

Crampton believes existing games will function on the new device, but that developers will undoubtedly want to design games that take advantage of the speed and efficiency improvements offered by the new chips. In fact, the recent lack of new EBOT games may be a sign that developers are already working on games for the new device. — [3] —.

Confuso regularly subsidizes the development of new games to coincide with product launches to ensure consumers have ample reason to upgrade. Confuso, which develops games under its Whadabot subsidiary, has not released a new product in over eight months. Ms. Puente cited this to support her forecast, though she notes that Whatabot is not expected to be a major profit center for the company. — [4] —.

第 172 到 175 題請參照下面這篇文章。

康福梭的新裝置即將推出？

瑪莎・魏爾斯報導

東京（七月二十一日）——分析師們預測，當紅的手持遊戲裝置製造商康福梭工業準備在今年秋天的某個時候推出一個新的裝置。分析師迪內希・柯藍普敦透過好幾個經銷網追蹤康福梭最新裝置的銷售與庫存，他發現 EBOT 5 在北美、非洲和歐洲的供應量正在縮減。— [1] — 該公司顯然是在刻意減少存貨。

在佐蒙德證券所發表的一項研究紀要中，柯藍普敦主張，即將問世的裝置很可能不是 EBOT 6，而是另一個全新的裝置。— [2] — 另一位分析師，安提希普研究的瑪莉亞・普恩特，也表示認同。「康福梭收到了幾大批埃索鐵克的 TR50 微晶片。」普恩特在一次訪談中說。「使用這麼強大的晶片明顯表示康福梭正在做一個重大的改變。」

柯藍普敦認為，現有的遊戲可適用於新裝置，但開發人員無疑會想要設計出能夠善用新晶片所提供之快速與高效率的遊戲。事實上，EBOT 近期未推出新遊戲或許就是開發人員已經在為新裝置製作遊戲的一個徵兆。— [3] —

康福梭會固定補助新遊戲的開發來配合產品的推出，以確保消費者有充分的理由去升級。以其子公司瓦達巴特來開發遊戲的康福梭已經超過八個月沒有推出新產品。普恩特小姐舉出了這點來佐證她的預測，雖然她表示，瓦達巴特並不會是該公司的主要利潤中心。— [4] —

第 2 回完全解析

PART 7

Vocabulary

☐ **track** 追蹤　☐ **inventory** 清單；庫存　☐ **distribution** 分配；經銷　☐ **diminishing** 正在減少的　☐ **intentionally** 故意地　☐ **stock** 存貨；股票
☐ **forthcoming** 即將來臨的　☐ **shipment** （被運送的）一批貨物　☐ **efficiency** 效率　☐ **subsidize** 補貼；補助　☐ **coincide** 同時發生；符合
☐ **release** 發行；推出　☐ **cite** 舉出；引用　☐ **stock price** 股價　☐ **go out of business** 停業；倒閉　☐ **decline** 婉拒

What is indicated about Confuso Industries?
(A) They are running out of essential components.
(B) They are launching a device in a new market.
(C) They are manufacturing a new computer chip.
(D) They are encouraging developers to create new products.

文中指出了康福梭工業的什麼事？
(A) 他們的基本組件快要用完了。
(B) 他們正在新市場上推出一個裝置。
(C) 他們正在製造一個新的電腦晶片。
(D) 他們正鼓勵開發人員打造新產品。

> **解析** 文章一開始就提到 "... Confuso Industries is preparing to launch a new device ...."「……康福梭工業準備……推出一個新的裝置。」第二段末尾提到 "Confuso received ... large shipments of ... microchips."「康福梭收到了……大批……微晶片。」並指出 "... Confuso is making a significant change."「……康福梭正在做一個重大的改變。」第三段中則推斷道 "... developers will undoubtedly want to design games that take advantage of the speed and efficiency improvements offered by the new chips."「……開發人員無疑會想要設計出能夠善用新晶片所提供之快速與高效率的遊戲。」最後一段更說 "Confuso regularly subsidizes the development of new games to coincide with product launches ...."「康福梭會固定補助新遊戲的開發來配合產品的推出……。」由此可見，康福梭目前應該是正在鼓勵開發人員打造新產品，故正解為 (D)。

What is NOT given as evidence that Confuso will launch a new device?
(A) Falling stock prices
(B) Diminishing supplies
(C) Upgraded microchips
(D) The lack of new products

哪一點「未」被提出作為康福梭將推出新裝置的證據？
(A) 股價下跌
(B) 供應量縮減
(C) 微晶片升級
(D) 新產品的缺乏

> **解析** 在第一段中就提到有分析師發現該公司在北美、非洲和歐洲的供應量正在縮減 (diminishing supplies ... in North America, Africa, and Europe)，因此選項 (B) 不可選。接著在第二段中則提到該公司使用了強大的微晶片 (The use of such powerful chips)，所以選項 (C) 亦不可選。之後在第三段中則提及該公司最近並未推出新遊戲 (the recent lack of new ... games)，而在第四段中也有相同的論點："Confuso ... has not released a new product in over eight months."「……康福梭已經超過八個月沒有推出新產品。」故選項 (D) 同樣為誤。本題應選無中生有的 (A)「股價下跌」。注意，"stock" 為多義字，原文第一段最後提到的 "reducing its stock" 指的是「減少存貨」，與「股價下跌」毫不相干。

What is reported about Whadabot?
(A) It often publishes market forecasts.
(B) It is going out of business.
(C) It is owned by Confuso.
(D) It is a major source of revenue.

文中報導了瓦達巴特的什麼事？
(A) 它經常發表市場預測。
(B) 它快停業了。
(C) 它為康福梭所擁有。
(D) 它是主要的營收來源。

> **解析** 本題考細節。由最後一段第二句中提到的 "Confuso, which develops games under its Whadabot subsidiary ...."「以其子公司瓦達巴特來開發遊戲的康福梭……。」即可知，瓦達巴特屬於康福梭，因此本題選 (C) It is owned by Confuso.。

In which of the positions marked [1], [2], [3], and [4] does the following sentence best belong?

"MiG Gaming Studio, which has created dozens of games for Confuso devices, declined to comment for this article but has recently hired over twenty game developers to work on 'an exciting new project.'"

(A) [1]
(B) [2]
(C) [3]
(D) [4]

下面這個句子插入文中標示的 [1]、[2]、[3]、[4] 四處當中的何處最符合文意？

「曾為康福梭的裝置打造過數十款遊戲的 MiG 遊戲工作室婉拒為本篇報導做評論，但近期它雇用了超過二十位遊戲開發人員進行『一個令人興奮的新案子』。」

(A) [1]
(B) [2]
(C) [3]
(D) [4]

> **解析** 由題目插入句的重點「曾為康福梭打造過數十款遊戲的 MiG 最近雇用了二十多位遊戲開發人員進行一個新案子」來推斷，此句最適合用來接續提及「未推出新遊戲或許就是開發人員已經在為新裝置製作遊戲的一個徵兆」(the ... lack of new ... games may be a sign that developers are already working on games for the new device.) 的第三段最後一句，即標示 [3] 之處。答案是 (C)。其他位置，不論其前或其後，則皆未觸及「開發人員為新裝置設計遊戲」這個關鍵要點，故皆不可選。

Questions 176-180 refer to the following webpage and contact form.

第 176 到 180 題請參照下列網頁和聯絡表單。

簡介	家具	家電	估價	聯絡我們

佛洛伊德室內陳設

新款與二手家具擺設

設計師款折扣價

由家族擁有、經營近五十年，佛洛伊德住宅家具擺設是您所有家具需求的一站式商店。我們販售優質當代家具，但也買賣高品質的二手物件。所以無論您是需要為整個住宅配置家具，還是只是想把地下室那具舊五斗櫃給處理掉，佛洛伊德都能幫上忙。

當然不止於此。我們還買賣上等的優質小地毯、燈具和比如像冰箱、烤箱、洗碗機等電器。由於我們的品味高雅且選擇繁多，有很高的機率我們的現貨就恰好有您想尋找的東西，也恰如您所喜歡的風格。從傳家之物到空調，從溫馨、舒適到時髦、現代，我們應有盡有。

顧客都非常喜歡我們的免費估價服務。做法很簡單。只要將您想要出售的物件的照片上傳，我們隔天就會開個價給您。

佛洛伊德合理的送貨服務也很受歡迎。我們親切的送貨司機可將您購買的物品直送家中，並且只須支付少許的額外費用，他們便可以幫忙組合或安裝我們所售出的每樣物件。我們向您收購的物件則會依您方便，到大安娜堡地區的任何一個地方取件。我們說到做到！

- 請注意，我們從不買賣二手床墊。另，由於供應過剩，我們目前不收床架。

48104 密西根安娜堡南第五大道 343 號
(734) 327-4200　service@floydsfurnishings.com

第 2 回完全解析　PART 7

Vocabulary

☐ **furnishings** 屋內陳設（複數形）　☐ **appliance** 器具（多指家電）　☐ **appraisal** 評估；估價　☐ **carry**（商店）有⋯⋯出售
☐ **contemporary** 當代的；現代的　☐ **furnish** 為⋯⋯配備家具　☐ **chest of drawers** 五斗櫃　☐ **light fixture** 燈具　☐ **thanks to** 多虧；由於
☐ **exquisite** 精緻的；高雅的　☐ **stock** 有現貨；進貨　☐ **heirloom** 祖傳遺物；傳家寶　☐ **cozy** 溫馨的；舒適的　☐ **classy** 高級的；時髦的
☐ **assemble** 組合；裝配　☐ **mattresses** 床墊　☐ **bed frame** 床架

Contact Us

Name *	Ted Rexroth
Email *	t.rex@ohnochicxulub.com
Phone	(734) 794-6320
Subject	In-Person Appraisal?
Message *	I'm planning to move overseas for work in the near future and need to sell all of my furniture as soon as possible. I live in a small two-bedroom home, but over the years I've amassed quite a large collection. I noticed on your website that you offer free digital appraisals, but I wonder if the process would be less cumbersome if someone from your store visited my home in person. My place is on the Old West Side, within walking distance of your location downtown. I have some antiques from my grandmother that would be best appreciated in person. There are also some pieces in the attic, which has poor lighting for photography. Also, I noticed that you said you don't take beds at the moment, but it would be a great help if you could remove the one from my apartment. My landlord insists that the place be completely empty when I leave. I understand that you would be unable to compensate me for it, and I would even gladly provide a reasonable removal fee.

SEND MESSAGE * Required

聯絡我們

姓名 *	泰德・瑞世樂
Email*	t.rex@ohnochicxulub.com
電話	(734) 794-6320
主旨	親自估價？
訊息 *	在不久的將來我打算移居海外工作，因此需要盡快把家具全部賣掉。我住在一棟兩房的小宅裡，但多年下來累積了不少物品。 我在貴網站上看到，你們提供免費的數位估價，但我在想，假如貴店的人員親自到我的住處來的話，過程會不會比較不繁瑣。我的住所在舊西城，在貴公司市區據點的步行距離內。我有一些骨董得自祖母，親自鑑價會最妥當。還有一些物件收在閣樓，要拍照的話恐怕光線不足。 另外，我留意到你們說這陣子不收床，但假如你們能把我的床搬出我的公寓的話，對我而言會大有幫助。我的房東堅持，住處在我離開時要全部清空。我明白你們將無法因此補償我，而我甚至會樂意支付合理的搬運費。

送出訊息 * 必填

---

176 正解 D

What is NOT suggested about Floyd's?
(A) It stocks a diverse range of merchandise.
(B) It purchases stuff from the public.
(C) It is currently selling bed frames.
(D) It guarantees low prices on used items.

網頁中「未」暗示佛洛伊德如何？
(A) 它庫存的商品種類繁多。
(B) 它會向大眾收購東西。
(C) 它目前在賣床架。
(D) 它保證二手物件絕對便宜。

解析 由網頁第二段最後一句 "From heirlooms to air conditioners, from cozy and comfortable to classy and contemporary, we have it all." 「從傳家之物到空調，從溫馨、舒適到時髦、現代，我們應有盡有。」可知，佛洛伊德擁有各式各樣的商品，故 (A) 為誤。而由第一段第二句中提到的 "We ... also buy and sell high-quality used items." 「我們……也買賣高品質的二手物件。」則可知，佛洛伊德會跟民眾收購舊貨，故 (B) 亦為誤。另，在網頁最後的附註中提到 "... due to oversupply, we are not currently accepting bed frames." 「……由於供應過剩，我們目前不收床架。」換言之，佛洛伊德此時應該是想盡快將手中的床架賣掉，因此 (C) 亦非正解。正確答案是 (D)，因為網頁從頭到尾皆未觸及二手貨的價格。

Vocabulary

☐ **amass** 累積；積聚 ☐ **cumbersome** 笨重的；麻煩的 ☐ **antique** 骨董 ☐ **appreciate** 正確地評價 ☐ **attic** 閣樓 ☐ **landlord** 房東
☐ **compensate** 補償；賠償

What is indicated about Floyd's?
(A) It offers a free delivery service.
(B) It specializes in heirlooms and antiques.
(C) It recently opened a new location.
(D) It sells household electric appliances.

網頁中指出了佛洛伊德如何？
(A) 它提供免費的送貨服務。
(B) 它專攻傳家之物和骨董。
(C) 它最近開設了一個新據點。
(D) 它有販售家用電器。

解析 由網頁第二段第二句中提到的 "We also buy and sell ... appliances like refrigerators, ovens, and washing machines." 「我們還買賣……比如像冰箱、烤箱、洗碗機等電器。」即可知，本題應選 (D) It sells household electric appliances.。注意，在網頁第四段一開始所提到的 "Floyd's reasonable delivery service" 「佛洛伊德合理的送貨服務」並不表示佛洛伊德會提供「免費」的送貨服務，因此不可誤選 (A)。

Why does Ted Rexroth request an in-person meeting?
(A) He believes it would be more convenient.
(B) He intends to purchase a large collection.
(C) His landlord insists that he do so.
(D) His grandmother prefers to stay home.

泰德‧瑞世樂為什麼會要求親自會面？
(A) 他認為這樣會比較方便。
(B) 他有意購買大量的收藏品。
(C) 他的房東堅持要他這麼做。
(D) 他的祖母偏好待在家。

解析 本題考點落在「細節」。泰德‧瑞世樂在聯絡表單「訊息」部分的第二段第一句中提及 "... I wonder if the process would be less cumbersome if someone from your store visited my home in person." 「……我在想，假如貴店的人員親自到我的住處來的話，過程會不會比較不繁瑣。」顯然泰德‧瑞世樂認為見面討論會較為簡單方便，因此本題選 (A) He believes it would be more convenient.。

What is suggested about Ted Rexroth?
(A) His family owns a business.
(B) He frequently travels abroad.
(C) He lives close to Floyd's.
(D) He owns his own home.

表單中暗示了泰德‧瑞世樂如何？
(A) 他家擁有一項事業。
(B) 他經常出國。
(C) 他住得離佛洛伊德很近。
(D) 他擁有自己的住宅。

解析 本題屬「推論」題。由「訊息」第二段第二句中的 "My place is ... within walking distance of your location downtown." 「我的住所……在貴公司市區據點的步行距離內。」即可斷定，泰德‧瑞世樂住的地方離佛洛伊德並不遠，故正解為 (C) He lives close to Floyd's.。

What does Ted Rexroth offer to do?
(A) Photograph some antiques
(B) Pay for a service
(C) Walk to the store
(D) Purchase a bed

泰德‧瑞世樂表示願意做什麼？
(A) 為一些骨董拍照
(B) 為服務付費
(C) 走去店裡
(D) 買一張床

解析 本題同樣考細節。由「訊息」第三段最後一句中提到的 "... I would even gladly provide a reasonable removal fee." 「……我甚至會樂意支付合理的搬運費。」可知，泰德‧瑞世樂願意為對方的服務付費。正確答案是 (B) Pay for a service。

Vocabulary

□ **diverse** 不同的；多樣的   □ **household** 家庭的；家用的

第2回完全解析

PART 7

223

From:	Justine Kemp <cto@megaopticaldevices.com>
To:	<All Employees>
Subject:	Professional Development
Date:	December 17

Dear All,

As most of you know, senior management meets annually to identify the key skills Mega team members need to strengthen to increase our competitiveness in the coming year. This system has worked well enough, but it has also led to some inefficiencies. Not all employees needed the training that was provided to them; other employees didn't receive the training they required to thrive in their positions.

To address this issue, we have partnered with Chase/Bender Analytics, a consulting company that specializes in understanding and improving corporate training processes. We want to hear about your experiences, expectations, and suggestions about professional development at Mega Optical. All employees will soon receive another email with a link to an online survey at the Chase/Bender website. Please complete it before the end of the day tomorrow. We won't be making any immediate decisions, but we would like to have some preliminary data this week to help us determine the professional development budget for next year.

Mega Optical values the contributions of all of our team members. I firmly believe that your support of this endeavor will make our professional development program even stronger.

Justine Kemp,
Chief Talent Officer, Mega Optical Devices

第 181 到 185 題請參照下列電子郵件和報告。

寄件者：Justine Kemp <cto@megaopticaldevices.com>
收件者：＜全體同仁＞
主　旨：專業發展
日　期：12 月 17 日

大家好：

誠如各位大部分的人所知，公司高層主管們每年都會開會找出梅加的團隊成員所須強化的關鍵技能，以增進我們在來年的競爭力。這套制度至今運作得還不錯，但也導致了一些效率不彰的情況。並非全體員工都需要提供給他們的訓練；其他有些員工則未獲得能讓他們在職位上成長茁壯所必需的訓練。

為了因應這個問題，我們已經和專門研究了解和改良企業訓練流程的顧問公司確斯／本德分析攜手合作。針對在梅加光學的專業發展我們想聽聽各位的經驗、期待和建議。全體員工很快就會收到另一封電子郵件，裡面有確斯／本德網站之線上調查的連結。請在明天結束前填妥。我們不會立刻就做出什麼決定，但我們希望本週就有一些初步的資料可以幫助我們決定明年的專業發展預算。

梅加光學非常重視全體團隊成員的貢獻。我堅信，有各位的支持這項努力將使我們的專業發展計畫更加強大。

賈斯汀・坎普
梅加光學裝置人才長

Vocabulary

☐ **senior management** 公司高層　☐ **annually** 每年　☐ **competitiveness** 競爭力　☐ **inefficiency** 無效率；低效率　☐ **thrive** 茁壯成長
☐ **corporate**（大）公司的　☐ **contribution** 貢獻

Mega Optical Devices Professional Development Survey
Preliminary Report ◀ ▶ December 20

DISCLAIMER: Chase/Bender Analytics is still evaluating the survey data and still receiving new data (the response rate as of December 20 stands at 87%). Significant decisions should not be made until the full report with formal recommendations is submitted on January 12.

The conclusions drawn here are tentative, but there are enough signals in the data to allow us to observe a few trends. Two areas in particular stood out as relevant: desired training content and the preferred frequency and duration of instruction.

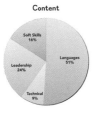
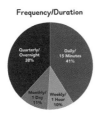

CONTENT: Previous professional development efforts focused on technical skills, but current interest in such training is minimal. A slight majority of employees expressed an interest in foreign languages, though there is no agreement about which languages should be taught. In situations where employees have diverse needs, companies often encourage employees to seek out their own classes and then offer them either full or partial tuition reimbursement.

FREQUENCY/DURATION: Employees overwhelmingly prefer either short daily classes or a quarterly overnight retreat. The frequency and duration of training has a bearing on how the instruction is provided. Short daily lessons are most efficiently delivered as part of an automated learning system. Conversely, an overnight retreat is as much an occasion for socializing and team building as it is for professional development. Moreover, some types of content (like language learning) are best acquired in short daily lessons, while others (such as a leadership workshop) are more suited to an all-day seminar.

梅加光學裝置專業發展調查

初步報告 ◀ ▶ 十二月二十日

免責聲明：確斯／本德分析仍在評估調查資料，並仍在收取新資料（截至十二月二十日，回覆率為 87%）。在一月十二日完整的報告以及正式建議提交之前，不應做出重大決定。

此處所得為暫時性之結論，但資料中的訊息足以讓我們觀察出幾個趨勢。有兩個相關的部分特別引人注目：希望獲得的訓練內容和偏好的授課頻率與時間長度。

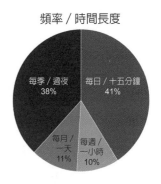

內容：先前為專業發展做的努力聚焦在技術性的技能上，但目前員工對這類訓練的興趣極低。略多於半數的員工對外語表示感興趣，雖然他們在該教哪種語言上並沒有共識。在員工有多元需求的情況下，許多公司常會鼓勵員工自尋課程，然後提供全額或部分的學費核銷。

頻率／時間長度：員工一面倒地偏好短期的每日課程，或是每季的過夜度假進修。訓練的頻率與時間長度則與授課的提供方式有關。若作為自動化學習系統的一部分，短期的每日課程在教學上最具效率。相反地，過夜度假進修既是社交和建立團隊的場合，同時也是提供員工專業發展訓練的好時機。此外，有些類型的內容（像是學語言）以短期的每日上課的學習效果最好，有的（諸如領導工坊）則比較適合全天的研討會。

---

181 正解 A

What is the purpose of the email?
(A) To explain an assignment
(B) To request some professional training
(C) To introduce a company
(D) To announce a budget

電子郵件的目的是什麼？
(A) 解釋說明一項指定任務
(B) 要求做一些專業訓練
(C) 介紹一家公司
(D) 宣布一項預算

解析　本題為「推論」題，問電子郵件之目的為何。寄件者賈斯汀·坎普在第一段先提到公司為了提高競爭力所採用的制度雖然還不錯但也導致了一些效果不彰的情況 (... it has also led to some inefficiencies.)。因此，他在第二段中就提出要與一家顧問公司合作以便找出更好的方法來幫助公司，而為了達成此目標員工則必須上該顧問公司的網站填寫問卷，且必須在明天結束之前填妥 (Please complete it before the end of the day tomorrow.)。由此可見，這封電子郵件的目的即 (A) To explain an assignment「解釋說明一項指定任務」。

Vocabulary

☐ **disclaimer** 免責聲明　☐ **evaluate** 評估；評價　☐ **recommendation** 建議　☐ **draw** 得出（結論等）　☐ **tentative** 試探的；暫時的
☐ **stand out** 突出；顯眼　☐ **relevant** 相關的　☐ **quarterly** 按季的　☐ **seek out** 找出　☐ **tuition** 學費　☐ **reimbursement** 核銷
☐ **overwhelmingly** 壓倒性地　☐ **retreat** 度假進修　☐ **have a bearing on** 與～有關　☐ **conversely** 相反地

第 2 回完全解析

PART 7

225

In the email, the word "endeavor" in paragraph 3, line 2, is closest in meaning to
(A) progress
(B) effort
(C) strategy
(D) attempt

電子郵件第三段第二行的 "endeavor" 這個字的意思最接近
(A) 進展
(B) 努力
(C) 策略
(D) 企圖

> 解析 本題考單字的含意，"endeavor" 指「努力」、「盡力」，與選項 (B) effort 的意思相同，不過前者屬較正式的用字，後者則為通俗字眼。

What is NOT mentioned about the survey?
(A) It was conducted online.
(B) It was required of all employees.
(C) It was administered by an outside company.
(D) It was written by Justine Kemp.

關於意見調查，哪一點「未」被提及？
(A) 它是在線上進行的。
(B) 它是全體員工必做的。
(C) 它是由外面的公司負責實施的。
(D) 它是賈斯汀‧坎普所撰寫的。

> 解析 本題屬「細節」題。由電子郵件第二段第三句 "All employees will soon receive another email with a link to an online survey at the Chase/Bender website."「全體員工很快就會收到另一封電子郵件，裡面有確斯／本德網站之線上調查的連結。」可知，選項 (A)、(B)、(C) 皆包括在內，因此皆不可選。本題應選無中生有的 (D) It was written by Justine Kemp.。

What is suggested in the preliminary report about Mega Optical Devices?
(A) It should focus on employees' technical skills.
(B) Not all of its employees completed the survey.
(C) It offers tuition reimbursement to its staff.
(D) Employees are expected to know more than one language.

關於梅加光學裝置，初步報告中暗示了什麼？
(A) 它應該聚焦在員工技術性的技能上。
(B) 員工並非全都完成了該項調查。
(C) 它有提供員工學費核銷。
(D) 員工被期待要懂不只一種語言。

> 解析 本題屬「推論」題。由該報告在「免責聲明」中所說的 "Chase/Bender Analytics is still evaluating the survey data and still receiving new data (the response rate as of December 20 stands at 87%)."「確斯／本德分析仍在評估調查資料，並仍在收取新資料（截至十二月二十日，回覆率為 87%）。」即可斷定，不是所有的梅加光學裝置的員工都已經完成該項調查。正確答案是 (B) Not all of its employees completed the survey.。

According to the report, what type of training is best provided by computer?
(A) Technical training
(B) Daily classes
(C) Leadership workshops
(D) All-day seminars

根據報告，哪一類訓練由電腦來提供最好？
(A) 技術訓練
(B) 每日課程
(C) 領導工坊
(D) 全天的研討會

> 解析 本題同樣屬「細節」題，但必須做些許推論。由該報告 "FREQUENCY/DURATION"「頻率／時間長度」說明中的第三句話 "Short daily lessons are most efficiently delivered as part of an automated learning system."「若作為自動化學習系統的一部分，短期的每日課程在教學上最具效率。」可推知，就每日課程而言，員工們認為「非實體」的上課方式較能達到學習效果；也就是說，他們認為「線上學習」乃為最佳方式，因此本題選 (B)。

Vocabulary

☐ **conduct** 進行；施作　☐ **administer** 執行；實施

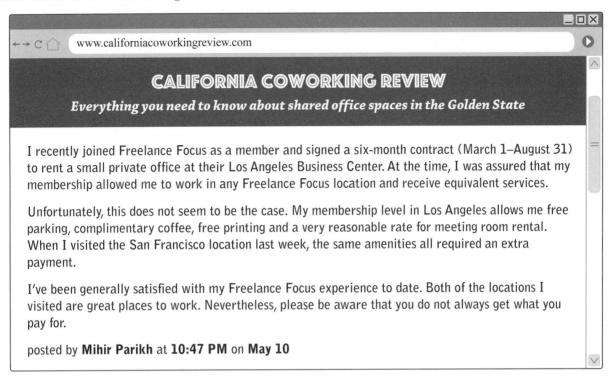

加州共工評論

你對金州共享辦公空間所需要知道的每一件事

我最近加入了「自由接案焦點」成為會員，簽了六個月的合約（三月一日到八月三十一日）租用他們在洛杉磯商業中心的小型私人辦公室。當時我獲得保證，我的會員身分可以讓我在「自由接案焦點」的任何據點工作，並得到同等的服務。

令人遺憾地，情況 似乎並非如此。我在洛杉磯的會員等級可讓我免費停車、獲贈免費咖啡、免費列印，並可以非常合理的價錢租用會議室。而我上週造訪舊金山的據點時，同樣的設備卻全都必須額外付費。

我在「自由接案焦點」的體驗至今大致滿意。我造訪過的兩個據點都是很棒的工作場所。儘管如此，請注意，不是你付了錢就一定會得到你應該得到的東西。

米希爾‧派立克張貼於五月十日 10:47 PM

Vocabulary

□ **assure** 向～保證 □ **equivalent** 相等的 □ **to date** 迄今

Freelance Focus Workspaces
Rates and Services effective Jan. 1

Type		Schedule		Locations (California)	
☐ Desk Rental		☐ Daily		☑ San Francisco	
☑ Small Office		☐ Weekly		☑ Los Angeles	
☐ Large Office		☑ Monthly		☐ San Diego	

San Francisco					
Status	Rate	Parking	Drinks	Meeting Room	Printing
Visitor	$710	$12/Day	$1	$45/hour	$0.20
Temporary	$790	$65/Month	$1	$40/hour	$0.10
Associate	$840	$55/Month	$1	$35/hour	$0.05
Collaborator	$950	$45/Month	No charge	$20/hour	No charge
Los Angeles					
Status	Rate	Parking	Drinks	Meeting Room	Printing
Visitor	$600	$6/Day	$1	$30/hour	$0.10
Temporary	$710	$2/Day	$1	$30/hour	$0.05
Associate	$790	No charge	No charge	$20/hour	No charge
Collaborator	$840	No charge	No charge	No charge	No charge

「自由接案焦點」工作空間
費率與服務，一月一日生效

類型		時程		據點（加州）	
☐ 租用辦公桌		☐ 按日		☑ 舊金山	
☑ 小型辦公室		☐ 按週		☑ 洛杉磯	
☐ 大型辦公室		☑ 按月		☐ 聖地牙哥	

舊金山					
身分	費率	停車	飲料	會議室	列印
訪客	$710	$12 / 日	$1	$45 / 小時	$0.20
短期	$790	$65 / 月	$1	$40 / 小時	$0.10
同事	$840	$55 / 月	$1	$35 / 小時	$0.05
協作者	$950	$45 / 月	不收費	$20 / 小時	不收費
洛杉磯					
身分	費率	停車	飲料	會議室	列印
訪客	$600	$6 / 日	$1	$30 / 小時	$0.10
短期	$710	$2 / 日	$1	$30 / 小時	$0.05
同事	$790	不收費	不收費	$20 / 小時	不收費
協作者	$840	不收費	不收費	不收費	不收費

Vocabulary
☐ **temporary** 暫時的；短期的　☐ **collaborator** 合作者

From:	customerexperience@freelancefocusworkspaces.com
To:	Mihir Parikh <mp@MHPinfomatics.com>
Subject:	Small Office Rates and Services
Date:	May 11

Dear Mr. Parikh,

I read the comments you posted yesterday about Freelance Focus on the California Coworking Review website. I'd like to apologize for the incorrect information you received when signing up and explain the steps we're taking to resolve the issue you raised.

The company sets minimum standards for each membership level but recognizes that local conditions can vary considerably. This is why we allow each location to set its own rates. I've made our human resources department aware of your concerns and they have committed to ensuring that staff nationwide communicate clearly about this issue with current and prospective members.

At no additional charge to you, I have upgraded your membership to Collaborator level for the duration of your current contract. This ensures that your experiences at the Los Angeles and San Francisco locations will be more uniform.

Please contact me directly if you have any additional questions or concerns.

Duncan Jones,
Director of Customer Experience

寄件者：customerexperience@freelancefocusworkspaces.com
收件者：Mihir Parikh <mp@MHPinfomatics.com>
主　旨：小型辦公室費率與服務
日　期：5 月 11 日

派利克先生您好：

我拜讀了您昨天在加州共工評論的網站上所張貼的關於「自由接案焦點」的留言。我想對您在簽約時得到了不正確資訊一事表示歉意，並解釋我們將採取什麼樣的步驟來解決您所提出的問題。

本公司對各等級的會員身分都訂定了最低標準，但也承認各地的條件可能差異很大。這就是為什麼我們容許各據點自訂費率的原因。我已經將您的疑慮告知了人資部，他們承諾會確保全國各地的員工向現有和可能的會員清楚溝通此問題。

在不另外收費的情況下，我已經將您在現有合約期間的會員身分升到了協作者的等級。這可確保您在洛杉磯和舊金山兩個據點的體驗更加一致。

如果您還有任何其他的疑問或疑慮，請直接與我聯絡。

鄧肯‧瓊斯
顧客體驗主任

186 正解 B

Why did Mr. Parikh write this review?
(A) To request an upgrade
(B) To warn of a problem
(C) To schedule a meeting
(D) To change a policy

派利克先生為什麼會寫這則評論？
(A) 為了要求升等
(B) 為了提醒注意一個問題
(C) 為了排定一場會議的時間
(D) 為了改變一個政策

解析　派利克先生在文章中先是敘述了他在與商家簽訂合約成為該公司會員並被告知享有的權利之後，竟被無理要求額外付費的情事。但由他在最後一句中所說的 "... please be aware that you do not always get what you pay for." 「……請注意，不是你付了錢就一定會得到你應該得到的東西。」來推斷，他寫這則評論的主要目的應該是想藉自己的經驗提醒大家注意這個問題，因此本題選 (B) To warn of a problem。

Vocabulary
☐ **resolve** 解決；決議　☐ **vary** 有變化；相異　☐ **considerably** 相當地　☐ **nationwide** 全國的　☐ **uniform** 一致的

What is suggested about Mr. Parikh?
(A) He works in more than one location.
(B) He wants to rent a larger office.
(C) He currently lives in San Francisco.
(D) He has recently changed jobs.

文中暗示了派利克先生如何？
(A) 他在不只一個據點工作。
(B) 他想租一間更大的辦公室。
(C) 他目前住在舊金山。
(D) 他最近換了工作。

解析	本題和上題一樣為「推論」題。由派利克先生加入「自由接案焦點 (Freelance Focus)」成為會員並獲保證可在該公司的任何據點 (location) 工作，且確實到過不同據點（洛杉磯與舊金山）這幾點來看，派利克先生應該不只在一個據點工作。正確答案是 (A)。

How much is Mr. Parikh's rent each month?
(A) $710
(B) $790
(C) $840
(D) $950

派利克先生每月的租金是多少？
(A) $710
(B) $790
(C) $840
(D) $950

解析	派利克先生在評論的第二段中提到 "My membership level in Los Angeles allows me free parking, complimentary coffee, free printing and a very reasonable rate for meeting room rental."「我在洛杉磯的會員等級可讓我免費停車、獲贈免費咖啡、免費列印，並可以非常合理的價錢租用會議室。」而依據表單上所提供的資訊，符合這些資格的洛杉磯會員等級是「同事」(Associate)，因此派利克先生每個月須支付的金額為 (B) $790。

What is true about the two locations?
(A) All members have to pay for printing in San Francisco.
(B) Los Angeles members enjoy a greater range of services.
(C) San Francisco charges less for some services.
(D) Some members pay for parking in Los Angeles.

關於兩個據點的敘述，下列何者為真？
(A) 所有的會員在舊金山列印都必須付費。
(B) 洛杉磯的會員享有的服務範圍較大。
(C) 舊金山的某些服務收費較低。
(D) 有些會員在洛杉磯停車要付費。

解析	本題和上題一樣為「細節」題。由表單上所列出的資訊可知，在洛杉磯據點並非所有會員等級的人都有資格享受免費停車；換句話說有些會員是必須付錢的。正確答案是 (D) Some members pay for parking in Los Angeles.。其他選項內容則皆與表單上的資訊不相符。

What is provided by the company as a response to the review?
(A) A change in pricing policy
(B) A new training initiative
(C) A membership fee discount
(D) A statewide uniform standard

該公司提供了什麼來作為對評論的回應？
(A) 定價政策的改變
(B) 一個新的訓練措施
(C) 會費折扣
(D) 一個全州的統一標準

解析	本題亦考細節。該公司的顧客體驗主任鄧肯‧瓊斯在電子郵件的第二段中提到說 "I've made our human resources department aware of your concerns and they have committed to ensuring that staff nationwide communicate clearly about this issue with current and prospective members."「我已經將您的疑慮告知了人資部，他們承諾會確保全國各地的員工向現有和可能的會員清楚溝通此問題。」換言之，為避免再產生誤會，該公司會針對這個新議題教導員工如何做妥善的處理，因此本題選 (B) A new training initiative。其他選項內容則皆屬無中生有。

Vocabulary

☐ **range** 範圍　☐ **initiative** 主動性；措施　☐ **statewide** 全州的

GYM NIGHTS

Tristero Pharmaceuticals & The San Narciso Scorpions

Join us for "Gym Nights," when Tristero employees get together after work at the San Narciso High School Gymnasium for a little exercise and a lot of fun. Now in its fifth year, Gym Nights is the centerpiece of our Employee Wellness program. With four different activities featured each week, you're sure to find something to get your body moving. All employees are welcome and there's no need to sign up in advance. All activities are 7–9 PM.

Monday Nights	**Line Dancing** *with* Damian Jones	Whether you're a beginner or an experienced pro, professional dancer Damian "DJ" Jones will get you up and moving around the dance floor. Please wear soft-soled shoes.
Tuesday Nights	**Basketball** *with* Jeff Rambis	Lace up your sneakers and take your game to the next level as the coach of the San Narciso Scorpions leads you through intense drills and fun scrimmages.
Wednesday Nights	No activities scheduled	The San Narciso Scorpions welcome Tristero employees to root for the county's most exciting high school basketball players. The boys' and girls' teams use the gym on alternate Wednesdays.
Thursday Nights	**Yoga** *with* Radha Patel	Practice a pose or simply do some breathing exercises with the owner of the San Narciso Yoga Studio. Please bring a mat.
Friday Nights	**Badminton** *with* Leslie Firth	No racket, no problem! San Narciso Scorpions Athletic Director has everything you need for a friendly game of badminton.

第 191 到 195 題請參照下列時程表、手機訊息和電子郵件。

體育館之夜

崔斯特羅製藥與
聖納西索天蠍隊

請加入我們「體育館之夜」的行列，崔斯特羅的員工下班後都會齊聚在聖納西索高中體育館，做一些運動並大大享受其樂趣。如今已邁入第五年的體育館之夜是我們員工保健計畫最重要的部分。由於我們每一週都特別安排了不同的四種活動，你必定能找到喜歡的項目讓身體動起來。歡迎全體員工參加，無須事先報名。所有的活動皆在晚上七點到九點。

週一夜	排舞 達米安·瓊斯	不論你是初學者還是經驗老道的行家，專業舞者達米安 "DJ" 瓊斯都會讓你願意起身在舞池裡轉轉。請著軟底鞋。
週二夜	籃球 傑夫·蘭比斯	把運動鞋的鞋帶綁好，將球賽到帶下一個層級，聖納西索天蠍隊的教練將一路帶著你做激烈的訓練並參加樂趣十足的練習賽。
週三夜	未排活動	聖納西索天蠍隊歡迎崔斯特羅的員工來為本郡最令人興奮的高中籃球隊員加油。男子隊和女子隊隔週輪流在週三使用體育館。
週四夜	瑜珈 拉妲·巴特爾	跟著聖納西索瑜珈教室的業主練習姿勢，或是純粹做一些呼吸鍛鍊。請自備瑜珈墊。
週五夜	羽球 萊絲莉·佛斯	沒球拍，沒問題！聖納西索天蠍隊的體育運動主任已經為你備好一場羽球友誼賽所需要的一切。

第 2 回完全解析

PART 7

Vocabulary

☐ **pharmaceuticals** 藥品（複數形） ☐ **scorpion** 蠍子 ☐ **centerpiece** 最重要的部分 ☐ **wellness** 保健；健全；健康
☐ **line dancing** 排舞（美國西部的一種舞蹈） ☐ **soft-soled** 軟鞋底的 ☐ **sneakers** 運動鞋（複數形） ☐ **drill** 練習；訓練
☐ **scrimmage**（籃球）練習賽 ☐ **root for** 為～加油 ☐ **racket**（網球）球拍 ☐ **athletic** 運動的；體育的

Leslie Firth [9:05 AM]
Hi, Ed. I'm afraid we have to make a few changes to the Gym Nights schedule next week.

Edward van Exel [9:16 AM]
Oh, OK. What's going on?

Leslie Firth [9:18 AM]
A couple things. Jeff is taking next week off to attend a wedding.
Could you get someone to fill in? Or maybe you just want to cancel?

Edward van Exel [9:26 AM]
It's kind of short notice, but I may be able to find someone. What's the other thing?

Leslie Firth [9:31 AM]
The school is going to need the gym on Friday night for an academic awards ceremony.
I should have put it on the schedule at the beginning of the year, but I forgot. That's on me.

Edward van Exel [9:33 AM]
Don't worry about it Leslie. Though I have to say I was looking forward to a rematch. We came so close last week!

Leslie Firth [9:35 AM]
Ha! Maybe next time. At least I'll finally be able to have a Friday night off.
I've already made plans to go out to dinner.

Edward van Exel [9:39 AM]
Enjoy it. I'll let everyone know what's going on and see what I can do about Tuesday.

萊絲莉・佛斯 [9:05 AM]
嗨，艾德。體育館之夜下週的時程恐怕必須做些許變動。

艾德華・范埃克塞爾 [9:16 AM]
噢，好的。發生了什麼事嗎？

萊絲莉・佛斯 [9:18 AM]
兩件事。傑夫下週要請假去參加婚禮。你能不能找人來代班？
或者也許你想乾脆取消掉？

艾德華・范埃克塞爾 [9:26 AM]
通知得有點臨時，但我或許能找到人。另一件事呢？

萊絲莉・佛斯 [9:31 AM]
因為要舉行學術獎的頒獎典禮，學校星期五晚上會需要用體育館。
我在年初就該把它排進時程表裡，但我忘了。都怪我。

艾德華・范埃克塞爾 [9:33 AM]
別擔心了，萊絲莉。雖然我必須說，我原本很期待再次交手。
我們上星期還真是旗鼓相當！

萊絲莉・佛斯 [9:35 AM]
哈！也許下次吧。至少我總算能休星期五晚上了。
我已經計畫好要出去吃晚餐。

艾德華・范埃克塞爾 [9:39 AM]
好好享受吧。我會告知每個人是怎麼回事，並看看我能怎麼處理星期二的事。

Vocabulary

☐ **fill in** 暫代　☐ **short notice** 臨時通知　☐ **academic** 學術的　☐ **ceremony** 典禮；儀式　☐ **rematch** 重賽；再度交手

From:	Edward van Exel <EvE@ tristeropharmaceuticals.com>
To:	<allemployees@tristeropharecuticals.com>
Subject:	Gym Nights
Date:	May 16

Dear All,

I just want to let everyone know about a few changes to the Gym Nights schedule next week.

Due to a previously scheduled event at San Narciso High, there will be no badminton practice on Friday, May 27. Also, because Coach Rambis will be out of town on personal business next week, our very own Stacey Fox from IT will be leading basketball activities on Tuesday. For those who don't know, Stacey is a former Scorpions player who later led the South State Sparks to a collegiate championship. Come prepared! It should be fun.

Other activities will not be affected, and everything should be back to normal for the week starting May 30.

Best,
Edward van Exel
Health and Wellness Program Supervisor
Human Resources Division, Tristero Pharmaceuticals

寄件者：Edward van Exel <EvE@ tristeropharmaceuticals.com>
收件者：<allemployees@tristeropharecuticals.com>
主　旨：體育館之夜
日　期：5 月 16 日

大家好：

我只是想通知每個人，體育館之夜下週的時程表有些許變動。

由於聖納西索高中先前就排定了一項活動，五月二十七日星期五將不會有羽球練習。另外，因為蘭比斯教練下週會出城處理私事，所以星期二的籃球活動將會由我們的自家人資訊科技部的史黛西‧福克斯來帶領。如果有人不知道的話，史黛西可是前天蠍隊員，後來帶領南州火花隊拿到了大學賽冠軍。請準備好再來！應該會充滿樂趣。

其他活動將不受影響，而五月三十日開始的那一週起，一切應該就會恢復正常。

艾德華‧范埃克塞爾敬上
崔斯特羅製藥人資部健康與健身計畫督導

191　正解 D

According to the information given on the schedule, what activity provides all the necessary equipment?	根據時程表上所提供之資訊，哪一項活動會提供所有必要裝備？
(A) Line dancing	(A) 排舞
(B) Basketball	(B) 籃球
(C) Yoga	(C) 瑜珈
(D) Badminton	(D) 羽球

解析　本題為「細節」題，問根據時程表上的資訊哪一項活動會提供所有的裝備。由時程表中週五夜羽球一欄的說明："No racket, no problem! San Narciso Scorpions Athletic Director has everything you need for a friendly game of badminton."「沒球拍，沒問題！聖納西索天蠍隊的體育運動主任已經為你備好一場羽球友誼賽所需要的一切。」即可知，正確答案是 (D)。

Vocabulary

☐ **spark** 火花　☐ **collegiate** 大學的

192 正解 A

What is true about San Narciso High School?
(A) It has two basketball teams.
(B) It sponsors "Gym Nights."
(C) It closes its gym every Wednesday night.
(D) It provides free transportation for Tristero employees.

關於聖納西索高中的敘述，下列何者為真？
(A) 它擁有兩支籃球隊。
(B) 它贊助「體育館之夜」。
(C) 它每週三晚上關閉體育館。
(D) 它提供免費交通工具給崔斯特羅的員工。

解析 本題考細節。由時程表中週三夜（未排活動）一欄之說明：" The San Narciso Scorpions welcome Tristero employees to root for the county's most exciting high school basketball players. The boys' and girls' teams use the gym on alternate Wednesdays." 「聖納西索天蠍隊歡迎崔斯特羅的員工來為本郡最令人興奮的高中籃球隊員加油。男子隊和女子隊隔週輪流在週三使用體育館。」即可確定，本題應選 (A)「它擁有兩支籃球隊。」其他選項不是無中生有（選項 (B) 與 (D)），就是與事實不符（選項 (C)）。

193 正解 A

Why did Leslie Firth start the text message chain?
(A) To remedy a problem
(B) To respond to an email
(C) To request a day off
(D) To recommend a replacement

萊絲莉‧佛斯為什麼會起動這段手機訊息？
(A) 為了補救一個問題
(B) 為了回覆電子郵件
(C) 為了要求休假一天
(D) 為了推薦替代人選

解析 本題屬「推論」題，問萊絲莉‧佛斯為何開始傳這段訊息。萊絲莉‧佛斯一開始就跟艾德華‧范埃克塞爾說："I'm afraid we have to make a few changes to the Gym Nights schedule next week." 「體育館之夜下週的時程恐怕必須做些許變動。」而在萊絲莉‧佛斯說明了問題之後，兩人接著就針對該如何處理問題交換意見，因此可合理推斷，萊絲莉‧佛斯之所以會起動這段訊息的原因就是 (A)「為了補救一個問題」。

194 正解 B

In the text message chain, at 9:31 AM, what does Leslie Firth mean when she writes, "That's on me"?
(A) She intends to pay for the meal.
(B) She takes responsibility for the mistake.
(C) She is required to attend the ceremony.
(D) She will buy a gift for Jeff Rambis.

手機訊息中九點三十一分時，萊絲莉‧佛斯打的 "That's on me." 是什麼意思？
(A) 她有意要用餐付費。
(B) 她要為錯誤負責。
(C) 她非出席典禮不可。
(D) 她會買禮物給傑夫‧蘭比斯。

解析 本題考的是詞句解釋。"That's on me." 這句話有「算在我身上」的含意，一般用於表示說話者願意承認錯誤、願意為錯誤負責。選項 (B) She takes responsibility for the mistake. 即為正解。注意，英文中還有一句類似的話："It's on me."，意思則是「算我的」、「我請客」。

195 正解 C

Who is going to substitute for Coach Rambis?
(A) Damian Jones
(B) Radha Patel
(C) Stacey Fox
(D) Edward van Exel

誰將會代蘭比斯教練的班？
(A) 達米安‧瓊斯
(B) 拉妲‧巴特爾
(C) 史黛西‧福克斯
(D) 艾德華‧范埃克塞爾

解析 由艾德華‧范埃克塞爾在電子郵件第二段第二句中所提到的 "... because Coach Rambis will be out of town ... next week, ... Stacey Fox from IT will be leading basketball activities on Tuesday." 「……因為蘭比斯教練下週會出城……所以星期二的籃球活動將會由……資訊科技部的史黛西‧福克斯來帶領。」即可知，正確答案是 (C)。

Vocabulary
☐ **remedy** 補救　☐ **sponsor** 贊助；資助

Questions 196-200 refer to the following webpage, news article, and letter.

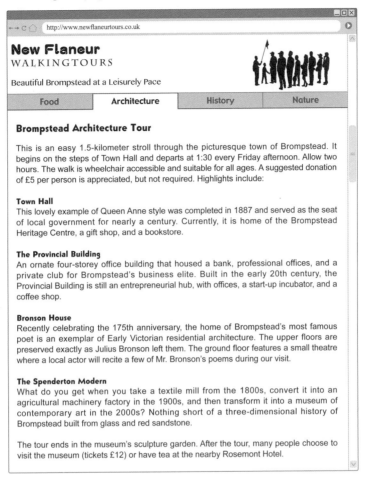

第 196 到 200 題請參照下列網頁、新聞報導和信件。

新漫遊者 步行遊覽 踏著悠閒的步伐欣賞美麗布隆普史特德			
美食	建築	歷史	自然

布隆普史特德建築之旅
這是輕鬆的 1.5 公里漫步，穿過如畫般的布隆普史特德鎮。遊覽由鎮公所的台階開始，每週五下午 1:30 出發。酌留兩小時。坐輪椅亦可參加，並適合各年齡層。每人建議捐款五英磅，不勝感激但非屬必要。亮點包括：

鎮公所
這座安妮女王風的美麗範例落成於 1887 年，被作為地方政府的所在地近一世紀。目前它則是布隆普史特德文化遺產中心的所在地，也有一間禮品店和一間書店。

省府大樓
華麗的四層辦公大樓，曾設有一家銀行、專業辦公室和布隆普史特德商業菁英的一個私人俱樂部。建於二十世紀初的省府大樓至今仍是企業家聚集之處，內有辦公室、一個新創業者育成所和一家咖啡館。

布朗森之家
近期歡慶 175 周年，這是布隆普史特德最著名詩人的家，為維多利亞初期住宅建築的典範。上面幾層以朱里斯·布朗森所留下的原樣加以保留。一樓則改成一個有特色的小型劇場，在我們參觀的期間，會由一位本地的演員朗誦幾首布朗森先生的詩。

現代史班德頓
若將 1800 年代的紡織廠轉型為 1900 年代的農機廠，再把它改造成 2000 年代的當代藝術博物館，樣貌會是如何？簡直就是布隆普史特德從玻璃和紅砂岩中建立起來的三度空間史。

遊覽在博物館的雕像花園結束。遊覽之後，很多人會選擇參觀博物館（門票十二英磅），或是到附近的羅斯蒙特飯店喝茶。

• Vocabulary 見下頁

A New Business for Historical Brompstead

By Alex Cruz

April 22 (Bristol)—I met Abigail Gleason whilst queuing for coffee on the ground floor of the building where I work. Five minutes later, I had a broad understanding of the past century of local history and learned that my office had once been occupied by Chester T. Dunford, a barrister who served as Mayor of Brompstead in the late 1920s.

This was no accident. Ms. Gleason is an historian of some renown. Her company, New Flaneur Walking Tours, is less than a year old, but Ms. Gleason has long been fascinated with historical Brompstead. "I've been collecting stories about this place ever since I can remember," she says. "I'm so pleased to be able to share them."

Ms. Gleason personally leads the History (Thursday) and Architecture (Friday) tours, but she has help on the weekends. Restauranteur Stephanie Liu leads the popular Food Tour on Saturdays and Shannon Quayle, a member of the Brompstead Land Trust, leads a four-hour Nature Walk through Mystic Woods.

A graduate of the University of Bristol History Department, Ms. Gleason was a long-time employee of the Brompstead Heritage Centre. She loves writing but wanted a more personal way to share her knowledge. "I've written countless pamphlets, blog posts, and even a short biography of Julius Bronson, but nothing beats spending time with people," she told me. "I was made for walking and talking, and that's why I started giving tours."

布隆普史特德悠久歷史下的新商機

艾力克斯·克魯茲報導

四月二十二日（布里斯托）——我與艾碧嘉·葛里森是在工作所在大樓的底層排隊買咖啡時結織的。五分鐘之後，我對於過去一世紀的本地史便有了廣泛的了解，而且得知我的辦公室曾經是柴斯特T.·鄧福德的辦公室，他是一位大律師並在一九二○年代後期擔任過布隆普史特德的市長。

這絕非偶然。葛里森女士是一位頗富盛名的史學家。她的公司新漫遊者步行遊覽成立還不足一年，但葛里森女士長久以來一直對歷史悠久的布隆普史特德深深著迷。「從我能記得以來，我就在蒐羅這個地方的故事了，」她說。「我好高興能把它分享出去。」

葛里森女士親自帶領歷史（週四）與建築（週五）之旅，但週末則有幫手。餐館老闆史蒂芬妮·劉在週六時會帶領熱門的美食之旅，而布隆普史特德土地信託的成員珊儂·奎爾則會帶領為時四小時穿越秘之林的自然漫步。

畢業於布里斯托大學歷史系的葛里森女士曾是布隆普史特德文化遺產中心的長期員工。她熱愛寫作，但想要以更個人的方式來分享她的知識。「我寫了無數的小冊子、部落格貼文，甚至是朱里斯·布朗森的短傳記，但什麼都比不上與眾人共度時光，」她跟我說。「我非常適合邊走邊說，而這就是我為什麼會開始為人做導覽。」

Vocabulary

- **flaneur**（法文）四處閒逛者；漫遊者
- **leisurely** 悠閒的
- **stroll** 散步；閒逛
- **picturesque** 美麗如畫的
- **town hall** 鎮公所
- **seat** 所在地
- **heritage**（文化）遺產
- **provincial** 省的
- **ornate** 裝飾華麗的
- **house** 給～房子住；給～提供場所
- **elite** 社會菁英
- **entrepreneurial** 企業家的
- **hub** 中心；樞紐
- **incubator** 孵化器；育成中心
- **exemplar** 典範；榜樣
- **residential** 居住的；住宅區的
- **preserve** 保留
- **ground floor**（英國）一樓
- **recite** 朗誦
- **textile mill** 紡織廠
- **convert** 轉換；轉變
- **nothing short of** 簡直是；無疑是
- **three-dimensional** 三度空間的
- **sculpture** 雕像
- **whilst** 在～時（與 "while" 同義，但為正式用法）
- **queue** 排隊（等候）
- **occupy** 占用；居住
- **barrister**（英國）大律師
- **renown** 名望；聲譽
- **fascinated** 著迷的
- **restauranteur** 餐廳老闆
- **mystic** 神秘的
- **countless** 無數的
- **pamphlet** 小冊子
- **biography** 傳記
- **be made for** 非常適合

Dear Brompstead Editor,

I was delighted by your story about Abigail Gleason and her company. At my advanced age, I get around by wheelchair, not on foot, but it seems I can still join one of Ms. Gleason's walking tours. It may interest your readers to know that Chester T. Dunford was my grandfather, and that in addition to his government service he was also instrumental in founding the Brompstead Land Trust. He worked tirelessly for the conservation of the Mystic Woods, which is why we can all enjoy that enchanting place today.

If Ms. Gleason has any plans to write another biography, I can think of nobody more worthy than Grandad Dunford!

Sincerely,
Oliver Dunford

《布隆普史特德郵報》編輯鈞鑑：

我非常高興看到您那篇關於艾碧嘉‧葛里森和她的公司的報導。我年事已高，我是靠輪椅而非步行四處活動，不過看來我還是可以參加葛里森女士步行遊覽的其中一場。您的讀者或許會有興趣知道，柴斯特 T.‧鄧福德是我的祖父，而除了任公職之外，他還曾大力協助創立布隆普史特德土地信託公司。他不遺餘力地致力於保育秘之林，這就是為什麼今天我們所有的人都能享受這個迷人地方的原因。

如果葛里森女士有任何計畫要再寫另一本傳記的話，我想不到有誰會比我祖父鄧福德更值得她這麼做！

奧利佛‧鄧福德敬上

---

196 正解 B

What is one common feature of all the buildings on the tour?
(A) They were initially built for commercial purposes.
(B) They have been adapted for contemporary use.
(C) They were constructed in the 1800s.
(D) They are not generally open to the public.

包括在遊覽行程中的所有建築物的一個共同特點是什麼？
(A) 它們最初是為了商用目的而建造。
(B) 它們經過了修改以符合現代的用途。
(C) 它們興建於 1800 年代。
(D) 它們通常不對大眾開放。

| 解析 | 本題屬「推論」題。根據網頁上的介紹，行程中會參觀的建築物皆為十九世紀或二十世紀初所建造；這些建築有的原是地方政府所在地 (the seat of local government)，有的為商辦大樓，有的為住宅，有的曾是紡織廠 (textile mill)、農機廠 (agricultural machinery factory)。後由於時代的變遷，這些「古蹟」也有了新的風貌：有的變成文化遺產中心 (Heritage Centre)，有的仍是企業家聚集之處 (entrepreneurial hub)，有的則成為劇場、博物館；而這些舊建築的共通點當然就是，它們肯定都經過一番改造才符合了現代的用途。正確答案是 (B)。 |

Vocabulary

☐ **delighted** 高興的　☐ **get around** 四處走動　☐ **instrumental** 有幫助的；起關鍵作用的　☐ **enchanting** 迷人的；令人陶醉的

Where does Alex Cruz most likely work?
(A) Town Hall
(B) The Provincial Building
(C) Bronson House
(D) The Spenderton Modern

艾力克斯・克魯茲最有可能是在哪裡工作？
(A) 鎮公所
(B) 省府大樓
(C) 布朗森之家
(D) 現代史班德頓

解析　本題亦屬「推論」題。艾力克斯・克魯茲在他的報導的第一段中提到 "... my office had once been occupied by Chester T. Dunford, a barrister who served as Mayor of Brompstead in the late 1920s." 「……我的辦公室曾經是柴斯特 T.・鄧福德的辦公室，他是一位大律師並在一九二○年代後期擔任過布隆普史特德的市長。」而在被列出的四棟建築物當中只有「省府大樓」以前有辦公室，且現在還是有辦公室。由此可推知，艾力克斯・克魯茲應該是在 (B) The Provincial Building 工作。

What is indicated in the news article about Ms. Gleason?
(A) She was a restaurant owner.
(B) She teaches History and Architecture at a university.
(C) She used to work in the Town Hall building.
(D) She is a native of Bristol.

新聞報導中指出了葛里森女士的什麼事？
(A) 她當過餐館老闆。
(B) 她在一所大學教歷史與建築。
(C) 她曾經在鎮公所那棟建築裡上班。
(D) 她是布里斯托本地人。

解析　本題考點落在「細節」部分，問報導中指出葛里森女士如何。報導的第四段第一句中提到 "... Ms. Gleason was a long-time employee of the Brompstead Heritage Centre." 「……葛里森女士曾是布隆普史特德文化遺產中心的長期員工。」而根據網頁上的資訊，布隆普史特德文化遺產中心的所在地乃當年的「鎮公所」，故正解為 (C) She used to work in the Town Hall building.。

In the letter, the word "founding" in paragraph 1, line 4, is closest in meaning to
(A) fabricating
(B) preserving
(C) discovering
(D) establishing

信件第一段第四行的 "founding" 這個字的意思最接近
(A) 製造
(B) 保存
(C) 發掘
(D) 成立

解析　本題考單字的含意。"founding" 是動詞 "found" 的動名詞或現在分詞，而 "found" 指的是「建立」、「創立」，因此本題選 (D) establishing。注意，勿將原形動詞 "found" 與另一動詞 "find"「發現」、「找到」的過去式與過去分詞 "found" 混淆。

What is probably true about Oliver Dunford?
(A) He has visited the New Flaneur website.
(B) He was once elected to public office.
(C) He wants to write a book about a family member.
(D) He will apply to become a tour guide.

關於奧利佛・鄧福德的敘述，下列何者可能為真？
(A) 他造訪過新漫遊者的網站。
(B) 他曾經當選擔任公職。
(C) 他想要寫一本關於家族成員的書。
(D) 他會申請成為一個導遊。

解析　在奧利佛・鄧福德寫給艾力克斯・克魯茲的信中（第一段第二句）他說："At my advanced age, I get around by wheelchair, not on foot, but it seems I can still join one of Ms. Gleason's walking tours." 「我年事已高，我是靠輪椅而非步行四處活動，不過看來我還是可以參加葛里森女士步行遊覽的其中一場。」由此可合理推斷，他很可能上過新漫遊者的網站，看到了布隆普史特德建築之旅的相關報導中提及該步行遊覽坐輪椅者也可參加 (The walk is wheelchair accessible)，因此本題選 (A)。

Vocabulary
☐ **initially** 最初　☐ **adapt** 適應；修改；改編　☐ **native** 本地人

ACTUAL TEST 1

Track 01-01 – 01-58

曲目編號	內　容	曲目編號	內　容
01-01	Part 1. Directions	01-30	No.28
01-02	No.1	01-31	No.29
01-03	No.2	01-32	No.30
01-04	No.3	01-33	No.31
01-05	No.4	01-34	Part 3. Directions
01-06	No.5	01-35	No.32-34
01-07	No.6	01-36	No.35-37
01-08	Part 2. Directions	01-37	No.38-40
01-09	No.7	01-38	No.41-43
01-10	No.8	01-39	No.44-46
01-11	No.9	01-40	No.47-49
01-12	No.10	01-41	No.50-52
01-13	No.11	01-42	No.53-55
01-14	No.12	01-43	No.56-58
01-15	No.13	01-44	No.59-61
01-16	No.14	01-45	No.62-64
01-17	No.15	01-46	No.65-67
01-18	No.16	01-47	No.68-70
01-19	No.17	01-48	Part 4. Directions
01-20	No.18	01-49	No.71-73
01-21	No.19	01-50	No.74-76
01-22	No.20	01-51	No.77-79
01-23	No.21	01-52	No.80-82
01-24	No.22	01-53	No.83-85
01-25	No.23	01-54	No.86-88
01-26	No.24	01-55	No.89-91
01-27	No.25	01-56	No.92-94
01-28	No.26	01-57	No.95-97
01-29	No.27	01-58	No.98-100

★ **下載音檔**
請刮開書內刮刮卡，上網啟用序號後即可下載聆聽。
網址：https://bit.ly/3d3P7te，或掃描 QR code

貝塔會員網

ACTUAL TEST 2

Track 02-01 – 02-58

曲目編號	內　容	曲目編號	內　容
02-01	Part 1. Directions	02-30	No.28
02-02	No.1	02-31	No.29
02-03	No.2	02-32	No.30
02-04	No.3	02-33	No.31
02-05	No.4	02-34	Part 3. Directions
02-06	No.5	02-35	No.32-34
02-07	No.6	02-36	No.35-37
02-08	Part 2. Directions	02-37	No.38-40
02-09	No.7	02-38	No.41-43
02-10	No.8	02-39	No.44-46
02-11	No.9	02-40	No.47-49
02-12	No.10	02-41	No.50-52
02-13	No.11	02-42	No.53-55
02-14	No.12	02-43	No.56-58
02-15	No.13	02-44	No.59-61
02-16	No.14	02-45	No.62-64
02-17	No.15	02-46	No.65-67
02-18	No.16	02-47	No.68-70
02-19	No.17	02-48	Part 4. Directions
02-20	No.18	02-49	No.71-73
02-21	No.19	02-50	No.74-76
02-22	No.20	02-51	No.77-79
02-23	No.21	02-52	No.80-82
02-24	No.22	02-53	No.83-85
02-25	No.23	02-54	No.86-88
02-26	No.24	02-55	No.89-91
02-27	No.25	02-56	No.92-94
02-28	No.26	02-57	No.95-97
02-29	No.27	02-58	No.98-100

ANSWER SHEET

Admission No.

NAME

LISTENING TEST (PART 1-4)

1	Ⓐ Ⓑ Ⓒ Ⓓ	21	Ⓐ Ⓑ Ⓒ Ⓓ	41	Ⓐ Ⓑ Ⓒ Ⓓ	61	Ⓐ Ⓑ Ⓒ Ⓓ	81	Ⓐ Ⓑ Ⓒ Ⓓ
2	Ⓐ Ⓑ Ⓒ Ⓓ	22	Ⓐ Ⓑ Ⓒ Ⓓ	42	Ⓐ Ⓑ Ⓒ Ⓓ	62	Ⓐ Ⓑ Ⓒ Ⓓ	82	Ⓐ Ⓑ Ⓒ Ⓓ
3	Ⓐ Ⓑ Ⓒ Ⓓ	23	Ⓐ Ⓑ Ⓒ Ⓓ	43	Ⓐ Ⓑ Ⓒ Ⓓ	63	Ⓐ Ⓑ Ⓒ Ⓓ	83	Ⓐ Ⓑ Ⓒ Ⓓ
4	Ⓐ Ⓑ Ⓒ Ⓓ	24	Ⓐ Ⓑ Ⓒ Ⓓ	44	Ⓐ Ⓑ Ⓒ Ⓓ	64	Ⓐ Ⓑ Ⓒ Ⓓ	84	Ⓐ Ⓑ Ⓒ Ⓓ
5	Ⓐ Ⓑ Ⓒ Ⓓ	25	Ⓐ Ⓑ Ⓒ Ⓓ	45	Ⓐ Ⓑ Ⓒ Ⓓ	65	Ⓐ Ⓑ Ⓒ Ⓓ	85	Ⓐ Ⓑ Ⓒ Ⓓ
6	Ⓐ Ⓑ Ⓒ Ⓓ	26	Ⓐ Ⓑ Ⓒ Ⓓ	46	Ⓐ Ⓑ Ⓒ Ⓓ	66	Ⓐ Ⓑ Ⓒ Ⓓ	86	Ⓐ Ⓑ Ⓒ Ⓓ
7	Ⓐ Ⓑ Ⓒ	27	Ⓐ Ⓑ Ⓒ Ⓓ	47	Ⓐ Ⓑ Ⓒ Ⓓ	67	Ⓐ Ⓑ Ⓒ Ⓓ	87	Ⓐ Ⓑ Ⓒ Ⓓ
8	Ⓐ Ⓑ Ⓒ	28	Ⓐ Ⓑ Ⓒ Ⓓ	48	Ⓐ Ⓑ Ⓒ Ⓓ	68	Ⓐ Ⓑ Ⓒ Ⓓ	88	Ⓐ Ⓑ Ⓒ Ⓓ
9	Ⓐ Ⓑ Ⓒ	29	Ⓐ Ⓑ Ⓒ Ⓓ	49	Ⓐ Ⓑ Ⓒ Ⓓ	69	Ⓐ Ⓑ Ⓒ Ⓓ	89	Ⓐ Ⓑ Ⓒ Ⓓ
10	Ⓐ Ⓑ Ⓒ	30	Ⓐ Ⓑ Ⓒ Ⓓ	50	Ⓐ Ⓑ Ⓒ Ⓓ	70	Ⓐ Ⓑ Ⓒ Ⓓ	90	Ⓐ Ⓑ Ⓒ Ⓓ
11	Ⓐ Ⓑ Ⓒ	31	Ⓐ Ⓑ Ⓒ Ⓓ	51	Ⓐ Ⓑ Ⓒ Ⓓ	71	Ⓐ Ⓑ Ⓒ Ⓓ	91	Ⓐ Ⓑ Ⓒ Ⓓ
12	Ⓐ Ⓑ Ⓒ	32	Ⓐ Ⓑ Ⓒ Ⓓ	52	Ⓐ Ⓑ Ⓒ Ⓓ	72	Ⓐ Ⓑ Ⓒ Ⓓ	92	Ⓐ Ⓑ Ⓒ Ⓓ
13	Ⓐ Ⓑ Ⓒ	33	Ⓐ Ⓑ Ⓒ Ⓓ	53	Ⓐ Ⓑ Ⓒ Ⓓ	73	Ⓐ Ⓑ Ⓒ Ⓓ	93	Ⓐ Ⓑ Ⓒ Ⓓ
14	Ⓐ Ⓑ Ⓒ	34	Ⓐ Ⓑ Ⓒ Ⓓ	54	Ⓐ Ⓑ Ⓒ Ⓓ	74	Ⓐ Ⓑ Ⓒ Ⓓ	94	Ⓐ Ⓑ Ⓒ Ⓓ
15	Ⓐ Ⓑ Ⓒ	35	Ⓐ Ⓑ Ⓒ Ⓓ	55	Ⓐ Ⓑ Ⓒ Ⓓ	75	Ⓐ Ⓑ Ⓒ Ⓓ	95	Ⓐ Ⓑ Ⓒ Ⓓ
16	Ⓐ Ⓑ Ⓒ	36	Ⓐ Ⓑ Ⓒ Ⓓ	56	Ⓐ Ⓑ Ⓒ Ⓓ	76	Ⓐ Ⓑ Ⓒ Ⓓ	96	Ⓐ Ⓑ Ⓒ Ⓓ
17	Ⓐ Ⓑ Ⓒ	37	Ⓐ Ⓑ Ⓒ Ⓓ	57	Ⓐ Ⓑ Ⓒ Ⓓ	77	Ⓐ Ⓑ Ⓒ Ⓓ	97	Ⓐ Ⓑ Ⓒ Ⓓ
18	Ⓐ Ⓑ Ⓒ	38	Ⓐ Ⓑ Ⓒ Ⓓ	58	Ⓐ Ⓑ Ⓒ Ⓓ	78	Ⓐ Ⓑ Ⓒ Ⓓ	98	Ⓐ Ⓑ Ⓒ Ⓓ
19	Ⓐ Ⓑ Ⓒ	39	Ⓐ Ⓑ Ⓒ Ⓓ	59	Ⓐ Ⓑ Ⓒ Ⓓ	79	Ⓐ Ⓑ Ⓒ Ⓓ	99	Ⓐ Ⓑ Ⓒ Ⓓ
20	Ⓐ Ⓑ Ⓒ	40	Ⓐ Ⓑ Ⓒ Ⓓ	60	Ⓐ Ⓑ Ⓒ Ⓓ	80	Ⓐ Ⓑ Ⓒ Ⓓ	100	Ⓐ Ⓑ Ⓒ Ⓓ

READING TEST (PART 5-7)

101	Ⓐ Ⓑ Ⓒ Ⓓ	121	Ⓐ Ⓑ Ⓒ Ⓓ	141	Ⓐ Ⓑ Ⓒ Ⓓ	161	Ⓐ Ⓑ Ⓒ Ⓓ	181	Ⓐ Ⓑ Ⓒ Ⓓ
102	Ⓐ Ⓑ Ⓒ Ⓓ	122	Ⓐ Ⓑ Ⓒ Ⓓ	142	Ⓐ Ⓑ Ⓒ Ⓓ	162	Ⓐ Ⓑ Ⓒ Ⓓ	182	Ⓐ Ⓑ Ⓒ Ⓓ
103	Ⓐ Ⓑ Ⓒ Ⓓ	123	Ⓐ Ⓑ Ⓒ Ⓓ	143	Ⓐ Ⓑ Ⓒ Ⓓ	163	Ⓐ Ⓑ Ⓒ Ⓓ	183	Ⓐ Ⓑ Ⓒ Ⓓ
104	Ⓐ Ⓑ Ⓒ Ⓓ	124	Ⓐ Ⓑ Ⓒ Ⓓ	144	Ⓐ Ⓑ Ⓒ Ⓓ	164	Ⓐ Ⓑ Ⓒ Ⓓ	184	Ⓐ Ⓑ Ⓒ Ⓓ
105	Ⓐ Ⓑ Ⓒ Ⓓ	125	Ⓐ Ⓑ Ⓒ Ⓓ	145	Ⓐ Ⓑ Ⓒ Ⓓ	165	Ⓐ Ⓑ Ⓒ Ⓓ	185	Ⓐ Ⓑ Ⓒ Ⓓ
106	Ⓐ Ⓑ Ⓒ Ⓓ	126	Ⓐ Ⓑ Ⓒ Ⓓ	146	Ⓐ Ⓑ Ⓒ Ⓓ	166	Ⓐ Ⓑ Ⓒ Ⓓ	186	Ⓐ Ⓑ Ⓒ Ⓓ
107	Ⓐ Ⓑ Ⓒ Ⓓ	127	Ⓐ Ⓑ Ⓒ Ⓓ	147	Ⓐ Ⓑ Ⓒ Ⓓ	167	Ⓐ Ⓑ Ⓒ Ⓓ	187	Ⓐ Ⓑ Ⓒ Ⓓ
108	Ⓐ Ⓑ Ⓒ Ⓓ	128	Ⓐ Ⓑ Ⓒ Ⓓ	148	Ⓐ Ⓑ Ⓒ Ⓓ	168	Ⓐ Ⓑ Ⓒ Ⓓ	188	Ⓐ Ⓑ Ⓒ Ⓓ
109	Ⓐ Ⓑ Ⓒ Ⓓ	129	Ⓐ Ⓑ Ⓒ Ⓓ	149	Ⓐ Ⓑ Ⓒ Ⓓ	169	Ⓐ Ⓑ Ⓒ Ⓓ	189	Ⓐ Ⓑ Ⓒ Ⓓ
110	Ⓐ Ⓑ Ⓒ Ⓓ	130	Ⓐ Ⓑ Ⓒ Ⓓ	150	Ⓐ Ⓑ Ⓒ Ⓓ	170	Ⓐ Ⓑ Ⓒ Ⓓ	190	Ⓐ Ⓑ Ⓒ Ⓓ
111	Ⓐ Ⓑ Ⓒ Ⓓ	131	Ⓐ Ⓑ Ⓒ Ⓓ	151	Ⓐ Ⓑ Ⓒ Ⓓ	171	Ⓐ Ⓑ Ⓒ Ⓓ	191	Ⓐ Ⓑ Ⓒ Ⓓ
112	Ⓐ Ⓑ Ⓒ Ⓓ	132	Ⓐ Ⓑ Ⓒ Ⓓ	152	Ⓐ Ⓑ Ⓒ Ⓓ	172	Ⓐ Ⓑ Ⓒ Ⓓ	192	Ⓐ Ⓑ Ⓒ Ⓓ
113	Ⓐ Ⓑ Ⓒ Ⓓ	133	Ⓐ Ⓑ Ⓒ Ⓓ	153	Ⓐ Ⓑ Ⓒ Ⓓ	173	Ⓐ Ⓑ Ⓒ Ⓓ	193	Ⓐ Ⓑ Ⓒ Ⓓ
114	Ⓐ Ⓑ Ⓒ Ⓓ	134	Ⓐ Ⓑ Ⓒ Ⓓ	154	Ⓐ Ⓑ Ⓒ Ⓓ	174	Ⓐ Ⓑ Ⓒ Ⓓ	194	Ⓐ Ⓑ Ⓒ Ⓓ
115	Ⓐ Ⓑ Ⓒ Ⓓ	135	Ⓐ Ⓑ Ⓒ Ⓓ	155	Ⓐ Ⓑ Ⓒ Ⓓ	175	Ⓐ Ⓑ Ⓒ Ⓓ	195	Ⓐ Ⓑ Ⓒ Ⓓ
116	Ⓐ Ⓑ Ⓒ Ⓓ	136	Ⓐ Ⓑ Ⓒ Ⓓ	156	Ⓐ Ⓑ Ⓒ Ⓓ	176	Ⓐ Ⓑ Ⓒ Ⓓ	196	Ⓐ Ⓑ Ⓒ Ⓓ
117	Ⓐ Ⓑ Ⓒ Ⓓ	137	Ⓐ Ⓑ Ⓒ Ⓓ	157	Ⓐ Ⓑ Ⓒ Ⓓ	177	Ⓐ Ⓑ Ⓒ Ⓓ	197	Ⓐ Ⓑ Ⓒ Ⓓ
118	Ⓐ Ⓑ Ⓒ Ⓓ	138	Ⓐ Ⓑ Ⓒ Ⓓ	158	Ⓐ Ⓑ Ⓒ Ⓓ	178	Ⓐ Ⓑ Ⓒ Ⓓ	198	Ⓐ Ⓑ Ⓒ Ⓓ
119	Ⓐ Ⓑ Ⓒ Ⓓ	139	Ⓐ Ⓑ Ⓒ Ⓓ	159	Ⓐ Ⓑ Ⓒ Ⓓ	179	Ⓐ Ⓑ Ⓒ Ⓓ	199	Ⓐ Ⓑ Ⓒ Ⓓ
120	Ⓐ Ⓑ Ⓒ Ⓓ	140	Ⓐ Ⓑ Ⓒ Ⓓ	160	Ⓐ Ⓑ Ⓒ Ⓓ	180	Ⓐ Ⓑ Ⓒ Ⓓ	200	Ⓐ Ⓑ Ⓒ Ⓓ

ANSWER SHEET

Admission No.

N A M E

LISTENING TEST (PART 1-4)

#	A	B	C	D	#	A	B	C	D	#	A	B	C	D	#	A	B	C	D
1	Ⓐ	Ⓑ	Ⓒ	Ⓓ	21	Ⓐ	Ⓑ	Ⓒ		41	Ⓐ	Ⓑ	Ⓒ		61	Ⓐ	Ⓑ	Ⓒ	Ⓓ
2	Ⓐ	Ⓑ	Ⓒ	Ⓓ	22	Ⓐ	Ⓑ	Ⓒ		42	Ⓐ	Ⓑ	Ⓒ		62	Ⓐ	Ⓑ	Ⓒ	Ⓓ
3	Ⓐ	Ⓑ	Ⓒ	Ⓓ	23	Ⓐ	Ⓑ	Ⓒ		43	Ⓐ	Ⓑ	Ⓒ	Ⓓ	63	Ⓐ	Ⓑ	Ⓒ	Ⓓ
4	Ⓐ	Ⓑ	Ⓒ	Ⓓ	24	Ⓐ	Ⓑ	Ⓒ		44	Ⓐ	Ⓑ	Ⓒ	Ⓓ	64	Ⓐ	Ⓑ	Ⓒ	Ⓓ
5	Ⓐ	Ⓑ	Ⓒ	Ⓓ	25	Ⓐ	Ⓑ	Ⓒ		45	Ⓐ	Ⓑ	Ⓒ	Ⓓ	65	Ⓐ	Ⓑ	Ⓒ	Ⓓ
6	Ⓐ	Ⓑ	Ⓒ	Ⓓ	26	Ⓐ	Ⓑ	Ⓒ		46	Ⓐ	Ⓑ	Ⓒ	Ⓓ	66	Ⓐ	Ⓑ	Ⓒ	Ⓓ
7	Ⓐ	Ⓑ	Ⓒ		27	Ⓐ	Ⓑ	Ⓒ		47	Ⓐ	Ⓑ	Ⓒ	Ⓓ	67	Ⓐ	Ⓑ	Ⓒ	Ⓓ
8	Ⓐ	Ⓑ	Ⓒ		28	Ⓐ	Ⓑ	Ⓒ		48	Ⓐ	Ⓑ	Ⓒ	Ⓓ	68	Ⓐ	Ⓑ	Ⓒ	Ⓓ
9	Ⓐ	Ⓑ	Ⓒ		29	Ⓐ	Ⓑ	Ⓒ		49	Ⓐ	Ⓑ	Ⓒ	Ⓓ	69	Ⓐ	Ⓑ	Ⓒ	Ⓓ
10	Ⓐ	Ⓑ	Ⓒ		30	Ⓐ	Ⓑ	Ⓒ		50	Ⓐ	Ⓑ	Ⓒ	Ⓓ	70	Ⓐ	Ⓑ	Ⓒ	Ⓓ
11	Ⓐ	Ⓑ	Ⓒ		31	Ⓐ	Ⓑ	Ⓒ		51	Ⓐ	Ⓑ	Ⓒ	Ⓓ	71	Ⓐ	Ⓑ	Ⓒ	Ⓓ
12	Ⓐ	Ⓑ	Ⓒ		32	Ⓐ	Ⓑ	Ⓒ		52	Ⓐ	Ⓑ	Ⓒ	Ⓓ	72	Ⓐ	Ⓑ	Ⓒ	Ⓓ
13	Ⓐ	Ⓑ	Ⓒ		33	Ⓐ	Ⓑ	Ⓒ		53	Ⓐ	Ⓑ	Ⓒ	Ⓓ	73	Ⓐ	Ⓑ	Ⓒ	Ⓓ
14	Ⓐ	Ⓑ	Ⓒ		34	Ⓐ	Ⓑ	Ⓒ		54	Ⓐ	Ⓑ	Ⓒ	Ⓓ	74	Ⓐ	Ⓑ	Ⓒ	Ⓓ
15	Ⓐ	Ⓑ	Ⓒ		35	Ⓐ	Ⓑ	Ⓒ		55	Ⓐ	Ⓑ	Ⓒ	Ⓓ	75	Ⓐ	Ⓑ	Ⓒ	Ⓓ
16	Ⓐ	Ⓑ	Ⓒ		36	Ⓐ	Ⓑ	Ⓒ		56	Ⓐ	Ⓑ	Ⓒ	Ⓓ	76	Ⓐ	Ⓑ	Ⓒ	Ⓓ
17	Ⓐ	Ⓑ	Ⓒ		37	Ⓐ	Ⓑ	Ⓒ		57	Ⓐ	Ⓑ	Ⓒ	Ⓓ	77	Ⓐ	Ⓑ	Ⓒ	Ⓓ
18	Ⓐ	Ⓑ	Ⓒ		38	Ⓐ	Ⓑ	Ⓒ		58	Ⓐ	Ⓑ	Ⓒ	Ⓓ	78	Ⓐ	Ⓑ	Ⓒ	Ⓓ
19	Ⓐ	Ⓑ	Ⓒ		39	Ⓐ	Ⓑ	Ⓒ		59	Ⓐ	Ⓑ	Ⓒ	Ⓓ	79	Ⓐ	Ⓑ	Ⓒ	Ⓓ
20	Ⓐ	Ⓑ	Ⓒ		40	Ⓐ	Ⓑ	Ⓒ		60	Ⓐ	Ⓑ	Ⓒ	Ⓓ	80	Ⓐ	Ⓑ	Ⓒ	Ⓓ

#	A	B	C	D
81	Ⓐ	Ⓑ	Ⓒ	Ⓓ
82	Ⓐ	Ⓑ	Ⓒ	Ⓓ
83	Ⓐ	Ⓑ	Ⓒ	Ⓓ
84	Ⓐ	Ⓑ	Ⓒ	Ⓓ
85	Ⓐ	Ⓑ	Ⓒ	Ⓓ
86	Ⓐ	Ⓑ	Ⓒ	Ⓓ
87	Ⓐ	Ⓑ	Ⓒ	Ⓓ
88	Ⓐ	Ⓑ	Ⓒ	Ⓓ
89	Ⓐ	Ⓑ	Ⓒ	Ⓓ
90	Ⓐ	Ⓑ	Ⓒ	Ⓓ
91	Ⓐ	Ⓑ	Ⓒ	Ⓓ
92	Ⓐ	Ⓑ	Ⓒ	Ⓓ
93	Ⓐ	Ⓑ	Ⓒ	Ⓓ
94	Ⓐ	Ⓑ	Ⓒ	Ⓓ
95	Ⓐ	Ⓑ	Ⓒ	Ⓓ
96	Ⓐ	Ⓑ	Ⓒ	Ⓓ
97	Ⓐ	Ⓑ	Ⓒ	Ⓓ
98	Ⓐ	Ⓑ	Ⓒ	Ⓓ
99	Ⓐ	Ⓑ	Ⓒ	Ⓓ
100	Ⓐ	Ⓑ	Ⓒ	Ⓓ

READING TEST (PART 5-7)

#	A	B	C	D	#	A	B	C	D	#	A	B	C	D	#	A	B	C	D
101	Ⓐ	Ⓑ	Ⓒ	Ⓓ	121	Ⓐ	Ⓑ	Ⓒ	Ⓓ	141	Ⓐ	Ⓑ	Ⓒ	Ⓓ	161	Ⓐ	Ⓑ	Ⓒ	Ⓓ
102	Ⓐ	Ⓑ	Ⓒ	Ⓓ	122	Ⓐ	Ⓑ	Ⓒ	Ⓓ	142	Ⓐ	Ⓑ	Ⓒ	Ⓓ	162	Ⓐ	Ⓑ	Ⓒ	Ⓓ
103	Ⓐ	Ⓑ	Ⓒ	Ⓓ	123	Ⓐ	Ⓑ	Ⓒ	Ⓓ	143	Ⓐ	Ⓑ	Ⓒ	Ⓓ	163	Ⓐ	Ⓑ	Ⓒ	Ⓓ
104	Ⓐ	Ⓑ	Ⓒ	Ⓓ	124	Ⓐ	Ⓑ	Ⓒ	Ⓓ	144	Ⓐ	Ⓑ	Ⓒ	Ⓓ	164	Ⓐ	Ⓑ	Ⓒ	Ⓓ
105	Ⓐ	Ⓑ	Ⓒ	Ⓓ	125	Ⓐ	Ⓑ	Ⓒ	Ⓓ	145	Ⓐ	Ⓑ	Ⓒ	Ⓓ	165	Ⓐ	Ⓑ	Ⓒ	Ⓓ
106	Ⓐ	Ⓑ	Ⓒ	Ⓓ	126	Ⓐ	Ⓑ	Ⓒ	Ⓓ	146	Ⓐ	Ⓑ	Ⓒ	Ⓓ	166	Ⓐ	Ⓑ	Ⓒ	Ⓓ
107	Ⓐ	Ⓑ	Ⓒ	Ⓓ	127	Ⓐ	Ⓑ	Ⓒ	Ⓓ	147	Ⓐ	Ⓑ	Ⓒ	Ⓓ	167	Ⓐ	Ⓑ	Ⓒ	Ⓓ
108	Ⓐ	Ⓑ	Ⓒ	Ⓓ	128	Ⓐ	Ⓑ	Ⓒ	Ⓓ	148	Ⓐ	Ⓑ	Ⓒ	Ⓓ	168	Ⓐ	Ⓑ	Ⓒ	Ⓓ
109	Ⓐ	Ⓑ	Ⓒ	Ⓓ	129	Ⓐ	Ⓑ	Ⓒ	Ⓓ	149	Ⓐ	Ⓑ	Ⓒ	Ⓓ	169	Ⓐ	Ⓑ	Ⓒ	Ⓓ
110	Ⓐ	Ⓑ	Ⓒ	Ⓓ	130	Ⓐ	Ⓑ	Ⓒ	Ⓓ	150	Ⓐ	Ⓑ	Ⓒ	Ⓓ	170	Ⓐ	Ⓑ	Ⓒ	Ⓓ
111	Ⓐ	Ⓑ	Ⓒ	Ⓓ	131	Ⓐ	Ⓑ	Ⓒ	Ⓓ	151	Ⓐ	Ⓑ	Ⓒ	Ⓓ	171	Ⓐ	Ⓑ	Ⓒ	Ⓓ
112	Ⓐ	Ⓑ	Ⓒ	Ⓓ	132	Ⓐ	Ⓑ	Ⓒ	Ⓓ	152	Ⓐ	Ⓑ	Ⓒ	Ⓓ	172	Ⓐ	Ⓑ	Ⓒ	Ⓓ
113	Ⓐ	Ⓑ	Ⓒ	Ⓓ	133	Ⓐ	Ⓑ	Ⓒ	Ⓓ	153	Ⓐ	Ⓑ	Ⓒ	Ⓓ	173	Ⓐ	Ⓑ	Ⓒ	Ⓓ
114	Ⓐ	Ⓑ	Ⓒ	Ⓓ	134	Ⓐ	Ⓑ	Ⓒ	Ⓓ	154	Ⓐ	Ⓑ	Ⓒ	Ⓓ	174	Ⓐ	Ⓑ	Ⓒ	Ⓓ
115	Ⓐ	Ⓑ	Ⓒ	Ⓓ	135	Ⓐ	Ⓑ	Ⓒ	Ⓓ	155	Ⓐ	Ⓑ	Ⓒ	Ⓓ	175	Ⓐ	Ⓑ	Ⓒ	Ⓓ
116	Ⓐ	Ⓑ	Ⓒ	Ⓓ	136	Ⓐ	Ⓑ	Ⓒ	Ⓓ	156	Ⓐ	Ⓑ	Ⓒ	Ⓓ	176	Ⓐ	Ⓑ	Ⓒ	Ⓓ
117	Ⓐ	Ⓑ	Ⓒ	Ⓓ	137	Ⓐ	Ⓑ	Ⓒ	Ⓓ	157	Ⓐ	Ⓑ	Ⓒ	Ⓓ	177	Ⓐ	Ⓑ	Ⓒ	Ⓓ
118	Ⓐ	Ⓑ	Ⓒ	Ⓓ	138	Ⓐ	Ⓑ	Ⓒ	Ⓓ	158	Ⓐ	Ⓑ	Ⓒ	Ⓓ	178	Ⓐ	Ⓑ	Ⓒ	Ⓓ
119	Ⓐ	Ⓑ	Ⓒ	Ⓓ	139	Ⓐ	Ⓑ	Ⓒ	Ⓓ	159	Ⓐ	Ⓑ	Ⓒ	Ⓓ	179	Ⓐ	Ⓑ	Ⓒ	Ⓓ
120	Ⓐ	Ⓑ	Ⓒ	Ⓓ	140	Ⓐ	Ⓑ	Ⓒ	Ⓓ	160	Ⓐ	Ⓑ	Ⓒ	Ⓓ	180	Ⓐ	Ⓑ	Ⓒ	Ⓓ

#	A	B	C	D
181	Ⓐ	Ⓑ	Ⓒ	Ⓓ
182	Ⓐ	Ⓑ	Ⓒ	Ⓓ
183	Ⓐ	Ⓑ	Ⓒ	Ⓓ
184	Ⓐ	Ⓑ	Ⓒ	Ⓓ
185	Ⓐ	Ⓑ	Ⓒ	Ⓓ
186	Ⓐ	Ⓑ	Ⓒ	Ⓓ
187	Ⓐ	Ⓑ	Ⓒ	Ⓓ
188	Ⓐ	Ⓑ	Ⓒ	Ⓓ
189	Ⓐ	Ⓑ	Ⓒ	Ⓓ
190	Ⓐ	Ⓑ	Ⓒ	Ⓓ
191	Ⓐ	Ⓑ	Ⓒ	Ⓓ
192	Ⓐ	Ⓑ	Ⓒ	Ⓓ
193	Ⓐ	Ⓑ	Ⓒ	Ⓓ
194	Ⓐ	Ⓑ	Ⓒ	Ⓓ
195	Ⓐ	Ⓑ	Ⓒ	Ⓓ
196	Ⓐ	Ⓑ	Ⓒ	Ⓓ
197	Ⓐ	Ⓑ	Ⓒ	Ⓓ
198	Ⓐ	Ⓑ	Ⓒ	Ⓓ
199	Ⓐ	Ⓑ	Ⓒ	Ⓓ
200	Ⓐ	Ⓑ	Ⓒ	Ⓓ

ANSWER SHEET

LISTENING TEST (PART 1-4)

#					#					#					#				
1	Ⓐ Ⓑ Ⓒ Ⓓ				21	Ⓐ Ⓑ Ⓒ				41	Ⓐ Ⓑ Ⓒ Ⓓ				61	Ⓐ Ⓑ Ⓒ Ⓓ				81	Ⓐ Ⓑ Ⓒ Ⓓ
2	Ⓐ Ⓑ Ⓒ Ⓓ	22	Ⓐ Ⓑ Ⓒ	42	Ⓐ Ⓑ Ⓒ Ⓓ	62	Ⓐ Ⓑ Ⓒ Ⓓ	82	Ⓐ Ⓑ Ⓒ Ⓓ
3	Ⓐ Ⓑ Ⓒ Ⓓ	23	Ⓐ Ⓑ Ⓒ Ⓓ	43	Ⓐ Ⓑ Ⓒ Ⓓ	63	Ⓐ Ⓑ Ⓒ Ⓓ	83	Ⓐ Ⓑ Ⓒ Ⓓ
4	Ⓐ Ⓑ Ⓒ Ⓓ	24	Ⓐ Ⓑ Ⓒ Ⓓ	44	Ⓐ Ⓑ Ⓒ Ⓓ	64	Ⓐ Ⓑ Ⓒ Ⓓ	84	Ⓐ Ⓑ Ⓒ Ⓓ
5	Ⓐ Ⓑ Ⓒ Ⓓ	25	Ⓐ Ⓑ Ⓒ Ⓓ	45	Ⓐ Ⓑ Ⓒ Ⓓ	65	Ⓐ Ⓑ Ⓒ Ⓓ	85	Ⓐ Ⓑ Ⓒ Ⓓ
6	Ⓐ Ⓑ Ⓒ Ⓓ	26	Ⓐ Ⓑ Ⓒ	46	Ⓐ Ⓑ Ⓒ Ⓓ	66	Ⓐ Ⓑ Ⓒ Ⓓ	86	Ⓐ Ⓑ Ⓒ Ⓓ
7	Ⓐ Ⓑ Ⓒ	27	Ⓐ Ⓑ Ⓒ	47	Ⓐ Ⓑ Ⓒ Ⓓ	67	Ⓐ Ⓑ Ⓒ Ⓓ	87	Ⓐ Ⓑ Ⓒ Ⓓ
8	Ⓐ Ⓑ Ⓒ	28	Ⓐ Ⓑ Ⓒ	48	Ⓐ Ⓑ Ⓒ Ⓓ	68	Ⓐ Ⓑ Ⓒ Ⓓ	88	Ⓐ Ⓑ Ⓒ Ⓓ
9	Ⓐ Ⓑ Ⓒ	29	Ⓐ Ⓑ Ⓒ	49	Ⓐ Ⓑ Ⓒ Ⓓ	69	Ⓐ Ⓑ Ⓒ Ⓓ	89	Ⓐ Ⓑ Ⓒ Ⓓ
10	Ⓐ Ⓑ Ⓒ	30	Ⓐ Ⓑ Ⓒ	50	Ⓐ Ⓑ Ⓒ Ⓓ	70	Ⓐ Ⓑ Ⓒ Ⓓ	90	Ⓐ Ⓑ Ⓒ Ⓓ
11	Ⓐ Ⓑ Ⓒ	31	Ⓐ Ⓑ Ⓒ	51	Ⓐ Ⓑ Ⓒ Ⓓ	71	Ⓐ Ⓑ Ⓒ Ⓓ	91	Ⓐ Ⓑ Ⓒ Ⓓ
12	Ⓐ Ⓑ Ⓒ	32	Ⓐ Ⓑ Ⓒ	52	Ⓐ Ⓑ Ⓒ Ⓓ	72	Ⓐ Ⓑ Ⓒ Ⓓ	92	Ⓐ Ⓑ Ⓒ Ⓓ
13	Ⓐ Ⓑ Ⓒ	33	Ⓐ Ⓑ Ⓒ	53	Ⓐ Ⓑ Ⓒ Ⓓ	73	Ⓐ Ⓑ Ⓒ Ⓓ	93	Ⓐ Ⓑ Ⓒ Ⓓ
14	Ⓐ Ⓑ Ⓒ	34	Ⓐ Ⓑ Ⓒ	54	Ⓐ Ⓑ Ⓒ Ⓓ	74	Ⓐ Ⓑ Ⓒ Ⓓ	94	Ⓐ Ⓑ Ⓒ Ⓓ
15	Ⓐ Ⓑ Ⓒ	35	Ⓐ Ⓑ Ⓒ	55	Ⓐ Ⓑ Ⓒ Ⓓ	75	Ⓐ Ⓑ Ⓒ Ⓓ	95	Ⓐ Ⓑ Ⓒ Ⓓ
16	Ⓐ Ⓑ Ⓒ	36	Ⓐ Ⓑ Ⓒ	56	Ⓐ Ⓑ Ⓒ Ⓓ	76	Ⓐ Ⓑ Ⓒ Ⓓ	96	Ⓐ Ⓑ Ⓒ Ⓓ
17	Ⓐ Ⓑ Ⓒ	37	Ⓐ Ⓑ Ⓒ	57	Ⓐ Ⓑ Ⓒ Ⓓ	77	Ⓐ Ⓑ Ⓒ Ⓓ	97	Ⓐ Ⓑ Ⓒ Ⓓ
18	Ⓐ Ⓑ Ⓒ	38	Ⓐ Ⓑ Ⓒ	58	Ⓐ Ⓑ Ⓒ Ⓓ	78	Ⓐ Ⓑ Ⓒ Ⓓ	98	Ⓐ Ⓑ Ⓒ Ⓓ
19	Ⓐ Ⓑ Ⓒ	39	Ⓐ Ⓑ Ⓒ	59	Ⓐ Ⓑ Ⓒ Ⓓ	79	Ⓐ Ⓑ Ⓒ Ⓓ	99	Ⓐ Ⓑ Ⓒ Ⓓ
20	Ⓐ Ⓑ Ⓒ	40	Ⓐ Ⓑ Ⓒ	60	Ⓐ Ⓑ Ⓒ Ⓓ	80	Ⓐ Ⓑ Ⓒ Ⓓ	100	Ⓐ Ⓑ Ⓒ Ⓓ

READING TEST (PART 5-7)

#					#					#					#					#				
101	Ⓐ Ⓑ Ⓒ Ⓓ	121	Ⓐ Ⓑ Ⓒ Ⓓ	141	Ⓐ Ⓑ Ⓒ Ⓓ	161	Ⓐ Ⓑ Ⓒ Ⓓ	181	Ⓐ Ⓑ Ⓒ Ⓓ
102	Ⓐ Ⓑ Ⓒ Ⓓ	122	Ⓐ Ⓑ Ⓒ Ⓓ	142	Ⓐ Ⓑ Ⓒ Ⓓ	162	Ⓐ Ⓑ Ⓒ Ⓓ	182	Ⓐ Ⓑ Ⓒ Ⓓ
103	Ⓐ Ⓑ Ⓒ Ⓓ	123	Ⓐ Ⓑ Ⓒ Ⓓ	143	Ⓐ Ⓑ Ⓒ Ⓓ	163	Ⓐ Ⓑ Ⓒ Ⓓ	183	Ⓐ Ⓑ Ⓒ Ⓓ
104	Ⓐ Ⓑ Ⓒ Ⓓ	124	Ⓐ Ⓑ Ⓒ Ⓓ	144	Ⓐ Ⓑ Ⓒ Ⓓ	164	Ⓐ Ⓑ Ⓒ Ⓓ	184	Ⓐ Ⓑ Ⓒ Ⓓ
105	Ⓐ Ⓑ Ⓒ Ⓓ	125	Ⓐ Ⓑ Ⓒ Ⓓ	145	Ⓐ Ⓑ Ⓒ Ⓓ	165	Ⓐ Ⓑ Ⓒ Ⓓ	185	Ⓐ Ⓑ Ⓒ Ⓓ
106	Ⓐ Ⓑ Ⓒ Ⓓ	126	Ⓐ Ⓑ Ⓒ Ⓓ	146	Ⓐ Ⓑ Ⓒ Ⓓ	166	Ⓐ Ⓑ Ⓒ Ⓓ	186	Ⓐ Ⓑ Ⓒ Ⓓ
107	Ⓐ Ⓑ Ⓒ Ⓓ	127	Ⓐ Ⓑ Ⓒ Ⓓ	147	Ⓐ Ⓑ Ⓒ Ⓓ	167	Ⓐ Ⓑ Ⓒ Ⓓ	187	Ⓐ Ⓑ Ⓒ Ⓓ
108	Ⓐ Ⓑ Ⓒ Ⓓ	128	Ⓐ Ⓑ Ⓒ Ⓓ	148	Ⓐ Ⓑ Ⓒ Ⓓ	168	Ⓐ Ⓑ Ⓒ Ⓓ	188	Ⓐ Ⓑ Ⓒ Ⓓ
109	Ⓐ Ⓑ Ⓒ Ⓓ	129	Ⓐ Ⓑ Ⓒ Ⓓ	149	Ⓐ Ⓑ Ⓒ Ⓓ	169	Ⓐ Ⓑ Ⓒ Ⓓ	189	Ⓐ Ⓑ Ⓒ Ⓓ
110	Ⓐ Ⓑ Ⓒ Ⓓ	130	Ⓐ Ⓑ Ⓒ Ⓓ	150	Ⓐ Ⓑ Ⓒ Ⓓ	170	Ⓐ Ⓑ Ⓒ Ⓓ	190	Ⓐ Ⓑ Ⓒ Ⓓ
111	Ⓐ Ⓑ Ⓒ Ⓓ	131	Ⓐ Ⓑ Ⓒ Ⓓ	151	Ⓐ Ⓑ Ⓒ Ⓓ	171	Ⓐ Ⓑ Ⓒ Ⓓ	191	Ⓐ Ⓑ Ⓒ Ⓓ
112	Ⓐ Ⓑ Ⓒ Ⓓ	132	Ⓐ Ⓑ Ⓒ Ⓓ	152	Ⓐ Ⓑ Ⓒ Ⓓ	172	Ⓐ Ⓑ Ⓒ Ⓓ	192	Ⓐ Ⓑ Ⓒ Ⓓ
113	Ⓐ Ⓑ Ⓒ Ⓓ	133	Ⓐ Ⓑ Ⓒ Ⓓ	153	Ⓐ Ⓑ Ⓒ Ⓓ	173	Ⓐ Ⓑ Ⓒ Ⓓ	193	Ⓐ Ⓑ Ⓒ Ⓓ
114	Ⓐ Ⓑ Ⓒ Ⓓ	134	Ⓐ Ⓑ Ⓒ Ⓓ	154	Ⓐ Ⓑ Ⓒ Ⓓ	174	Ⓐ Ⓑ Ⓒ Ⓓ	194	Ⓐ Ⓑ Ⓒ Ⓓ
115	Ⓐ Ⓑ Ⓒ Ⓓ	135	Ⓐ Ⓑ Ⓒ Ⓓ	155	Ⓐ Ⓑ Ⓒ Ⓓ	175	Ⓐ Ⓑ Ⓒ Ⓓ	195	Ⓐ Ⓑ Ⓒ Ⓓ
116	Ⓐ Ⓑ Ⓒ Ⓓ	136	Ⓐ Ⓑ Ⓒ Ⓓ	156	Ⓐ Ⓑ Ⓒ Ⓓ	176	Ⓐ Ⓑ Ⓒ Ⓓ	196	Ⓐ Ⓑ Ⓒ Ⓓ
117	Ⓐ Ⓑ Ⓒ Ⓓ	137	Ⓐ Ⓑ Ⓒ Ⓓ	157	Ⓐ Ⓑ Ⓒ Ⓓ	177	Ⓐ Ⓑ Ⓒ Ⓓ	197	Ⓐ Ⓑ Ⓒ Ⓓ
118	Ⓐ Ⓑ Ⓒ Ⓓ	138	Ⓐ Ⓑ Ⓒ Ⓓ	158	Ⓐ Ⓑ Ⓒ Ⓓ	178	Ⓐ Ⓑ Ⓒ Ⓓ	198	Ⓐ Ⓑ Ⓒ Ⓓ
119	Ⓐ Ⓑ Ⓒ Ⓓ	139	Ⓐ Ⓑ Ⓒ Ⓓ	159	Ⓐ Ⓑ Ⓒ Ⓓ	179	Ⓐ Ⓑ Ⓒ Ⓓ	199	Ⓐ Ⓑ Ⓒ Ⓓ
120	Ⓐ Ⓑ Ⓒ Ⓓ	140	Ⓐ Ⓑ Ⓒ Ⓓ	160	Ⓐ Ⓑ Ⓒ Ⓓ	180	Ⓐ Ⓑ Ⓒ Ⓓ	200	Ⓐ Ⓑ Ⓒ Ⓓ

ANSWER SHEET

LISTENING TEST (PART 1-4)

#					#					#					#				
1	Ⓐ	Ⓑ	Ⓒ	Ⓓ	21	Ⓐ	Ⓑ	Ⓒ		41	Ⓐ	Ⓑ	Ⓒ		61	Ⓐ	Ⓑ	Ⓒ	Ⓓ
2	Ⓐ	Ⓑ	Ⓒ	Ⓓ	22	Ⓐ	Ⓑ	Ⓒ		42	Ⓐ	Ⓑ	Ⓒ		62	Ⓐ	Ⓑ	Ⓒ	Ⓓ
3	Ⓐ	Ⓑ	Ⓒ	Ⓓ	23	Ⓐ	Ⓑ	Ⓒ		43	Ⓐ	Ⓑ	Ⓒ	Ⓓ	63	Ⓐ	Ⓑ	Ⓒ	Ⓓ
4	Ⓐ	Ⓑ	Ⓒ	Ⓓ	24	Ⓐ	Ⓑ	Ⓒ		44	Ⓐ	Ⓑ	Ⓒ	Ⓓ	64	Ⓐ	Ⓑ	Ⓒ	Ⓓ
5	Ⓐ	Ⓑ	Ⓒ	Ⓓ	25	Ⓐ	Ⓑ	Ⓒ		45	Ⓐ	Ⓑ	Ⓒ	Ⓓ	65	Ⓐ	Ⓑ	Ⓒ	Ⓓ
6	Ⓐ	Ⓑ	Ⓒ	Ⓓ	26	Ⓐ	Ⓑ	Ⓒ		46	Ⓐ	Ⓑ	Ⓒ	Ⓓ	66	Ⓐ	Ⓑ	Ⓒ	Ⓓ
7	Ⓐ	Ⓑ	Ⓒ		27	Ⓐ	Ⓑ	Ⓒ		47	Ⓐ	Ⓑ	Ⓒ	Ⓓ	67	Ⓐ	Ⓑ	Ⓒ	Ⓓ
8	Ⓐ	Ⓑ	Ⓒ		28	Ⓐ	Ⓑ	Ⓒ		48	Ⓐ	Ⓑ	Ⓒ	Ⓓ	68	Ⓐ	Ⓑ	Ⓒ	Ⓓ
9	Ⓐ	Ⓑ	Ⓒ		29	Ⓐ	Ⓑ	Ⓒ		49	Ⓐ	Ⓑ	Ⓒ	Ⓓ	69	Ⓐ	Ⓑ	Ⓒ	Ⓓ
10	Ⓐ	Ⓑ	Ⓒ		30	Ⓐ	Ⓑ	Ⓒ		50	Ⓐ	Ⓑ	Ⓒ	Ⓓ	70	Ⓐ	Ⓑ	Ⓒ	Ⓓ
11	Ⓐ	Ⓑ	Ⓒ		31	Ⓐ	Ⓑ	Ⓒ		51	Ⓐ	Ⓑ	Ⓒ	Ⓓ	71	Ⓐ	Ⓑ	Ⓒ	Ⓓ
12	Ⓐ	Ⓑ	Ⓒ		32	Ⓐ	Ⓑ	Ⓒ		52	Ⓐ	Ⓑ	Ⓒ	Ⓓ	72	Ⓐ	Ⓑ	Ⓒ	Ⓓ
13	Ⓐ	Ⓑ	Ⓒ		33	Ⓐ	Ⓑ	Ⓒ		53	Ⓐ	Ⓑ	Ⓒ	Ⓓ	73	Ⓐ	Ⓑ	Ⓒ	Ⓓ
14	Ⓐ	Ⓑ	Ⓒ		34	Ⓐ	Ⓑ	Ⓒ		54	Ⓐ	Ⓑ	Ⓒ	Ⓓ	74	Ⓐ	Ⓑ	Ⓒ	Ⓓ
15	Ⓐ	Ⓑ	Ⓒ		35	Ⓐ	Ⓑ	Ⓒ		55	Ⓐ	Ⓑ	Ⓒ	Ⓓ	75	Ⓐ	Ⓑ	Ⓒ	Ⓓ
16	Ⓐ	Ⓑ	Ⓒ		36	Ⓐ	Ⓑ	Ⓒ		56	Ⓐ	Ⓑ	Ⓒ	Ⓓ	76	Ⓐ	Ⓑ	Ⓒ	Ⓓ
17	Ⓐ	Ⓑ	Ⓒ		37	Ⓐ	Ⓑ	Ⓒ		57	Ⓐ	Ⓑ	Ⓒ	Ⓓ	77	Ⓐ	Ⓑ	Ⓒ	Ⓓ
18	Ⓐ	Ⓑ	Ⓒ		38	Ⓐ	Ⓑ	Ⓒ		58	Ⓐ	Ⓑ	Ⓒ	Ⓓ	78	Ⓐ	Ⓑ	Ⓒ	Ⓓ
19	Ⓐ	Ⓑ	Ⓒ		39	Ⓐ	Ⓑ	Ⓒ		59	Ⓐ	Ⓑ	Ⓒ	Ⓓ	79	Ⓐ	Ⓑ	Ⓒ	Ⓓ
20	Ⓐ	Ⓑ	Ⓒ		40	Ⓐ	Ⓑ	Ⓒ		60	Ⓐ	Ⓑ	Ⓒ	Ⓓ	80	Ⓐ	Ⓑ	Ⓒ	Ⓓ

#					#				
81	Ⓐ	Ⓑ	Ⓒ	Ⓓ	91	Ⓐ	Ⓑ	Ⓒ	Ⓓ
82	Ⓐ	Ⓑ	Ⓒ	Ⓓ	92	Ⓐ	Ⓑ	Ⓒ	Ⓓ
83	Ⓐ	Ⓑ	Ⓒ	Ⓓ	93	Ⓐ	Ⓑ	Ⓒ	Ⓓ
84	Ⓐ	Ⓑ	Ⓒ	Ⓓ	94	Ⓐ	Ⓑ	Ⓒ	Ⓓ
85	Ⓐ	Ⓑ	Ⓒ	Ⓓ	95	Ⓐ	Ⓑ	Ⓒ	Ⓓ
86	Ⓐ	Ⓑ	Ⓒ	Ⓓ	96	Ⓐ	Ⓑ	Ⓒ	Ⓓ
87	Ⓐ	Ⓑ	Ⓒ	Ⓓ	97	Ⓐ	Ⓑ	Ⓒ	Ⓓ
88	Ⓐ	Ⓑ	Ⓒ	Ⓓ	98	Ⓐ	Ⓑ	Ⓒ	Ⓓ
89	Ⓐ	Ⓑ	Ⓒ	Ⓓ	99	Ⓐ	Ⓑ	Ⓒ	Ⓓ
90	Ⓐ	Ⓑ	Ⓒ	Ⓓ	100	Ⓐ	Ⓑ	Ⓒ	Ⓓ

READING TEST (PART 5-7)

#					#					#					#				
101	Ⓐ	Ⓑ	Ⓒ	Ⓓ	121	Ⓐ	Ⓑ	Ⓒ	Ⓓ	141	Ⓐ	Ⓑ	Ⓒ	Ⓓ	161	Ⓐ	Ⓑ	Ⓒ	Ⓓ
102	Ⓐ	Ⓑ	Ⓒ	Ⓓ	122	Ⓐ	Ⓑ	Ⓒ	Ⓓ	142	Ⓐ	Ⓑ	Ⓒ	Ⓓ	162	Ⓐ	Ⓑ	Ⓒ	Ⓓ
103	Ⓐ	Ⓑ	Ⓒ	Ⓓ	123	Ⓐ	Ⓑ	Ⓒ	Ⓓ	143	Ⓐ	Ⓑ	Ⓒ	Ⓓ	163	Ⓐ	Ⓑ	Ⓒ	Ⓓ
104	Ⓐ	Ⓑ	Ⓒ	Ⓓ	124	Ⓐ	Ⓑ	Ⓒ	Ⓓ	144	Ⓐ	Ⓑ	Ⓒ	Ⓓ	164	Ⓐ	Ⓑ	Ⓒ	Ⓓ
105	Ⓐ	Ⓑ	Ⓒ	Ⓓ	125	Ⓐ	Ⓑ	Ⓒ	Ⓓ	145	Ⓐ	Ⓑ	Ⓒ	Ⓓ	165	Ⓐ	Ⓑ	Ⓒ	Ⓓ
106	Ⓐ	Ⓑ	Ⓒ	Ⓓ	126	Ⓐ	Ⓑ	Ⓒ	Ⓓ	146	Ⓐ	Ⓑ	Ⓒ	Ⓓ	166	Ⓐ	Ⓑ	Ⓒ	Ⓓ
107	Ⓐ	Ⓑ	Ⓒ	Ⓓ	127	Ⓐ	Ⓑ	Ⓒ	Ⓓ	147	Ⓐ	Ⓑ	Ⓒ	Ⓓ	167	Ⓐ	Ⓑ	Ⓒ	Ⓓ
108	Ⓐ	Ⓑ	Ⓒ	Ⓓ	128	Ⓐ	Ⓑ	Ⓒ	Ⓓ	148	Ⓐ	Ⓑ	Ⓒ	Ⓓ	168	Ⓐ	Ⓑ	Ⓒ	Ⓓ
109	Ⓐ	Ⓑ	Ⓒ	Ⓓ	129	Ⓐ	Ⓑ	Ⓒ	Ⓓ	149	Ⓐ	Ⓑ	Ⓒ	Ⓓ	169	Ⓐ	Ⓑ	Ⓒ	Ⓓ
110	Ⓐ	Ⓑ	Ⓒ	Ⓓ	130	Ⓐ	Ⓑ	Ⓒ	Ⓓ	150	Ⓐ	Ⓑ	Ⓒ	Ⓓ	170	Ⓐ	Ⓑ	Ⓒ	Ⓓ
111	Ⓐ	Ⓑ	Ⓒ	Ⓓ	131	Ⓐ	Ⓑ	Ⓒ	Ⓓ	151	Ⓐ	Ⓑ	Ⓒ	Ⓓ	171	Ⓐ	Ⓑ	Ⓒ	Ⓓ
112	Ⓐ	Ⓑ	Ⓒ	Ⓓ	132	Ⓐ	Ⓑ	Ⓒ	Ⓓ	152	Ⓐ	Ⓑ	Ⓒ	Ⓓ	172	Ⓐ	Ⓑ	Ⓒ	Ⓓ
113	Ⓐ	Ⓑ	Ⓒ	Ⓓ	133	Ⓐ	Ⓑ	Ⓒ	Ⓓ	153	Ⓐ	Ⓑ	Ⓒ	Ⓓ	173	Ⓐ	Ⓑ	Ⓒ	Ⓓ
114	Ⓐ	Ⓑ	Ⓒ	Ⓓ	134	Ⓐ	Ⓑ	Ⓒ	Ⓓ	154	Ⓐ	Ⓑ	Ⓒ	Ⓓ	174	Ⓐ	Ⓑ	Ⓒ	Ⓓ
115	Ⓐ	Ⓑ	Ⓒ	Ⓓ	135	Ⓐ	Ⓑ	Ⓒ	Ⓓ	155	Ⓐ	Ⓑ	Ⓒ	Ⓓ	175	Ⓐ	Ⓑ	Ⓒ	Ⓓ
116	Ⓐ	Ⓑ	Ⓒ	Ⓓ	136	Ⓐ	Ⓑ	Ⓒ	Ⓓ	156	Ⓐ	Ⓑ	Ⓒ	Ⓓ	176	Ⓐ	Ⓑ	Ⓒ	Ⓓ
117	Ⓐ	Ⓑ	Ⓒ	Ⓓ	137	Ⓐ	Ⓑ	Ⓒ	Ⓓ	157	Ⓐ	Ⓑ	Ⓒ	Ⓓ	177	Ⓐ	Ⓑ	Ⓒ	Ⓓ
118	Ⓐ	Ⓑ	Ⓒ	Ⓓ	138	Ⓐ	Ⓑ	Ⓒ	Ⓓ	158	Ⓐ	Ⓑ	Ⓒ	Ⓓ	178	Ⓐ	Ⓑ	Ⓒ	Ⓓ
119	Ⓐ	Ⓑ	Ⓒ	Ⓓ	139	Ⓐ	Ⓑ	Ⓒ	Ⓓ	159	Ⓐ	Ⓑ	Ⓒ	Ⓓ	179	Ⓐ	Ⓑ	Ⓒ	Ⓓ
120	Ⓐ	Ⓑ	Ⓒ	Ⓓ	140	Ⓐ	Ⓑ	Ⓒ	Ⓓ	160	Ⓐ	Ⓑ	Ⓒ	Ⓓ	180	Ⓐ	Ⓑ	Ⓒ	Ⓓ

#				
181	Ⓐ	Ⓑ	Ⓒ	Ⓓ
182	Ⓐ	Ⓑ	Ⓒ	Ⓓ
183	Ⓐ	Ⓑ	Ⓒ	Ⓓ
184	Ⓐ	Ⓑ	Ⓒ	Ⓓ
185	Ⓐ	Ⓑ	Ⓒ	Ⓓ
186	Ⓐ	Ⓑ	Ⓒ	Ⓓ
187	Ⓐ	Ⓑ	Ⓒ	Ⓓ
188	Ⓐ	Ⓑ	Ⓒ	Ⓓ
189	Ⓐ	Ⓑ	Ⓒ	Ⓓ
190	Ⓐ	Ⓑ	Ⓒ	Ⓓ
191	Ⓐ	Ⓑ	Ⓒ	Ⓓ
192	Ⓐ	Ⓑ	Ⓒ	Ⓓ
193	Ⓐ	Ⓑ	Ⓒ	Ⓓ
194	Ⓐ	Ⓑ	Ⓒ	Ⓓ
195	Ⓐ	Ⓑ	Ⓒ	Ⓓ
196	Ⓐ	Ⓑ	Ⓒ	Ⓓ
197	Ⓐ	Ⓑ	Ⓒ	Ⓓ
198	Ⓐ	Ⓑ	Ⓒ	Ⓓ
199	Ⓐ	Ⓑ	Ⓒ	Ⓓ
200	Ⓐ	Ⓑ	Ⓒ	Ⓓ

Notes

New TOEIC 新制多益奇蹟筆記書：
全真練題本

作　　者 / David Katz、王復國
執行編輯 / 游玉旻

出　　版 / 波斯納出版有限公司
地　　址 / 100 台北市館前路 26 號 6 樓
電　　話 / (02) 2314-2525
傳　　真 / (02) 2312-3535
客服專線 / (02) 2314-3535
客服信箱 / btservice@betamedia.com.tw
郵撥帳號 / 19493777
帳戶名稱 / 波斯納出版有限公司

總 經 銷 / 時報文化出版企業股份有限公司
地　　址 / 桃園市龜山區萬壽路二段 351 號
電　　話 / (02) 2306-6842

出版日期 / 2022 年 1 月初版一刷
定　　價 / 680 元
I S B N / 978-986-06892-4-2

貝塔網址：www.betamedia.com.tw

喚醒你的英文語感！

Get a Feel for English !